By William Dietrich

WILLIAM DIETRICH

THE
ROSETTA KEY

AN ETHAN GAGE ADVENTURE

HARPER

NEW YORK • LONDON • TORONTO • SYDNEY

HARPER

A hardcover edition of this book was published in 2008 by HarperCollins Publishers.

HarperCollins books may be purchased for educational, business, or sales promotional use. For information please write: Special Markets Department, HarperCollins Publishers, 10 East 53rd Street, New York, NY 10022.

FIRST HARPER PAPERBACK PUBLISHED 2012.

Library of Congress Cataloging-in-Publication Data is available upon request.

ISBN 978-0-06-219157-1(pbk.)

12 13 14 15 16   RRD   10 9 8 7 6 5 4 3 2 1

To my daughter, Heidi

*The possession of knowledge does not kill
the sense of wonder and mystery.
There is always more mystery.*

— ANAÏS NIN

Napoleon and the Holy Land, 1799

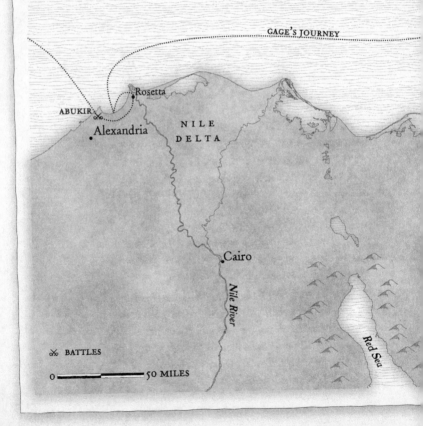

MEDITERRANEAN SEA

GAGE'S JOURNEY

Rosetta

ABUKIR

Alexandria

NILE
DELTA

Cairo

Nile River

Red Sea

✂ BATTLES

0 ⎯⎯⎯⎯ 50 MILES

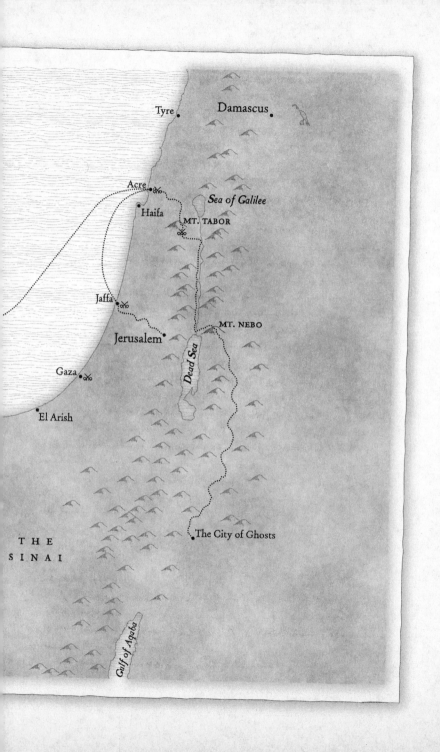

PART ONE

CHAPTER 1

Eyeing a thousand musket barrels aimed at one's chest does tend to force consideration of whether the wrong path has been taken. So I did consider it, each muzzle bore looking as wide as the bite of a mongrel stray in a Cairo alley. But no, while I'm modest to a fault, I have my self-righteous side as well—and by my light it wasn't me but the French army that had gone astray. Which I could have explained to my former friend, Napoleon Bonaparte, if he hadn't been up on the dunes out of hailing distance, aloof and annoyingly distracted, his buttons and medals gleaming in the Mediterranean sun.

The first time I'd been on a beach with Bonaparte, when he landed his army in Egypt in 1798, he told me the drowned would be immortalized by history. Now, nine months later outside the Palestinian port of Jaffa, history was to be made of *me*. French grenadiers were getting ready to shoot me and the hapless Muslim captives I'd been thrown in with, and once more I, Ethan Gage, was trying to figure out a way to sidestep destiny. It was a mass execution, you see, and I'd run afoul of the general I once attempted to befriend.

How far we'd both come in nine brief months!

I edged behind the biggest of the wretched Ottoman prisoners I could find, a Negro giant from the Upper Nile who I calculated might be just thick enough to stop a musket ball. All of us had been herded like bewildered cattle onto a lovely beach, eyes white and round in the darkest faces, the Turkish uniforms of scarlet, cream, emerald, and sapphire smeared with the smoke and blood of a savage sacking. There were lithe Moroccans, tall and dour Sudanese, truculent pale Albanians, Circassian cavalry, Greek gunners, Turkish sergeants—the scrambled levies of a vast empire, all humbled by the French. And me, the lone American. Not only was I baffled by their babble; they often couldn't understand each other. The mob milled, their officers already dead, and their disorder a defeated contrast to the crisp lines of our executioners, drawn up as if on parade. Ottoman defiance had enraged Napoleon—you should never put the heads of emissaries on a pike—and their hungry numbers as prisoners threatened to be a crippling drag on his invasion. So we'd been marched through the orange groves to a crescent of sand just south of the captured port, the sparkling sea a lovely green and gold in the shallows, the hilltop city smoldering. I could see some green fruit still clinging to the shot-blown trees. My former benefactor and recent enemy, sitting on his horse like a young Alexander, was (through desperation or dire calculation) about to display a ruthlessness that his own marshals would whisper about for many campaigns to come. Yet he didn't even have the courtesy to pay attention! He was reading another of his moody novels, his habit to devour a book's page, tear it out, and pass it back to his officers. I was barefoot, bloody, and only forty miles as the crow flies from where Jesus Christ had died to save the world. The past several days of persecution, torment, and warfare hadn't persuaded me that our Savior's efforts had entirely succeeded in improving human nature.

"Ready!" A thousand musket hammers were pulled back.

Napoleon's henchmen had accused me of being a spy

and a traitor, which was why I'd been marched with the other prisoners to the beach. And yes, circumstance had given a grain of truth to that characterization. But I hadn't set out with that intent, by any means. I'd simply been an American in Paris, whose tentative knowledge of electricity—and the need to escape an utterly unjust accusation of murder—resulted in my being included in the company of Napoleon's scientists, or savants, during his dazzling conquest of Egypt the year before. I'd also developed a knack for being on the wrong side at the wrong time. I'd taken fire from Mameluke cavalry, the woman I loved, Arab cutthroats, British broadsides, Muslim fanatics, French platoons—and I'm a likable man!

My latest French nemesis was a nasty scoundrel named Pierre Najac, an assassin and thief who couldn't get over the fact that I'd once shot him from beneath the Toulon stage when he tried to rob me of a sacred medallion. It's a long story, as an earlier volume will attest. Najac had come back into my life like a bad debt, and had kept me marching in the prisoner rank with a cavalry saber at my back. He was anticipating my imminent demise with the same feeling of triumph and loathing that one has when crushing a particularly obnoxious spider. I was regretting that I hadn't aimed a shave higher and two inches to the left.

As I've remarked before, it all seems to start with gambling. Back in Paris, it had been a card game that won me the mysterious medallion and started the trouble. This time, what had seemed a simple way to get a new start—taking the bewildered seamen of HMS *Dangerous* for every shilling they had before the British put me ashore in the Holy Land—had solved nothing and, it could be argued, had actually led to my present predicament. Let me repeat: gambling is a vice, and it is foolish to rely on chance.

"Aim!"

But I'm getting ahead of myself.

I, Ethan Gage, have spent most of my thirty-four years trying to keep out of too much trouble and away from too much work. As my mentor and onetime employer, the late, great Benjamin Franklin, would no doubt observe, these two ambitions are as at odds as positive and negative electricity. The pursuit of the latter, no work, is almost sure to defeat the former, no trouble. But that's a lesson, like the headache that follows alcohol or the treachery of beautiful women, forgotten as many times as learned. It was my dislike of hard labor that reinforced my fondness for gambling, gambling that got me the medallion, the medallion that got me to Egypt with half the planet's villains at my heels, and Egypt that got me my lovely lost Astiza. She in turn had convinced me that we had to save the world from Najac's master, the French-Italian count and sorcerer Alessandro Silano. All this, without my quite expecting it to, put me on the wrong side of Bonaparte. In the course of things I fell in love, found a secret way into the Great Pyramid, and made the damndest discoveries ever, only to lose everything I held dear when forced to escape by balloon.

I told you it was a long story.

Anyway, the gorgeous and maddening Astiza—my would-be assassin, then servant, then priestess of Egypt—had fallen from the balloon into the Nile along with my enemy, Silano. I've been desperately trying to learn their fate ever since, my anxiety redoubled by the fact that my enemy's last words to Astiza were, "You know I still love you!" How's *that* for prying at the corners of your mind at night? Just what *was* their relationship? Which is why I'd agreed to allow the English madman Sir Sidney Smith to put me ashore in Palestine just ahead of Bonaparte's invading army, to make inquiries. Then one thing led to another and here I stood, facing a thousand gun muzzles.

"Fire!"

¤   ¤   ¤

But before I tell you what happened when the muskets blazed, perhaps I should go back to where my earlier tale left off, in late October of 1798, when I was trapped on the deck of the British frigate *Dangerous*, making for the Holy Land with her sails bellied and a bone in her teeth, cutting the frothy deep. How hearty it all was, English banners flapping, burly seamen pulling at their stout lines of hemp with lusty chants, stiff-necked officers in bicorne hats pacing the quarterdeck, and bristling cannon dewed by the spray of the Mediterranean, droplets drying into stars of salt. In other words, it was just the kind of militant, masculine foray I've learned to detest, having narrowly survived the hurtling charge of a Mameluke warrior at the Battle of the Pyramids, the explosion of *L'Orient* at the Battle of the Nile, and any numbers of treacheries by an Arab snake worshipper named Achmed bin Sadr, who I finally sent to his own appropriate hell. I was a little winded from brisk adventure and more than ready to scuttle back home to New York for a nice job as a bookkeeper or a dry goods clerk, or perhaps as a solicitor attending to dreary wills clutched by black-clad widows and callow, undeserving offspring. Yes, a desk and dusty ledgers—that's the life for me! But Sir Sidney would hear none of it. Worse, I'd finally figured out what I cared about in this world: Astiza. I couldn't very well take passage home without finding out if she'd survived her fall with that villain Silano and could, somehow, be rescued.

Life was simpler when I had no principles.

Smith was gussied up like a Turkish admiral, plans building in his brain like an approaching squall. He'd been given the job of helping the Turks and their Ottoman Empire thwart the further encroachment of Bonaparte's armies from Egypt into Syria, since young Napoleon's hope was to carve an eastern empire out for himself. Sir Sidney needed allies and intelligence, and, after fishing me out of the Mediterranean, he'd told me it would work to both our advantage if I joined his cause. It was foolhardy for me to try to return to Egypt and face the angry French alone, he pointed out. I could make inquiries about Astiza from Palestine, while simultaneously assessing the various sects that might be lined up to fight Napoleon. "Jerusalem!" he'd cried. Was he mad? That half-forgotten city, an Ottoman backwater encrusted by dirt, history, religious lunatics, and disease, had—by all reports—survived only by foisting obligatory tourism on the credible and easily cheated pilgrims of three faiths. But if you're an English schemer and warrior like Smith, Jerusalem had the advantage of being a crossroad of the complicated culture of Syria, a polyglot den of Muslim, Jew, Greek Orthodox, Catholic, Druze, Maronite, Matuwelli, Turk, Bedouin, Kurd, and Palestinian, all of them remembering slights from each other going back several thousand years.

Frankly, I'd never have ventured within a hundred miles of the place, except that Astiza was convinced that Moses had stolen a sacred book of ancient wisdom from the bowels of the Great Pyramid and that his descendants had carried it to Israel. That meant Jerusalem was the likeliest place to look. So far this Book of Thoth, or the rumors of it, had been nothing but trouble. Yet if it did hold keys to immortality and mastery of the universe, I couldn't quite forget about it, could I? Jerusalem did make a perverse kind of sense.

Smith imagined me a trusted accomplice, and in truth we did have an alliance of sorts. I'd met him in a gypsy camp after I'd shot Najac. The signet ring he gave had saved me from a yardarm noose when I was hauled before Admiral Nelson after the fracas at the Nile. And Smith was a genuine hero who'd burned French ships and escaped from a Paris prison by signaling one of his former bedmates from a barred window. After I'd picked up a pharaoh's treasure under the Great Pyramid, lost it again to keep from drowning, and stolen a balloon from my friend and fellow savant Nicolas-Jacques Conte, I'd crash-landed into the sea and found myself wet and penniless on the quarterdeck of the *Dangerous*, fate putting me face-to-face with Sir Sidney once more, and as much at the mercy of the British as I'd been the French. My own feelings—that I'd had quite enough of war and treasure and was ready to go home to America—were blithely ignored.

"So while you make inquiries from Syrian Palestine about this woman you took a fancy to, Gage, you can also feel out the Christians and Jews for possible resistance to Bonaparte," Smith was telling me. "They might side with the frogs, and if he's taking an army that way, our Turkish allies need all the help they can get." He put his arm around my shoulder. "You're just the man for this kind of work, I judge: clever, affable, rootless, and without any scruples or belief. People tell you things, Gage, because they figure it doesn't matter."

"It's just that I'm American, not British or French . . ."

"Exactly. Perfect for our uses. Djezzar will be impressed that even a man as shallow as you has enlisted."

Djezzar, whose name meant "the Butcher," was the notoriously cruel and despotic pasha in Acre whom the British were depending on to fight Napoleon. Charmed, I'm sure.

"But my Arabic is crude and I know nothing of Palestine," I pointed out reasonably.

"Not a problem for an agent with wit and pluck like you, Ethan. The Crown has a confederate in Jerusalem by the code name of Jericho, an ironmonger by trade who once served in our own navy. He can help you search for this Astiza and work for us. He has contacts in Egypt! A few days of your artful diplomacy, a chance to walk in the footsteps of Jesus Christ hisself, and you're back with nothing more than dust on your boots and a holy relic in your pocket, your other problems solved. It's really quite splendid how these things work out. Meanwhile I'll be helping Djezzar organize the defense of Acre in case Boney marches north, as you've warned. In no time we'll both be bloody heroes, feted in the chambers of London!"

Whenever people start complimenting you and using words like "splendid," it's time to check your purse. But, by Bunker Hill, I was curious about the Book of Thoth and tortured by the memory of Astiza. Her sacrifice to save me was the worst moment of my life—worse, honestly, than when my beloved Pennsylvania long rifle blew up—and the hole in my heart was so big you could fire a cannonball through it and not hit a thing. Which is a good line to use on a woman, I figured, and I wanted to try it out on her. So of course I said yes, the most dangerous word in the English language.

"I *am* lacking clothes, weapons, and money," I pointed

out. The only things I'd managed to retain from the Great Pyramid were two small gold seraphim, or kneeling angels, which Astiza contended came from the staff of Moses and which I'd stuffed rather ingloriously into my drawers. My initial thought had been to pawn them, but they'd acquired sentimental value despite their tendency to make me scratch. At the very least they were a reserve of precious metal I preferred not to reveal. Let Smith give an allowance, if he was so anxious to enlist me.

"Your taste for Arab rags is perfect," the British captain said. "That's quite the swarthy tan you've developed, Gage. Add a cloak and turban in Jaffa and you'll blend like a native. As for an English weapon, *that* might get you clapped in a Turkish prison if they suspect you of spying. It's your wits that will keep you safe. I *can* lend you a small spyglass. It's splendidly sharp and just the thing to sort out troop movements."

"You didn't mention money."

"The Crown's allowance will be more than adequate."

He gave me a purse with a scattering of silver, brass, and copper: Spanish reales, Ottoman piastres, a Russian kopek, and two Dutch rix-dollars. Government budgeting.

"This will hardly buy breakfast!"

"Can't give you pound sterling, Gage, or it will give you away in an instant. You're a man of resources, eh? Stretch the odd penny! Lord knows the Admiralty does!"

Well, resourcefulness can start right now, I said to myself, and I wondered if I and the off-duty crewmen might while away the hours with a friendly game of cards. When I was still in good standing as a savant on Napoleon's Egyptian expedition, I'd enjoyed discussing the laws of probability with famed mathematicians such as Gaspard Monge and the geographer Edmé François Jomard. They'd encouraged me to think in a more systematic way about odds and the house advantage, sharpening my gambling skills.

"Perhaps I can interest your men in a game of chance?"

"Haw! Be careful they don't take your breakfast, too!"

CHAPTER 2

I started with *brelan*, which is not a bad game to play with simple sailors, contingent as it is on bluff. I had some practice at this in the salons of Paris—the Palais Royale alone had one hundred gambling chambers on a mere six acres—and the honest British seamen were no match for the man they soon called a Frankish dissembler. So after taking them for as much as they'd tolerate by pretending I had better cards—or letting slip my vulnerability when the hand actually left me better armed than the weapon-stuffed sash of a Mameluke bey—I offered games that seemed to be more straightforward luck. Ensigns and gunner mates who'd lost half a month's pay at a card game of skill eagerly came forward with a full month's wager on a game of sheer chance.

Except that it wasn't, of course. In simple *lansquenet*, the banker—me—places a bet that other players must match. Two cards are turned, the one to the left my card, the one to my right the player's. I then start revealing cards until there's a match with one of the first two. If the right card is matched first, the player wins; if the left card is matched first, the dealer wins. Even odds, right?

But if the first two cards are the same, the banker wins immediately, a slight mathematical advantage that gave me a margin after several hours, and finally had them pleading for a different game.

"Let's try *pharaon*," I offered. "It's all the rage in Paris, and I'm sure your luck will turn. You are my rescuers, after all, and I am in your debt."

"Yes, we'll have our money back, Yankee sharp!"

But *pharaon* is even more advantageous to the banker, because the dealer automatically wins the first card. The last card in the deck of fifty-two, a player's card, is not counted. Moreover, the dealer wins all matching cards. Despite the obviousness of my advantage they thought they'd wear me down through time, playing all night, when exactly the opposite was true—the longer the game went on, the greater my pile of coins. The more they thought my loss of luck to be inevitable, the more my advantage became inexorable. Pickings are slim on a frigate that has yet to take a prize, yet so many wanted to best me that by the time the shores of Palestine hove into view at dawn, my poverty was mended. My old friend Monge would simply have said that mathematics is king.

It's important when taking a man's money to reassure him of the brilliance of his play and the caprice of ill fortune, and I daresay I distributed so much sympathy that I made fast friends of the men I most deeply robbed. They thanked me for making four high-interest loans back to the most abject losers, while tucking away enough surplus to put me up in Jerusalem in style. When I gave back a sweetheart's locket that one of the fools had pawned, they were ready to elect me president.

Two of my opponents remained stubbornly uncharmed, however. "You have the devil's luck," a huge, red-faced marine who went by the descriptive name of Big Ned observed with a glower, as he counted and recounted the two pennies he had left.

"Or the angels," I suggested. "Your play has been masterful, mate, but providence, it seems, has smiled on me this long night." I grinned, trying to look as affable as Smith had described me, and then tried to stifle a yawn.

"No man is that lucky, that long."

I shrugged. "Just bright."

"I want you to play with me dice," the lobsterback said, his look as narrow and twisted as an Alexandrian lane. "Then we'll see how lucky you are."

"One of the marks of an intelligent man, my maritime friend, is reluctance to trust another man's ivory. Dice are the devil's bones."

"You afraid to give me a chance of winning back?"

"I'm simply content to play my game and let you play yours."

"Well, now, I think the American is a bit the poltroon," the marine's companion, a squatter and uglier man called Little Tom, taunted. "Scared to give two honest marines a fighting chance, he is." If Ned had the bulk of a small horse, Tom carried himself with the compact meanness of a bulldog.

I began to feel uneasy. Other sailors were watching this exchange with growing interest, since they weren't going to get their money back any other way. "To the contrary, gentlemen, we've been at arms over cards all night. I'm sorry you lost, I'm sure you did your best, I admire your perseverance, but perhaps you ought to study the mathematics of chance. A man makes his own luck."

"Study the what?" Big Ned asked.

"I think he said he cheated," Little Tom interpreted.

"Now, there's no need to talk of dishonesty."

"And yet the marines are challenging your honor, Gage," said a lieutenant whom I'd taken for five shillings, putting in with more enthusiasm than I liked to hear. "The word is that you're quite the marksman and fought well enough with the frogs. Surely you won't let these redcoats impugn your reputation?"

"Of course not, but we all know it was a fair . . ."

Big Ned's fist slammed down on the deck, a pair of dice jumping from his grip like fleas. "Gives us back our money, play these, or meet me on the waist deck at noon." It was a growl with just enough smirk to annoy. Clearly he was of a size not accustomed to losing.

"We'll be in Jaffa by then," I stalled.

"All the more leisure to discuss this between the eighteen-pounders."

Well. It was clear enough what I must do. I stood. "Aye, you need to be taught a lesson. Noon it is."

The gathering roared approval. It took just slightly longer for the news of a fight to reach from stem to stern of *Dangerous* than it takes a rumor of a romantic tryst to fly from one end of revolutionary Paris to the other. The sailors assumed a wrestling match in which I'd writhe painfully in the grip of Big Ned for every penny I'd won. When I'd been sufficiently kneaded, I'd then plead for the chance to give all my winnings back. To distract my all-too-fervent imagination from this disagreeable future, I went up to the quarterdeck to watch our approach to Jaffa, trying my new spyglass.

It was a crisp little telescope, and the principal port of Palestine, months before Napoleon was to take it, was a beacon on an otherwise flat and hazy shore. It crowned a hill with forts, towers, and minarets, its dome-topped buildings terracing downward in all directions like a stack of blocks. All was surrounded by a wall that meets the harbor quay on the seaward side. There were orange groves and palms landward, and golden fields and brown pastures beyond that. Black guns jutted from embrasures, and even from two miles out we could hear the wails of the faithful being called to prayer.

I'd had Jaffa oranges in Paris, famed because their thick skin makes them transportable to Europe. There were so many fruit trees that the prosperous city looked like a castle in a forest. Ottoman banners flapped in the warm autumn breeze, carpets hung from railings, and the smell of charcoal fires carried on the water. There were some nasty-looking reefs just offshore, marked by ringlets of white, and the little harbor was jammed with small dhows and feluccas. Like the other large ships, we anchored in open water. A small flotilla of Arab lighters set out to see what business they could solicit, and I readied to leave.

After I'd dealt with the unhappy marine, of course.

"I hear your famous luck got you into a tangle with Big Ned, Ethan," Sir Sidney said, handing me a bag of hard biscuit that was supposed to get me to Jerusalem. The English aren't known for their cooking. "Regular bull of a man with a head like a ram, and just as thick, I wager. Do you have a plan to fox him?"

"I'd try his dice, Sir Sidney, but I suspect that if they were weighted any more, they'd list this frigate."

He laughed. "Aye, he's cheated more than one pressed wretch, and has the muscle to shut complaints about it. He's not used to losing. There's more than a few here pleased you've taken him. Too bad your skull has to pay for it."

"You could forbid the match."

"The men are randy as roosters and won't get ashore until Acre. A good tussle helps settle them. You look quick enough, man! Lead him a dance!"

Indeed. I went below to seek out Big Ned and found him near the galley hearth, using lard to slick his imposing muscles so he'd slide out of my grip. He gleamed like a Christmas goose.

"Might we have a word in private?"

"Trying to back from it, eh?" He grinned. His teeth seemed as big as the keys of a newfangled piano.

"I've just given the whole matter some thought and realized our enemy is Bonaparte, not each other. But I do have my pride. Come, let's settle out of sight of the others."

"No. You'll pay not just me back, but every jack-tar of this crew!"

"That's impossible. I don't know who is owed what. But if you follow right now, and promise to leave me alone, I'll pay *you* back double."

Now the gleam of greed came to his eyes. "Damn your eyes, it will be triple!"

"Just come to the orlop where I can show my purse without causing a riot."

He shambled after me like a dim but eager circus bear. We descended to the lowest part of the frigate, where the stores are kept.

"I hid the money down here so no one could thieve it," I said, lifting a hatch to the bilge. "My mentor Ben Franklin said riches increase cares, and I daresay he had a point. You should remember it."

"Damn the rebel Franklin! He should have hanged!"

I reached down. "Oh dear, it shifted. Fell, I think." I peered about and looked up at the looming Goliath, using the same art of feigned helplessness that any number of wenches had used on me. "Your losses were what, three shillings?"

"Four, by God!"

"So triple that . . ."

"Aye, you owe me ten!"

"Your arm is longer than mine. Can you help?"

"Reach it yourself!"

"I can just brush it with my fingertips. Maybe we could find a gaff?" I stood, looking hapless.

"Yankee swine . . ." He got down and poked his head in. "Can't see a bloody thing."

"There, to the right, don't you see that gleam of silver? Reach as far as you can."

He grunted, torso through the hatch, stretching and groping.

So with a good hearty heave I tipped him the rest of the way. He was heavy as a flour sack, but once I got him going that was an advantage. He fell, there was a clunk and a splash, and before he could get off a good howl about greasy bilgewater, I had the hatch shut and bolted. Gracious, the language coming from below! I rolled some water casks over the hatch to muffle it.

Then I took the purse from where it was really hidden between two biscuit barrels, tucked it in my trousers, and bounded up to the waist deck, sleeves rolled. "It's noon by the ship's bells!" I cried. "In the name of King George, where is he?"

A chorus of shouts for Big Ned went up, but no answer came.

"Is he hiding? Can't blame him for not wanting to face me." I boxed the air for show.

Little Tom was glowering. "By Lucifer, *I'll* thrash you."

"You will not. I'm not matching every man on this ship."

"Ned, give this American what he deserves!" Tom cried. But there was no answer.

"I wonder if he's napping in the topgallants?" I looked up at the rigging, and then had the amusement of watching Little Tom clamber skyward, shouting and sweating.

I spent some minutes below behaving like an impatient rooster, and then as soon as I dared I turned to Smith. "How long do we have to wait for this coward? We both know I've business ashore."

The crew was clearly frustrated, and deeply suspicious. If I didn't get off *Dangerous* soon, Smith knew he'd likely lose his newest, and only, American agent. Tom dropped back down to the deck, panting and frustrated. Smith checked the hourglass. "Yes, it's a quarter past noon and Ned had his chance. Be gone, Gage, and accomplish your task for love and freedom."

There was a roar of disappointment.

"Don't play cards if you can't afford to lose!" Smith shouted.

They jeered, but let me pass to the ship's ladder. Tom had disappeared below. I'd not much time, so I dropped onto the dirty fishing nets of an Arab lighter like an anxious cat. "To shore now, and an extra coin if you make it fast," I whispered to the boatman. I pushed us off myself, and the Muslim captain began sculling for Jaffa's harbor with twice his usual energy, meaning half what I preferred.

I turned to wave back to Smith. "Can't wait until we meet again!" Blatant lie, of course. Once I learned Astiza's fate and satisfied myself about this Book of Thoth, I had no intention of going near either the English or the French, who'd been at each other's throats for a millennium. I'd sail for China first.

Especially when there was a boil of men at the gun deck and Big Ned's head popped up like a gopher, red from rage and exertion. I gave him a look from the new glass and saw he was wearing a baptism of slime.

"Come back here, yellow dog! I'll rip you limb from limb!"

"I think the yellow is yours, Ned! You didn't keep our appointed time!"

"You tricked me, Yankee sharp!"

"I educated you!" But it was getting hard to hear as we bobbed away. Sir Sidney lifted his hat in wry salute. The English marines scrambled to lower a longboat.

"Can you go a little faster, Sinbad?"

"For another coin, effendi."

It was a sharp little race, given that the beefy marines churned the waves like a waterwheel, Big Ned howling at the bow. Still, Smith had told me about Jaffa. It has just one land gate in, and you needed a guide to find your way back out. Given a head start, I'd hide well enough.

So I took one of my ferryman's fishing nets and, before he could object, heaved it in the path of the closing long-boat, snarling their starboard oars so they began turning in circles, roaring insults in language that would make a drill sergeant blush.

My ferryman protested, but I had coins enough to pay double for his sorry net and keep him rowing. I leapt onto the stone quay a good minute ahead of my complainants, determined to find Astiza and get back out—and vowing never to see Big Ned or Little Tom again.

CHAPTER 3

Jaffa rises like a loaf from the Mediterranean shore, empty beaches curving north and south into haze. Its importance as a trading port had been superseded by Acre to the north, where Djezzar the Butcher has his headquarters, but it is still a prosperous agricultural town. There is a steady stream of Jerusalem-bound pilgrims in and oranges, cotton, and soap back out. Its streets are a labyrinth leading to the towers, mosques, synagogues, and churches that form its peak. House additions arch illegally over dim lanes. Donkeys clatter up and down stone steps.

Questionably gotten though my gambling gains might be, they quickly proved invaluable when a street urchin invited me to the upstairs inn of his disappointingly homely sister. The money bought me pita bread, falafel, an orange, and a screened balcony to hide behind while the gang of British marines rushed up one alley and down another, in futile search of my vile carcass. Blown and hot, they finally settled in a Christian quayside inn to discuss my perfidy over bad Palestinian wine. Meanwhile, I snuck about to spend more winnings. I bought a sleeved Bedouin robe of maroon and white stripes, new boots, bloused trousers (so much more comfortable in the heat than tight European breeches!) sash, vest, two cotton shirts, and cloth for a turban. As Smith had predicted, the result made me look like one more exotic member of a polyglot empire, so long as I took care to stay away from the arrogant, questioning Ottoman janissaries in their red and yellow boots.

I learned there was no coach to the holy city, or even a decent highway. I was too financially prudent—Ben, again—to buy or feed a horse. So I purchased a docile donkey sufficient to get me there, and not much farther. For a meager weapon, I economized with a curbed Arab knife with a handle of camel horn. I have little skill with swords, and I couldn't bear to purchase one of the Muslims' long, clumsy, elaborately decorated muskets. Their inlaid mother-of-pearl is lovely, but I'd seen how indifferently they performed against the French musket during Napoleon's battles in Egypt. And any musket is far inferior to the lovely Pennsylvania rifle I'd sacrificed at Dendara in order to escape with Astiza. If this Jericho was a metallurgist, maybe he could make a replacement!

For guide and bodyguard to Jerusalem I chose a bearded, sharp-bargaining entrepreneur named Mohammad, a moniker seemingly given to half the Muslim men in this town. Between my elementary Arabic and Mohammad's primitive French, learned because Frankish merchants dominated the cotton trade, we could communicate. Still conscious of money, I figured that if we left early enough I could shave a day off his fee. I'd also slip out of town unseen, in case any Royal Marines were still lurking about.

"Now then, Mohammad, I would prefer to depart about midnight. Steal a march on the traffic and enjoy the brisk night air, you see. Early to rise, Ben Franklin said."

"As you wish, effendi. You are fleeing enemies, perhaps?"

"Of course not. I'm told I'm affable."

"It must be creditors then."

"Mohammad, you know I've paid half your extortionate fee in advance. I've money enough."

"Ah, so it is a woman. A bad wife? I have seen the Christian wives." He shook his head and shuddered. "Satan couldn't placate them."

"Just be ready at midnight, will you?"

Despite my sorrow at losing Astiza and my anxiety to learn her fate, I'll confess it crossed my mind to seek an hour or two of female companionship in Jaffa. All varieties of sex from the dullest to the most perverse were advertised with distracting persistence by Arab boys, despite condemnation from any number of religions. I'm a man, not a monk, and it *had* been some days. But Smith's ship remained anchored offshore, and if Big Ned had any persistence it would be just my luck that he'd find me entwined with a trollop, too single-minded to outwit him. So I thought better of it, congratulated myself for my piety, and decided I would wait for relief in Jerusalem, even though copulating in the Holy Land was the kind of deed that would choke my old pastor. The truth is, abstinence and loyalty to Astiza made me feel good. My trials in Egypt had made me determined to work on self-discipline, and here I was, past the first test. "A good conscience is a continual Christmas," my mentor Franklin liked to say.

Mohammad was an hour late, but finally led me through the dark maze of alleys to the landward gate, its paving stained with dung. A bribe was required to get it opened at night, and I passed through its archway with that curious exhilaration that comes from starting a new adventure. I had, after all, survived eight kinds of hell in Egypt, restored myself to temporary solvency with gambling skills, and was off on a mission that bore no resemblance to real work, despite my fantasies of becoming a ledger clerk. The Book of Thoth, which believers contended could confer anything from scientific wisdom to life everlasting, probably no longer existed . . . and yet it *might* just be found somewhere, giving my trip the optimism of a treasure hunt. And despite my lustful instincts, I truly longed for Astiza. The opportunity to somehow learn her fate through Smith's confederate in Jerusalem made me impatient.

So off we strode through the gate—and stopped.

"What are you doing?" I asked the suddenly recumbent Mohammad, wondering if he'd had a fainting spell. But no, he lay down with the deliberation of a dog circling a fireplace rug. No one can relax like an Ottoman, their very bones melting.

"Bedouin gangs infest the road to Jerusalem and will rob any unarmed pilgrim, effendi," my guide said blithely in the dark. "It's not just risky to proceed alone, it is insane. My cousin Abdul is leading a camel caravan there later today, and we will join him for safety. Thus do I and Allah look after our American guest."

"But what about our early start?"

"You have paid, and we have started." And with that he went back to sleep.

Well, tarnation. It was the middle of the night, we were fifty yards outside the walls, I had little notion which way to go, and it was entirely possible he was right. Palestine was notorious for being overrun by brigands, feuding warlords, desert raiders, and thieving Bedouins. So I stewed and steamed for three hours, worried the marines might somehow wander this way, until at last Abdul and his snorting camels did indeed congregate at the gate, well before the sun rose. Introductions were made, I was loaned a Turkish pistol, charged five more English shillings both for it and my added escort, and then another shilling for feed for my donkey. I'd been in Palestine less than twenty-four hours and already my purse was growing thin.

Next we brewed some tea.

At last there was a glimmer of light as the stars faded, and we were off through the orange groves. After a mile we passed into fields of cotton and wheat, the road lined with date palms. The thatched farmhouses were dark in early morning, barking dogs signaling their location. Camel bells and creaking saddles marked our own passage. The sky lightened, bird call and rooster crow started up, and as the dawn pinked I could see the rugged hills ahead where so much biblical history had taken place. Israel's trees had been depleted for charcoal and ashes to make soap, yet after the waterless Egyptian desert this coastal plain seemed as fat and pleasant as Pennsylvania Dutch country. Promised Land, indeed.

The Holy Land, I learned from my guide, was nominally a part of Syria, a province of the Ottoman Empire, and its provincial capital of Damascus was under the control of the Sublime Porte in Constantinople. But just as Egypt had really been under the control of the independent Mamelukes until Bonaparte threw them out, Palestine was really under the control of the Bosnian-born Djezzar, an ex-Mameluke himself who'd ruled from Acre with notorious cruelty for a quarter century, ever since putting down a revolt of his own mercenary troops. Djezzar had strangled several of his wives rather than put up with rumors of infidelity, maimed his closest advisers to remind them who was boss, and drowned generals or captains who displeased him. This ruthlessness, Mohammad opined, was necessary. The province was splintered among too many religious and ethnic groups, each about as comfortable with the other as a Calvinist at a Vatican picnic. The invasion of Egypt had hurled even more refugees into the Holy Land, with Ibrahim Bey's fugitive Mamelukes seeking a toehold. Fresh Ottoman levies were pouring in to anticipate a French invasion, while British gold and promises of naval aid were stirring the pot even thicker. Half the population was spying on the other half, and every clan, sect, and cult was weighing its best chances between Djezzar and the so-far-invincible French. Word of the astonishing Napoleonic victories in Egypt, the latest of which had been suppression of a revolt in Cairo, had shaken the Ottoman Empire.

I knew, too, that Napoleon still hoped to eventually link up with Tippoo Sahib, the Francophile sultan fighting Wellesley and the British in India. The fervently ambitious Bonaparte was organizing a camel corps he hoped could eventually cross the eastern deserts more efficiently than Alexander had done. The thirty-year-old Corsican wanted to do the Greek one better by galloping all the way to southern India to link with Citizen Tippoo and deprive Britain of its richest colony.

According to Smith, I was to make sense of this porridge.

"Palestine sounds like a regular rat's nest of righteousness," I remarked to Mohammad as we rode along, me three sizes too big for my donkey, which had a spine like a hickory rail. "As many factions here as a New Hampshire town council."

"All men are holy here," Mohammad said, "and there is nothing more irritating than a neighbor, equally holy, of a different faith."

Amen to that. For another man to be convinced he is right is to suggest you may be wrong, and there is the root of half the world's bloodshed. The French and British are perfect examples, firing broadsides at each other over who is the most democratic, the French republicans with their bloody guillotine, or the British parliamentarians with their debtor prisons. Back in my Paris days, when all I had to care about was cards, women, and the occasional shipping contract, I can't recall being very upset with anybody, or they with me. Then along came the medallion, the Egyptian campaign, Astiza, Napoleon, Sidney Smith, and here I was, urging my diminutive steed toward the world capital of obstinate disagreement. I wondered for the thousandth time how I'd gotten to such a point.

Because of our delay and the caravan's stately pace, we were three long days getting to Jerusalem, arriving at dusk on the third. It's a tiresome, winding route on roads that would be snubbed by any self-respecting goat—there obviously hadn't been a repair since Pontius Pilate—and in little time the brown, scrub-cloaked hills had acquired the steepness of the Appalachians. We climbed up the valley of the Bab al-Wad into pine and juniper, the grass brown this fall season. The air got noticeably cooler and drier. Up and down and roundabout we went, past braying donkeys, farting, foam-flecked camels, and cart drovers whose oxen butted head-to-head while the two drivers argued. We passed brown-robed friars, cassocked Armenian missionaries, Orthodox Jews with beards and long

sidelocks, Syrian merchants, one or two French expatri-
ate cotton traders, and Muslim sects beyond number, tur-
baned and carrying staffs. Bedouin drove flocks of sheep
and goats down hillsides like a spill of water, and village
girls swayed interestingly by on the road's fringe, clay jars
balanced carefully on their heads. Bright sashes swung to
the rock of their hips, and their dark eyes were bright as
black stones on the bottom of a river.

What passed for hostels, called *khans*, were consider-
ably less appealing: little more than walled courts that served
chiefly as corrals for fleas. We also encountered bands of
tough-looking horsemen who on four different occasions
demanded a toll for passing. Each time I was expected by
my companions to contribute more than what seemed my
fair share. These parasites looked like simple robbers to
me, but Mohammad insisted they were local village toughs
who kept even worse bandits away, and each village had a
right to a portion of this toll, called a *ghafar*. He was probably telling the truth, since being taxed for protection
against robbers is something all governments do, isn't it?
These armed louts were a cross between private extortion-
ists and the police.

When I wasn't grumbling about the unceasing drain
upon my purse, however, Israel had its charm. If Palestine
didn't quite carry the atmosphere of antiquity that Egypt
had, it still seemed well-trodden, as if we could hear the
echoes of long-past Hebrew heroes, Christian saints, and
Muslim conquerors. Olive trees had the girth of a wine
cask, the wood twisted by countless centuries. Odd bits of
historic rubble jutted from the prow of every hill. When we
paused for water, the ledges leading down to spring or well
were concave and smooth from all the sandals and boots that
had gone before us. As in Egypt, there was a clarity to the
light, very different from foggy Europe. The air had a dusty
taste as well, as if it had been breathed too many times.

It was at one of these *khans* that I was reminded that I
hadn't left the world of the medallion entirely behind. A
geezer of indeterminate faith and age was given meager

sustenance by the innkeeper for doing the odd chore about the place, and he was so meek and unassuming that none of us paid him much mind except to ask for a cup of water or an extra sheepskin to sprawl on. I would have had eyes for a serving wench, but a raggedy man pushing a twig broom did not capture my attention, so when I was undressing in the wee hours and had my golden seraphim momentarily exposed, I backed into him and jumped before I knew he was there. He was staring goggle-eyed at my little angels, wings outstretched, and at first I thought the old beggar had spied something he longed to steal. But instead he stepped back in consternation and fear.

I flipped my linen over the seraphim, the brightness vanishing as if light had gone out.

"The compass," he whispered in Arabic.

"What?"

"Satan's fingers. Allah's mercy be upon you."

He was clearly as addled as a loon. Still, his look of dismay made me uneasy. "They're personal relics. Not a word of this, now."

"My imam whispered of these. From the den."

"The den?" They'd come from under the Great Pyramid.

"Apophis." And with that, he turned and fled.

Well, I hadn't been so flabbergasted since the danged medallion had actually worked. Apophis! That was the name of a snake god, or demon, that Astiza had claimed was down in the bowels of Egypt. I didn't take her seriously—I am a Franklin man, after all, a man of reason, of the West—but *something* had been down in a smoky pit I'd had no desire to get closer to, and I thought I'd left it and its name long behind in Egypt. . . . Yet here it had been spoken again! By the snout of Anubis, I'd had quite enough of stray gods and goddesses, mucking up my life like unwanted relatives tracking the floor with mud on their boots. Now a senescent handyman had brought the name up again. Surely it made no sense, but the coincidence was unnerving.

I hurriedly redressed, secreting the seraphim again in my clothing, and hurried outside my cubicle to seek the old man out and ask him what the name meant.

But he was nowhere to be found. The next morning, the innkeeper said the servant had apparently packed his meager belongings and fled.

¤   ¤   ¤

And then at last we came to fabled Jerusalem. I'll admit it was a striking sight. The city is perched on a hill set amid hills, and on three sides the ground falls steeply to narrow valleys. It is on the fourth side, the north, from which invaders always come. Olives, vineyards, and orchards clothe the hillsides, and gardens provide clusters of green within. Formidable walls two miles long, built by a Muslim sultan called Suleiman the Magnificent, entirely enclose the city's inhabitants. Fewer than nine thousand people lived there when I arrived, subsisting economically on pilgrims and a desultory pottery and soap industry. I'd learn soon enough that about four thousand were Muslims, three thousand Christians, and two thousand Jews.

What picked the place out were its buildings. The primary Muslim mosque, the Dome of the Rock, has a golden cupola that glows like a lighthouse in the setting sun. Closer to where we stood, the Jaffa Gate was the old military citadel, its crenellated ramparts topped by a round tower like a lighthouse. Stones as colossal as the ones I'd seen in Egypt made up the citadel's base. I'd find similar rocks at the Temple Mount, the old Jewish temple plateau that now served as the base of the city's great mosque. Apparently, Jerusalem's foundations had been laid by Titans.

The skyline was punctuated everywhere by domes, minarets, and church towers bequeathed by this crusader or that conqueror, each trying to leave a holy building to make up for his own national brand of slaughter. The effect was as competitive as rival vegetable stalls at a Saturday market, Christian bells tolling as muzzeins wailed and Jews chanted their prayers. Vines, flowers, and shrubs erupted from the ill-maintained wall, and palms marked squares and gardens. Outside, ranks of olive trees marched down to twisting, rocky valleys that were smoky from burning garbage. From this terrestrial hell-dump one lifted the eye to heaven, birds wheeling in front of celestial cloud palaces, everything sharp and detailed. Jerusalem, like Jaffa, was the color of honey in the low sun, its limestone fermenting in the yellow rays.

"Most men come here looking for something," Mohammad remarked as we gazed across the Citadel Valley toward the ancient capital. "What do you seek, my friend?"

"Wisdom," I said, which was true enough. That's what the Book of Thoth was supposed to contain, and by Franklin's spectacles I could use some. "And news of one I love, I hope."

"Ah. Many men search their entire lives without finding wisdom *or* love, so it is well you come here, where prayers for both might be answered."

"Let's hope so." I knew that Jerusalem, precisely because it was reputed to be so holy, had been attacked, burned, sacked, and pillaged more times than any place on earth. "I'll pay you now and seek out the man I'm to stay with." I tried not to jingle my purse too much as I counted out the rest of his fee.

He took his pay eagerly and then reacted with practiced shock. "Not a gift for sharing my expertise about the Holy Land? No recompense for the safety or your arrival? No affirmation of this glorious view?"

"I suppose you want credit for the weather, as well."

He looked hurt. "I have tried to be your servant, effendi."

So, twisting in my saddle so he couldn't see how little was left, I gave him a tip I could ill afford. He bowed and gave effusive thanks. "Allah smiles on your generosity!"

I wasn't able to keep the grumpiness from my "Godspeed."

"And peace be upon you!"

A blessing that had no power, it turned out.

CHAPTER 4

Jerusalem was half ruin, I saw when I rode down the dirt track and crossed a wooden bridge to the black iron of the Jaffa Gate, and through it to a market beyond. A *subashi*, or police officer, checked me for weapons—they were not allowed in Ottoman cities—but allowed me to keep my poor dagger. "I thought Franks carried something better," he muttered, taking me for European despite my clothing.

"I'm a simple pilgrim," I told him.

His look was skeptical. "See that you remain one."

Then I sold my donkey for what I'd paid for it—a few coins back, at least!—and got my bearings.

The gate had a steady stream of traffic. Merchants met caravans, and pilgrims of a dozen sects shouted thanksgiving as they entered the sacred precincts. But Ottoman authority had been in decline for two centuries, and powerless governors, raiding Bedouin, extortionate tax collection, and religious rivalry had left the town's prosperity as stunted as cornstalks on a causeway. Market stalls lined major streets, but their faded awnings and half-empty shelves only emphasized the historical gloom. Jerusalem was somnolent, birds having occupied its towers.

My guide Mohammad had explained the city was divided into quarters for Muslims, Christians, Armenians, and Jews. I followed twisting lanes as best I could for the northwest quadrant, built around the Church of the Holy Sepulcher and Franciscan headquarters. The route was depopulated enough that chickens skittered out of my way. Half the houses appeared abandoned. The inhabited homes, built of ancient stone with haphazard wooden sheds and terraces jutting like boils, sagged liked the skin of grandmothers. As in Egypt, any fantasies of an opulent East were disappointed.

Smith's vague directions and my own inquiries took me to a two-story limestone house with a solid wooden wagon gate topped by a horseshoe, its façade otherwise featureless in the Arab fashion. There was a smaller wooden door to one side, and I could smell the charcoal from Jericho's smithy. I pounded on the small entry door, waited, and pounded again, until a small peephole opened. I was surprised when a feminine eye looked out: I'd become accustomed in Cairo to bulky Muslim doormen and sequestered wives. Moreover, her pupils were pale gray, of a translucence unusual in the East.

On Smith's instruction, I started in English. "I'm Ethan Gage, with a letter of introduction from a British captain to a man they call Jericho. I'm here . . ."

The eyehole shut. I stood, wondering after some minutes whether I even had the right house, when finally the door swung open as if of its own accord and I stepped cautiously through. I was in the work yard of an ironmonger, all right, its pavers stained gray with soot. Ahead I could see the glow of a forge, in a ground-story shed with walls hung with tools. The left of the courtyard was a sales shop stocked with finished implements, and to the right was storage for metal and charcoal. Slightly overhanging these three wings were the living apartments above, reached by an unpainted wooden stair and fronted by a balcony, faded roses cascading from iron pots. A few petals had fallen to the ashes below.

The gate closed behind me, and I realized the woman had been hidden by it. She ghosted by without speaking, her eyes inspecting me with a sidewise glance and an intense curiosity that surprised me. It's true I'm a handsome rogue, but was I really that interesting? Her dress fell from neck to ankles, her head was covered by a scarf in the custom of all faiths here in Palestine, and she modestly averted her face, but I saw enough to make a key judgment. She was pretty.

Her face had the rounded beauty of a Renaissance painting, her complexion pale for this part of the world, with an eggshell smoothness. Her lips were full, and when I caught her gaze she looked down demurely. Her nose had that slight Mediterranean arch, that subtle curve of the south that I find seductive. Her hair was hidden except for a few escaping strands that hinted at a surprisingly fair coloring. Her figure was trim enough, but it was hard to tell more than that. Then she disappeared through a doorway.

And with that instinctive scouting done, I turned around to see a bearded, hard-muscled man striding from the smithy in a leather apron. He had the forearms of a smith, thick as hams and marked with the inevitable burns of the forge. The smudge from his work didn't hide his sandy hair and startling blue eyes that looked at me with some skepticism. Had Vikings washed ashore in Syria? Yet his build was softened somewhat by a fullness to his lips and ruddiness behind his bearded cheeks (a cherubic youthfulness he shared with the woman), which suggested the earnest gentleness I've always imagined of Joseph the Carpenter. He shed a leather glove and held out a callused hand. "Gage."

"Ethan Gage," I confirmed as I shook a palm hard as wood.

"Jericho." The man might have a woman's mouth, but he had a grip like a vise.

"As your wife might have explained . . ."

"Sister."

"Really?" Well, that was a step in the right direction. Not that I was forgetting about Astiza for a moment—it's just that female beauty arouses a natural curiosity in any healthy male, and it's safest to know where one stands.

"She is shy of strangers, so do not make her uncomfortable."

That was clear enough, from a man sturdy as an oak stump. "Of course. Yet it is commendable that she apparently understands English."

"It would be more remarkable if she didn't, since she lived in England. With me. She has nothing to do with our business."

"Charming yet unavailable. The very best ladies are."

He reacted to my wit with as much animation as a stone idol. "Smith sent word of your mission, so I can offer temporary lodging and time-tested advice: any foreigner who pretends to understand the politics of Jerusalem is a fool."

I remained my affable self. "So my job might be brief. I ask, don't understand the answer, and go home. Like any pilgrim."

He looked me up and down. "You prefer Arab dress?"

"It's comfortable, anonymous, and I thought it might help in the souk and the coffee shop. I speak a little Arabic." I was determined to keep trying. "As for you, Jericho, I don't see you falling down anytime soon."

I'd merely puzzled him.

"The biblical story, about the walls of Jericho coming down? Solid as a rock, you seem to be. Good man to have on one's side, I hope?"

"My home village. There are no walls now."

"And I didn't expect to find blue eyes in Palestine," I stumbled on.

"Crusader blood. The roots of my family go far back. We should be a paintbox mix, but in our generation the paleness came out. Every race comes through Jerusalem: Crusaders, Persians, Mongols, Ethiopians. Every creed, opinion, and nation. And you?"

"American, ancestry brief and best forgotten, which is one of the advantages of the United States. I understand you learned your English through their navy?"

"Miriam and I were orphaned by the plague. The Catholic fathers who took us in told us something of the world, and at Tyre I signed onto an English frigate and learned ironwork repairs. The sailors gave me my nickname, I apprenticed to a smith in Portsmouth, and sent for her. I felt obligated."

"But didn't stay, obviously."

"We missed the sun; the British are white as worms. I'd met Smith while in the navy. For passage back and some pay, I agreed to keep my ears open here. I host his friends. They do his bidding. Little useful is ever learned. My neighbors think I'm simply capitalizing on my English to take in the occasional lodger, and they're not far wrong."

Bright and blunt, this blacksmith. "Sidney Smith thinks he and I can help each other. I got caught up with Bonaparte in Egypt. Now the French are planning to come this way."

"And Smith wants to know what the Christians and the Jews and the Druze and the Matuwelli might do."

"Exactly. He's trying to help Djezzar mount resistance to the French."

"With people who hate Djezzar, a tyrant who keeps his slipper on their neck. More than a few will regard the French as liberators."

"If that's the message, I'll take it back. But I also need help for my own cause. I met a woman in Egypt who disappeared. Fell into the Nile, actually. I want to learn if she's dead or alive and, if alive, how to rescue her. I'm told you may have contacts in Egypt."

"A woman? Close to you?" He seemed reassured by my interest in someone other than his sister. "That kind of inquiry is more costly than listening to political gossip in Jerusalem."

"How much more costly?"

He looked me up and down. "More, I suspect, than you can afford to pay."

"So you won't help me?"

"It's my contacts in Egypt who won't help you, not without coin."

I judged he wasn't trying to cheat me, just tell me the truth. I needed a partner if I was going to get anywhere in my quest, and who better than this blue-eyed blacksmith? So I gave him a hint of what else I was after. "Maybe *you* can contribute. What if I promised, in return, a share of the greatest treasure on earth?"

He finally laughed. "Greatest treasure? Which is?"

"A secret. But it could make a man a king."

"Ah. And where might this treasure be?"

"Right under our noses in Jerusalem, I hope."

"Do you know how many fools have hoped to find treasure in Jerusalem?"

"It's not the fools who will find it."

"You want me to spend *my* money looking for *your* woman?"

"I want you to invest in your future."

He licked his lips. "Smith found a bold, impudent, rascal, didn't he?"

"And you are a judge of character!" He might be skeptical, but he was also curious. Paying for word of Astiza would not really cost him much, I bet. And he had the same avarice as all of us: Everyone dreams of buried treasure.

"I could see if it's affordable."

I'd hooked him. "There's another thing I need as well. A good rifle."

¤   ¤   ¤

Jericho lived simply, despite some prosperity from his ironmonger trade. Because he was a Christian his house had more furnishings than a Muslim abode: Muhammadans rely on cushions that can be moved so the women can be sequestered when a male guest arrives. The habit of the Bedouin tent has never been left behind. We Christians, in contrast, are accustomed to having our heads closer to the warm ceiling than the cooler floor, and so sit high and formal, in stationary clutter. Jericho had a table, chairs, and armoires instead of Islamic cushions and chests. The carpentry was plain, however, with a Puritan simplicity. The plank floors were bare of carpets, and any decoration on the plaster walls was limited to the odd crucifix or picture of a saint: clean as a convent, and just as disconcerting. Miriam, the sister, kept it spotless. Food was plentiful, but basic: bread, olives, wine, and what greens the woman could buy each day in the market stalls. Occasionally she'd bring meat for her muscled, hungry brother, but it was relatively rare and expensive. Winter was coming, but there was no provision for heat except that given off by the charcoal of the cooking hearth and the forge below. There was no glass in the screened windows, so the coldest were blocked up by bags of sawdust for the season, adding to the autumn gloom. The basin water was cold, winds penetrating, candles and oil precious, and we slept and rose at farmer hours. For a Parisian layabout like me, Palestine was a shock.

It was the forging of my new rifle that first bonded us. Jericho was steady, skilled, quiet, diligent (all things I should emulate, I suppose) and had earned the town's respect. You could see it in the eyes of the men who came into the sooty courtyard to buy iron implements: Muslims, Christians, and Jews alike. I thought I might have to tutor him in the design of a good gun, but he was ahead of me. "You mean like the German jaegar, the hunting rifle?" he said when I described the piece I'd lost. "I've worked on some. Show me on the sand how long you want the piece to be."

I sketched out a forty-two-inch barrel.

"Won't that be clumsy?"

"The length gives it accuracy and killing power. Just forty-five caliber is enough; the rifle velocity makes up for bullets smaller than a musket's. I can carry more ammunition for a given weight of shot and powder. Soft iron, deep grooving, a drop to the stock to bring the sights up to my eye for aiming but keep my brow out of the pan flash. The best I've seen can drive a tack three times out of five at fifty yards. It takes a full minute to load and ram, but the first shot will actually hit something."

"Smoothbores are the rule here. Quick to load and you can shoot with anything—pebbles, if need be. For this gun, we'll need precise bullets."

"Precision means accuracy."

"In a close fight, sometimes speed wins." He had the prejudice of the sailors he had served with, who fought in sharp brawls when boarding.

"And the right shot can keep them from getting close at all. To my mind, trying to fight with an ordinary musket is like going to a brothel blindfolded—you might get the result you want, but you can miss by a mile, too."

"I wouldn't know about that." Damned if I could get him to joke. He looked at the pattern in the sand. "Four hundred hours of work. For which you'll pay me out of this treasure of yours?"

"Double. I'm going to be searching hard while you craft the rifle."

"No." He shook his head. "Easy to promise money you don't have. You'll help, and not just with this but other projects. It will be a new experience for you, doing real work. On slow days you can hunt for buried treasure or learn enough gossip to satisfy Sidney Smith. You can bill *him* to satisfy your debt to *me*."

Honest work? The idea was intriguing—truth be told, I'm sometimes envious of solid men like Jericho—but daunting, too. "I'll help at your forge," I bargained, "but you have to guarantee me enough hours to peck about. Get me the rifle by the end of winter, when Napoleon comes, and by that time I'll find the treasure and get Smith's money, too." Squeezing anything out of the Admiralty is like getting gravy from a shoelace, but spring was far off. Things could happen.

"Then bellow that fire." And when I leaped to obey, and shoveled charcoal, and shifted enough metal to make my shoulders ache, he grudgingly nodded. "Miriam thinks you're a good man."

And with her endorsement, I knew I had some trust.

Jericho first fetched a round metal rod, or mandrel, slightly smaller than the intended bore of my future rifle. He heated a bar of carbonized Damascus steel, called a skelp, the same length as my gun barrel. This he would wrap around the mandrel. I held the rod and handed tools while he placed these on a groove in a barrel anvil and began to beat to fuse the barrel's cylinder. He'd do an inch at a time, removing the rod while the metals were still slightly pliable, then plunging the result into sizzling water. Then it was reheat, wrap another inch of the steel, hammer, and reweld: inch by inch. It was tedious, painstaking work, but curiously enthralling too. This lengthening tube would become my new companion. The duty kept me warm, and hard physical work was its own satisfaction. I ate simply, slept well, and even came to feel comfortable in the pious simplicity of my lodging. My muscles, already toughened by Egypt, became harder still.

I tried to draw him out. "You're not married, Jericho?"

"Have you seen a wife?"

"A handsome, prosperous man like you?"

"I have no one I wish to marry."

"Me neither. Never met the right girl. Then this woman in Egypt . . ."

"We'll get word of her."

"So it's just you and your sister," I persisted.

He stopped his hammering, annoyed. "I was married once. She died carrying my child. Other things happened. I went to the British ship. And Miriam . . ."

Now I saw it. "Takes care of you, the grieving brother."

His gaze held mine. "As I take care of her."

"So if a suitor would appear?"

"She has no wish for suitors."

"But she's such a lovely girl. Sweet. Demure. Obedient."

"And you have your woman in Egypt."

"You need a wife," I advised. "And some children to make you laugh. Maybe I can scout about for you."

"I don't need a foreigner's eye. Or a wastrel's."

"Yet I might as well offer it, since I'm here!"

And I grinned, he grumped, and we went back to pounding metal.

When work was light I explored Jerusalem. I'd vary my dress slightly depending on which quarter I was in, trying to glean useful information through my Arabic, English, and French. Jerusalem was used to pilgrims, and my accents were unremarkable. The city's crossroads were its markets, where rich and poor mingled and janissary warriors casually shared meals with common artisans. The *khaskiyya*, or soup kitchens, provided welfare for the destitute, while the coffeehouses attracted men of all faiths to sip, smoke water pipes, and argue. The air, heady with the dark beans, rich Turkish tobacco, and hashish, was intoxicating. Occasionally I'd coax Jericho to come along. He needed a cup of wine or two to get going, but once started, his reluctant explanations of his homeland were invaluable.

"Everyone in Jerusalem thinks they're three steps closer to heaven," he summarized, "which means that together they create their own little hell."

"It is a weaponless city of peace and piety, is it not?"

"Until someone steps on someone else's piety."

If anyone questioned my own presence I'd explain I was a trade representative for the United States, which had been true in Paris. I was waiting to make deals with the winner, I said. I wanted to be friends with everyone.

The city was so filled with rumor of Napoleon's coming that it buzzed like a hive, but there was no consensus about which side was likely to prevail. Djezzar had been in ruthless control for a quarter century. Bonaparte had yet to be beaten. The English controlled the sea, and Palestine was but an islet in a vast Ottoman lake. While the Shiite and Sunni sects of the Muslim communities were at bitter odds with each other, and both Christians and Jews were restless minorities and mutually suspicious, it was not at all clear who might take arms against who. Would-be religious despots from half a dozen faiths dreamed of carving out their own puritanical utopias. While Smith hoped I might recruit for the British cause, I'd no real intention of doing so. I still liked French republican ideals and the men I'd served with, and I didn't necessarily disagree with Napoleon's dreams of reforming the Near East. Why should I take the side of the arrogant British, who had so bitterly fought my own nation's independence? All I really wanted was to hear of Astiza and find out if there was any chance this fabled

Book of Thoth might improbably have survived over three thousand years. And then flee this madhouse.

So I learned what I could in their hookah culture. It was a small town, and word inevitably spread of the infidel in Arab clothes who worked at the forge of a Christian, but there were any number of people with foggy pasts seeking any number of things. I was just one more, who did what life chiefly consists of: waiting.

CHAPTER 5

To pass the winter, I did my best to tease Miriam. I'd found a piece of amber in the market, an insect preserved inside. It was being sold as a slick and shiny good-luck charm, but I saw it as an artifact of science. I stole up behind her once when she was cleaning a chicken, rubbed the amber briskly on my robes, and then lifted my hand above the downy feathers. Some floated up to my down-turned palm.

She whirled. "How are you doing that?"

"I bring mysterious powers from France and America," I intoned.

She crossed herself. "It's evil to bring magic into this house."

"It's not magic, it's an electrical trick I learned from my mentor Franklin." I turned my palm so she could see the amber I held. "Even the ancient Greeks did this. If you rub amber, it will attract things. We call the magic electricity. I am an electrician."

"What a foolish idea," she said uncertainly.

"Here, try it." I took her hand, despite her hesitation, and put the amber in her fingers, enjoying the excuse to touch her. Her fingers were strong, red from work. Then I rubbed it on her sleeve and held it over the feathers. Sure enough, a few levitated to stick.

"Now you're an electrician, too."

She sniffed and gave it back to me. "How do you find time for useless games?"

"But perhaps they're not useless."

"If you're so clever, use your amber to pluck the next chicken!"

I laughed, and ran the amber past her cheek, pulling with it strands of her lovely hair. "It can serve as a comb, perhaps." I had created a blond veil, her eyes suspicious above it.

"You are an impudent man."

"Simply a curious one."

"Curious about what?" She blushed when she said it.

"Ah. Now you're beginning to understand me." I winked.

But she wouldn't allow things to go any further. I'd hoped to while away spare time by finding a card game or two, but I was in the worst city in the world for that. Jerusalem had fewer amusements than a Quaker picnic. Nor did there turn out to be much sexual temptation in a town where women were wrapped as tightly as a toddler in a Maine blizzard: my celibacy in Jaffa was involuntarily extended. Oh, women would give me a fetching eye now and again—I've got a bit of dash—but their allure was poisoned by lurid stories one heard in the coffeehouses of genital mutilation by angry fathers or brothers. It does give one pause.

In time I was so frustrated and bored that I took inspiration from my amber play and decided to tinker with electricity as Franklin had taught me. What had seemed a clever Parisian hobby to charm salons with an electric kiss—I could make a spark pass between a couple's lips, once I'd given a woman a charge with my machines—had taken on more seriousness after my sojourn in Egypt. Was it possible ancient people had turned such mysteries into powerful magic? Was that the secret of their civilizations? Science was also a way to give myself status during my winter of discontent in Jerusalem. Electricity was novel here.

With Jericho's reluctant tolerance, I built a frictional hand crank, with a glass disk to make a generator. When I rotated it against pads connected to a wire, the static charge was passed to glass jugs I lined with lead: my makeshift Leyden jars. I used strands of copper to wire these spark batteries in sequence and sent enough electricity to a chain to make customers jump if they touched it, numbing their limbs for hours. Students of human nature won't be surprised that men lined up to be jolted, shaking their tingling extremities in awe. I gained even more of a reputation as a sorcerer when I electrified my own arms and used my fingers to attract flakes of brass. I'd become a Count Silano, I realized, a conjurer. Men began to whisper about my powers, and I admit I enjoyed the notoriety. For Christmas I evacuated the air from a glass globe, spun it with my crank, and laid my palm on it. The ensuing purple glow lit the shed and entranced neighborhood children, though two old women fainted, a rabbi stormed from the room, and a Catholic priest held up a cross in my direction.

"It's just a parlor trick," I reassured them. "We did it all the time in France."

"And what are the French but infidels and atheists?" the priest rejoined. "No good will come from electricity."

"On the contrary, learned doctors in France and Germany believe electric shocks may be able to cure illness or madness." But since everyone knows physicians kill more than they cure, Jericho's neighbors were hardly impressed by this promise.

Miriam also remained dubious. "It seems like a lot of trouble just to sting someone."

"But why does it sting? That's what Ben Franklin wanted to understand."

"It comes from your cranking, does it not?"

"But why? If you churn milk or hoist a well bucket, do you get electricity? No, there is something special here, which Franklin thought might be the force that animates the universe. Perhaps electricity animates our souls."

"That is blasphemous!"

"Electricity is in our bodies. Electricians have tried to animate dead criminals with electricity."

"Ugh!"

"And their muscles actually moved, though their spirits had departed. Is electricity what gives us life? What if we could harness that force the way we harness fire, or the muscles of a horse? What if the ancient Egyptians did? The person who knew how might have unimaginable power."

"And is that what you seek, Ethan Gage? Unimaginable power?"

"When you've seen the pyramids, you wonder if men didn't have such power in the past. Why can't we relearn it today?"

"Perhaps because it caused more harm than good."

Meanwhile, Jerusalem worked its own spell. I don't know if human history can soak into soil like winter rain, but the places I visited had a palpable, haunting sense of time. Every wall held a memory, every lane a story. Here Jesus fell, there Solomon welcomed Sheba, into this square the Crusaders charged, and across that wall Saladin took the city back. Most extraordinary was the southeastern corner of the city, consisting of a vast artificial plateau built atop the mount where Abraham offered to sacrifice Isaac: the Temple Mount. Built by Herod the Great, it's a paved platform a quarter mile long and three hundred yards wide that covers, I was told, thirty-five acres. To hold a mere temple? Why did it have to be so big? Was it covering something—*hiding* something—more critical? I was reminded of our endless speculation about the true purpose of the pyramids.

Solomon's Temple was on this mount until first the Babylonians and then the Romans destroyed it. And then the Muslims built their golden mosque on the same spot. On the south end was another mosque, El-Aqsa, its form distorted by Crusader additions. Each faith had tried to leave its stamp, but the overall result was a serene emptiness, elevated above the commercial city like heaven itself. Children played and sheep grazed. I'd stride up sometimes through the Chain Gate and stroll its perimeter, viewing the surrounding hills with my little spyglass. The Muslims left me alone, whispering that I was a genie who tapped dark powers.

Despite my reputation, or perhaps because of it, I'd occasionally be allowed to enter the blue-tiled Dome of the Rock itself, taking off my boots before stepping on its red and green carpet. Perhaps they hoped I'd convert to Islam. The dome was held up by four massive piers and twelve columns, its interior decorated with mosaics and Islamic script. Beneath it was the sacred rock, Kubbet es-Sakhra, root stone of the world, where Abraham had offered to sacrifice his son, and where Muhammad had ascended for a tour of heaven. There was a well on one side of the rock, and reportedly a small cave underneath it. Was anything hidden *there*? If this was where Solomon's Temple once stood, wouldn't any Hebrew treasures have been secreted in the same place? But none were allowed to descend to the cave, and when I lingered too long, a Muslim caretaker would shoo me away.

So I speculated, and labored with Jericho to beat out horseshoes, sickles, fire tongs, hinges, and all the sundry hardware of everyday life. I had ample opportunity to interrogate my host.

"Are there any underground places in this city where something valuable might be hidden for a long time?"

Jericho barked a laugh. "Underground places in Jerusalem? Every cellar leads to a maze of abandoned tunnels and forgotten streets. Don't forget that this city has been sacked by half the world's nations, including your own Crusaders. So many throats have been cut that the groundwater should be blood. It is ruin built atop ruin atop ruin, not to mention a honeycomb of caves and quarries. Underground? There may be more Jerusalem down there than up here!"

"This thing I'm looking for was brought by the ancient Israelites."

He groaned. "Don't tell me you're looking for the Ark of the Covenant! That's a lunatic's myth. It may have been in Solomon's Temple once, but there's been no mention of it since Nebuchadnezzar destroyed Jerusalem and carried the Jews into exile in 586 B.C."

"No, no, I don't mean *that*." But I did mean it, or at least hope that the ark could lead me to the Book, or that they were one and the same. "Ark" means "box," and the Ark of the Covenant was supposedly the gold-plated acacia wood box where the Hebrews who escaped from Egypt kept the Ten Commandments. By reputation it had mysterious powers and was a help in defeating their enemies. Naturally I wondered if the Book of Thoth was in the container as well, since Astiza believed Moses had taken it. But I said none of this, yet.

"Good. It would take you all of eternity to dig up Jerusalem, and I suspect in the end you'd have no more than when you started. Crawl down holes if you will, but all you'll find are pot shards and rat bones."

¤   ¤   ¤

Miriam was a quiet woman, but gradually I realized that this quiet was a veil over a keen intelligence, with intense curiosity about the past. As different as she and Astiza were in personality, in intellect they were twins. In the early days of my stay she cooked and served our meals but ate apart. It wasn't until I'd worked awhile with Jericho at his forge, winning some small measure of trust, that I was able to cajole the two of them into letting her join us at the table. We weren't Muslims bound to segregate the sexes, after all, and their reluctance was curious. At first she spoke only when spoken to—she was again the opposite of Astiza in that way—and seemed to have little in need of saying. As I'd suspected, she was truly lovely—a beauty that always put me in mind of fruit and cream—but only with reluctance did she shed her scarf at table. When she did, her hair was a golden waterfall, as light as Astiza's was dark, her neck high, her cheeks lovely. I continued to pride myself on my chastity (since trying to find an adventuress in Jerusalem was like trying to find a virgin in the

card cozies of Paris, I might as well take satisfaction in my
enforced virtue) but I was astonished that this beauty hadn't
already been swept off by some persistent swain. At night I
could hear the sounds of her splashing as she carefully
bathed while standing in a wooden tub, and I couldn't help
but wonder about her breasts and belly, the roundness of her
rump, and the slim strong legs that my all-too-frustrated
brain imagined, runnels of soapy water cascading down the
perfect topography of her thighs and calves and ankles.
And then I'd groan, try to think about electricity, and finally resort to my fist.

At supper Miriam enjoyed our talk, her eyes quick and
lively. Brother and sister were people who'd seen some of
the world, and so they enjoyed my own stories of life in
Paris, growing up in America, my early fur-trading forays
on the Great Lakes, and my journeys down the Mississippi
to New Orleans and to the Caribbean Sugar Isles. They
were curious about Egypt as well. I didn't tell them about
the secrets of the Great Pyramid, but I described the Nile,
the great land and sea battles of the year before, and the
Temple of Dendara that I'd visited far to the south. Jericho
told me more of Palestine, of Galilee where Jesus walked,
and of the Christian sites I might visit on the Mount of Olives. After some hesitation, Miriam began to make shy sug-
gestions as well, hinting that she knew a great deal more
about historic Jerusalem than I would have guessed—more,
in fact, than her brother. Not only could she read—rare
enough for a woman in Muslim lands—but she did read,
avidly, and spent much of her quiet days, shielded from men
and free from children, in study of books she bought in the
market or borrowed from the nunneries.

"What are you reading?" I'd ask her.

"The past."

Jerusalem was a place pregnant with the past. I roamed
the hills outside the walls in chilly winter, when the light
cast long shadows across anonymous ruins. Once the bitter
wind brought light snow, the white coverlet followed by
pale blue skies, and a sun as heatless as a kite. It lit the landscape into sugar.

Meanwhile work on the rifle proceeded, and I could tell Jericho was enjoying the craftsmanship required. When the barrel was completely forged we drilled it out to the correct diameter, I turned the hand crank while he fed the clamped barrel toward me. It's hard work. When that was done he stretched a line through its bore, drawing it tight with a bent bow, and then sighted down its middle for shadows and ridges that would signal imperfections. Adept heating and hammering made the tube even straighter.

The grooved rifling that would spin the bullet was painstaking. There were seven grooves, each cut by a bit rotated through the barrel. Since it could not cut deeply, the bit had to be hand-twisted through the gun two hundred times per groove.

That was only the beginning. There was polishing, the bluing of the metal, and then the myriad metal parts for the flintlock, trigger, patch box, ramrod, and so on. My hands helped, but the skill was pure Jericho, his meaty paws able to produce results worthy of a maiden with a needle. He was happiest when silently working.

Maid Miriam surprised me one day by asking to measure my arm and shoulder. She, it turned out, would shape the rifle's stock, which has to be fitted to the rifleman's size like a coat. She'd volunteered for the job. "She has an artist's eye," Jericho explained. "Show her the drop and offset you want in the stock." There was no maple in Palestine, so she used desert acacia, the same wood used in the ark: heavier than I preferred, but hard and tight-grained. After I'd roughly sketched how I wanted the wood to differ from the design of Arab firearms, she translated my suggestion into graceful curves, reminiscent of Pennsylvania. When she measured my size to get the dimensions of the butt right, I trembled like a schoolboy at the touch of her fingers.

That's how chaste I'd become.

So I existed, sending vague political and military assessments to Smith that would have confused any strategist foolish enough to pay attention to them, until finally one evening our supper was interrupted by a hammering at

Jericho's door. The blacksmith went to check, and came back with a dusty, bearded traveler from the day's market caravan. "I bring the American word from Egypt," the visitor announced.

My heart hammered in my breast.

We sat him at the plain wood trestle table, gave him some water—he was Muslim, and refused any wine—and some olives and bread. While he gave uneasy thanks for our hospitality and ate like a wolf, I waited apprehensively, surprised at the flood of emotion rushing through my veins. Astiza had shrunken in memory during these weeks with Miriam. Now feelings buried for months pounded in my head as if I were still holding Astiza, or watching her desperately dangle on a rope below. I flushed impatiently, feeling the prickle of sweat. Miriam watched me.

There were the obligatory greetings, wishes for prosperity, thanks to the divine, a report on health—"How are you?" is one of the most profound queries of my age, given the prevalence of gout, ague, dropsy, chilblains, ophthalmia, aches, and faints—and recitation of the hardships of the journey.

Finally, "What news of this man's woman friend?"

The messenger swallowed, flicking bread crumbs from his beard. "There are reports of a French balloon lost during the October revolt in Cairo," he began. "Nothing about the American aboard; he is said to have simply disappeared, or deserted from the French army. There are a number of stories placing him at this location or that, but no agreement about what happened to him." He glanced at me, then down at the table. "No one confirms his story."

"But surely there are reports of the fate of Count Silano," I said.

"Count Alessandro Silano has similarly disappeared. He was reported investigating the Great Pyramid, and then vanished. Some suspect he may have been killed in the pyramid. Others think that he returned to Europe. The credulous think he disappeared by magic."

"No, no!" I objected. "He fell from the balloon!"

"There is no report of that, effendi. I am only telling you what is being said."

"And Astiza?"

"We could find no trace of her at all."

My heart sank. "No trace?"

"The house of Qelab Almani, the man you call Enoch, where you claimed to have stayed, was empty after his murder and has since been requisitioned as a French barracks. Yusuf al-Beni, who you said hosted this woman in his harem, denies that she ever stayed there. There was rumor of a beautiful woman accompanying General Desaix's expeditionary force to Upper Egypt, but if so, she too vanished. Of the wounded Mameluke Ashraf that you mentioned, we heard no word. No one remembers Astiza's presence in either Cairo or Alexandria. There is soldier talk of an attractive woman, yes, but no one claims to have seen her, or known her. It is almost as if she never existed."

"But she fell into the Nile too! An entire platoon saw it!"

"If so, my friend, she must never have emerged. Her memory is like a mirage."

I was stunned. Her death, the burial of her drowned body, I had braced for. Her survival, even if she was imprisoned, I had hoped for. But her complete disappearance? Had the river carried her away, never to be seen again or decently buried? What kind of answer was that? Silano gone too? That was even more suspicious. Had she somehow survived and gone with him? That was even greater agony!

"You must know something more than that! My God, the entire army knew her! Napoleon remarked on her! Key savants took her on their boat! Now there's no word at all?"

He looked at me with sympathy. "I am sorry, effendi. Sometimes God leaves more questions than answers, does he not?"

Humans can adapt to anything but uncertainty. The worst monsters are the ones we haven't yet encountered. Yet here I was, hearing her last words that rang in my head,

"Find it!" and then her cutting the rope, falling away with Silano, the screams, the blinding sun as the balloon soared away . . . was it all just a nightmare? No! It had been as real as this table.

Jericho was looking at me gloomily. Sympathy, yes, but also the knowledge that the Egyptian woman had kept me at a distance from his sister. Miriam's gaze was more direct than it ever had been before, and in her eyes I read sorrowful understanding. In that instant I realized she'd lost someone too. This was why no suitors were encouraged, and why her brother remained her closest companion. We were all bonded by grief.

"I just wanted a clear answer," I whispered.

"Your answer is, what is past is past." Our visitor stood. "I am sorry that I could not bring better news, but I am only the messenger. Jericho's friends will keep their ears open, of course. But do not hope. She is gone."

And with that, he, too, left.

CHAPTER 6

My first reaction was to depart Jerusalem, and the cursed East, immediately and forever. The bizarre odyssey with Bonaparte—escaping Paris, sailing from Toulon, the assault on Alexandria, meeting Astiza, and on and on through horrific battles, the loss of my friend Antoine Talma, and the bitter secret of the Great Pyramid—was like a mouthful of ashes. Nothing had come of it—no riches, no pardon for a crime in Paris I'd never committed, no permanent membership with the esteemed savants who had accompanied Napoleon's expedition, and no lasting love with the woman who'd entranced and bewitched me. I'd even lost my rifle! My only real reason for coming to Palestine was to learn Astiza's fate, and now that word was that there was no word (could any message be crueler?) my mission seemed futile. I didn't care about the coming invasion of Syria, the fate of Djezzar the Butcher, the career of Sir Sidney Smith, or the political calculations of Druze, Matuwelli, Jew, and all the rest trapped in their endless cycles of revenge and envy. How had I found myself in such a crazy necropolis of hatred? It was time to go home to America and start a normal life.

And yet . . . my resolution to get out and be done was paralyzed by the very fact of not knowing. If Astiza seemed not alive, neither was she definitely dead. There was no body. If I sailed away I'd be haunted the rest of my life. I had too many memories of her—of her showing me the star Sirius as we sailed up the Nile, her help in wrestling down Ashraf during the fury of the Battle of the Pyramids, her beauty when seated in Enoch's courtyard, or her vulnerability and eroticism when chained at the Temple of Dendara. And then possessing her body by the banks of the Nile! With a century or two to spare you might get over memories like that—but you wouldn't forget them. She haunted me.

As for the Book of Thoth, it might well be a myth—all we'd found in the pyramid, after all, was an empty repository for it, and perhaps Moses' taunting staff—and yet what if it wasn't, and really rested somewhere under my feet? Jericho was nearing completion on a rifle that I'd had a hand in building, and which seemed likely to be superior to the one I'd lost. And then there was Miriam, who I guessed had suffered a tragic loss before mine, and who was a partner in sorrow. With Astiza vanished, the woman whose house I shared, whose food I ate, and whose hands were shaping the wood of my own weapon, suddenly seemed more wondrous. Who did I have to return to in America? No one. So despite my frustration I found myself deciding to stay a little longer, at least until the gun was completed. I was a gambler, who waited for a turn of the cards. Maybe a new card would come now.

And I was curious who Miriam had lost.

She treated me with proper reserve as she had before, and yet our eye contact lingered longer now. When she set my plate she stood perceptibly closer, and the tone of her voice—was it my imagination?—was softer, more sympathetic. Jericho was watching both of us more closely, and would sometimes interrupt our conversations with gruff interjections. How could I blame him? She was a beautiful helpmate, loyal as a hound, and I was a shiftless foreigner, a treasure hunter with an uncertain future. I couldn't help but dream of having her, and Jericho was a man too: he knew what any man would wish. Worse, I might take her away to America. I noticed that he began devoting more hours to my rifle. He wanted to get it finished, and me gone.

We endured the late winter rains, Jerusalem gray and quiet. Reports came that Bonaparte's best general, Desaix, had reported fresh triumphs and seen spectacular new ruins far up the Nile. Smith was roving at sea between Acre, the blockade off Alexandria, and Constantinople, all to prepare for Napoleon's spring assault. French troops were assembling at El-Arish, near the border with Palestine. The strengthening sun slowly warmed the city stone, war drew nearer, and then one dusky evening when Miriam set out to the city's markets to fetch a missing spice for our evening's supper, I impulsively decided to follow. I wanted an opportunity to speak with her away from Jericho's protective presence. It was unseemly for a man to trail a single woman in Jerusalem, but perhaps some opportunity for conversation would present itself. I was lonely. What did I intend to say to Miriam? I didn't know.

I followed at a distance, trying to think of some plausible reason to approach, or a way to circle ahead so our meeting would seem to be coincidence. How odd that we humans have to think so deviously about ways to express our heart. She walked too quickly, however. She skirted the Pools of Hezekiah, descended to the long souk that divided the city, bought food once, passed up goods at two other stalls, and then took the lanes toward the markets of the Muslim Bezetha District, beyond the pasha's residence.

And then Miriam disappeared.

One moment she was descending the Via Dolorosa, toward the Temple Mount's Gate of Darkness and the El-Ghawanima Tower, and the next she was gone. I blinked, confused. Had she noticed me following, and was she trying to avoid me? I accelerated my pace, hurrying past locked doorways, until finally realizing I must have gone too far. I retraced my steps and then, from the courtyard adjacent to an ancient Roman arch that bridged the street, I heard talking, rough and urgent. It's odd how a sound or smell can jar memory, and I could swear there was something familiar about the male voice.

"Where does he go? Where is he looking?" The tone was threatening.

"I don't know!" She sounded terrified.

I stepped past iron grillwork into a dark, rubble-strewn courtyard, the ruins sometimes used as a goat pen. Four brutes, in French cloaks and European boots, surrounded the frightened young woman. I was, as I have said, weaponless, except for the Arab dagger I carried in my sash. But they hadn't seen me yet, so I had the advantage of surprise. These didn't look like the kind of men to bluff, so I glanced around for a better weapon. "To be thrown upon one's own resources is to be cast into the very lap of fortune," Ben Franklin used to say. But then he had more resources than most.

I finally spied a discarded stone Cupid, long since defaced and castrated by either Muslims or Christians trying to obey edicts about false idols and pagan penises. It lay on its side in the debris like a forgotten doll.

The sculpture was a third my height—heavy enough— and fortunately not held down by anything but its own weight. I could just barely lift it over my head. So I did, said a prayer to love, and heaved. It struck the huddled rascals in their back like pins in a bowl and they went down in a heap, cursing.

"Run for home!" I cried to gentle Miriam. They'd already ripped her clothing.

So she gave me a fearful nod, took a step to leave, and then swung back as one villain grabbed at her again. I thought maybe he'd pull her down, but even as he clawed she kicked him hard in his cockles as neatly as dancing a jig. I could hear the thump of the impact, and it froze him like a flamingo in a Quebec snowstorm. Then she broke free and sprang past out the gate. Brave girl! She had more pluck, and better knowledge of male anatomy, than I'd imagined.

Now the pack of ruffians rose against me, but meanwhile I'd hauled Cupid up again and had taken the cherub by his head. I swung him in a circle and let go. Two of the devils crashed down again and the statuary shattered. Meanwhile neighbors had heard the ruckus and were raising a hue and cry. A third villain began to draw a hidden sword—obviously sneaked past the police of Jerusalem—so I charged him with my Arab knife before he could clear his scabbard, ramming the blade home. For all my scuffles, I'd never stabbed anyone before, and I was surprised how readily it plunged in, and how eerily it scraped a rib when it did so. He hissed and twisted away so violently that I lost my grip. I staggered. Now I had no weapon at all.

Meanwhile the one who'd been interrogating Miriam had dragged out a pistol. Surely he wouldn't risk a shot in the sacred city, violating all laws, voices rising!

But the piece went off with a roar, its flash like a flicker of lightning, and something seared the side of my head. I lurched away, half-blinded. It was time to retreat! I tottered out to the street but now the bastard was coming after me, dark, his cape flying like wings, his own sword drawn. Who the devil *was* this? The blow of the pistol ball had left me so woozy I was wading in syrup.

And then, as I turned in the lane to meet him as best I could, a blunt staff thrust past me and struck the bastard smack where throat meets chest. He gave an awful cough and his feet slid out ahead of him, landing him on his backside. He looked up in amazement, gulping. It was Miriam, who'd taken a pole from a market awning and hefted it like a lance! I do have a knack for finding useful women.

"You!" he gagged, his eyes on me, not her. "Why aren't you dead?"

Neither are you, I thought, my own shock as great as his. For in the dusky light of the cobbled lane, I recognized first the emblem that Miriam's thrust had knocked out of his shirt—a Masonic compass and square, with the letter G inside—and then the swarthy face of the "customs inspector" who had accosted me on the stage to Toulon during my flight from Paris last year. He'd tried to take my medallion and I'd ended up shooting him with my rifle, while Sidney

Smith had shot another bandit in unseen support. I'd left this one howling, wondering if the wound had been mortal. Obviously not. What the devil was he doing in Jerusalem, armed to the teeth?

But I knew, of course, knew with dread that he had the same purpose as me, to search for ancient secrets. This was a confederate of Silano, and the French hadn't given up. He was here to look for the Book of Thoth. And, apparently, for me.

Before I had any chance to confirm this, however, he scrambled upward, listened to the shrieks of the neighbors and the cries of the watchmen, and fled, wheezing.

We ran the other way.

¤   ¤   ¤

Miriam was shaking as we made our way back to Jericho's house, my arm around her shoulder. We'd never been physically close, but now we clung instinctively. I took some of the less obvious back alleys I'd learned in my wanderings of Jerusalem, rats skittering away as I looked over my shoulder for pursuit. It was a climb back to Jericho's—none of the city is level, and the Christian quarter is higher than the Muslim—so after a while we paused for a moment in an alcove, to catch our breath and make sure that with my throbbing head I was taking the right direction. "I'm sorry about that," I told her. "It isn't you they are after, it's me."

"Who *are* those men?"

"The one who shot at me is French. I've seen him before."

"Seen him where?"

"In France. I shot *him*, actually."

"Ethan!"

"He was trying to rob me. Shame I didn't kill him then."

She looked as if seeing me for the first time.

"It wasn't about money, it was something more impor-

tant. I haven't told you and your brother the whole story."
Her mouth was half open. "I think it's time to."

"And this woman Astiza was part of it?" Her voice was
soft.

"Yes."

"Who was she?"

"A student of ancient times. A priestess, actually, but of
an old, old Egyptian goddess. Isis, if you've heard of her."

"The Black Madonna." It was a whisper.

"Who?"

"There has long been a cult of worshippers around the
statues of the Virgin carved in black stone. Some simply
saw it as a variation of Christian artwork, but others said it
was really a continuation of the cult of Isis. The White Madonna and the Black."

Interesting. Isis had turned up repeatedly during my
search in Egypt. And now this quiet woman, by all appear-
ances a pious Christian, knew something of her as well. I'd
never heard of a pagan goddess who got around so well.

"But why white and black?" I was reminded of the checkerboard pattern of the Paris Masonic lodges where I'd done
my best at grasping Freemasonry. And the twin pillars, one
black and one white, which flanked the lodge altar.

"Like night and day," Miriam said. "All things are dual,
and this is a teaching from the oldest times, long before Jerusalem and Jesus. Man and woman. Good and evil. High
and low. Sleep and wakefulness. Our secret mind and our
conscious mind. The universe is in constant tension, and
yet opposites must come together to make a whole."

"I heard the same from Astiza."

She nodded. "That man who shot at you had a medal
expressing this, did he not?"

"You mean the Masonic symbol of overlapping square
and compass?"

"I've seen that in England. The compass draws a circle,
while the carpenter's angle makes a square. Again, the
dual. And the G stands for God, in English, or *gnosis*,
knowledge, in Greek."

"The heretic Egyptian Rite began in England," I said.

"So what do those men want?"

"The same thing I seek. That Astiza and I sought. They might have held you for ransom to get to me."

She was still trembling. "His fingers were like talons."

I felt guilty at what I'd inadvertently dragged her into. What had been a treasure-hunting lark was now a perilous quest. "We're in a race to learn the truth before they do. I'm going to need Jericho's help."

She took my arm. "Let's go get it, then."

"Wait." I pulled her back into the darkness. I felt our scrape had given us some measure of emotional intimacy, and thus permission to ask a more personal question. "You lost someone too, didn't you?"

She was impatient. "Please, we must hurry."

"I could see it in your eyes when the messenger told me there's no trace of Astiza. I've wondered why you're not married, or betrothed: You're too pretty. But there was someone, wasn't there?"

She hesitated, but the peril had breached her reserve as well. "I'd met a man through Jericho, an apprentice smith in Nazareth. We were engaged in secret because my brother became jealous. Jericho and I were close as orphans, and suitors pain him. He found out and there was a row, but I was determined to marry. Before we could do so, my fiancé was pressed into Ottoman service. He was eventually sent to Egypt and never came back. He died at the Battle of the Pyramids."

I, of course, had been on the opposite side in that battle, watching the efficient slaughter the European troops carried out. What a waste. "I'm sorry," I said inadequately.

"That is war. War and fate. And now Bonaparte may come this way." She shuddered. "Is this secret you seek, will it help?"

"Help what?"

"Stop all the killing and violence. Make this city holy again."

Well, that was the question, wasn't it? Astiza and her

allies had never been certain whether they could use this mysterious Book of Thoth for good or must simply ensure it didn't fall into the wrong hands for evil.

"I only know it will hurt if that bastard who shot at us gets it first." And with that, I decided to kiss her.

It was a stolen kiss that took advantage of our emotional turmoil, and yet she didn't immediately pull away, even though I was hard against her thigh. I couldn't help my arousal, the action and intimacy had excited me, and the way she kissed back I knew it was reciprocated, at least a little. When she did pull away it was with a little gasp.

To keep me from pressing against her again, she looked from my eyes to my temple. "You're bleeding." It was a way to not talk of what we'd just done.

Indeed, the side of my head was wet and warm, and I had the damndest headache. "It's a scratch," I said, more bravely than I felt. "Let's go talk to your brother."

¤   ¤   ¤

W e'd better finish this rifle of yours," Jericho said when I told him our story.

"Capital idea. I might get you to forge me a tomahawk, too. *Ouch!*" Miriam was dressing my wound. It stung a little, but her strong fingers were wonderfully gentle as she wrapped my head. The pistol ball had only grazed me, but it shakes a man to come that close. Truth to tell, I also enjoyed being nursed. The woman and I had touched more in the last hour than the previous four months. "There's nothing more useful than those hatchets, and I lost mine. We're going to need every advantage we can get."

"We'll need to stand watch in case these ruffians come around. Miriam, you're not to leave this house."

She opened her mouth, then closed it.

Jericho was pacing. "I have an idea to improve the gun, if the rifle is as accurate as you claim. You said it is difficult to focus on targets at its farthest range, correct?"

"Once I aimed at an enemy and hit his camel."

"I've noticed you peer around the city with your spy-glass. What if we used it to help you aim?"

"But how?"

"By attaching it to the barrel."

Well, that was a perfectly ridiculous idea. It would add to the weight, make the gun clumsier, and get in the way of loading. It *must* be a bad idea because no one had done it before. And yet what if it would really help to see distant targets up close? "Could that work?" Franklin, I knew, would have been intrigued by this kind of tinkering. The unknown, which frightens most men, lured him like a siren.

"We can try. And we need allies if that gang of men is still in the city. You think you killed one?"

"Stabbed him. Who knows? I shot their leader in France, and here he is, big as life. I seem to have a hard time finishing people off." I thought of Silano and Achmed bin Sadr in Egypt, who both kept coming at me after various wounds. I not only needed that rifle, I needed practice with it.

"I'm going to send word to Sir Sidney," Jericho said. "The French agents here may be important enough for the British to send help. And Miriam said all this has something to do with that treasure you keep promising. What's really going on?"

It was past time to bring them into my confidence. "There may be something buried here in Jerusalem that could affect the course of the entire war. We hunted for it in Egypt, but decided in the end that it must have come to Israel. Yet every time I find a stair or a ladder leading downward, I come to a dead end. The city is a rubble heap. My quest may be impossible. Now the French are here, undoubtedly after the same thing."

"They asked about you," Miriam reminded.

"Yes, and did they just discover my presence or hear of it from afar? Jericho, could the people who asked about Astiza in Egypt have let slip my own existence?"

"They weren't supposed to . . . but wait. Find *what*, exactly? What is this treasure you seek?"

I took a breath. "The Book of Thoth."

"A book?" He was disappointed. "I thought you said it was treasure. I've spent the winter making a rifle for a book?"

"Books have power, Jericho. Look at the Bible or the Koran. And this book is different, it's a book of wisdom, power and . . . magic."

"Magic." His expression was flat.

"You don't have to believe me. All I know is that people have shot at me, thrown snakes in my bed, and chased me on camels and boats to get this book—or rather a medallion I had that was a clue to where the book was kept. It turned out the medallion was a key to a secret door in the Great Pyramid, which Astiza and I entered. We found an underground lake heaped with treasure, a marble pavilion, and a golden repository for this book."

"So you already have the treasure?"

"No. The only way to escape the pyramid was to swim through a tunnel. The weight of the gold and jewels threatened to drown me. I lost it all. The Jews might have hidden a different treasure here in Jerusalem."

He had the same skeptical look I used to get from Madame Durrell in Paris when I explained the lateness of my rent. "And the book?"

"The repository was empty. All that was left was a shepherd's crook lying next to it. Astiza convinced me that the crook had been carried by the man who stole the book, and that that man must have been . . ." I hesitated, knowing what this all must sound like.

"Who?"

"Moses."

For a moment he simply blinked, in consternation. Then he laughed, a scornful bark. "So! I have been hosting a madman! Does Sidney Smith know you are insane?"

"I haven't told him all this, and wouldn't tell *you* if we hadn't seen that Frenchman. I know it sounds odd, but that villain was allied with my greatest enemy, Count Silano. Which means time is short. We have to find the book before he does."

"A book Moses stole."

"Is it that impossible? An Egyptian prince kills an overseer in a fit of rage, flees the country, and then comes back after conversations with a burning bush to free the Hebrew slaves. All this you believe, correct? Yet suddenly Moses has the power to call down plagues, part the waters, and keep the Israelites fed in the wilderness of Sinai. Most men call it a simple miracle, a gift from God, but what if he discovered instructions to tell him how to do so? This is what Astiza believed. As a prince, he knew how to get in and out of the pyramid, which was but a decoy and a marker to protect the book from the unworthy. Moses takes it, and when Pharaoh discovers it gone, he pursues Moses and the Hebrew slaves with six hundred chariots, only to be swallowed by the Red Sea. Later, this tribe of ex-slaves enters the Promised Land and proceeds to conquer it from its civilized, established inhabitants. How? By an ark with mysterious powers or a book of ancient wisdom? I know it sounds improbable, and yet the French believe it too. Otherwise, these men wouldn't have seized your sister. This is a crisis as real as the bruises on her arms and shoulders."

The blacksmith looked at me, drumming his fingers. "You *are* mad."

I shook my head in frustration. "Then why do I have these?" And I reached in my robe to bring out the two golden seraphim, each four inches long. Miriam gasped and Jericho's eyes went wide. It wasn't just the brilliance of the gold, I knew, still vivid after thousands of years. It was the fact that these kneeling angels, their wings outstretched toward each other, were a tiny model of the ones that had once decorated the top of the Ark of the Covenant. This wasn't a cheap trick I could have had made up in an artisan's shop. The workmanship was too good, and the gold too heavy.

"One old man I met called these a compass," I went on. "I don't know what he meant. I don't know how much any of this is true. I've been operating on science, faith, and speculation since I fled Paris a year ago. But the pyramids seem to encode sophisticated mathematics that no primitive people would know. And where did civilization come from? In Egypt, it seemed to spring wholly formed. The legend is that human knowledge of architecture, writing, medicine, and astronomy came from a being called Thoth, who became an Egyptian god, predecessor of the Greek god Hermes. Thoth supposedly wrote a book of wisdom, a book so powerful that it could be used for evil as well as good. The Egyptian pharaohs, realizing its potency, safeguarded it under the Great Pyramid. But if Moses stole it, the book may have— must have—been brought here by the Jews."

"Moses didn't even get to the Promised Land," objected Miriam. "He died on Mount Nebo, looking across the river Jordan. He was not allowed by God to enter."

"But his successors came, with the ark. What if this book was part of the ark, or supplemented it? What if it was secreted under Solomon's Temple? And what if it survived the destruction of the First Temple by Nebuchadnezzar and the Babylonians and the Second Temple by Titus and the Romans? What if it's still here, waiting to be rediscovered? And what if it is found first by Bonaparte, who dreams of being another Alexander? Or by the followers of Count Alessandro Silano, who dream of enriching themselves and their corrupt Egyptian Rite of Freemasonry? What if Silano survived his fall from my balloon, even if Astiza did not? This book could tip the balance of power. It must be found and safeguarded or, if worse comes to worst, destroyed. All I'm saying is we have to look in every likely place before those French do."

"You live in my house, and work at my forge, and not until now do you tell me this?" Jericho was annoyed, and yet was looking curiously at my seraphim.

"I've tried to leave you and Miriam out of all this. It's a nightmare, not a privilege. But now, if you know of underground tunnels you must help me find them. The French will not give up. We're in a race."

"I'm a smith, not an explorer."

"And I'm a mere trade representative caught up in distant wars, not a soldier. Sometimes we're called to things, Jericho. You've been called to help me with this."

"To find Moses' magic book."

"Not Moses. Thoth."

"Ah. To find a book written by a mythical god, a false idol."

"No! To prevent the wrong people—the renegade Egyptian Rite of Freemasonry—from harnessing its power for evil." My frustration was rising because I knew how insane I sounded.

"The Egyptian Rite?"

"You remember the rumors of them in England, brother," Miriam said. "A secret society, said to have dark practices. Other Masons abhorred them."

"Yes, that's right," I encouraged. "I suspect the man who attacked your sister is one of them."

"But I work with hard iron and hot fire," Jericho protested. "Tangible things. I know nothing of ancient Jerusalem or hidden tunnels or lost books or renegade Masons."

I grimaced. How could I enlist him?

"Yet we know there is a scholar in this city who has researched the ancient pathways," Miriam allowed.

"You don't mean the usurer!"

"He's a student of the past, brother."

"A historian?" I interrupted. It sounded like Enoch, who had helped me in Egypt.

"More like a mutilated tax collector, but no one knows more about the history of Jerusalem," Jericho conceded. "Miriam has befriended him. We need lanterns, picks, help from Sidney Smith . . . and the counsel of Haim Farhi."

"And who is he?" I said cheerfully, relieved the blacksmith was helping.

"A man who knows more than anyone about the treasure hunters who came before you—the Christian knights who may have beaten you to your quest."

CHAPTER 7

I expected Haim Farhi would have some of the Aristotle-like gravity and dignity of Enoch, the mentor and antiquarian in Egypt who was murdered by my enemies. Instead, I was struggling not to gape. It wasn't just that this short, slight, middle-aged Jew with corkscrew sidelocks and dour, dark clothing lacked Enoch's majesty. It was that he had been mutilated into one of the most hideous men I'd ever seen. Part of his nose was carved away, leaving a piglike snout. His right ear was missing. And his right eye had been gouged, leaving a socket closed by a scar.

"My God, what happened to him?" I whispered to Jericho as Miriam took the man's cloak at the door.

"He incurred the ire of Djezzar the Butcher," the smith replied quietly. "Do not express pity. He carries his survival like a badge of honor. He's one of the most powerful bankers in Palestine and has Djezzar's trust, having remained loyal after torture."

"People use him for their savings and loans?"

"It was his face that was damaged, not his mind."

"Rabbi Farhi is one of the province's foremost historians," Miriam said more loudly as they came toward us, both guessing the reason for our whispers. "He's also a student of Jewish mysteries. Anyone delving into the past is wise to seek his counsel."

"So I appreciate his help," I said diplomatically, trying not to stare.

"As I appreciate your tolerance of my misfortune," Farhi replied in a serene voice. "I know my effect on people. I see my disfigurement mirrored in the look of every frightened child. But mutilation's isolation gives me time for this city's legends. Jericho tells me you're searching for lost secrets of strategic significance, yes?"

"Possibly."

"Possibly? Come, if we're to make progress we must trust each other, must we not?"

I was learning not to trust much of anyone, but didn't say that, or anything else.

"And these items may have some connection with the Ark of the Covenant," Farhi persisted. "Is this not so as well?"

"It is." Obviously he knew what I'd told Jericho.

"I can understand why you've journeyed so far, with such excitement. Yet it is my sad responsibility to warn that you may be seven hundred years too late. Men have come to Jerusalem before, seeking the same powers you have."

"And you're going to tell me they tried their best and didn't find them."

"On the contrary, I am going to tell you they possibly found exactly what you are looking for. Or, that if they didn't, it's unlikely you could succeed either. They searched for years. Jericho tells me you have days, at most."

What did this mutilated man know? "Found what, exactly?"

"Curiously, scholars still argue about that. A group of Christian knights came away from Jerusalem with inexplicable powers, and yet they proved powerless when they were betrayed. So did they find something? Or not?"

"A fairy story," Jericho scoffed.

"But one grounded in history, brother," Miriam said quietly.

"Those stories of tunnels are musty legends," Jericho insisted to Miriam.

"And what is legend but an echo of truth?" his sister answered.

I looked among the three of them. They'd argued this before. "*What* legends?"

"Of our ancestors, the Knights Templar," Miriam said. "Their full name was the Poor Knights of Christ on the Temple of Solomon. Not all the warrior monks were celibate, and tradition holds that our blood descends from theirs. They sought what you seek, and some think they found it."

"Do they now?"

"It's a curious story," Farhi said. "I understand you have lived in Paris, Mr. Gage? Are you familiar with the Champagne region of France, southeast of Paris and north of Troyes?"

"I've passed through, and enjoyed its products."

"More than thirteen hundred years ago, one of the most terrible battles in all history was fought there. The last of the Romans defeated Attila, the great Hun."

"The Battle of Chalons," I said, grateful that Franklin had mentioned this ancient scrape once or twice. He was a fount of oddball information, and read history books thick enough for three doorstops, written by some Englishman named Gibbon.

"At this battle Attila had a mysterious ancient sword with mystical powers, dating far, far back in time. Legends of such enchantments, and the idea that there are greater powers in this world than mere muscle and steel, carried down to the generations of Franks who came to inhabit Champagne. These were people who thought there might be more to the world than what we easily see and touch. The great saint and teacher Saint Bernard of Clairvaux was one who heard these stories."

That name struck a bell too. I remembered the French

savant Jomard evoking him when we first climbed the Great Pyramid. "Wait, I've heard of him. He said something about God being height and breadth—being dimensions. That you could incorporate divine dimensions into holy buildings."

"Yes. 'What is God? He is length, width, height and depth,' the saint said. And the powerful knight André de Montbard, Bernard's uncle, shared the idea that ancients who knew such things might have buried powerful secrets in the East. Buried, perhaps, beneath Solomon's Temple, which occupied the Temple Mount a short distance from where we sit."

"Freemasons believe that to this day," I said, remembering my dead journalist friend, Antoine Talma, and his enthusiastic theories.

"In 1119," Farhi went on, "Bernard's uncle, Montbard, was one of nine knights who journeyed to the Holy Land on a special mission. Jerusalem had already been captured by the Crusaders, and these nine arrived in the city and asked to form a new military order of warrior-monks called the Templars. Yet from the very beginning their purpose seemed mysterious. They proposed to protect Christian pilgrims, but these men from Champagne initially recruited no followers and did little patrolling of the Jaffa road. Instead, they got extraordinary permission from the ruler of Jerusalem, King Baldwin II, to set up their headquarters in the El-Aqsa Mosque, on the southern end of the Temple Mount."

"Nine newcomers get to camp on the Temple Mount?"

Farhi nodded, fixing me with his one good eye. "Curious, isn't it?"

"And what do these Templars have to do with Moses and the ark?" I asked.

"Here we come to speculation," Farhi said. "The rumors are that they tunneled into the roots of what had been Solomon's Temple and found . . . *something*. After their sojourn here, they returned to Europe, were given special status by the pope, and became the continent's first bankers and most powerful military order. Recruits flocked to them. They were rich beyond imagination, and kings trembled before the Templar Order. And then on one, single, terrible night—on Friday, October 13, 1309—the Templar leaders were arrested in a massive purge by the king of France. Hundreds were tortured and burned. With them died the secrets of what they'd found in Jerusalem. So legends began: how did an obscure order of knights grow so rich and powerful so quickly?"

"You think they found the Ark?"

"No trace of it has ever been seen."

"Soon after," Miriam added, "stories began to be sung of knights in search of a Holy Grail."

"The cup of the Last Supper," I said.

"That's one story," Farhi said. "But the Grail has also been described in various accounts as a cauldron, a platter, a stone, a sword, a spear, a fish, a table . . . and even a secret book." He was watching me carefully.

"The Book of Thoth!"

"I haven't heard it called that, until now. And yet the story you've told Jericho and Miriam is intriguing. The god Thoth was the precursor of the Greek god Hermes. Did you know that?"

"Yes, I learned that in Egypt."

"In the legend of Parzival, finished in 1210, the hero seeks counsel from a wise old hermit named Treurizent. Do you recognize that name?"

I shook my head.

"Some scholars believe it comes from the French *treble escient.*"

Now I felt a warm surge of excitement. "Thrice knowing! Which is what the Greek name Hermes Trismegistus means, Hermes the thrice knowing, master of all crafts, who in turn is the Egyptian god Thoth!"

"Yes. Three Times Greatest, the First Intelligence, the originator of civilization. He was the first great author, the one we Jews know as Enoch."

"Enoch was the name my mentor in Egypt took."

"I'm not surprised. Now, when the Templars were arrested they were accused of heresy. They were charged with obscene rituals, sex with other men, and worshipping a mysterious figure named Baphomet. Have you ever heard of him?"

"No."

"He's been portrayed as a goat-headed demon, or devil. Yet there is a curiosity about that name. If it came from Jerusalem, it could be a corruption of the Arabic word *abufihamat*, pronounced 'bufihimat.' It means 'father of wisdom.' And who could that be, to men who called themselves Knights of the Temple?"

I thought a moment. "King Solomon."

"Yes! The connections continue. The ancient Jews also had the habit, during foreign occupation, of sometimes writing secret codes using substitution ciphers. In the Atbash cipher, each letter of the Hebrew alphabet actually represents another letter. The first letter becomes the last in the alphabet, the second letter the second-to-the-last, and so on. If you spell Baphomet in Hebrew, and then translate it using this Atbash cipher, it comes out reading *sophia*, the Greek word for wisdom."

"Baphomet. Solomon. Sophia. So the knights were pledging themselves to wisdom, not to a demon?"

"That is my theory," Farhi said modestly.

"Then why were they persecuted?"

"Because the king of France feared them and wanted their wealth. What better way to discredit your enemies than to accuse them of blasphemy?"

"The knights may have pledged themselves to something more tangible," Miriam said. "Did you not tell us, Ethan, that *thoth* is allegedly the origin of the English word for 'thought'?"

"Yes."

"And so the chain is even longer. Baphomet is the Father of Wisdom, is Solomon, is Sophia . . . but could he also not be thought, Thoth, your original god of all learning?"

I was stunned. Had the Knights Templar, the reputed ancestors of my own fraternal Masonic lodges, know of this ancient Egyptian deity? Had they even worshipped it? Was all this nonsense connected, in ways that stretched from Masons to Templars, and from Templars back through Greeks, Romans, Jews, to ancient Egypt? Was there a secret history that wound through all the world's time, paralleling the commonly known one?

"And how did Solomon become so wise?" Jericho said slowly. "If this book were real, and the king had it in his possession. . . ."

"There were dark rumors Solomon had the power to summon demons," Miriam said. "And so the stories loop on themselves—that pious men sought only knowledge, or that the knowledge itself was corrupting, leading to riches and evil. Is knowledge good or bad? Look at the story of the Garden of Eden and the Tree of Knowledge of Good and Evil. Back and forth the legends and arguments go."

I was dazed with the possibilities. "You think the Knights Templar already found this book?"

"If they did they may have lost it in the purge that followed," Farhi said. "Your particular Grail may be nothing but ashes, or in other hands. Yet no power followed the Templars. No group of knights ever equaled them, and no fraternity ever again became so widespread over Europe. And when Jacques de Molay, the last grand master, was burned at the stake for refusing to betray Templar secrets, he levied a terrible curse by promising that the king of France and the pope would follow him to the grave within a year. Both did so. So was the book found to begin with? Was it lost? Or was it . . ."

"Re-hidden," Miriam said.

"In the Temple Mount!" I cried.

"Possibly, but in places so deep it cannot be easily found again. Moreover, when Saladin recaptured Jerusalem from the Crusaders, the possibility of penetrating the mount seemed lost. Even now, the Muslims guard it zealously. No doubt they've heard some of the stories we have. Yet they allow no exploration. These secrets could shake all religions to their foundations, and Islam is an enemy of witchcraft."

"You mean we can't get in there?"

"If we tried and were found, we'd be executed. It is

sacred ground. Excavations in the past have caused riots. It would be as if we tried to excavate St. Peter's."

"Then why are we talking?"

They glanced at each other in mutual understanding.

"Ah. So we must not be found."

"Exactly," Jericho said. "Farhi has suggested a possible path."

"Why hasn't he taken this path himself?"

"Because it is wet, filthy, dangerous, confined, and probably futile," Farhi said cheerfully. "We were, after all, dealing only with vague historical legend until you come with claims that something extraordinary really existed in ancient Egypt, and was perhaps carried here. Do I believe it? No. You may be an entertaining liar, or a credulous fool. But do I *disbelieve*, when its existence may have represented great power to my people? I can't afford to."

"So you will lead us?"

"As well as a disfigured bookkeeper can."

"For a share of the treasure, I presume."

"For truth and knowledge, as Thoth would be content with."

"Which Miriam said could be used for good or evil."

"The same could be said about money, my friend."

Well, anytime a stranger announces altruism, and calls me friend, I wonder what pocket he's reaching into. But in my own months of searching I hadn't found a clue, had I? Maybe he and I could use each other. "Where do we start?"

"Between the Dome of the Rock and the El-Aqsa Mosque is the Fountain of El-Kas," Farhi said crisply. "It draws its water from ancient rain cisterns deep within the Temple Mount. Those cisterns are connected by tunnels, to feed each other. Some writers have speculated they are part of a vein of passages that may extend even under the holy rock Kubbet es-Sakhra itself, where Abraham offered his sacrifice to God: the foundation stone of the world. Moreover, these cisterns must also be connected to springs, not just rainwater. Accordingly, a decade ago I was asked by Djezzar to search the ancient records for underground passageways into Temple Mount. I told him I found none."

"You lied?"

"It was a costly admission of failure. I was mutilated as punishment. But the reason is that I *did* find old records, fragmentary accounts, suggesting a secret route to powers so great that a man such as Djezzar must never get them. The Spring of Gihon that feeds the Pool of Siloam, outside the city walls, may offer a way. If so, the Muslims would never see us."

"The cisterns," said Miriam, "might lead to the deepest places where the Jews may have hid the ark, the book, and other treasures."

"Until, perhaps, they were uncovered by the Knights Templar," Farhi added. "And, perhaps, re-hidden—after Jacques de Molay burned at the stake. There is one other problem, however, that has also discouraged me from pursuing any exploration."

"The tunnels are blocked by water?" I had grim memories of my escape from the Great Pyramid.

"Possibly. But even if they are not, one record I found made reference to doors that are sealed. What was once open may now be closed."

"Determined men can force any locked door, with enough muscle or gunpowder," Jericho said.

"Not gunpowder!" Farhi said. "Do you want to arouse the city?"

"Muscle, then."

"What if the Muslims hear us poking around down there?" I asked.

"That," the banker said, "would be most unfortunate."

¤   ¤   ¤

My rifle was complete. Jericho had carefully pasted two of Miriam's hairs on its telescope to give an aiming point, and when I tested the gun outside the city I found I could reliably hit a plate at two hundred yards. A musket, in contrast, was inaccurate after fifty. But when I took the piece up to watch for the French brigands from our rooftop, peering until my eye ached, I saw nothing. Had they left? I fantasized that they hadn't, that Alessandro Silano was here, secretly directing them, and that I could capture and interrogate him about Astiza.

But it was as if the gang had never existed.

Miriam has used bright brass to inset two replica seraphim on each side of the wooden stock as patch boxes where I kept my greased wadding. Pushed by the bullet, it cleans the barrel of powder residue with each shot. The seraphim crouched with wings outstretched like those on the Ark. She also made me a new tomahawk. I was so pleased I gave a dubious Jericho some instruction on how to win at *pharaon*, should he ever find a game, and bought a small golden Spanish cross for Miriam. I also wasn't entirely surprised, when our evening of adventure came, that Miriam insisted she come along, despite the custom to cloister women in Jerusalem. "She knows old legends that bore me," Jericho admitted. "She sees things I don't, or won't. And I don't want to leave her alone with the French thieves skulking about."

"We agree on that," I said.

"Besides, the two of you need a woman's sense," she said.

"It's important we move stealthily," Jericho added. "Miriam said you have red Indian skills."

Truth be told, my red Indian skills had consisted primarily of avoiding the savages whenever I could, and buying them off with presents when I couldn't. My few scrapes with them had been terrifying. But I had exaggerated my frontier exploits to Miriam (a bad habit of mine), and it wouldn't do to set the record straight now.

Farhi also came, dressed in black. "My presence may be even more important than I thought," he said. "There are Jewish mysteries too, and since our conversation I've been studying what the Templars studied, including the numerology of the Jewish kabbalah and its Book of Zohar."

"Another book? What's this one for?"

"Some of us believe the Torah, or your Bible, can be read at two levels. One is the stories we all know. The second is that there is another story, a mystery, a sacred story—a story hidden between the lines—embedded in a number code. That is Zohar."

"The Bible is a code?"

"Each letter of the Hebrew alphabet can be represented by a number, and there are ten more numbers beyond, representing the sacred *sefiroth*. These are the code."

"Ten what?"

"*Sefiroth*. They are the six directions of reality—the four cardinals of east, west, north, and south, plus up and down—and the makings of the universe, being fire, water, ether, and God. These ten *sefiroth* and twenty-two letters represent the thirty-two ways of wisdom, which in turn point toward the seventy-two sacred names of God. Can this Book of Thoth perhaps be read in the same way? What is its key? We will see."

Well, here was more of the same gibberish I'd encountered ever since I'd won the damned Egyptian medallion in Paris. Lunacy, apparently, is contagious. So many people seem to believe in legends, numerology, and mathematical marvels that I'd begun to believe too, even if I could rarely make heads or tails of what people were talking about. But if a disfigured banker like Farhi was willing to muck about in the bowels of the earth because of Jewish numerology, then it seemed worth my time, too.

"Well, welcome. Try to keep up." I turned to Jericho. "Why are you shouldering a bag of mortar?"

"To brick up whatever we break into. The secret to stealing things is to make it look like no theft has occurred."

That's the kind of thinking I admire.

We slipped out the Dung Gate after dark. It was early March, and Napoleon's invasion had already begun. Word had come that the French had marched from El-Arish at the border between Egypt and Palestine on February 15, won a quick victory at Gaza, and were approaching Jaffa. Time was short. We made our way down the rocky slope to the Pool of Siloam, a plumbing fixture since King David's time, me breezily giving advice to crouch here and scurry there as if it were really trusty Algonquin lore. The truth is, I'm more at home in a gambling salon than wilderness, but Miriam seemed impressed.

There was a new moon, a sliver that left the hillside dark, and the early spring night air was cold. Dogs barked from the hovels of a few shepherds and goatherds as we clambered over old ruins. Behind us, forming a dark line against the sky, were the city walls that enclosed the south side of the Temple Mount. I could see the form of El-Aqsa up there, and the walls and arches of its Templar additions.

Were Muslim sentries peering down? As we crept along, I had an uneasy feeling of being watched. "Someone's out there," I whispered to Jericho.

"Where?"

"I don't know. I feel them, but can't see them."

He looked around. "I've heard nothing. I think you frightened the French away."

I fingered my tomahawk and took my rifle in both hands. "You three go ahead. I'll see if I can catch anyone behind."

But the night seemed as empty as a magician's black bag. At length, knowing the others were waiting, I went on to the Pool of Siloam, a rectangular ink pit near the valley floor. Worn stone steps led downward to a stone platform from which women could dip their jars. Sparrows, which nested in the pit's stone walls, rustled uneasily. Only the faintest gleam of faces showed me where the others huddled.

And our group had grown.

"Sir Sidney *did* send help," Jericho explained.

"British?" Now I understood my foreboding.

"We'll need their labor underground."

"Lieutenant Henry Tentwhistle of HMS *Dangerous* at your service, Mr. Gage," their crouched commander whispered in the dark. "You will recall, perhaps, your success at outbluffing me in our games of *brelan*."

I groaned inwardly. "I was lucky in the face of your boldness, Lieutenant."

"This is Ensign Potts, who you bested in *pharaon*. Took six months' wages."

"Surely not that much." I shook his hand. "How desperately I have needed it to complete the Crown's mission here in Jerusalem."

"And these two lads you know as well, I believe."

Even in the midnight gloom of the Pool of Siloam, I could recognize the barricade gleam of a memorably wide and hostile smile of piano-key teeth.

"You owes me a tussle, after this," the owner said.

"And our money back besides."

But of course. It was Big Ned and Little Tom.

CHAPTER 8

Y ou should be honored, guv'nor," Big Ned said.

"This is the only mission we's ever volunteered for," said Little Tom.

"Sir Sidney thought it best for us all to work together."

"It's because of *you* we're along."

"Flattered, I'm sure," I said weakly. "You couldn't advise me of this, Jericho?"

"Sir Sidney teaches: the fewer to speak, the better."

Indeed. Old Ben himself said, "Three may keep a secret if two of them are dead."

"So he sent four more along?"

"The way we figured it, there must be money at stake to draw in a weasel like you," Little Tom said cheerfully. "Then they issued us picks and we say to each other, well, it must be buried treasure! And this Yankee, he can settle with Ned here as he promised on the frigate—or he can give us his share."

"We're not as simple as you think," Big Ned added.

"Clearly. Well," I said, looking at the decidedly unfriendly squad of sailors, trying to ignore my instinct that this was all going to turn out badly, "it's good to have allies, lads, who've met over friendly games of chance. Now then. There's a bit of danger here, and we must be quiet as mice, but there's a real chance to make history, too. No treasure, but a chance to find a secret corridor into the heart of the enemy, should Boney seize this town. That's our mission. My philosophy is that what's past is past, and what comes, comes best to men who stand with each other, don't you think? Every penny I have goes into the Crown's business, after all."

"Crown's business? And what's that fine firearm you're bearing, then?" Little Tom pointed.

"This rifle?" It did gleam ostentatiously. "Why, a foremost example. For your protection, since it's my responsibility that none of you come to harm."

"Costly little piece, it looks to me. As made up as a high-class tart, that gun is. Lot of our money went into that, I'll wager."

"It cost hardly a trifle here in Jerusalem," I insisted. "Eastern manufacture, no knowledge of real gunnery. . . . Pretty piece of rubbish, actually." I avoided Jericho's glare. "Now, I can't promise we'll find anything of value. But if we do, then of course you lads can have my share and I'll just content myself with the odd scroll or two. That's the spirit of cooperation I'd like to enter with, eh? All cats are gray in the dark, as Ben Franklin liked to say."

"Who said?" asked Tom.

"Bloody rebel who should have hanged," Big Ned rumbled.

"And what the devil does it mean?"

"That we're a bag of bloody cats, or something."

"That we're all one until the mission is over," Tentwhistle corrected.

"And who's this damsel, then?" Little Tom said, poking at Miriam. She stepped distastefully away.

"My sister," Jericho growled.

"Sister!" Tom stepped back as if he'd been given a jolt of electricity. "You take your *sister* on a treasure hunt? What the devil for?"

"She sees things," I said.

"The hell she does," Ned said. "And who's that back there?"

"Our Jewish guide."

"A Jew, too?"

"Molls are bad luck," Tom said.

"Nor are we carrying her," his companion added.

"As if I'd let you," Miriam snapped.

"Be careful, Ned," I warned. "Her knee knows where your cockles are."

"Does it now?" He looked at her with more interest.

By the lawns of Lexington, wasn't this a fine mess? I couldn't have made a worse stew if I'd invited anarchists to draw up a constitution. So, thoroughly unsettled, we stepped into the shallow pool and waded knee-deep water to its end. Current issued from a cavelike opening secured by an iron grate.

"Built to keep out children and animals," Jericho said, hefting his iron pry bar. "Not us." He applied muscle and leverage and there was a snap, the rusty grill swinging inward with a screech. Once inside, our ironmonger closed the gate behind us, securing it with his own new padlock. "For this one I have a key."

I looked behind at the well's long rim. Had someone ducked out of sight? "Did you see anything?" I whispered to Farhi.

"I haven't been able to see since we left Jericho's house," the old banker grumbled. "This is not my habit, splashing in the dark."

Soon the water was thigh-deep, cool but not cold. The tunnel passage we were wading into was as wide as my outstretched arms and from ten to fifteen feet high, bearing the texture of ancient picks. This was a man-made tube built to bring natural spring water into King David's old city, Farhi told us. Its bottom was uneven, making us stumble. When we were far enough into the tunnel for Jericho to risk lighting the first lantern, I splashed up to Tentwhistle. "There's no chance you were followed down here, was there?" I asked.

"We paid our guides to keep their mouths shut," the lieutenant said.

"Aye, and didn't breathe a word in Jerusalem, neither," Ned put in.

"Wait. The four of you English sailors went *inside* the city?"

"Just to get some tack."

"I told you to lie low until dark!" Jericho hissed with exasperation.

"We were in Arab sheets, and kept to ourselves," Tentwhistle said defensively. "By the pulpit, I'm not getting all the way to Jerusalem and not have a look around. Famous town, it is."

"Arab sheets!" I exclaimed. "All of you look as Arab as Father Christmas! Your beet-red faces couldn't be any more obvious if you'd marched in with the Union Jack!"

"So we was s'posed to starve ourselves until nightfall and then dig *you* a hole?" Big Ned countered. "Meet us with some tucker if you're so determined to keep us out of your precious city."

Well, what could we do about it now? I turned to Jericho, his face gloomy in the amber lantern light. "I think we'd better hurry."

"I left a strong padlock at the grate. But you're our rear guard, with your rifle."

Suddenly Miriam yelped from the shadows. "Don't touch me!"

"Sorry, did I brush against?" Little Tom said salaciously.

"Here, doll, I'll keep you safe," Ned added.

Jericho started to raise his pick, but I stayed his hand. "I'll handle this." As I pushed my way back to the rear of the file, I let the barrel of my new rifle drive into Ned's groin. "Bloody hell!" he gasped.

"My clumsiness," I said, swinging the stock away so abruptly that it nicely clipped the side of Little Tom's face.

"Bastard!"

"I'm sure if we all keep our distance, we won't bump."

"I'll stand where I bloody well . . ." Then Tom yelped and jumped. "That bitch snuck up behind!"

"Sorry, did I brush against?" Miriam was holding a pry bar.

"I warned you, gentlemen. Keep distant if you value your manhood."

"I'll geld you myself if you touch my sister again," Jericho added.

"And I'll give you both a dance with the lash," Tentwhistle said. "Ensign Potts! Keep discipline!"

"Yes sir! You two—behave!"

"Ah, we was just playing . . . Lord on high! What happened to *him*?" Farhi had passed through the lantern light, and the startled sailors had their first look at his mutilated face: the cratered eye, the snoutlike nose, the butchered ear.

"I touched his sister," the Jew said slyly.

The sailors went white and kept as far from Miriam as they could.

¤   ¤   ¤

If there was any advantage to the long slog through thigh-deep water, it was that it took some starch out of the panting sailors. They weren't used to close places or land work, and only their assumption of ancient coin kept them from balking entirely. To keep them wheezing, I suggested to Tentwhistle that Ned and Tom help carry Jericho's bag of mortar.

"Why don't we all just carry a hod of bloody bricks while we're at it?" Ned complained. But he plodded on like a mule, all of us wading in a cocoon of lantern light. I paused once to listen while the others pushed ahead, darkness growing as they receded. There—was that the echo of a clang, of a padlock being broken far behind? Yet at such a distance it was hardly more audible than the drop of a pin, and I heard nothing else. At length I gave up and hurried to catch the others.

Finally there was the sound of running water and the tunnel began lowering toward the water surface. Soon we'd be crawling.

"We are nearing the natural spring," Farhi said. "Legend says that somewhere above is the navel of Jerusalem."

"I think we're in the bloody arse, meself," Little Tom muttered.

We hunted with our lanterns until we indeed found a dark slit overhead, tight as a purser's pocket. I wouldn't have guessed it led anywhere, but once we'd boosted each other up it opened and a passage angled back toward the main city, dry this time. We crawled over boulders fallen from the ceiling, Miriam more agile than any of us. There was another mouse hole and the woman led the way, Big Ned cursing as he barely squeezed through, pushing the sack of mortar. He was covered in a sweaty sheen. Then the tunnel became regular again, man-made. It led upward at a steady slope, its ceiling only a foot above our heads and its diameter too narrow for two men to easily pass. Ned kept bumping his crown and cursing.

"Legend has it that this passage was built just wide enough for a shield," Farhi said. "A single man could hold it against an army of invaders. We're on the right path."

As we advanced the air grew stale and the lanterns dimmer. I had no idea how far we'd come or what time it was. I wouldn't have been surprised to have been told we'd walked, waded and crawled back to Paris. Finally we came to dressed stone, not cave walls. "Herod's wall," Jericho murmured. "We're passing under it, and thus under the Temple Mount platform itself, far above."

We pressed on, and once more I heard water ahead. Suddenly our passageway ended in a large cave barely bridged by our feeble light. Jericho had me hold his lantern while he cautiously lowered himself into a pool below. "It's all right, only chest deep and clean," he announced. "We've found the cisterns. Be as quiet as you can."

At the other side the tunnel went on. We came to a second cistern and then a third, each about ten yards across. "In a wetter season all these passages would be underwater," Jericho said.

Finally the passageway led upward again to a dry cavern, and at last our path abruptly ended. The ceiling was higher because of a cave-in of stone that half-filled the chamber, raising its floor as well. Beyond, we could see the top of an arched doorway made of stone. Trouble was, its door was gone and the opening had been entirely filled with mortared stone blocks, our way plugged.

"Bloody hell, it's all for nothing then," Ned wheezed.

"Is it?" Jericho said. "What's behind this wall that its builders didn't want us to get to?"

"Or let out," Miriam added.

"We needs a keg of powder," the sailor said, throwing down the mortar.

"No, quiet is the key," said Farhi. "You must dig through before dawn prayers."

"And seal it back up," Miriam put in.

"Bollocks," said Ned.

I tried to focus the oaf. "Lost time is never found again, old Ben would say."

"And men that cheats at cards should give back what they wrongfully took, Big Ned says." He squinted at me. "There better be something on the other side of that wall, guv'nor, or I'll empty you by shaking from the ankles." But despite his bluster he and Little Tom finally pitched in, the eight of us forming a chain, passing loose rock to make a trench to the base of the blocked arch. It took two hours of backbreaking work to push enough rubble aside to see the entrance whole. A broad underground gate was stoppered like a bottle by different-colored limestone.

"It made sense to seal it," Tentwhistle offered. "This could be an entry point for enemy armies."

"The ancient Jews built the arch," Farhi guessed, "and Arabs, Crusaders, or Templars bricked it up. Some earthquake brought down the ceiling, and it's been forgotten ever since, except for legend."

Jericho wearily hefted a bar. "Let's get to it, then."

The first stone is always the hardest. We didn't dare pound and break, so we chiseled out mortar and put Ned on one side and Jericho on the other to pry. Their muscles bulged, the block slid out like a stuck, stubborn drawer, and finally they caught its fall and set it quietly as a slipper.

Farhi kept looking at the ceiling as if he could somehow see the reaction of Muslim guards far above us.

I bent to the puff of stale air that came out our hole. Blackness. So we worked on adjacent stones, cracking their mortar and leveraging them one by one. Finally the hole was big enough to crawl through.

"Jericho and I will scout," I said. "You sailors stand guard. If there's anything here, we'll bring it to you."

"Bloody 'ell with *that!*" Big Ned protested.

"I'm afraid I must agree with my subordinate," Tent-whistle said crisply. "We are on a naval mission, gentlemen, and like it or not, we're all agents of the Crown. By the same token, any property taken belongs to the Crown for later distribution under the prize laws. Your contributions will be fully taken into account, of course."

"We're not in your navy anymore," Jericho objected.

"But you're in the pay of Sir Sidney Smith, are you not?" Tentwhistle said. "And Gage is his agent as well. Which means that we go through this hole together, in the name of king and country, or not at all."

I put my hand on my rifle barrel, which I'd leaned against the cave wall. "You were sent as underground labor, not a prize crew," I tried.

"And you, sir, were sent to Jerusalem as the Crown's agent, not a private treasure hunter." His hand went to his pistol, as did that of Ensign Potts. Ned and Tom grasped the hilt of their cutlasses. Jericho raised his pry bar like a spear.

We quivered like rival dogs in a butcher shop.

"Stop!" Farhi hissed. "Are you insane? Start a fight down here and we'll have every Muslim in Jerusalem waiting for us! We can't afford to quarrel."

We hesitated, then lowered our hands. He was right. I sighed. "So which of you wants to go first? There were snakes and crocodiles behind every hole in Egypt."

Uneasy silence. "Sounds like you're the one with experience, guv'nor."

So I wriggled through the hole, waited a moment to make sure nothing was biting me, and then pulled through a lantern to lift.

I started. Skulls grinned back at me.

They weren't real skulls, just sculpture. Still, it was disquieting to see a carved row of skulls and crossbones running like a molding around the junction of walls and ceiling. I'd seen nothing like that in Egypt. The others were crawling in behind me, and as they spied the morbid frieze the sailors' exclamations ranged from "Jesus!" to a more anticipatory "Pirate treasure!"

Farhi had a more prosaic explanation. "Not pirates, gentlemen. A Templar style, that skeletal molding. You knew, Mr. Gage, that the skull and crossbones dates back at least to the Poor Knights?"

"I've seen it in connection with Masonic rites as well. And in church graveyards."

"Mortality occupies us all, doesn't it?"

The skulls decorated a corridor, and we passed down it to a larger room. There I saw other decorations that I assumed had originated with Masons as well. The floor was paved with marble tile in the familiar black-and-white checkerboard of the Dionysian architects, except down the center was a curious pattern. Black tiles zigzagged against white to make a slashing symbol, like an enormous lightning bolt. Odd. Why lightning?

The entrance we'd come through was flanked on this side by two enormous pillars, one black and one white.

In alcoves on either side were two statues of what looked like the Virgin, one alabaster and the other ebony: The white and black Virgins. Mary the Mother and Mary Magdalene? Or the Virgin Mary and ancient Isis, goddess of the Sirian star?

"All things are dual," Miriam murmured.

The roof was a vaulted barrel, rather plain, but sturdy enough to hold up the Herodian platform somewhere above. At the far end was a stone altar, with a dark alcove beyond. The rest of the room was barren. It had the scale of a dining hall, and perhaps the knights had feasted here when they weren't busy tunneling into the earth in search of Solomon's hoard. Other than that, it was disappointingly empty.

We walked across the room, fifty paces in length. Mounted on the face of the altar was a double plaque. On one side was a crude drawing of a domed church. On the other, two knights were mounted on a single horse.

"The Templar seal!" Farhi exclaimed. "This confirms they built this. See, there's the Dome of the Rock, just like the mosque above us, symbolizing the site of Solomon's Temple, origin of the Templar name. And two knights on a single horse? Some believe it was a sign of their voluntary poverty."

"Others contend that it means the two are aspects of the one," Miriam said. "Male and female. Forward and backward. Night and day."

"There's bloody nothing here," Big Ned interjected, looking around.

"An astute observation," Tentwhistle said. "It appears we've gone to a lot of labor for nothing, Mr. Gage."

"Except the Crown's business," I shot back sourly.

"Aye, the American has given us the business all right," Little Tom muttered.

"But look at this, then!" Ensign Potts called. He'd gone over to examine the White Madonna. "A servant's door, maybe? Or a secret passageway!"

We clustered around. The ensign had pushed on the Madonna's outstretched hand, raised as if in blessing, and she had pivoted. When she did so, stone had slid away behind her to reveal a winding circular stair, with an opening so narrow you had to squeeze sideways to enter it. It climbed steeply upward.

"That would go to the Temple platform above," Farhi said. "Communication with the old Templar quarters, in El-Aqsa Mosque. It's probably blocked, but we must be quieter than ever. Sound would carry up that like a chimney."

"Who cares what they 'ear," Ned said. "There's nothing down here anyway."

"You're on Muslim holy ground, fool, and sacred Jewish soil as well. If either group hears us they'll bind us, circumcise us, torture us for trespassing, and then tear us limb from limb."

"Ah."

"Let's try the Black Madonna as well," Miriam said.

So we went to the opposite side of the room, but this time no matter how hard Potts pushed on the arm, the statue didn't move. Miriam's dualism didn't seem in effect. We stood, frustrated.

"Where's the Temple treasure, Farhi?" I asked.

"Did I not warn that the Templars got here before you?"

"But this chamber looks European, like something they built, not something they discovered. Why would they construct this? It's a laborious way to get a dining hall."

"No windows down here," Potts observed.

"So this was for ceremonies," Miriam reasoned. "But the real business, the research, must have been in another chamber. There must be another door."

"The walls are blank and solid," her brother said.

I remembered my experience at Dendara in Egypt and glanced at the floor. The black-and-white tiles formed diagonals that radiated out from the altar. "I think Big Ned should push on this stone table here," I said. "Hard!"

At first nothing happened. Then Jericho joined him, and finally Little Tom, Potts, and me, all of us grunting. Finally there was a scrape and the altar began to rotate on a pivot set at one corner. As it slid sideways across the floor, a hole was revealed underneath. Stairs led down into darkness.

"This is more like it, then," Ned said, panting.

We descended, crowding into an anteroom below the main chamber. At its end was a great iron door, red and black with rust. It was marked by ten brass disks the size of dinner plates, green with age. There was one disk at the top, then two rows of three each descending. Between them but lower was a vertical column of three more. In the center of each was a latch.

"Ten doorknobs?" Tentwhistle asked.

"Or ten locks," Jericho said. "Each of these latches might turn a bar into this jamb of iron." He tried one handle but it didn't move. "We've no tools to dent *this*."

"Which means that maybe it ain't been opened and ain't been robbed," Ned reasoned, more shrewdly than I would have given him credit for. "That's good news, it seems to me. The guv'nor may have found something after all. What would you have that's so precious that you'd put a door like this in front of it, eh, and down at the bottom of a rabbit hole to boot?"

"Ten locks? There are no keyholes," I pointed out.

And as Jericho and Ned pulled and pushed on the massive door, it didn't quiver. "It's frozen in place," the blacksmith said. "Maybe it's not a door after all."

"And time is growing short," Farhi warned. "It will be dawn on the platform above, and Muslims will be coming to pray. If we start pounding on that iron, someone is bound to hear us."

"Wait," I said, remembering the mystery of the medallion in Egypt. "It's a pattern, don't you think? Ten discs, shaped like the sun . . . ten is a sacred number. This meant something to the Templars, I'm guessing."

"But what?"

"*Sefiroth*," Miriam said slowly. "It's the tree."

"A tree?"

Farhi suddenly stepped back. "Yes, yes, I see it now! The Etz Hayim, the Tree of Life!"

"The kabbalah," Miriam confirmed. "Jewish mysticism and numerology."

"The Knights Templar were *Jews*?"

"Certainly not, but ecumenical when it came to searching for ancient secrets," Farhi reasoned. "They'd have studied the Jewish texts for clues for where to dig in the mount. Muslim too, and any other. They would have been interested in all symbols aiding their quest for knowledge. This is the pattern of the ten *sefiroth*, with *keter*, the crown, at the top, and then *binah*, intuition, opposite *chokhmah*, wisdom—and so on."

"Greatness, mercy, strength, glory, victory, majesty, foundation, and sovereignty, or kingdom," Miriam recited. "All aspects of a God that is beyond understanding. We cannot grasp him, but only these manifestations of his being."

"But what does it mean on this door?"

"It's a puzzle, I think," Farhi said. He had brought his

lantern closer. "Yes, I can see the Jewish names engraved in Hebrew. *Chesed, tiferet, netzach . . .*"

"The Egyptians believed words were magic," I remembered. "That reciting them could summon a god or powers . . ."

Big Ned crossed himself. "By our Lord, heathen blasphemy! These knights of yours adopted the works of the Jew? No wonder they were burned at the stake!"

"They didn't adopt, they used," Jericho said patiently. "Here in Jerusalem we respect other faiths, even when we quarrel with them. The Templars meant something by this. Perhaps the latches are to be turned in the correct succession."

"The crown first," I offered. "*Keter* there, at the top."

"I'll try it." Yet that latch budged no more than the others.

"Wait, think," Farhi said. "If we make a mistake perhaps none will work."

"Or we'll trigger some trap," I said, remembering the descending stone monoliths that almost pinned me in the pyramid. "This might be a test to keep out the unworthy."

"What would a Templar choose first?" Farhi asked. "Victory? They were warriors. Glory? They found fame. Wisdom? If the treasure were a book. Intuition?"

"Thought," Miriam said. "Thought, like Thoth, like the book Ethan is seeking."

"Thought?"

"If you draw lines from disc to disc they intersect here in the center," she pointed. "Does not that center represent to the kabbalistic Jews the unknowable mind of God? Is not that center thought itself? Essence? What we Christians might call soul?"

"You're right," Farhi said, "but there is no latch there."

"Yes, the only place without a latch is the heart." She traced lines from the ten disks to this central point. "But here is a small engraved circle." And before anyone could stop her, she took the pry bar she had poked Little Tom with and rammed the end of the barrel against the iron at precisely that point. There was a dull, echoing boom that made us all jump. Then the engraved circle sank, there was a click, and suddenly all ten latches on all ten brass disks began to turn in unison.

"Get ready!" I raised my rifle. Tentwhistle and Potts held up their naval pistols. Ned and Tom unsheathed their cutlasses.

"We're all going to be rich," Ned breathed.

When the latches stopped turning Jericho gave a shove and, with a grinding rattle, the great door pivoted inward and down like a drawbridge, its top held by chains, ponderously lowering until it landed with a soft whump on a floor of dust beyond. A gray puff flew upward, momentarily obscuring what lie beyond, and then we saw the door had bridged a crevice in the floor. The chasm extended downward into blackness.

"Some fundamental fault in the earth," Farhi guessed, peering down. "This has been a sacred mountain since time began, a rock that addresses heaven, but perhaps it has roots to the underworld as well."

"All things are dual," Miriam said again.

Cool air wafted upward from the stone crevasse. All of us were uneasy, and I for one remembered that pit of hell in the pyramid. Our greed made us step across anyway.

This chamber was much smaller than the Templar hall above, not much bigger than a drawing room, with a low, domed ceiling. The dome was painted with a riot of stars, zodiacal signs, and weird creatures from some primordial time, a swirl of symbolism that reminded me of the ceiling I'd seen in Egypt at Dendara. At its apex was a seemingly gilded orb that likely represented the sun. In the center of the room was a waist-high stone pedestal, like the base for a statue or a display stand, but it was empty. The walls bore writing in an alphabet I'd never seen before, neither Arabic, Hebrew, Greek, nor Latin. It was different than what I'd seen in Egypt, too. Many characters were geometrical in shape, squares and triangles and circles, but others were twisting worms or tiny mazes. Wood and brass chests were heaped around the room's periphery, dry and corroded from age. And inside them there was . . .

Nothing.

Again, I was reminded of the Great Pyramid, where the book's depository was empty. Cruelty upon cruelty. First the book gone, then Astiza, and now this joke. . . .

"Bloody hell!" It was Ned and Tom, kicking at the chests. Ned hurled one against the stone wall, a great crash turning it into a spray of splinters. "There's nothing here! It's all been robbed!"

Robbed, retrieved, or removed. If there had ever been treasure here—and I suspected there had been—it was long gone: taken by the Templars to Europe, perhaps, or hidden elsewhere when their leaders went to the stake. Maybe it had gone missing since the Jews were enslaved by Nebuchadnezzar.

"Silence, you fools!" Farhi pleaded. "Do you have to break things so Muslim guards can hear? This Temple Mount is a sieve of caves and passages!" He turned on Tentwhistle. "Are English sailors' *brains* of oak, too?"

The lieutenant flushed.

"What do the walls say?" I asked, looking at the curious characters.

No one answered, because not even Farhi knew. But then Miriam, who'd been counting, pointed at a small ledge where walls and dome joined. There were sconces sculpted out of the stone, as if to hold candles or oil lamps.

"Farhi, count them," she said.

The mutilated banker did so. "Seventy-two," he said slowly. "Like the seventy-two names of God."

Jericho went closer. "There's oil dripping into them," he said with wonder. "How could that be, after so many years?"

"It's a mechanism triggered by the door," Miriam suggested.

"We're to light them," I said with sudden conviction. "Light them to understand." This was Templar magic, I guessed, some way to illuminate the mystery we'd discovered. And so Jericho lit a scrap of trunk wood with the wick of his lantern, and touched the oil in the nearest sconce. It lit, and then a tendril of flame moved along an oily channel to light the next one.

One by one they flared to life, igniting in a chain around the circle of the dome, until what had been dim was now a place pulsing with light and shadow. Nor was this all. The dome had stone ribs reaching upward to its apex, I saw, and in each rib was a groove. Now these grooves began to glow from the heat or light below, an eerie purple color similar to what I'd seen in electrical experiments with vacuumed tubes of glass.

"Lucifer's den," Little Tom breathed.

At the dome's highest point, a sunlike orb I thought had been merely gilded began to glow as well. And from it issued a beam of purple light, like the gleam I'd conjured from electricity at Christmas, which fell straight back down to the pedestal in the room's center.

Where a book or scroll might have been kept, to be read.

Jericho and Miriam were crossing themselves.

There was a hole in the pedestal's center, I saw, which would have been blocked had a book or scroll rested there. Without them, the light from above could shine through. . . .

And then there was a grinding squeal, like a rusted wheel turning. The sailors stopped and listened. I looked at the ceiling for signs of collapse.

"It's the Black Virgin!" Ensign Potts shouted from the stairs leading back into the Templar meeting room. "She's turning!"

CHAPTER 9

We ran back upstairs to the statue as if to witness a miracle. The arm that had been immobile before was now pivoting, the Black Madonna turning with it, and a door similar to one behind the White Madonna was opening. When the statue stopped, she seemed to be pointing to the newly opened door.

"By the saints," Ned declared. "It's got to be the treasure!"

Potts had his pistol out and ducked in first, climbing a steep, winding passageway.

"Wait!" I cried. If the weird display of light had somehow triggered this opening, it was only because the book was missing from the pedestal, allowing the beam to penetrate that hole. So was the pedestal hole some kind of key that led to more treasure—or a Templar alarm, set off when the book was gone? "We don't know what this means!"

But all four sailors were charging up the passageway, and Jericho and I reluctantly followed, Miriam and Farhi bringing up the rear. The stairway's rough-hewn walls reminded me of the workmanship of the water tunnel from the Pool of Siloam: it was old, far older than the Templars. Did it date from Solomon's time, or even Abraham's? The tunnel climbed, spiraling, and then it ended at a stone slab with a great iron ring in it. "Pull, Ned!" Tentwhistle commanded. "Pull like the devil and let's finish this business! It's almost dawn!"

The sailor did so, and as he slowly hauled the portal open I noticed the far side of the door was uneven rock. This latest door would seem, from its other side, to merely be part of the wall of a cave. Had people above ever known this passage existed?

"Where the bloody hell are we?" Potts asked.

There was a wider cave ahead, and light. "I'm guessing we've come out in the cave under the holy rock itself," I said with a whisper. "We're right under Kubbet es-Sakhra, the sacred stone, root of the world, and the Dome of the Rock."

"Right under what once was Solomon's Temple," Farhi said excitedly, gasping from exertion at the tail of our party. "Where Temple treasures might have been kept, or even the ark itself . . ."

"Right where any guardians of the mosque can hear intruders below," Jericho warned. This was all going too fast.

"You mean the Muslims . . ."

The seamen weren't waiting. "Treasure, boys!" Ned and his comrades pushed into the corridor. Then there was an Arabic cry and a shot and poor Pott's head exploded.

One moment the ensign was dragging me with him in mad enthusiasm, and the next his brains sprayed us all. He dropped like a puppet with cut strings. Gun smoke filled the narrow passage with its familiar stink. "Get down!" I shouted, and we dropped.

Then a roar of gunfire and bullets pinged madly around us.

"Allah akbar!" God is great! The Muslims had heard us blundering into their most sacred precincts and had called their janissary guard! We'd stirred up a hornet's nest, all right. Through the smoke I could see a cluster of men reloading.

So I fired, and there was a scream in response. Tentwhistle's pistol went off, too, hitting another, and now it was the janissaries' turn to tumble to cover.

"Retreat!" I shouted. "Hurry, by God! Back through that door!"

Yet even as we began to swing it shut, the janissaries charged and a dozen Muslim hands grasped the rim from the other side. Ned gave a great cry and cleaved at some with his cutlass, severing fingers, but more guns went off and Little Tom took a ball in the arm. He bucked backward, cursing. The door was inexorably being pushed open, so Ned roared like a bear and waded into them, chopping like a dervish until the arms disappeared. Then he slammed it shut, taking one of our pry bars to jam it temporarily closed until they could ram it open. We ran back down the twisting stairway to the empty Templar room. Behind and above, we could hear the heavy slam of a hammer as the Muslims beat on the stone door.

If they caught us, they'd butcher us for sacrilege.

Only through the archway might we have a chance. In the passage back to the spring, Farhi had said, one man could block an army. We sprinted through the corridor with its frieze of skulls to the hole we'd excavated just an hour before. I'd buy time while the others fled, using cutlass and rifle. What a bloody mess!

Yet something had changed. The opening we'd made through the stone archway had shrunken. The stones were somehow reassembling themselves and the hole was too small to crawl through. What magic was this?

"Au revoir, Monsieur Gage!" a familiar voice called through the shrunken hole. Once again, it was the voice of the so-called customs inspector who'd tried to rob me in France, and who I'd fought in Jerusalem when his henchmen accosted Miriam. This time he was calling through what was now the space of a single block! So there was no magic after all, just Silano's perfidy. The final stone slid back into place in our faces, sealing us in. The French must have followed us as I feared, broken Jericho's lock on the grating at the Pool of Siloam, and heard our cries when we found no treasure. Then they'd started to brick up our escape route with the bag of mortar Big Ned had carried. We were trapped by our own foresight.

"The mortar can't have set!" Ned roared. But either the lime fused quickly, or the stonework was braced from the other side with rubble and beams. He bounced off like a ball. The sailor began beating on the blocked archway with his fists, while Little Tom staggered like a drunk, holding his arm with a hand that dripped blood from his fingertips.

"We've no time for this!" Tentwhistle snapped. "The Muslims are going to get through the stone door above and come down the stairs of the Black Madonna!"

"The stairs of the White Madonna!" Farhi cried. "It's our only chance!"

Back to the Templar hall we ran. There was a crash, and an echo of warlike Arabic cries spilled down from the stairway of the black statue. They were through! Tentwhistle and I ran to the bottom of it and fired blindly upward, the balls pinging and forcing some hesitation. On the opposite side Farhi squeezed past the White Madonna and began climbing those stairs, Jericho pushing his sister hard on the Jew's heels. Then the rest of us retreated across the Templar hall too, squeezing upward one by one. Finally Big Ned shoved even me ahead of him. "I'll take care of that rabble!" The goliath seized the White Virgin, muscles almost bursting, and broke her loose. Now our pursuers were entering the Templar hall, looking about in wonder, and then shouting as they spotted us on the opposite side. Turning sideways, Ned barely squeezed into the stairway entrance while dragging the Madonna's head with him, jamming her stone body in the narrow entrance. That gave a partial plug between us and our pursuers. We turned and scrambled upward.

A wave of Muslims, running wildly, dashed against the obstruction and recoiled, howling with outrage and frustration. They began pulling to break the Madonna free.

We climbed as desperately as the damned. I could hear the mob below scream in frustration as they battered the statue blocking our escape route. More guns went off, but the bullets ricocheted harmlessly on the lower stairs. Alarms were called, no doubt alerting compatriots on the Temple

Mount above of our imminent emergence. We came to an iron grate that locked us in. Tentwhistle blew its lock apart with his pistol and slammed it aside. It rang like a gong. I used the pause to reload my own rifle. We emerged atop the Temple Mount in the El-Aqsa Mosque. I noticed how it had been modified by the Crusaders, its line of arches and high windows giving the cavernous space an architectural cross between an Arabic palace and a European church. As Farhi had guessed, the stairway of the White Madonna must have been built to allow secret access from the main Templar headquarters to the chambers and tunnels below.

We ran to the mosque's door. The vast temple platform, dimly lit by a predawn sky, was swarming with hundreds of crudely armed Muslims, like so many bees in a hive that's been disturbed. I could see the blue tile and golden crown of the serene Dome of the Rock beyond, its door boiling as men ran in and out in consternation. The mob was chanting, shouting alarms, and waving cudgels. Thankfully there were few janissaries and few guns. Finally some of them saw us, and with a great shout they turned as if one and began to charge.

"What a bollocks you make of things," Ned said to me.

So I took aim.

¤   ¤   ¤

El-Aqsa Mosque is illuminated at night by enormous hanging brass lamps that can be lowered from white cotton ropes for lighting. One of these lamps—with several dozen individual flames on metalwork ten feet wide, its grillwork weighing well over a ton—hung above the main door of the mosque. As the mob surged through, I sighted through my rifle-mounted spyglass, put the rope and its hook on the ornate ceiling in my crosshairs, and fired.

My shot shredded the rope and the lamp came down like a guillotine, landing with a great crash as it buried the head of the mob and scattered the rest. Our pursuers momentarily recoiled, looking warily upward. It was enough to give our crew of filthy, bleeding troglodytes the precious seconds necessary to retreat toward the back of the mosque.

"They have the sacred relics of Muhammad!" I heard the mob cry.

And I suddenly wondered if the Prophet's midnight journey to Jerusalem and his ascension to heaven was just a myth, or if he too had truly been here once, seeking and perhaps finding wisdom. Had he, too, heard of the Book of Thoth? What had Jesus learned in Egypt, or Buddha in his wanderings? Were all the faiths, myths, and stories an endless interweaving and embroidery of ancient texts, wisdom built on wisdom, and mystery concealed by yet more mystery? Heresy—but here at the religious center of the world, I couldn't help but wonder.

We raced over worn red carpets that covered the flagstones of the mosque and into the small anterooms beyond the great hall, dreading a dead-end that would trap us. But at the point where the El-Aqsa and the Temple Mount joined the city's periphery wall there was another locked door. Big Ned ran at it full tilt and this time smashed it open, the torn splinters like fresh wounds in old wood. We looked out. The wall led off the southern end of the Temple Mount at a downward slope, to enclose Jerusalem. At a tower it turned westward, encompassing the city below.

"If we get into the maze of streets we can lose them," Farhi gasped.

He, Miriam, and the injured Little Tom began trotting along the rampart toward the steps that led downward at the Dung Gate, staggering with exhaustion, while Tentwhistle and I reloaded on the rampart and Ned and Jericho stood ready with swords. When our first pursuers filled the doorway we'd just exited, we fired. Then our swordsmen charged into the smoke, swinging. There were howls, retreat, and Ned trotted back, speckled with blood.

"They're thinking now," he said with a toothy grin.

Jericho looked sickened, his blade wet. "This is evil you've brought," he told the sailor.

"If I remember, blacksmith, it's been you and your doxy sister leading the way."

And we retreated yet again.

If the mob had been better armed, we would have been dead. But we ran a gauntlet of only a few shots, bullets passing with that peculiar hot sizzle that paralyze if you stop to think about it. Then we were down the stairs of the wall and onto a Jerusalem street, the Dung Gate bolted shut by a squad of janissaries, scimitars ready so we couldn't run outside. Above us, the battlements were crammed with screaming Muslims racing for the stairs.

"Into the Jewish Quarter!" urged Farhi. "It's our only chance!"

Now there were calls of alarm from the minarets, and Christian bells were ringing. We'd roused the entire city. Shouting people streamed into the streets. Dogs were howling, sheep bleating. A terrified goat galloped past us, going the other way. Farhi, panting, led us uphill toward the Ramban Synagogue and Jaffa Gate, the Muslim mob behind lit by torches in a snake of fire. Even if I could find time to load again, my single shot would be no deterrent to the anger we'd aroused by trespassing under the Dome of the Rock. Unless we got help, we were doomed.

"They want to burn the Ramban and Yochanan ben Zakkai synagogues!" Farhi shouted to the anxious Jews as they poured into the streets. "Get Christian allies! The Muslims are rioting!"

"The synagogues! Save our holy temples!" And with that, we had a shield. Jews ran to block the mob surging into their quarter. Christians warned that their real goal was the Church of the Holy Sepulcher. Mob collided with mob. In moments there was chaos.

With it, Farhi disappeared.

I grabbed the others. "We split up! Jericho and Miriam, you live here. Go home!"

"I heard Muslims call my name," he said grimly. "We cannot stay in Jerusalem. I was recognized." He glared at me. "They'll sack and burn my house."

I felt sick with guilt. "Then take what you can and flee to the coast. Smith is organizing the defense of Acre. Seek protection with him there."

"Come with us!" Miriam pleaded.

"No, alone you two can likely travel unmolested, because you're native. The rest of us stand out like snowmen in July." I pressed the seraphim into her hands. "Take these and secrete them until we meet again. We Europeans can run or hide, sneaking when it's dark. We'll go the other way to give you time. Don't worry. We'll meet in Acre."

"I've lost my home and reputation for an empty room," Jericho said bitterly.

"There was something there," I insisted. "You know there was. The question is, where is it now? And when we find it, we'll be rich."

He looked at me with a combination of anger, despair, and hope.

"Go, go, before it's too late for your sister!"

At the same time, Tentwhistle pulled at me. "Come, before it's too late for us!"

So we parted. I looked back at brother and sister as we ran. "We'll find it!"

I and the British sailors headed toward the Zion Gate. I looked back once, but Jericho and Miriam were lost in the mobs like flotsam in a tossing sea. We stumbled on, too slow and desperate. Little Tom, his arm sticky with blood, couldn't hurry but kept manfully on. We entered the Armenian Quarter and came to the gate. Its soldiers had gone, probably to control the rioting or search for us: our first stroke of luck in this entire fiasco. We unbolted the great doors, pushed hard, and passed into open country. The sky was just pinking. Behind, flames, torchlight, and the coming dawn had turned the sky orange above the city's walls. Ahead was sheltering shadow.

To our right was Mount Zion and the Tomb of David. To the left was the Valley of Hinnom, the Pool of Siloam somewhere in the darkness below. "We'll circle the city wall to the north and take the Nablus Road," I said. "If we travel at night we can make Acre in four days and get word to Sidney Smith."

"What about the treasure?" Tentwhistle asked. "Is that it? Do we give up?"

"You saw it wasn't there. We have to figure where next to look. I hope to God they didn't catch Farhi. He'll know where to try next."

"No, I think he's betraying us. Why'd he slip off like that?"

I wondered that too.

"It's our own skins first," said Big Ned.

And with that his lieutenant jerked and the sound of a shot echoed up the hill. Then another and another, bullets whapping into the dust. Tentwhistle sat down with a grunt. Then I heard the words in French: "There they are! Spread out! Cut them off!"

It was the group that had tried to brick us up in the tunnels, the same Frenchmen who had accosted Miriam. They'd crawled back out of the Pool of Siloam, heard the chaos, and waited under the wall for someone to appear.

I crouched by Tentwhistle and aimed. My lens found one of our ambushers and I fired. He went down. Pretty rifle. I feverishly reloaded.

Ned had taken Tentwhistle's pistol and he fired too, but our assailants were not within pistol range. "All you'll do is draw their aim with your flash," I told him. "Get Tom and the lieutenant back through the gate. I'll hold them here a moment and then we can lose them in the Armenian Quarter."

Another bullet whined overhead. Tentwhistle was coughing blood, his eyes glazed. He would not live long.

"Right, guv'nor, you buy us time." Ned began dragging Tentwhistle back, Tom groggily following. "Potts dead, two more of us wounded. Bloody inspiration, you are."

It was getting lighter. Bullets pinged as the Frenchmen swarmed closer. I fired again, then glanced behind me. The sailors were back through the gate. No time to reload, time to go! In a crouch, I sidled backward toward it. Dark forms were closing like circling wolves. Then I heard a creak. The gate was closing! I scuttled rapidly, and just made it to the city wall when the gate boomed shut, locking me out. I heard the thud of its bar being slid home.

"Ned! Open up!" There was a French command and I

threw myself flat just before a volley went off. Bullets hammered against the iron like hail. I was like a condemned man at an execution wall. "Hurry, they're coming!"

"I think we'll be going our own way, guv'nor," Ned called.

"Own way? For God's sake . . ."

"I don't think these frogs will care that much about a couple of poor British sailors. You're the one with the treasure secrets, ain't you?"

"What, you're leaving me to them?"

"Maybe you can lead 'em on like you did us, eh?"

"Damn, Ned, let's stand together, as the lieutenant said!"

"He's done, and so are we. Doesn't pay to cheat honest seamen at cards, guv'nor. Lose your friends, you do."

"But I didn't cheat, I outsmarted you!"

"The same bloody thing."

"Ned, open this gate!"

But there was no reply, just the mute slab.

"Ned!" Lying prone, I hammered on the unyielding iron. "Ned! Let me in!"

But he didn't, of course, as I strained to hear their retreat over the city's tumult. I turned back. The French had crept to just yards away, and several muskets were trained on me. The tallest one smiled.

"We said good-bye beneath the Temple Mount and yet we meet again!" their leader cried. He doffed a tricorn hat and bowed. "You do have a talent of being everywhere, Monsieur Gage, but then so do I, do I not?" His was a torturer's grin. "Surely you remember me, from the Toulon stage? Pierre Najac, at your service."

"I remember you: The customs inspector who turned out to be a thief. So is Najac your real name?"

"Real enough. What happened to your friends, monsieur?"

Slowly I stood. "Disappointed in a game of cards."

CHAPTER 10

I knew I was in hell when Najac insisted on showing me his bullet wound. It was the one I'd given him the year before, red and scabby, on a torso that couldn't have seen soap or a washcloth for a month. The little crater was a few inches below his left nipple and toward his left side, confirming that my aim had been off by degrees. Now I knew he smelled bad, too.

"It broke a rib," he said. "Imagine my pleasure when I learned after my convalescence that you might be alive and that I could help my master track you down. First you were stupid enough to make inquiry in Egypt. Then, when we came here we caught a doddering old fool who squealed about meeting a Frank carrying Satan's gold angels, once we'd roasted him enough. That's when I knew you must be close. Revenge is sweeter the longer it is delayed, don't you think?"

"I'll let you know when I finally kill you."

He laughed at my little joke, stood, and then kicked the side of my head so hard that the night dissolved into bright bits of light. I toppled over by the fire, bound hand and foot, and it was the smoldering of my clothes and resulting pain that finally jarred me enough to wriggle away. This greatly amused my captors, but then I always did enjoy being the center of attention. Afterward the burn kept me feverish. It was the night after our departure from Jerusalem, and fear and pain were the only things keeping me conscious. I was exhausted, sore, and frightfully alone. Najac's party of bullyboys had somehow swelled to ten, half of them French and the rest bedraggled Bedouin who looked like the kitchen grease of Arabia, ugly as toads. Missing, besides half this complement's teeth, was the Frenchman I'd stabbed in the fight over Miriam. I hoped I'd finished him, a sign I was getting better at dispatching my enemies. But maybe he was convalescing too, dreaming of the day he could capture and kick me as well.

Najac's mood wasn't improved by his discovery that I carried nothing of value but my rifle and tomahawk, which, being a thief, he appropriated. My seraphim I'd entrusted to Miriam, and in all the excitement I hadn't noticed that someone—Big Ned or Little Tom, I assumed—had also relieved me of my purse. My insistence that we'd found nothing underground, that Jerusalem was as frustrating as Egypt, did not sit well.

What was I doing if nothing was to be found down there?

Seeing the root stone of the world from its other side, I answered.

They pounded on me but hesitated to kill me. The passageways under the Temple Mount were as stirred up as an ant nest, the Muslims probably puzzling over what we'd been looking for. The ruckus eliminated any chance of this French-Arab gang going back, so I was the only clue they had.

"I'd roast you right now if Bonaparte and the master didn't want you alive," Najac snarled. He let the Arabs amuse themselves by using their daggers to flick embers on my arms and legs, but not much more. Time enough later to make me scream.

So I finally lapsed into exhausted blackness until I was yanked painfully awake the next morning for a breakfast of chickpea paste and water. Then we continued down a trace from the Jerusalem hills to the coastal plain, the horizon marked by columns of smoke.

The French army was hard at work.

¤   ¤   ¤

Despite my captivity, I had an odd sense of homecoming when we reached Napoleon's camp. I'd marched with Bonaparte's army and encountered Desaix's division at Dendara. Now, pitching white tents before the walls of Jaffa, were men in European uniforms again. I smelled familiar food, and once more heard the lilting elegance of the French tongue. As we rode through the ranks, men looked curiously at Najac's gang and a few pointed at me in surprised recognition. Not long before I'd been one of their savants. Now here I was again, a deserter and a prisoner.

Jaffa itself was familiar, but viewed this time from the vantage of the besieger. Canopies and hanging carpets had disappeared, its ramparts bearing the fresh bite of cannonballs. Similarly, many of the orange trees that sheltered Napoleon's army showed raw wood where Ottoman fire had smashed their tops. Fresh earth and sand were being thrown up for siege works, and long lines of French cavalry horses shifted nervously where they were picketed in the shade, whinnying and shuffling as cannon popped. Their tails flicked at flies like metronomes, and their manure had that familiar sweet scent.

Najac went inside Napoleon's broad canvas pavilion while I stood hatless in the Mediterranean sun, thirsty, dazed, and feeling fatalistic. I'd fallen once on a cliff above the St. Lawrence River, pivoting endlessly, and felt this same vague sense of sickening regret that time—only to bounce off a bush, over the rocks, and into the river.

And here, perhaps, came my savior bush. "Gaspard!" I called.

It was Monge, the famed French mathematician, the man who'd helped solve some of the puzzle of the Great

Pyramid. He'd been a confidant of Napoleon since the general's triumphs in Italy and had mentored me like a wayward nephew. Now he was accompanying the army into Palestine.

"Gage?" Monge squinted as he came closer, his civilian dress increasingly shopworn, his knees patched, coat ragged, and face rough with stubble. The man was fifty-two, and tired. "What are you doing here? I thought I told you to go home to America!"

"I tried. Listen. Do you have word of Astiza?"

"The woman? But she went with you."

"Yes, but we were separated."

"Took a balloon, the two of you did—that's what Conte told me. Oh, how furious he was at that prank! Floated away, how the rest of us envied you . . . and now you're back in this asylum? Good God, man, I knew you weren't a true savant, but you seem to have no sense at all."

"On that point we can agree, Doctor Monge."

Not only did he know nothing of Astiza's fate, he clearly didn't know of our entry into the pyramid, and I quickly decided it best not to tell him. If the French ever became aware there were things of value down there, they'd blow the edifice apart. Better to let Pharaoh rest in peace.

"Astiza fell into the Nile and the balloon eventually came down in the Mediterranean," I explained. "Is Nicolas here too?" I was a little nervous at meeting Conte, the expedition's aeronaut, having stolen his observation balloon.

"Fortunately for you he's back in the south, organizing the shipment of our siege artillery. He had a rather brilliant plan to construct multiwheeled wagons to carry the guns across the desert, but Bonaparte has no time for new inventions. We're risking bringing the train by sea." He stopped, realizing he was relating secrets. "But what are you doing here, with your hands tied?" He looked puzzled. "You're filthy, burned, friendless—my God, what's happened to you?"

"He's an English spy," said Najac, emerging from the tent. "And you risk suspicion too, scientist, simply by talking to him."

"English spy? Don't be ridiculous. Gage is a dilettante, a

hanger-on, a dabbler, a wanderer. No one could take him seriously as a spy."

"No? Our general would."

And with that Bonaparte himself appeared, the tent flap billowing grandly as if infused with his electricity. Like all of us he was browner than when we'd left Toulon nearly a year before, and while he was still just thirty, success and responsibility had given new hardness to his face. Josephine was an adulteress, his plans to reform Egypt on French republican lines had been answered with his condemnation as an infidel, and he'd had to put down a bloody uprising in Cairo. His idealism was under siege, his romanticism breached. Now his gray eyes were icy, his dark hair shaggy, his countenance more hawklike, his stride impatient. He marched up to me and stopped. At five-foot-six he was shorter than me, and yet inflated with power. I couldn't help flinching.

"So. It *is* you! I'd thought you dead."

"He went to the British, *mon général*," Najac said. The man was like a schoolroom tattletale, and I was beginning to wish I'd shot him in the tongue.

Bonaparte leaned into me. "Is this true, Gage? Did you desert me for the enemy? Did you reject republicanism, rationality, and reform for royalism, reactionaries, and the Turk?"

"Circumstances forced us apart, General. I've simply been trying to discover the fate of the woman I'd acquired in Egypt. You remember Astiza."

"The one who shoots at people. My experience is that love does more harm than good, Gage. And you expected to find her in Jerusalem, where Najac caught you?"

"As a savant, I was trying to make some historical inquiry . . ."

He erupted. "No! If there is one thing I've learned, you are *not* a savant! Don't waste my time anymore with damned nonsense! You're a turncoat, a liar, and a hypocrite who fought in the company of English sailors! You probably *are* a spy, as Najac said. If you weren't so silly, as Monge also points out."

"Sir, Najac there tried to rob me of my critical medallion in France when I was already committed to your expedition. *He's* the traitor!"

"*He* shot *me*," Najac said.

"He's a henchman of Count Alessandro Silano and an adherent of the heretical Egyptian Rite, enemy of all true Freemasons. I'm certain of it!"

"Silence!" Bonaparte interrupted. "I'm well aware of your dislike of Count Silano, Gage. I also know he has shown admirable loyalty and perseverance despite his tumble at the pyramids." So, I thought: Silano is alive. The news was going from bad to worse in a hurry. Had the count pretended his fall from the balloon had been from the pyramids? And why did nobody say anything about Astiza?

"If you had Silano's loyalty, you wouldn't have condemned yourself now," Bonaparte went on. "By the saints, Gage, you were accused of murder, I gave you every opportunity, and yet you switch sides like a pendulum!"

"Character tells, *mon général*," Najac said smugly. I longed to strangle him.

"You were actually looking for treasure, weren't you?" Napoleon demanded. "That's what this is all about. American mercantilism and greed."

"Knowledge," I corrected, with some semblance of truth.

"And what *knowledge* have you found? Speak honestly, if you value your life."

"Nothing, General, as you can see from my condition. *That's* the truth. All I tell is the truth. I'm just an American investigator, caught up in a war not of my . . ."

"Napoleon, the man is clearly more fool than traitor," the mathematician Monge interrupted. "His sin is incompetence, not betrayal. Look at him. What does he know?"

I tried to grin stupidly—not easy for a man of my basic sense—but I figured the mathematician's assessment was an improvement over Najac's. "I can tell you the politics of Jerusalem are very confused," I offered. "It is unclear where the loyalty of the Christians and the Jews and the Druze truly lie . . ."

"Enough!" Bonaparte looked sourly at all of us. "Gage, I don't know whether to have you shot or let you take your chances with the Turk. I should send you into Jaffa and let you wait for my troops there. They are not patient men, my soldiers, not after the resistance at El-Arish and Gaza. Or perhaps I should send you to Djezzar, with a note saying you are a spy for me."

I swallowed. "Perhaps I could aid Doctor Monge . . ."

And then came the sound of gunfire, horns, and cheering. We all looked toward the city. On the south side, a column of Ottoman infantry was boiling out of Jaffa while Turkish guns thudded. Flags thrashed, men skittering down the hill toward a half-finished French artillery emplacement.

French bugles began to sound in response.

"Damn," Napoleon muttered. "Najac!"

"Oui, *mon général!!*"

"I've a sally to attend to. Can you find out what he really knows?"

The man grinned. "Oh yes."

"Then report back to me. If he's truly useless, I'll have him shot."

"General, let *me* talk to him . . ." Monge tried again.

"If you talk to him again, Doctor Monge, it will be only to hear his last words." And then Bonaparte ran toward the sound of the guns, calling his aides.

¤   ¤   ¤

I'm no coward, but there's something about being hung upside down above a sand pit in the Mediterranean dunes by a gang of hooting French-Arab cutthroats that made me want to tell them anything they want to hear. Just to stop the damned blood from welling in my head! The French had repulsed the Ottoman sally, but not before the plucky Turks overran the uncompleted battery and killed just enough Frenchmen to get the army's fire up. When told I was an English spy, several soldiers enthusiastically offered to help Najac's gang excavate the pit and construct the palm-log scaffold I was suspended from. Officially, the idea was to wring from me any secrets I hadn't already shared. Unofficially, my torture was a reward to Najac's particular assortment of sadists, perverts, lunatics, and thieves, who existed to do the invasion's dirty work.

I'd already told the truth a dozen times. "There's nothing down there!" And, "I failed!" And, "I didn't even know exactly what I'm looking for!"

But then truth isn't really the point of torture, given that the victim will say anything to get the pain to stop. Torture is about the torturer.

So they roped my ankles and hung me upside down from the crossbeam over the sandy pit, my arms free to flap. They'd dug the hole a good ten feet deep before striking something hard, declaring it good enough for my grave. Now one of the Bedouin came forward with a wicker basket and emptied its contents. Half a dozen snakes fell to the bottom of the pit and writhed in indignation, hissing.

"An interesting way to die, is it not?" Najac asked rhetorically.

"Apophis," I replied, my voice thickened by being where my feet should be.

"What?"

"Apophis!" I said it louder.

He pretended not to understand, but the Arabs did. They recoiled at the name, given that it was the moniker of that old Egyptian snake god revered by the renegade murderer Achmed bin Sadr. Yes, I'd encountered the same scaly bunch all right, and they twitched at my knowledge as if shedding their own skin. It put doubt in their heads. Just how much did I *really* know—I, the mysterious electrician of Jerusalem? Najac, however, pretended to be oblivious to the name.

"A snake bite is horribly painful and agonizingly slow. We'll kill you quicker, Monsieur Gage, if you tell us what you're really after, and what you really found."

"I've had more agreeable offers. Go to hell."

"You first, monsieur." He turned to the men holding my ropes. "Lower away!"

The rope began to unreel in jerky movements. My upside-down head descended to ground level, my body swaying above the pit, and all I could see was a line of boots and sandals, their owners jeering. Then more rope. I pulled my head back up, curving my back to look straight down. Yes, the snakes were there, slithering as snakes do. It reminded me of poor Talma's treacherous death, and all the rotten misdeeds Silano and his rabble had committed to get to the book.

"I'll curse you with the name of Thoth!" I shouted.

The rope stopped again, and an argument broke out in Arabic. I couldn't follow the furious flood of words but I heard fragments like "Apophis" and "Silano" and "sorcerer" and "electricity." So I *had* acquired a reputation! They were nervous.

Najac's own voice rose over that of his henchmen, angry and insistent. The rope was let down again another foot and stopped again, the arguing continuing. Suddenly there was the crack of a pistol shot, a jerk as I fell two more feet, and then a halt again. All of me was now in the pit, the snakes four feet below.

I looked up. A Bedouin who'd argued too long with Najac lay dead, one sandaled foot draped over the edge of my pit.

"The next man who argues with me shares the grave with the American!" Najac warned. The group had fallen silent. "Yes, you agree with me now? Lower him! Slowly, so he can beg!"

Oh, I begged all right, begged like a man possessed. I'm not proud when it comes to avoiding snakebite. But it did no good, except to keep my descent incremental so I could provide entertainment. They must have thought me born for the stage. I called out anything I thought they might want to hear, pleading, twisting, and sweating, my eyes stinging as perspiration ran. Then, when my abject wailing began to bore, someone pushed so I swung back and forth. It was dizzying. Much more of this and I would black out. I saw serpent after serpent coiling in excitement but then noticed something else.

"There's a shovel down here!"

"To fill your own grave, once you have been bitten, Monsieur Gage," Najac called. "Or would it be easier to explain what you saw under the Temple Mount?"

"I told you, *nothing!*"

So they lowered it a foot again. That's what telling the truth will get you.

The blasted snakes were hissing. It was unfair how angry the reptiles were, since it wasn't me who had put them down there.

"Well, maybe something," I amended.

"I am not a patient man, Monsieur Gage." The rope went down again.

"Wait, wait!" I was beginning to truly panic. "Haul me up and I'll tell you!" I'd think of something! A couple of the serpents were swaying upward, getting ready to strike at my head.

The sun had climbed, its illumination crawling across my grave. I saw the shovel again, snakes curling across it, and the scraped rock my grave excavators had stopped at. Except now I didn't think it was a rock at all because it had the red clay color of a jar or a roof tile. It was also regular in shape I saw, cylindrical if the hump of covering sand was any indication. It looked almost like a pipe. No—it *was* a pipe.

A pipe, now that I thought about it, which extended toward the sea.

"I think you can tell me from down there," Najac said, peering over the lip.

I extended my dangling arms downward as far as I could. I was still a foot too short to reach the abandoned shovel. My tormentors saw what I was trying to do and lowered me inches further. But then a snake struck toward my palm and I jerked my arms upward, half curling, a move that brought peals of laughter. Now they began betting on my ability to grab the shovel before I was bitten by crawling reptiles. Down I went another inch, and another. Oh, the fun my captors were having!

"If you kill me, you'll lose the greatest treasure on earth!" I warned.

"So tell me where it is." Down a few more inches.

"I can only lead you to it if you spare my life!" I was eyeing the shovel and the snakes, swinging myself by twisting my torso so I would pass over its wooden handle.

"And what is this treasure?"

Another snake struck toward me, I yelped, and there was another chorus of laughter. If only I could be so amusing to Paris courtesans.

"It's . . ." The rope dropped more, I reached, fingers straining, the snakes rose in readiness, and then as they jerked I seized the shovel and swung desperately. It caught two of the reptiles and threw them against the sand walls, starting a small cascade. They thrashed in fury as they fell back into the pit.

"Up, up, please, by the grace of God, get me *up!*"

"What is it, Monsieur Gage? What is the treasure?"

I could think of nothing else to do. I took the shovel in both hands, bent myself as far upward as I painfully could, took careful aim, and then dropped back down, letting my weight drive the crude shovel's wooden beak against the clay pipe. It shattered!

Liquid gushed into the pit.

No one was more surprised than I was.

The rope fell another foot as the men above cried out in surprise, and my hair was in effluent stinking of sewage and seawater. Was this some wretched outfall from Jaffa? I squeezed my eyes tight, ready for the bite of fangs on my nose or ears or eyelids. Instead, the angry hissing was receding.

I blinked open. The snakes had crawled to the sides of the pit to get away from the gushing stink. They were desert serpents, as unhappy about all this as I was.

My head dropped again, and now my forehead dragged in the greasy cesspool. By Hamilton's dollar, was I to escape the venom only to drown head down?

"The Grail!" I roared. "It's the Grail!"

And with that Najac snapped an order and they began to hoist me.

The Arabs were in an uproar, declaring I was a sorcerer

who'd performed some electric miracle by bringing water out of sand. Najac was looking at the shovel in my hands with disbelief. Below, the pit kept filling, the snakes trying to climb away and dropping back down.

And then my head was above ground level, my ankles still bound, my torso swaying like a hooked side of beef.

"*What* did you say?" Najac demanded.

"The Grail," I grasped weakly. "The Holy Grail. Now, will you please just shoot me?"

And of course he'd like to. But what if my claim proved important to Bonaparte? And then an angry mutter, growing to an indignant roar, began to rise from the entire besieging army.

CHAPTER 11

Atrocities cannot be justified, but sometimes they can be explained. Bona-
parte's troops had been struggling with disillusion since
landing in Egypt last summer. The heat, the poverty, and the
enmity of the population had all come as shocks. The French
had expected to be welcomed as republican saviors, bringing
the gifts of the Enlightenment. Instead they'd been resisted,
viewed as infidels and atheists, the remnants of the Mameluke armies raiding from the desert. Garrisons in villages
lived under the constant threat of poisoning or a knife in the
dark. Napoleon's answer was to march on.

There had been unexpectedly fierce resistance at Gaza.
Turkish prisoners had been paroled on the promise not to
fight again, but officers with telescopes had spied the same
units now manning the walls of Jaffa. This was a breach of
a fundamental rule of European warfare! Yet even this
might not have ignited the massacres to follow. What caused
the thunder roll of outrage was the decision by Ottoman
commander Aga Abdalla to answer Napoleon's offer of
surrender terms by killing the two French emissaries and
mounting their heads on poles.

It was rashness by a proud Muslim outnumbered three to one. The French army roared in protest, like a provoked lion.

Now there could be no mercy. Within minutes, the bombardment began. There would be a bark, a sizzle as a cannonball cut through the air, and then an eruption of dust and flying fragments as it struck the town's masonry. With each hit the troops cheered, until the pounding extended hour into hour and became monotonous in its steady erosion of Jaffa's defenses. On the east and north sides, each gun fired every six minutes. On the south, where cannon pointed across a thickly vegetated ravine that would give good cover to attacking troops, the guns roared every three minutes, slowly smashing a breech. Ottoman artillery replied, but with old ordnance and rusty aim.

Najac took the time to watch his snakes drown and then chained me to an orange tree while he watched the bombardment and considered what I'd said. The battle was mayhem he preferred not to miss, but I assume he found a minute to inform Bonaparte of my babbling about the Holy Grail. Night came, fires pulsing in Jaffa, but I got no food or water, just the monotonous thud of artillery. I fell asleep to its drums.

Dawn revealed a large breach in the city's southern wall. The wedding-cake stack of white houses was pockmarked by dark new holes, and smoke shrouded Jaffa. The French aimed their guns like surgeons, and steadily the breach widened. I could see dozens of spent shot lying in the rubble at the base of the wall, raisins in rumpled dough. Then two companies of grenadiers, accompanied by assault engineers carrying explosives, began assembling in the ravine. More troops readied behind them.

Najac unchained me. "Bonaparte. Prove your usefulness or die."

Napoleon was in a cluster of officers, shortest in stature, biggest in personality, and the one who gestured most vigorously. The grenadiers were filing past into the ravine, saluting as they approached the breach in Jaffa's wall. Ottoman cannonballs were crashing, thrashing the foliage like a prowling bear. The soldiers ignored the inaccurate fire and its rain of cut leaves.

"We'll see whose head ends on a pole!" one sergeant called as they tramped past, bayonets fixed.

Bonaparte smiled grimly.

The officers ignored us for a time, but as the advance troops began their assault, Napoleon abruptly swung his attention to me, as if to fill the anxious time waiting for success or failure. There was a rattle of musket fire as the grenadiers emerged from the grove and charged into the breach, but he didn't even look. "So, Monsieur Gage, I understand that now you are performing miracles, wringing water from stones and smothering serpents?"

"I found an old conduit."

"And the Holy Grail, I understand."

I took a breath. "It is the same thing I was looking for in the pyramids, General, and the same thing that Count Alessandro Silano and his corrupt Egyptian Rite of Freemasonry is pursuing to the possible harm of us all. Najac here is himself in league with scoundrels who . . ."

"Mr. Gage, I've endured your rambling over many months, and don't recall benefiting whatsoever. If you remember I offered you partnership, a chance to remake the world through the ideals of our two revolutions, French and American. Instead you deserted by balloon, is this not correct?"

"But only because of Silano . . ."

"Do you have this Grail or not?"

"No."

"Do you know where it is?"

"No, but we were looking when Najac here . . ."

"Do you know what it even is?"

"Not precisely, but . . ."

He turned to Najac. "He obviously knows nothing. Why did you pull him out?"

"But he said he did, in the pit!"

"Who wouldn't say anything, with your damned snakes snapping at his head? Enough of this nonsense from you and him! I want an example made of this man: he is not only useless, he is boring! He will be paraded before the infantry and shot like the turncoat he is. I am tired of Masons, sorcerers, snakes, moldering gods, and every other kind of imbecilic legend I have heard since starting this expedition. I am a member of the Institute! France is the embodiment of science! The only 'Grail' is firepower!"

And with that, a bullet plucked off the general's hat and slammed into the chest of a colonel behind, killing the man.

The general jumped, staring in shock as the officer toppled over.

"Mon dieu!" Najac crossed himself, which I considered the height of hypocrisy, given that his piety had as much value as a Continental dollar. "It's a sign! You should not speak as you did!"

Napoleon momentarily went pale, but regained his composure. He frowned at the enemy swarming on the walls, looked at the sprawled colonel, and then picked up his hat. "It was Lambeau who took the bullet, not me."

"But the power of the Grail!"

"This is the second time my stature has saved my life. If I had the height of our General Kléber, I would be dead twice over. There's your miracle, Najac."

My captor was transfixed by the hole in the general's hat.

"Perhaps it's a sign we can all still help each other," I tried.

"And I want the American gagged as well as bound. Another word, and I will have to shoot him myself."

And with that he stalked away, my plight unimproved. "All right, they have a foothold! Lannes, get a three-pounder into that breach!"

¤   ¤   ¤

I missed much of what happened next and am grateful for it. The Ottoman troops fought ferociously, so much so that a captain of engineers named Ayme had to find his way through Jaffa's cellars to take the enemy from behind with the bayonet. With that, angry French soldiers began fanning into Jaffa's alleys.

Meanwhile, General Bon on the northern side of town had turned his diversionary attack into a full-fledged assault that broke in from that direction. With French troops swarming, the defenders' morale collapsed and the Ottoman levies began to surrender. French fury at the foolish emissary beheadings hadn't been slaked, however, and killing and looting first went unchecked, then turned into mob frenzy. Prisoners were shot and bayoneted. Homes were ransacked. As the bloody afternoon gave way to concealing night, whooping soldiers staggered through the streets heavy with plunder. They fired muskets into windows and waved sabers wet with blood. The looters refused to even stop to help their own wounded. Officers who tried to stop the massacre were threatened and shoved aside. Women's veils were ripped from their faces, their clothes following. Any husband or brother who tried to defend them was shot down, the women raped in sight of the bodies. No mosque, church, or synagogue was respected, and Muslim, Christian, and Jew alike died in the flames. Children lay screaming on the corpses of their parents. Daughters pleaded for mercy while being violated on top of dying mothers. Prisoners were hurled from walls. Flames trapped the elderly, the sick, and the insane in the rooms where they hid. Blood ran down the gutters like rainwater. In one monstrous night, the fear and frustration of nearly a year's bitter campaigning was taken out on a single helpless city. An army of the rational, from the capital of reason, had gone insane.

Bonaparte knew better than to try to stem this release; the same anarchy had reigned in a thousand sackings before, from Troy to the Crusader pillages of Constantinople and Jerusalem. "One should never forbid what one lacks the power to prevent," he remarked. By dawn the men's emotion had been spent and the exhausted soldiers sprawled like their victims, stunned by what they'd done, but satiated as well, like satyrs after a debauch. A hungry, demonic anger had been fed.

In the aftermath, Bonaparte was left with more than three thousand sullen, hungry, terrified Ottoman prisoners.

Napoleon did not shrink from hard decisions. For all his admiration of poets and artists, he was at heart an artillery-man and an engineer. He was invading Syria and Palestine, a land with two and a half million people, with thirteen thousand French soldiers and two thousand Egyptian auxil-iaries. Even as Jaffa fell, some of his men were displaying symptoms of plague. His fantastic goal was to march to In-dia like Alexander before him, heading an army of re-cruited Orientals, carving out an empire in the East. Yet Horatio Nelson had destroyed his fleet and cut him off from reinforcements, Sidney Smith was helping organize the de-fense of Acre, and Bonaparte needed to frighten the Butcher into capitulation. He dared not free his prisoners, and he couldn't feed or guard them.

So he decided to execute them.

It was a monstrous decision in a controversial career, made more so by the fact that I was one of the prisoners he decided to execute. I wasn't even to have the dignity and fame of being paraded before assembled regiments as a noteworthy spy; instead I was herded by Najac into the mass of milling Moroccans and Sudanese and Albanians as if I were one more Ottoman levy. The poor men were still uncertain of what was happening, since they'd surren-dered on the assumption their lives would be spared. Was Bonaparte marching them to boats bound for Constanti-nople? Were they being sent as slave labor to Egypt? Were they merely to be camped outside the city's smoking walls until the French moved on? But no, it was none of these, and the grim ranks of grenadiers and fusiliers, muskets at parade rest, soon began to ignite rumor and panic. French cavalry were stationed at either end of the beach to prevent escape. Against the orange groves were the infantry, and at our back was the sea.

"They are going to kill us!" some began to cry.

"Allah will protect us," others promised.

"As he protected Jaffa?"

"Look, I haven't found the Grail yet," I whispered to Najac, "but it exists—it's a book—and if you'll kill me, you'll never find it either. It's not too late for partnership . . ."

He pressed the point of his saber into my back.

"This is a crime, what you're about to do!" I hissed. "The world will not forget!"

"Nonsense. There are no crimes in war."

I described the ensuing scene at the beginning of this story. One of the remarkable things about readying to be executed is how the senses sharpen. I could sense the fabric layers of the air as if I had butterfly wings, I could pick out the scents of sea, blood, and oranges, I could feel every grain of sand under my now bootless feet and hear every click and creak of weapons being readied, harness being twitched by impatient horses, the hum of insects, the cries of birds. How unwilling I was to die! Men pleaded and sobbed in a dozen languages. Prayers were a hum.

"At least I drowned your damned snakes," I remarked.

"You will feel the ball go into your body as I did," Najac replied. "Then another, and another. I hope it takes you time to bleed away, because the lead hurts very much. It flattens and tears. I would have preferred the snakes, but this is almost as good." He strode away as the muskets leveled.

"Fire!"

¤   ¤   ¤

There was a crash, and the rank of prisoners reeled. Bullets thwacked home, flesh and droplets flying. So what saved me? My Negro giant, arms lifted in supplication, ran after Najac as if the villain might grant reprieve, which put him between me and the muskets just as the volley went off. The bullets hurled him backward, but he formed a momentary shield. A line of prisoners collapsed, screaming, and I was spattered with so much blood that initially I feared some might be my own. Of those of us still standing, some fell to their knees, and some rushed at the ranks of the French. But most, including me, fled instinctively into the sea.

"Fire!" Another rank blasted and prisoners spun, toppled, tripped. One next to me gave an awful, bloody cough; another lost the crown of his head in a spray of red mist. The water splashed upward in blinding sheets as hundreds of us ran into it, trying to escape a nightmare too horrific to seem real. Some stumbled, crawling and bawling in the shallows. Others clutched wounded arms and legs. Pleas to Allah rang out hopelessly.

"Fire!"

As bullets whined over me, I dove and struck out, realizing as I did so that most of the Turks around me didn't know how to swim. They were paralyzed, chest deep in water. I went several yards and looked back. The pace of firing had slackened as the soldiers rushed forward with bayonets. The wounded and those frozen by fear were being stuck like pigs. Other French soldiers were calmly reloading and aiming at those of us farther out in the water, calling to each other and pointing targets. The volleys had dissolved into a general maelstrom of shooting.

Drowning men clutched at me. I pushed them off and kept going.

About fifty yards offshore was a flat reef. Waves rolled over its top, leaving shallows one or two feet in depth. Scores of us reached this jagged table, pulling ourselves up on it and staggering toward the deeper blue on the seaward side. As we did so we drew fire; men jerked, spun, and fell into froth that was turning pink. Behind me the sea was thick with the bobbing heads and backs of Ottomans shot or drowned, as French waded in with sabers and axes.

This was madness! I still was as miraculously unhurt as Napoleon, watching from the dunes. The reef ended and I plunged into deeper water with a wild hopelessness. Where could I go? I drifted, paddling feebly, down the outer edge of the reef, watching as men huddled until bullets finally found them. Was that Najac running up and down the sand, furiously looking for my corpse? There was a higher outcropping of reef that rose above the waves nearer Jaffa itself. Could I find some kind of hiding place?

Bonaparte, I saw, had disappeared, not caring to watch the massacre to its end.

I came to the rock where men clung, as pitifully exposed as flies on paper. The French were putting out in small boats to finish off survivors.

Not knowing what else to do, I put my head underwater and opened my eyes. I saw the thrashing legs of the prisoners clinging to our refuge, and the muted hues of blue as the edifice descended into the depths. And there, a hole, like a small underwater cave. If nothing else, it looked blessedly removed from the horrible clamor at the surface. I dove, entered, and felt with my arm. The rock was sharp and slimy. And then at my farthest reach my hand thrashed in empty air. I pulled myself forward and surfaced.

I could breathe! I was in an inner air pocket in an underwater cave, the only illumination a shaft of light from a narrow crack overhead. I could hear the screams and shots again, but they were muffled. I dared not call out my discovery, lest the French find me. There was only room for one, anyway. So I waited, trembling, while wooden hulls ground against the rocks, shots rang out, and the last blubbering prisoners were put to the sword or bayonet. The soldiers were methodical; they wanted no witnesses.

"There! Get that one!"

"Look at the vermin squirm."

"Here's another to finish off!"

Finally, it was quiet.

I was the only survivor.

So I existed, shivering with growing cold, as the curses and pleas faded. The Mediterranean has almost no tide, so I was in little danger of drowning. It was morning when we were marched to the beach and nightfall by the time I dared emerge, my skin as corrupted as a cadaver's from the long soaking. My clothes were in shreds, my teeth chattering.

Now what?

I numbly treaded water, bobbing out to sea. A corpse or two floated by. I could see that Jaffa was still burning, banked coals against the sky. The stars were bright enough to silhouette the line of vegetation along the beach. I spied the flicker of French campfires and heard the occasional shot, or shout, or ring of bitter laughter.

Something dark floated by that wasn't a corpse and I grabbed it: an empty powder keg, discarded by one side or the other during the battle. Hour followed hour, the stars wheeling overhead, and Jaffa grew dimmer. My strength was being leached by the chill.

And then in the glimmer of predawn, almost twenty-four hours since the executions had begun, I spied a boat. It was a small Arab lighter of the kind that had taken me from HMS *Dangerous* into Jaffa. I croaked and waved, coughing, and the boat came near, wide eyes peering at me over the gunwale like a watchful animal.

"Help." It was barely more than a mutter.

Strong arms seized me and hauled me aboard. I lay at the bottom, spineless as a jellyfish, exhausted, blinking at gray sky and not entirely certain if I was alive or dead.

"Effendi?"

I jerked. I knew that voice. "Mohammad?"

"What are you doing in the middle of the sea, when I deposited you in Jerusalem?"

"When did *you* become a sailor?"

"When the city fell. I stole this boat and sculled out of the harbor. Unfortunately, I have no idea how to sail it. I've just drifted."

Painfully, I sat up. We were well offshore I saw with relief, out of range of any French. The lighter had a mast and lateen sail, and I'd sailed craft not too dissimilar to this one on the Nile. "You are bread upon the waters," I croaked. "I can sail. We can go find a friendly ship."

"But what is happening in Jaffa?"

"Everyone is dead."

He looked stricken. No doubt he had friends or family that had been caught up in the siege. "Not *everyone*, of course." But I was more honest the first time.

Years from now historians will labor to explain the strategic reasoning for Napoleon's invasions of Egypt and Syria, for the slaughter at Jaffa and the marches with no clear goal. The scholars' task is futile. War is nothing about reason and everything about emotion. If it has logic, it is the mad logic of hell. All of us have some evil: deep in most, indulged by a few, universally released by war. Men sign away everything for this release, uncapping a pot they scarcely know is boiling, and then are haunted ever after. The French—for all their muddle of republican ideals, alliances with distant pashas, scientific study, and dreams of reform—achieved above all else an awful catharsis, followed by the sure knowledge that what they'd released must eventually consume them too. War is poisoned glory.

"But do you know a friendly ship?" Mohammad asked.

"The British, perhaps, and I have news I need to bring them." And some scores to settle, too, I thought. "Do you have water?"

"And bread. Some dates."

"Then we are shipmates, Mohammad."

He beamed. "Allah has his ways, does he not? And did you find what you were looking for in Jerusalem?"

"No."

"Later, I think." He gave me some water and food, as restorative as a tingle of electricity. "You are meant to find it, or you would not have survived."

How comforting it would be to have such faith! "Or I shouldn't have looked, and I've been punished by seeing too much." I turned away from the sad glow from shore. "Now then, help me set this sail. We'll set course for Acre and the English ships."

"Yes, once more I am your guide, effendi, in my new and sturdy boat! I will take you to the English!"

I lay back against a thwart. "Thanks for your rescue, friend."

He nodded, "And for this I will charge only ten shillings!"

PART TWO

CHAPTER 12

I came to Acre a hero, but not for escaping the mass execution at Jaffa. Rather, I paid back the French with timely information.

Mohammad and I found the British squadron the second day of our sail. The ships were led by the battleships *Tigre* and *Theseus*, and when we coasted into the lee of the flagship I hailed none less than that friendly devil himself, Sir Sidney Smith.

"Gage, is that really you?" he called. "We thought you'd gone back over to the frogs! And now you're back to us?"

"To the French by the treachery of your own British seamen, Captain!"

"Treachery? But they said you deserted!"

How's that for a cheeky lie by Big Ned and Little Tom? No doubt they thought me dead and unable to contradict them. It's just the kind of truth-twisting I might have thought of, which made me all the more indignant. "Hardly! Locked out from brave retreat by your own bully seamen, I was! You owe us a medal. Don't they, Mohammad?"

"The French tried to kill us," my boat mate said. "He owes me ten shillings."

"And here you are in the middle of the Mediterranean?" Smith scratched his head. "Damnation. For a man who turns up everywhere, it's hard to know where you belong. Well, come aboard and let's sort this out."

So up we climbed, the eighty-gun ship-of-the-line a behemoth compared to the feeble lighter we'd been sailing in, which was taken in tow. The British officers searched Mohammad as if he might produce a dagger at any moment, and gave sharp looks at me. But I'd already determined to act the wronged one, and had a trump besides. So I launched into my version of events.

". . . And then the iron gate slammed shut against me as the ring of French and Arab scoundrels closed in. . . ."

Yet instead of the outrage and sympathy I deserved, Smith and his officers regarded me with skepticism.

"Admit it, Ethan. You *do* seem to go too easily from one side to the other," Smith said. "And get out of the damndest fixes."

"Aye, he's an American rebel, he is," a lieutenant put in.

"Wait. You think the French *let* me escape from Jaffa?"

"The reports are that no one else did. It's rather remarkable, finding you."

"And who's this heathen, then?" another officer asked, pointing at Mohammad.

"He's my friend and savior, and a better man than you, I'll wager."

Now they bristled, and I was probably on the brink of being called out for a duel. Smith hurriedly intervened. "Now, there's no need for that. We have the right to ask hard questions, and you have the right to answer them. Frankly, Gage, I hadn't heard all that much useful from you in Jerusalem, despite the Crown's investment. Then my sailors report you'd acquired a quite expensive, rather remarkable rifle? Where's that?"

"Stolen by a blasted French thief and torturer named Najac," I said. "If I'd joined the French, what the devil am I doing in rags, wounded, burned, bobbing in a boat with a Muslim camel driver and without a weapon?" I was angry. "If I'd gone to the French, why am I not sipping claret in

Napoleon's tent right now? Aye, let's sort the truth. Call those rascal seamen up right now. . . ."

"Little Tom lost his arm and has been sent home," Smith said. Despite my indignation, the news gave me pause. To lose a limb was a sentence of poverty. "Big Ned has been assigned ashore, with much of the *Dangerous* crew, to bolster Djezzar's defenses in Acre. Perhaps you can discuss it with him there. We've got a stew of stout men to hold off Bonaparte, a mix of Turks, Mamelukes, mercenaries, rascals, and English bulldogs. We've even got a French royalist artillery officer who's joined our side, Louis-Edmond Phelipeaux. He's strengthening the fortifications."

"You're allied with a Frenchman, and you're questioning me?"

"He helped arrange my escape from Templar Prison in Paris and is as faithful a comrade as you could wish for. Curious how men choose up sides in a dangerous time, isn't it?" He looked at me closely. "Potts and Tentwhistle dead, Tom crippled, nothing gained, yet here you are. Jericho says he thought you dead or deserted as well."

"You've talked to Jericho, too?"

"He's in Acre, with his sister."

Well, there was glad news. I'd been distracted by my own problems, but I felt a flush of relief of hearing that Miriam was safe for the moment. I wondered if she still had my seraphim. I took a breath. "Sir Sidney, I'm done with the French, I can assure you. Hung me upside down over a snake pit, they did."

"By God, the barbarians! Didn't tell them anything, did you?"

"Of course not," I lied. "But they told me something, and I can prove my loyalty with it." It was time to play my trump.

"Told you what?"

"That Bonaparte's siege artillery is coming by water, and with luck we can capture it all before his troops reach Acre."

"Really? Well, that would change things, wouldn't it?" Smith beamed. "Find me those guns, Gage, and I *will* give you a medal. A fine Turkish one—they're bigger than ours and nicely gaudy. They hand them out by the basket load, and you can bet I'll spare one if you're telling the truth. For once."

¤   ¤   ¤

Of course it rained, dampening our chances of spying the French flotilla, and then fog moved in, lowering visibility even more. The murk soon had the English thinking I was a double agent again, as if I controlled the weather. But if we had difficulty finding the French, they had a worse time evading us. Fog was their enemy, too.

So the French stumbled upon us on the morning of March 18 when Captain Standelet tried to round Cape Carmel and enter the huge bay bounded by Haifa at the south and Acre at the north. Three boats, including that of Standelet, escaped. Six more did not, however, and siege guns, which fire a twenty-four-pound ball, were trussed in their holds. In a single blow, we'd captured Napoleon's most potent weapon. With a morning's work I was proclaimed bulwark of Acre, fox of Jaffa, and watchman of the deep. I got a jeweled medal, too, the Sultan's Order of the Lion, which Smith then bought back to cover my payment to Mohammad, plus a few coins besides. "If you know how to spend less than you get, you have the philosopher's stone," he lectured. "I've been reading your Franklin."

And so I came to the old Crusader city. Our route by water was paralleled on land by columns of smoke marking the advance of Napoleon's troops. Reports had come of a steady string of skirmishes between his regiments and the Muslims of the interior, but it was at Acre that the contest would be decided.

The city is on a peninsula that juts into the Mediterranean at the north end of the Bay of Carmel, and thus is two-thirds surrounded by sea. The peninsula extends southwest from the mainland, and its harbor is formed by a breakwater. Acre is smaller than Jerusalem, its sea and land walls less than a mile and a half in circumference, but is more prosperous and about as populous. By the time I arrived the French were already sealing off the city from the landward side, flapping tricolors marking the arc of their camps.

Acre is a lovely city in normal times, its seawalls bounded by aquamarine reefs and its land walls bordered by green fields. An ancient aqueduct, no longer in use, led from its moat to the French lines. The great copper green dome of its central mosque, coupled with a needle-like minaret, punctuate a charming skyline of tile, towers, and awnings. Upper stories arch over twisting streets. Markets shaded by bright awnings fill the main thoroughfares. The port smells of salt, fresh fish, and spices. There are three major inn-and-warehouse complexes for maritime visitors, the Khan el-Omdan, the Khan el-Efranj, and the Khan a-Shawarda. Balancing this prettiness is the ruler's palace on the northern wall, a grim Crusader block with a round tower at each corner, softened only because its harem windows look down on cool gardens between mosque and palace. The stout fort and rambling medieval town of tile roofs called to my mind a stern, forbidding headmaster overlooking a lively class of redheaded children.

The government and religious area occupies the northeastern quarter of the city, and the land walls face north and east, their corner joined at a massive tower. This would be so key to the ensuing siege that it would eventually be called by the French *la tour maudite*: the accursed tower. But could Acre be defended?

Clearly, many thought not. We took Mohammad's little boat ashore, following the *Tigre*'s longboat, and when we reached the quay the waterfront was jammed with refugees anxious to flee the city. Smith, Mohammad, and I pushed through a crowd close to panic. Most were women and children, but not a few were rich merchants who'd paid Djezzar steep bribes to leave. In war, money can mean survival, and stories of slaughter had raced up the coast. People clutched the few belongings they could carry and bid for passage on the merchantmen offshore. A sweating woman cradled a silver coffee service, her toddlers clutching at her gown and howling. A cotton merchant had stuffed loaded pistols into a sash sewn with golden coins. A lovely dark-eyed girl of ten with trembling mouth held a squirming puppy. A banker used a wedge of African slaves to push his way to the forefront.

"Never mind this rabble," Smith said. "We're better without them."

"Don't they trust their own garrison?"

"Their garrison doesn't trust itself. Djezzar has spine, but the French have crushed every army they've met. Your cannon will help. We'll have bigger guns than Boney has, and we'll put a battery of them right at the Land Gate, where the sea and land walls meet. But it will be the corner tower that's the nut the devil cracks his tooth on. It's the farthest from the support of our naval artillery, yet the strongest point in the wall. It's Acre's bloody knuckle, and our real secret is a man who hates Boney even more than we do."

"You mean Djezzar the Butcher."

"No, I mean Napoleon's classmate from the Ecole Royale Militaire in Paris. Our Louis-Edmond le Picard de Phelipeaux shared a desk with the Corsican rascal, believe it or not, and the aristocrat and provincial kicked each other's legs blue when they were teens. It was Phelipeaux who always bested Bonaparte on tests, Phelipeaux who graduated with higher honors, and Phelipeaux who got the best military assignments. If the revolution hadn't occurred, forcing our royalist friend out of France, he'd likely be Napoleon's superior. He slipped into France as a clandestine agent last year and rescued me from Temple Prison, posing as a police commissioner who pretended he was transferring me to a different cell. He's never lost to Napoleon, and won't this time. Come and meet him."

Djezzar's "palace" looked like a transplanted Bastille. The Crusader keep had been remodeled to include gunports, not charm, and two-thirds of the Butcher's ordinance was aimed at his own people, not the French. Square and stolid, the citadel was as implacable as Djezzar's iron-fisted rule.

"There's an armory in the basement, barracks on the ground floor, administrative offices in the next, Djezzar's palace above that, and the harem at the very top," Smith said, pointing. I could see grilled harem windows, like the cage of pretty birds. As if in sympathy, swallows flitted between them and the palms below. Having broken into a harem in Egypt, I had no desire to explore this one. Those women had been scary.

We passed hulking Ottoman sentries and a massive wooden door studded with iron, and entered the gloomy interior. After the dazzling light of the Levant, the inside had the air of a dungeon. I blinked as I looked about. This was the level that was quarters for Djezzar's loyalist guards, and there was a military sparseness about it. The soldiers looked at us shyly from the shadows, where they were cleaning muskets and sharpening blades. They looked about as cheerful as recruits at Valley Forge. Then there were quick footsteps from the stairs and a lithe and more energetic Frenchman bounded down, in a rather stained and careworn white uniform of the Bourbons. This must be Phelipeaux.

He was taller than Napoleon, elegant in his movements, and with that languid self-confidence that comes with high birth. Phelipeaux gave a courtly bow, his wan smile and dark eyes seeming to measure everything with an artilleryman's calculation. "Monsieur Gage, I am told you may have saved our city!"

"Hardly that."

"Your captured French guns will be invaluable, I assure you. Ah, the irony of it. And an American! We are Lafayette and Washington! What an international alliance we are forming here: British, French, American, Mameluke, Jew, Ottoman, Maronite . . . all against my former classmate!"

"Did you really school together?"

"He peeked at my answers." He grinned. "Come, let's peek at him now!"

I liked his dash already.

Phelipeaux led us up a winding stair until we came out on the roof of Djezzar's castle. What a magnificent view! After the rain of recent days the air was dazzling, distant Mount Carmel a blue ridge far across the bay. Nearer, the assembling French were as sharp as lead soldiers. Tents and awnings were blossoming like a spring carnival. From Jaffa, I knew what life would be like in their lines: plentiful food, imported drink to bolster the courage of assault groups, and cadres of prostitutes and servant women to cook, clean, and provide warmth at night, all at exorbitant prices cheerfully paid by men who felt there was a good chance they were about to die. About a mile inland was a hill a hundred feet in height, and there I could see a cluster of men and horses amid flapping banners, out of range of any of our fire.

"I suspect that is where Buonaparte will set his head-quarters," Phelipeaux said, drawing out the Italian pronun-ciation with aristocratic disdain. "I know him, you see, and know how he thinks. We both would do the same. He'll extend his trenches and try to mine our walls with sappers. So I know that he knows the tower is key."

I followed the sweep of his finger. Cannon were being swung up onto the walls, and there was a stone-lined dry moat just beyond, about twenty feet deep and fifty wide. "No water in the moat?"

"It hasn't been designed for it—the bottom is above sea level—but our engineers have an idea. We're building a reservoir on the Mediterranean near the city's Land Gate that we'll pump full of seawater. It could be released into the moat at a time of crisis."

"That plan, however, is still weeks from completion," Smith said.

I nodded. "So in the meantime, you've got your tower." It was massive, like a promontory at the edge of a sea. I imagined it looked even taller from the French side.

"It's the strongest on the wall," Phelipeaux said, "but it can also be fired upon and assaulted from two sides. If the republicans break it, they will be into the gardens and can fan out to seize our defenses from behind. If they cannot, their infantry will perish uselessly."

I tried to survey the scene with his engineer's eye. The ruined aqueduct ran off from the walls toward the French. It broke just short of our wall near the tower, having once delivered water. I saw the French were digging trenches alongside it because it provided cover from harassing fire. To one side was what looked like a dried pond. The French were setting survey stakes inside it.

"They've drained a reservoir to provide themselves a protective depression to site a battery," Phelipeaux said as if reading my mind. "Soon it will be filled with the lighter guns they brought overland."

I looked down. The garden was an oasis of shade amid the military preparation. The harem women were probably accustomed to visiting there. Now, with so many soldiers and sailors manning the ramparts above, they'd be locked away.

"We've added nearly a hundred cannon to the city's defenses," Phelipeaux said. "Now that we've captured the heaviest French guns, we must keep them at a distance."

"Which means not allowing Djezzar to give up," Smith amended. "And you, Gage, are the key to that."

"Me?"

"You've seen Napoleon's army. I want you to tell our ally it can be beaten, because it *can* be if he believes. But first you have to believe it yourself. Do you?"

I thought a moment. "Bonaparte buttons his breeches like the rest of us. He just hasn't met anyone yet as pugnacious as himself."

"Exactly. So come meet the Butcher."

We did not have to wait for an audience. After Jaffa, Djezzar recognized his own survival depended on his new European allies. We were ushered into his audience chambers, a finely decorated but nonetheless modest room with an ornately carved ceiling and a carpet of overlapping oriental rugs. Birds tweeted from golden cages, a small monkey hopped about on a leather leash, and some kind of large jungle cat, spotted, eyed us sleepily from a cushion, as if deciding whether we were worth the trouble of eating. I had much the same sense from the Butcher, who was sitting erect, his aging torso still conveying physical power. We sat cross-legged before him while his Sudanese bodyguards watched us carefully, as if we might be assassins instead of allies.

Djezzar was seventy-five and looked like a fiery prophet, not a kindly grandfather. His bushy beard was white, his eyes flint, and his mouth had a cruel set. A pistol was tucked in his sash, and a dagger lay near to hand. Yet his gaze also betrayed the self-doubt of a bully up against another tough: Napoleon.

"Pasha, this is the American I told you about," Smith introduced.

He took me in at a glance—my borrowed seaman's clothing, stained boots, skin leathered by too much sun and saltwater—and didn't try to hide his skepticism. Yet he was curious, too. "You escaped Jaffa."

"The French meant to kill me with the other prisoners," I said. "I swam out to sea and found a small cave in the rocks. The massacre was horrible."

"Still, survival is the mark of remarkable men." The Butcher himself was a wily survivor, of course. "And you helped capture the enemy's artillery?"

"Some of it, at least."

He studied me. "You are resourceful, I think."

"As are you, Pasha. As resourceful as any Napoleon."

He smiled. "More so, I think. I have killed more men and fucked more women. So now it is a test of wills. A siege. And Allah has forced me to use infidels to fight infidels. I don't trust Christians. They are always conspiring."

This seemed ungrateful. "Right now we're conspiring to save your neck."

He shrugged. "So tell me about this Bonaparte. Is he a patient man?"

"Not in the least."

"But he's energetic at pushing for what he wants," Phelipeaux amended.

"He'll come at your city hard, early, even without the guns," I said. "He believes in a quick strike of overpowering force to break an enemy's will. His soldiers are good at what they do, and their fire is accurate."

Djezzar took a date from a cup and examined it as if he'd never seen one before, then popped it in his mouth, chewing it to one side as he talked. "So perhaps I should surrender. Or flee. He outnumbers my garrison two to one."

"With the British ships you outgun him. He's hundreds of miles from his Egyptian base and two thousand miles from France."

"So we can beat him before he gets more cannon."

"He has almost no troops to garrison anything he captures. His soldiers are homesick and tired."

"Sick in another way, too," Djezzar said. "There have been rumors of plague."

"A few cases appeared even in Egypt," I confirmed. "I heard there were more at Jaffa." The Butcher was a shrewd one, I saw, not some Ottoman weakling imposed by the Sublime Porte in Constantinople. He gathered information about his enemies like a scholar. "Napoleon's weakness is time, Pasha. Every day he stays in front of Acre, the sultan in Constantinople can order more forces to surround him. He gets no reinforcements, and no resupply, while the British navy can bring both to us. He tries to accomplish in a day what other men require a year to complete, and that's his weakness. He's trying to conquer Asia with ten thousand men, and no one knows better than he that it's all bluff. The moment his enemies stop fearing him, he's finished. If you can hold . . ."

"He goes away," Djezzar finished. "This little man no one has beaten."

"We will beat him here," Smith vowed.

"Unless he finds something more powerful than artillery," another said from the shadows.

I started. I knew that voice! And indeed, emerging from the gloom behind Djezzar's cushioned perch was the hideous countenance of Haim Farhi! Smith and Phelipeaux blinked at this mutilation but did not recoil. They'd seen it before, too.

"Farhi! What are you doing in Acre?"

"Serving his master," Djezzar said.

"We left Jerusalem an uncomfortable place, Monsieur Gage. And with no book, there was no reason to stay there."

"You went with us for the pasha?"

"But of course. You know who modified my appearance."

"It was a favor to him," the Butcher rumbled. "Good looks allow vanity, and pride is the greatest sin. His scars let him concentrate on his numbers. And get into heaven."

Farhi bowed. "As always, you are generous, master."

"So you escaped Jerusalem!"

"Narrowly. I left you because my face draws too much attention, and because I knew further research was required. What do the French know of our secrets?"

"That Muslim outrage bars them from further exploration of the tunnels. They know nothing, and threatened me with snakes to try to learn what I knew. We've all come away empty-handed, I think."

"Empty-handed of what?" Smith asked.

Farhi turned to the British officer. "Your ally here did not go to Jerusalem merely to serve you, Captain."

"No, there was a woman he inquired about, if I recall."

"And a treasure desperate men are seeking."

"Treasure?"

"Not money," I said, annoyed at Farhi's casual sharing of my secret. "A book."

"A book of magic," the banker amended. "It's been rumored for thousands of years, and sought by the Knights Templar. When we asked for your sailor allies, we weren't looking for a siege door into Jerusalem. We were looking for this book."

"As were the French," I added.

"And me," said Djezzar. "Farhi was my ear."

It was appropriate he used the singular, since the scoundrel had cut off his minister's other one.

Smith was looking from one to the other of us.

"But it wasn't there," I said. "Most likely, it doesn't exist."

"And yet agents are making inquiries up and down the province of Syria," Farhi said. "Arabs, mostly, in the employ of some mysterious figure back in Egypt."

My skin prickled. "I was told Count Silano is still alive."

"Alive. Resurrected. Immortal." Farhi shrugged.

"What's your point, Haim?" Djezzar said, with the tone of a master long impatient with the meanderings of his subordinates.

"That, as Gage said, what all men seek might not exist. Yet if it does, we have no way to look for it, locked up as we are by Napoleon's army. Time is his enemy, yes. But it's our challenge too. If we are besieged too long, it may be too late to find first what Count Alessandro Silano is still seeking." He pointed at me. "This one must find a way to look for the secret again, before it is too late."

¤   ¤   ¤

I followed the smell of charcoal to find Jericho. He was in the bowels of the armory in the basement of Djezzar's palace, his muscles illuminated by the glow of a smithy furnace, hammering like Thor on the tools of war: swords, pikes, forked poles to push off scaling ladders, bayonets, ramrods. Lead cooled in bullet molds like black pearls, and scrap was piled for conversion into grapeshot and shrapnel. Miriam was working the bellows, her hair curled on her cheeks in sweaty tendrils, her shift damp and disturbingly clingy, perspiration glistening in that vale of temptation between neck and breasts. I didn't know what my reception would be, given that they'd lost their Jerusalem house in the tumult I'd caused, but when she saw me her eyes flashed bright greeting and she flew to me in the hellish glow, hugging. How good she felt! It was all I could do to keep my hand from slipping onto her round bottom, but of course her brother was there. Yet even taciturn Jericho allowed a reluctant smile.

"We thought you dead!"

She kissed my cheek, setting it on fire. I held her a safe distance away lest my own enthusiasm at our reunion be too physically obvious.

"And I feared the same for the two of you," I said. "I'm sorry our adventure has left you trapped here, but I really thought we'd find treasure. I escaped from Jaffa with my friend Mohammad in a boat." I looked at Miriam, realizing how much I'd missed her, and how angelically beautiful she really was. "The news of your survival was like nectar to a man dying of thirst."

I thought I saw a blush beyond the soot, and certainly I'd erased her brother's smile. No matter. I wouldn't release her waist, and she wouldn't release my shoulders.

"And now here we all are, alive," Jericho said. "All three of us."

I finally let her go and nodded. "With a man called the Butcher, a half-mad English sea captain, a mutilated Jew, a disgruntled schoolmate of Bonaparte, and a Muslim guide. Not to mention a burly blacksmith, his scholarly sister, and a ne'r-do-well American gambler. Quite the merry men, we are."

"And women," Miriam said. "Ethan, we heard what happened at Jaffa. What happens if the French break in here?"

"They won't," I said with more confidence than I felt. "We don't have to beat them—we just have to hold them off until they're compelled to retreat. And I have an idea for that. Jericho, is there any spare heavy chain in the city?"

"I've seen some about, used by ships, and to chain off the harbor mouth. Why?"

"I want to drape it from out towers to welcome the French."

He shook his head, convinced I was daft as ever. "To give them a hand up?"

"Yes. And then charge it with electricity."

"Electricity!" He crossed himself.

"It's an idea I had while in the boat with Mohammad. If we store enough spark in a battery of Leyden jars, we could transfer them with a wire to a suspended chain. It would give the same jolt I demonstrated in Jerusalem, but this time it would knock them into the moat where we could kill them." I'd become quite the sanguinary warrior.

"You mean they wouldn't be able to hold onto the chain?" Miriam asked.

"No more than if it were red hot. It would be like a barrier of fire."

Jericho was intrigued. "Could that really work?"

"If it doesn't, the Butcher will use the links to hang us."

CHAPTER 13

I needed to generate an electric charge on a scale even Ben Franklin had not dreamed of, so while Jericho set to work collecting and linking chain, Miriam and I set out to assemble glass, lead, copper, and jars in sufficient quantity to make a giant battery. I've seldom enjoyed a project so much. Miriam and I didn't just work together, we were partners, in a way which recaptured the alliance I'd had with Astiza. The demure shyness I'd first encountered had been lost somewhere in the tunnels beneath Jerusalem, and now she exhibited a brisk confidence that stiffened the courage of anyone she worked with. No man wants to be a coward around a woman. She and I worked shoulder to shoulder, brushing more than necessary, while I remembered exactly the spot on my cheek where her kiss had burned. There's nothing more desirable than a woman you haven't had.

While we labored we could hear the echo of the French guns, seeking the range as their first trenches advanced toward the walls. Even the bowels of Djezzar's palace would tremble when an iron ball crashed into the outer walls.

Franklin gave the name "battery" to lines of Leyden jars

because they reminded him of a battery of guns, set hub to hub to give concentrated fire. In our case, each additional jar could be connected to the last to add to the potential shock of French soldiers that I intended. We soon had so many that the task of energizing them all with friction—by turning a crank—looked Sisyphean, like rolling a boulder endlessly uphill.

"Ethan, how are we going to turn your glass disks long enough to power this huge contraption?" Miriam asked. "We need an army of grinders."

"Not an army, but a broader back and a dimmer mind." I meant Big Ned.

Ever since I had stepped ashore in Acre I'd been contemplating my reunion with the hulking, cranky sailor. He had to be paid back for his treachery at the Jerusalem gate, and yet he remained a dangerous giant still resentful about his gambling losses. The key was not to blunder into him when I was at a disadvantage, so I carefully planned my lesson. I learned he'd heard of my miraculous reappearance and boasted he still owed me a tussle, once I left the protection of my woman's skirts. When I was informed he'd been assigned to help hurriedly patch the moat masonry at the base on Acre's key tower, I appeared to give a hand from the sallyport above.

A wall is strongest without cracks for cannonballs to pry at, so that's why Smith and Phelipeaux wanted repairs made. It was a bold job, British marksmen traded sniper fire with French sharpshooters in their trenches while a few volunteers, including Ned, labored outside the walls below in the dark. Despite my problems with Ned and Tom, I'd come to admire the flinty determination of the English crew, a working man's porridge of the poor and illiterate who had little of the idealism of the French volunteers but a dogged loyalty to crown and country. Ned had that same starch. As muskets flashed and banged in the dark—how I missed my rifle!—baskets of stone, mortar, and water were lowered to the repair crew while they chipped, scraped, and fitted. Near dawn they finally scrambled back up a rope ladder like scurrying monkeys, bullets pinging, my arm giving each a hand inside. Finally there was only Ned below. He gave the ladder a good tug.

The look on his face when his escape route came loose and rattled down to make a heap at his feet was priceless. There's something to be said for revenge.

I leaned out. "Not fun to be locked out, is it, Ned?"

His head flamed like a red onion when he recognized me fifty feet above. "So you've dared come out of the pasha's palace, Yankee tinkerer! I thought you wouldn't come within a hundred miles of honest British seamen after the lesson I taught you at Jerusalem! And now you plan to leave me in this moat and let the French do your work for you?" He cupped his hands and shouted. "He's a coward, he is!"

"Oh, no," I countered. "I just want you to get a taste of your own base treachery, and see if you're man enough to face me honestly, instead of slamming gates in my face or hiding in a ship's bilge."

His eyes bulged as if pumped full of steam. "Face you honestly! By God, I'll rip you limb from limb, you cheat, if you ever have the pluck to stand toe to toe like a man!"

"It's a bully's way to rely on size, Big Ned," I called down. "Fight me fairly, sword to sword like gentlemen do, and I'll teach you a real lesson."

"Bloody thunder, indeed I will! I'll fight you with pistols, marlinspikes, cudgels, daggers, or cannon fire!"

"I said swords."

"Let me up then! If I can't strangle you, I'll cleave you in two!"

So with our duel set to my satisfaction I lowered a rope, hoisted the ladder back up, and got Ned back into Acre just before the dawn light would make him a target.

"I just showed you more mercy than you showed me," I lectured as he glowered, dusting mortar from his clothes.

"And I'm about to return the mercy you showed at cards. Let's cross blades and be done with our business once and for all! I wouldn't let you buy your way out now if you had money to pay me back ten times!"

"I'll meet you in the palace gardens. Do you want rapier, saber, or cutlass?"

"Cutlass, by God! Something to cut through bone! And I'll bring my bullyboys to watch you bleed!" He glared at the other men who were enjoying our exchange. "Nobody crosses Big Ned."

¤ ¤ ¤

My willingness to duel such an animal came from thinking a few cards ahead. Franklin was always an inspiration, and while working at Jericho's new forge I mused how the sage of Philadelphia might use ingenuity instead of brawn. Then I set to work.

Ned's sabotage was simple. I disassembled the cloth-and-wood handle from his cutlass, bolted on a copper replacement, roughened the handle to let my opponent take firm hold, and polished the entire assembly. Metal is conductive.

Mine was more complicated. I hollowed its haft, lined it with lead, doubled its wrapping for my own added insulation, and—just before my opponent arrived—held its butt end against a stout wire leading from the cranking machine I had built to generate a frictional charge. I was spinning away, storing electricity in the steel of my weapon, when my opponent appeared in the courtyard.

Ned squinted. "What's that then, you bloody Yankee tinkerer?"

"Magic," I said.

"Hey, I wants a fair fight now!"

"And you shall get it, blade to blade. Your muscle to my brain. Nothing fairer than that, eh?"

"Ethan, he'll split you like a bolt of wood," Jericho warned, as I'd coached. "This is madness. You stand no chance against Big Ned."

"Honor requires that we cross blades," I recited with equally rehearsed resignation, "no matter what his skill and size." I suppose it's not sporting to lead on a bull, but what matador doesn't wave a cape?

I gave some minutes for a crowd of assembled sailors to

bet against me—I covered them all, with a loan from the metallurgist, figuring I might as well make a profit from all this bother—and then took a fencing stance on the garden path where we'd duel. I liked to think the harem girls were watching from above, and I knew Djezzar was. "On guard, you big bully!" I cried. "If I lose I'll give you every shilling, but if you lose, then you're beholden to me!"

"If you lose, I'll *take* what I'm owed from the steaks and chops I'll have turned you into!" The crowd roared at this wit and Ned preened. Then he charged and swung.

I parried.

I wish I could report there was some gallant and expert swordplay as I deftly countered his brute force with athletic skill. Instead, as steel touched steel, there was simply a blaze of sparks and a sharp report like a gunshot that made the spectators cry and jump. Our blades merely touched, yet Ned flew backward as if he'd been kicked by a mule. His cutlass went flying, narrowly missing one of his shipmates, and he crashed down like Goliath and lay there, eyes rolled back in his head. The sword stung in my own hand, but I'd been insulated from the worst of the jolt. The air had a burning smell.

Was he dead?

I touched him with my sword tip. He jerked like one of Galvani's frogs.

The crowd was utterly silent, in awe.

Finally Ned shuddered, blinked, and cringed. "Don't touch me!"

"You shouldn't test your betters, Ned."

"Blimey, what did you do?"

"Magic," I said again. I pointed my sword at the others. "I won at cards fairly, and won this duel. Now. Who else wants to challenge me?"

They backed off as if I had leprosy. A boatswain hurriedly tossed me the purse of bets he'd held. God bless the foolish gambling instincts of British sailors.

Ned woozily sat up. "No one's ever bested me before. Not even my pappy, not once I got to be eight or nine and could thrash him."

"Will you respect me finally?"

He waggled his head to clear it. "I'm beholden, you said. You've got strange powers, guv'nor. I see that now. You always survive, no matter what side you're on."

"I just use my brain, Ned. If you'd ally with me, I'd teach you to do the same."

"Aye. I wants to serve *with* you, not fight." Clumsily, he struggled to his feet and swayed. I could imagine the unearthly tingling he still felt. Electricity hurts. "You others, you listen to me," he croaked. "Don't cross the American. And if you do, you have to deal with me. We's partners, we is." He gave me a hug, like a giant ape.

"Don't touch the sword, man!"

"Oh yes." He stepped hastily away.

"Now, I need your help making more magic, but this time against the French. I need a fellow who can crank my apparatus like the devil himself. Can you do that, Ned?"

"If you don't touch me."

"No, we're even," I confirmed. "Now we can be friends."

¤   ¤   ¤

There was an odd lull as the French burrowed like ants toward the walls of Acre, putting their remaining cannon in place. They dug and we waited, with that sluggish fatalism that wears down the besieged. It was Holy Week, so in the spirit of the holidays, Smith and Bonaparte agreed to a prisoner exchange, trading back the men taken in raids and skirmishing. Djezzar paced his walls like a restless cat, muttering about the damnation of Christians and all infidels, and then sat in a great chair on the corner tower to motivate his soldiers by glaring with his fierce eye. I labored on my electrical scheme, but it was difficult to get Jericho's help because the Butcher, Smith, and Phelipeaux kept sending down a steady stream of armory requests. In close combat on the ramparts, with little time to reload, steel would be as important as gunpowder.

The strain was showing. The metallurgist's somewhat cherubic face had grown tauter, his eyes shadowed. The French guns banged around the clock, he seldom saw daylight, and he was uneasy about my growing closeness to Miriam. And yet he was the kind of man who couldn't refuse anyone, nor allow a lapse in quality. He worked even when Miriam and I collapsed in opposite corners of the armory, in fitful, exhausted sleep.

Thus the ironmonger awakened us in the predawn darkness of March 28 when the tattoo of the French guns accelerated, signaling an impending attack. Even deep in Djezzar's cellar, the beams overhead trembled from the bombardment. Dust filtered down. The quaking made sparks fly up from the forge.

"The French are testing our defenses," I guessed groggily. "Keep your sister down here. You're both more valuable as metallurgists than targets."

"And you?"

"It's not ready yet, but I'm going to see how my chain might be used!"

It was four in the morning, the stairs and ramps lit by torches. I was swept up in a tide of Turkish soldiers and British sailors mounting the walls, everyone cursing in their own language. At the parapet the bombardment was a rolling thunder, punctuated by the occasional crash as a cannonball hit the wall, or a shriek as one sailed overhead. There were stabs of light on the French line, marking where their cannons were.

Smith was there, a weird smile on his lips, pacing behind a contingent of Royal Marines. Phelipeaux was racing madly up and down the walls, using a garbled mixture of French, English, Arabic, and anxious hand gestures to direct the city's cannon. At the same time signal lanterns were being hoisted on the corner tower to elicit naval support.

I looked into the gloom but couldn't see the enemy troops. I borrowed a musket and fired to where I guessed they might be, in hopes of drawing answering pinpricks of light, but the French were too disciplined. So I followed

Phelipeaux to the tower. It was trembling like a tree being chopped at.

Now our own cannon were beginning to bark back, their flashes interrupting the steady drum of French fire, but also giving the enemy artillerists a reference for aiming. Shot began flying higher, and then there was a bang as a cannon-ball clipped the wall's crenellation and rock fragments spewed like the pieces of a grenade. A Turkish cannon was dismounted and flopped over, blinded men screaming.

"What can I do?" I asked Phelipeaux, trying to contain the natural shake in my voice. The whole business hurt my ears. The walls and moat tended to echo and amplify the crashes, and there was that acrid, intoxicating stench of burnt powder.

"Get Djezzar. He's the only man his men are more frightened of than Napoleon."

I was grateful for an excuse to run back to the palace, and almost collided with Haim Farhi in the pasha's chambers.

"We need your master to help stiffen his soldiers!"

"He can't be disturbed. He's in the harem."

By Casanova's trousers, the ruler could rut at a time like this? But then a door opened on a stairway leading upward and the Butcher appeared, shirtless, bearded, his eyes bright, a cross between a satyr and the prophet Elijah. Two pistols had been stuffed into his sash and he held an old Prussian saber. A slave brought a rusty coat of medieval mail and a felt undershirt. Before he closed the door behind, I could hear the excited chattering and weeping of the women.

"Phelipeaux needs you," I said unnecessarily.

"Now the Franks will come close enough that I can kill them," he promised.

The first pale light was silhouetting Napoleon's observatory hill when we returned to the tower. British ships had moved close inshore in Acre Bay, I saw, but their fire couldn't reach the assault column. Now I could make out a mass of men in shallow trenches below, like a great dark centipede. Many were carrying ladders.

"They've made a breach in the tower just above the

moat," Phelipeaux reported. "It's not big, but if they get inside the Turks will bolt. There've been too many rumors about what happened at Jaffa. Our Ottomans are too nervous to fight and too frightened to surrender."

I leaned over the edge to look at the black pit of the dry moat far below. The French could get into it easily enough, but could they get out? "Use a barrel of gunpowder," I suggested. "Or half a barrel, and the rest nails and ball. Drop it on them when they try the breach."

The royalist colonel grinned. "Ah, my bloodthirsty *Américain*. You have a warrior's instincts! We will light the way for the Corsican!"

"Napoleon!" Djezzar roared, climbing to stand on his observatory chair so that he was visible as a flag. "Try this Mameluke now! I will fuck you like I just fucked my wives!" Bullets whizzed by, miraculously not hitting him. "Yes, fan me like my women!"

We dragged him down. "If you're killed, all is lost," Phelipeaux lectured.

The Butcher spat. "That is what I think of their marksmanship." His mail shirt swung at the hem as he strutted from side to side of the tower, making sure his soldiers stood fast. "Don't think my eye isn't upon you!"

As the landscape turned pale gray with the coming sun, I saw how hasty Bonaparte had been. His trenches were still too shallow and a score of his men had already been hit. Several French guns had been disabled in his reservoir battery because their earthworks were inadequate, and the old aqueduct was chewed by our fire, spraying his huddled troops with masonry. Their ladders looked absurdly short.

Nonetheless, there was a great shout, a waving of the tricolor, and the French charged. Always, they had élan.

This was the first time I'd seen their reckless courage from the other side, and it was a frightening sight. The centipede charged and swallowed the ground between trenches and moat with alarming swiftness. The Turks and British marines tried to slow them with gunfire, but the expert French covering fire forced our heads down. We picked off only a few. They spilled down the lip of the moat to its bottom.

Their ladders were too short to reach—their scouting had been hasty—but the bravest jumped down, braced the stunted ladders, and allowed comrades to follow. Others fired across the moat into the breach they'd made, killing some of our defenders. The Ottoman troops began to moan.

"Silence! You sound like my women!" Djezzar roared. "Do you want to learn what I will do to you if you run?"

Now the French infantry propped their scaling ladders on the other side of the moat. The tops were several feet short of the breach, an inexcusable miscalculation. This was the moment, when pulling themselves up, that they might grasp a suspended chain. Left uncharged, it would allow them to flood inside the city and Acre would suffer the fate of Jaffa. But if electrified . . .

The bravest Turks leaned over to fire or hurl down stones, but as soon as they did they were hit by Frenchmen aiming across the moat. One man gave a great cry and fell all the way to the bottom. I fired a musket myself, cursing its inaccuracy.

A few Ottomans began to desert their guns. The British sailors tried to stop them, but they were panicked. Then Djezzar descended from the top of the tower to block their exit, waving his Prussian saber and roaring. "What are you afraid of?" he shouted. "Look at them! Their ladders are too short! They can't get in!" He leaned out, discharged both pistols, and handed them to a Turk. "Do something, old woman! Reload these!"

His men, chastened, started firing again. As frightened as they were of the formidable French, they were terrified of Djezzar.

Then a flaming meteor fell from the tower.

It was the keg of gunpowder I'd suggested. It hit, bounced, and exploded.

There was a thunderous roar and a radiating cloud of wood splinters and metal bits. The clustered grenadiers reeled, the closest blown to bits, others severely wounded, and still more stunned by the blast. Djezzar's men whooped and began firing into the milling French in earnest, adding to the havoc below.

The assault thus ended before it could properly begin. With their own cannon unable to fire too close to their charge, their ladders too short, the breach too small, and the resistance newly stiffened, the French had lost momentum. Napoleon had gambled on speed over tedious siege preparation, and lost. The attackers turned and began scrambling back the way they'd come.

"See how they run?" Djezzar shouted to his men.

And indeed, the Turkish troops began to shout in amazement and new confidence. The ruthless Franks were retreating! They were not invincible after all! And from that moment a new confidence seized the garrison, a confidence that would sustain them in the long dark weeks to come. The tower would become the rallying point not just for Acre but for the entire Ottoman Empire.

When the sun finally crested the eastern hills and fully lit the scene, the havoc was apparent. Nearly two hundred of Napoleon's troops lay dead or wounded, and Djezzar refused to slacken fire to let the French recover their injured. Many died, screaming, before the survivors could finally be carried to safety the next night.

"We have taught the Franks Acre's hospitality!" the Butcher crowed.

Phelipeaux was less satisfied. "I know the Corsican. That was just a probe. Next time he will come stronger." He turned to me. "Your little experiment had better work."

¤   ¤   ¤

The failure of Napoleon's first assault had a curious effect on the garrison. The Ottoman soldiers were heartened by their successful repulse, and for the first time attended to their duties with proud determination instead of fatalistic resignation. The Franks could be beaten! Djezzar was invincible! Allah had answered their prayers!

The British sailors, in contrast, sobered. A long succession of naval victories had made them cocky about "facing the frogs." The courage of the French soldiers, however, was noted. Bonaparte had not retreated. Instead his trenches were being dug forward more vigorously than ever. The seamen felt trapped on land. The French used scarecrows to draw our fire and dug out our cannonballs to fire back at us.

It didn't help that Djezzar was convinced the Christians in Acre must be plotting against him, even though the attacking French were from a revolution that had abandoned Christianity. He had several dozen, plus two French prisoners, sewn into sacks and cast into the sea. Smith and Phelipeaux could no more stop the pasha than Napoleon could have stopped his troops at the sack of Jaffa, but many English concluded their ally was a madman who could not be controlled.

Djezzar's restless enmity was not limited to followers of the cross. Salih Bey, a Cairo Mameluke and old archenemy, had fled Egypt after Napoleon's victory there and came to make common cause with Djezzar against the French. The pasha greeted him warmly, gave him a cup of poisoned coffee, and threw his corpse into the sea within half an hour of his arrival.

Big Ned told his fellows to put their trust in "the magician"—me. The same trickery that had allowed me to defeat him, a man twice my size, would help us prevail against Napoleon, he promised. So at our direction, the sailors built two crude wooden capstans on either side of the tower. The chain would be hung like a garland across its face, the elevation controlled by these hoists. Next I moved my Leyden jars and cranking apparatus to a floor halfway up the tower, which contained the sally door from which I'd challenged Big Ned. A smaller chain with a hook would link with the larger one, and that chain in turn would be touched by a copper rod connected to my jars.

"When they come, Ned, you must crank like the very devil."

"I'll light the frogs up like a fire at All Hallows, guv'nor."

Miriam helped set the apparatus up, her quick fingers ideal for linking the jars. Had the ancient Egyptians known such sorcery, too?

"I wish old Ben was here to see me," I remarked when we rested in the tower one evening, our metal sorcery gleaming in the dim light from the tower's arrow slits.

"Who's old Ben?" she murmured, leaning against my shoulder as we sat on the floor. Such physical closeness no longer seemed remarkable, though I dreamt of more.

"An American wiseman who helped start our country. He was a Freemason who knew about the Templars, and some think he had their ideas in mind when he made the United States."

"What ideas?"

"Well, I don't know, exactly. That a country is supposed to stand for something, I guess. Believe in something."

"And what do you believe, Ethan Gage?"

"That's what Astiza used to ask me! Do all women ask that? I ended up believing in her, and as soon as I did, I lost her."

She looked at me sadly. "You miss her, don't you?"

"As you must miss your betrothed who died in the war. As Jericho misses his wife, Big Ned his Little Tom, and Phelipeaux the monarchy."

"So here we are, our circle of mourning." She was quiet a moment. Then, "Do you know what I believe in, Ethan?"

"The church?"

"I believe in the Otherness the church stands for."

"You mean God?"

"I mean there's more to life's madness than just madness. I believe that in every life there are rare moments when we sense that Otherness that is all around us. Most of the time we are sealed up, lonely and blind, like a chick in its egg, but occasionally we get to crack the shell for a peek. The blessed have many such moments, and the wicked not one. But when you do—when you've sensed what is truly real, far realer than the nightmare we live in—everything is bearable. And I believe that if you can ever find someone who believes like you do, who strains against the egg that constrains us—well, then the two of you together can smash the shell entirely. And that's the most we can hope for in this world."

I shivered inwardly. Was the monstrous war I'd been trapped in the past year some false dream, some enclosing shell? Did the ancients know how to crack open the egg? "I don't know if I've ever had even a single moment. Does that make me wicked?"

"The wicked would never admit it, not even to themselves." Her hand felt my stubbled jaw, her blue eyes like the abyss off the reef at Jaffa. "But when the moment comes you must seize it, to let in the light."

And so she kissed me, fully this time, her breath hot, her body straining against mine, her breasts flattened against me, and her torso trembling.

I fell in love then, not just with Miriam, but with everyone. Does that sound insane? For the briefest of breaths I felt linked to all the other troubled souls of our mad world, a weird sense of community that filled me with heartbreak and love. So I kissed her back, clinging. Finally, I was forgetting the pain of long-lost Astiza.

"I kept your golden angels, Ethan," she murmured, pulling a velvet pouch that she had hung between her breasts. "You can have them back now."

"Keep them, as a present." What use did I have for them?

And then there was a roar, a spit of mortar, and our entire tower quaked as if a giant hand was shaking it to spill us out. For a moment I feared it would go over, but it slowly stopped swaying and just settled slightly, its floor at a slight tilt. Bugles sounded.

"They set off a mine! They're coming!"

It was time to try the chain.

CHAPTER **14**

I peered out the sally port into a fog of smoke and dust. "Stay here," I told Miriam. "I'm going to try to see what's happening." Then I galloped for the top of the tower. Phelipeaux was already there, hatless, leaning over the edge of the parapet and heedless of French bullets pattering about.

"The sappers dug a tunnel under the tower and packed it with gunpowder," he told me. "They misjudged, I think. The moat is rubble, but we only breached. I don't see cracks all the way up." He pulled himself back and grasped my arm. "Is your devilry ready?" He pointed. "Bonaparte is determined."

As before a column of troops trotted beside the ancient aqueduct, but this time it looked like a full brigade. Their ladders were longer than last time, bobbing as they jogged. I leaned out myself. There was a large gap at the base of the tower and a new causeway of rubble in the moat.

"Rally your best men at the breach," I told Phelipeaux. "I'll hold them with my chain. When they bunch, hit them with everything we have from down there and up here." I turned to Smith, who'd come up breathless. "Sir Sidney, ready your bombs!"

He gulped air. "I'll drop the fire of Zeus on them."

"Don't hesitate. At some point, I'll lose power and they'll break my contraption."

"We'll finish them by then."

Down Phelipeaux and I dashed, he to the breach and I to my new companion. "Now, Ned, now! Come to our room and crank for all you're worth! They're coming, and our battery of jars must be fully charged!"

"You lower the chain, guv'nor, and I'll give it a spark."

I put a few sailors at each of the capstans, telling them to crouch until it was time to lower. A full-scale artillery duel had broken out since the mine explosion, and the scale and fury of the battle was breathtaking. Cannon were firing everywhere, making us shout against their thunder. As balls smashed into the city, bits of debris would fly into the air. Sometimes the shadowy stream of the missiles could be spied sailing overhead, and when they struck there was a great crash and puff of dust. Our own balls were throwing up great gouts of sand where they fell amid the French positions, occasionally flipping or destroying a field piece or powder wagon. The leading French grenadiers were breaking into a run, ladders like lances, making for the moat.

"Now, now!" I shouted. "Lower the chain!" At both ends, my sailors began letting the capstan cables out. The suspended chain, like a holiday garland, began scraping and sliding down the side of the tower toward the breach at its base.

When it reached the gap I had them tie it off, the chain hanging across the hole in the tower like an improbable entry bar. The French must have thought we'd gone mad. Whole companies of them were firing volleys at our heads atop the wall, while we returned the compliment with grapeshot. Metal whined and buzzed. Men screamed or gasped in shock as they were hit, and the ramparts were becoming slick with blood.

Djezzar appeared, still in his old mail like a crazed

Saracen, striding up and down past the sprawled or crouched bodies of his soldiers, heedless of enemy fire. "Shoot, shoot! They'll break when they realize we won't run! Their mine didn't work! See, the tower still stands!"

I dashed down the tower stairs to the room where my companions were. Ned was cranking furiously, his shirt off, his great torso gleaming with sweat. The glass disk spun like a galloping wheel, the frictional pads buzzing like a hive. "Ready, guv'nor!"

"We'll wait for them to get to the chain."

"They're coming," Miriam said, peering out an arrow slit.

Running madly despite the withering fire decimating their ranks, the lead grenadiers charged across the causeway of rubble that half filled the moat and began clambering toward the hole their mine had made, one of them holding a tricolor banner. I heard Phelipeaux shout a command and there was a rippling bang as a volley from our men inside the base of the tower went off. The lead attackers pitched backward and the standard fell. New attackers scrambled over their bodies, shooting back into the breach, and the flag was raised again. There was that familiar thud of lead hitting flesh, and the grunts and shouts of wounded men.

"Almost there, Ned."

"All my muscle is in those jars," he panted.

The leading attackers reached my iron garland and clung. Far from a barrier, it was more like a climbing aid as they reached back to hoist up comrades behind them. In no time the chain was thick with soldiers, like wasps on a line of treacle.

"Do it!" Miriam cried.

"Give a prayer to Franklin," I muttered. I pushed a wooden lever that rammed a copper rod from the batteries against the small chain connected to the big one. There was a flash and crackle.

The effect was instantaneous. There was a shout, sparks, and the grenadiers flew off the chain as if kicked. A few could not detach themselves, screaming as they burned, and then hanging on the chain shuddering, their muscles putty. It was ghastly. I could smell their meat. Instantly, confusion reigned.

"Fire!" Phelipeaux shouted from below. More shots from our tower, and more attackers fell.

"There is strange heat in that chain!" the grenadiers were shouting. Men touched it with their bayonets and recoiled. Soldiers tried to lift or tug it and dropped like stunned oxen.

The contraption was working, but how long would the charge hold? Ned was wheezing. At some point the attackers would notice how the chain was suspended and break it down, but now they were milling uncertainly, even as more troops poured into the moat behind them. As they bunched, more of them were shot down.

Suddenly I realized an absence and looked wildly about. "Where's Miriam?"

"She went to carry powder to Phelipeaux below," Ned grunted.

"No! I need her here!" The breach would be a butcher's shop. I ran for the door. "Keep cranking!"

He winced. "Aye."

Two floors below, I stepped into the full fury of battle. Phelipeaux and his band of Turks and English marines, with fixed bayonets, were jammed in the tower's base, firing and fencing through the ragged breach with French grenadiers trying to get under or over the chain. Both sides had hurled grenades, and at least half our number were down. On the French side, the dead lay like shingles. From here the breach looked like a yawning cave open to the entire French army, a hideous hole of light and smoke. I spied Miriam at the very front, trying to drag one of the wounded back from French bayonets. "Miriam, I need you above!"

She nodded, her dress torn and bloody, her hair a wild tangle, her hands red with gore. Fresh troops rushed, touched the chain and screamed, and hurled backward. *Crank, Ned, crank,* I prayed under my breath. I knew the charge would become exhausted.

Phelipeaux was slashing with his sword. He took a

lieutenant through the chest, then slashed at another's head. "Damned republicans!"

A pistol went off, narrowly missing his face.

Then there was a female scream and Miriam was being dragged from us. A soldier had crawled under and caught her legs. He began hauling her back with him as if to throw her on my device. She'd be cooked!

"Ned, stop cranking! Pull back the copper rod!" I shouted. But there was no chance he could hear me. I plunged after her.

It was a charge into a wedge of Frenchmen who had crawled under. I grabbed a dropped musket and swung wildly, knocking men aside like tenpins, until it broke at the stock's wrist. Finally I grabbed Miriam's kidnapper and the three of us began to writhe, she clawing at his eyes.

We stumbled in the debris, hands clutching at us from both sides, and then I received a blow and she was pulled from me and hurled against the chain.

I braced, waiting for my witchcraft to kill what I now loved.

Nothing happened.

The metal had gone dead.

There was a great cheer, and the French surged forward. They hacked at the chain ends and it fell. A dozen men dragged it away, inspecting it for the source of its mysterious powers.

Miriam had fallen with the chain. I tried to crawl under the surging grenadiers to reach her, but was simply trampled. I grasped the hem of her dress, even as booted soldiers charged and stumbled over the top of us. I could hear shots and cries in at least three languages, men snorting and going down.

And then there was another roar, this one even louder than the mine because it was not confined underground. A massive bomb made from gunpowder kegs had finally been hurled from the tower top by Sidney Smith. It fell into the mass of Frenchmen who had bunched before the chain and now it exploded, its force redoubled by the moat and tower that bounded it. I hugged the rubble as the world dissolved into fire and smoke. Limbs and heads flew like chaff. The men who had been trampling us turned into a bloody shield, their bodies falling on us like beams. I went briefly deaf.

And then hands were digging at us to drag us backward. Phelipeaux was mouthing something I couldn't hear, and pointing.

Once more, the French were retreating, their casualties far heavier than before.

I turned back, shouting a shout I couldn't hear myself. "Miriam! Are you alive?"

She was limp and silent.

¤   ¤   ¤

I carried her from the wreckage and out of the tower to the pasha's gardens, my ears ringing but beginning to clear. Behind, Phelipeaux was shouting orders for engineers and laborers to begin repairing the breach. The garden air was smoky. Ash sifted down.

I lay my helpmate on a bench beside a fountain and put my ear to her lips. Yes! A whisper of tremulous breath. She was unconscious, not dead. I dipped a handkerchief in the water, pink from blood, and wiped her face. So soft, so smooth, under the grime! Finally the coolness brought her back. She blinked, shivering a little, and then abruptly jerked up. "What happened?" She was shaking.

"It worked. They retreated."

She put her arms around my neck and clung. "Ethan, it's so horrible."

"Maybe they won't come back."

She shook her head. "You told me Bonaparte is implacable."

I knew it would take more than an electric chain to defeat Napoleon.

Miriam looked down at herself. "I look like a butcher."

"You look beautiful. Beautiful and bloody." It was true. "Let's get you inside." I boosted her up and she leaned against me, one arm around my shoulders for support. I wasn't quite sure where to take her, but I wanted to get away from Jericho's foundry and the combat wall. I began to walk us toward the mosque.

Then Jericho appeared, led by an anxious Ned.

"My God, what happened?" the ironmonger asked.

"She got caught up in the fighting in the breach. She performed like an Amazon."

"I'm all right, brother."

His voice was accusatory. "You said she'd simply help with your sorcery."

She interceded. "The men needed ammunition, Jericho."

"I could have lost you."

Then there was silence, and the strain of two men wanting a woman for different reasons. Ned stood mutely to one side, looking guilty as if it was his fault.

"Well, come back down to the foundry, then," Jericho said tightly. "No cannonballs will reach us there."

"I'm going with Ethan."

"Going? Where?"

They both looked at me, as if I knew. "Going," I said, "where she can get some rest. It's noisy as a factory at your forge, Jericho. Hot and dirty."

"I don't want you with her." His voice was flat.

"I'm with Ethan, brother." Her voice was soft but insistent.

And so we went, she leaning on me, the metallurgist left standing in the garden in frustration, his hands closing on nothing. Behind us, artillery rumbled like distant drums.

My friend Mohammad had taken quarters at Khan el-Omdan, the Pillars Inn, rather than sail away and leave us to Napoleon. In the excitement of working on the chain I'd forgotten about him, but I sought him out now. I'd wrapped a cloak around Miriam, but when we appeared at his apartment we both looked like refugees: smoke-stained, filthy, and torn.

"Mohammad, we need to find a place to rest."

"Effendi, all the rooms are taken!"

"Surely . . ."

"Yet something can always be found for a price."

I smiled wryly. "Could we share your room?"

He shook his head. "The walls are thin and water scarce. It's no place for a lady. You don't deserve better, but she does. Give me the rest of the money Sir Sidney gave you for your medal and your winnings at the duel." He held out his hand.

I hesitated.

"Come, you know I won't cheat you. What good is money, unless you use it?"

So I handed it over and he disappeared. In half an hour he was back, my purse empty. "Come. A merchant has fled the city and a young physician has been using his home to sleep, but rarely gets to. He rented me the keys."

The house was dark, its shutters drawn, its furnishing draped and pushed against the wall. Its desertion by its owner had left a desolate air, and the doctor who had taken his place was only camped there. He was a Christian Levantine from Tyre named Zawani. He shook my hand and looked curiously at Miriam. "I'll use the money for herbs and bandages." We were far enough from the walls that the guns were muted. "There's a bath above. Rest. I won't be back until tomorrow." He was handsome, his eyes kind, but already hollowed from exhaustion.

"The lady needs to recover . . ."

"There's no need to explain. I'm a doctor."

We were left alone. The top floor had a bathing alcove with a white masonry dome above its pool that was pierced by thick panes of colored glass. Light came through in shafts of multiple colors like a dismantled rainbow. There was wood to heat the water, so I set to work while Miriam dozed. The room was full of steam when I woke her. "I've prepared a bath." I made to leave but she stopped me, and undressed us both. Her breasts were small but perfect, firm, her nipples pink, her belly descending to a thatch of pale hair. She was a virginal Madonna, scrubbing both of us of the dirt of battle until she was once more alabaster.

The merchant's mattress was elevated as high as my waist on an ornately carved bed, with drawers underneath and a canopy overhead. She crawled up first and lay back, so I could see her in the pale light. There's no sight lovelier than a welcoming woman. The sweetness of her swallows you, like the embrace of a warm sea. The topography of her body was a snowy mountain range, mysterious and unexplored. Did I even remember what to do? It felt like a thousand years. An odd, sudden memory of Astiza intruded—a knife to the heart—but then Miriam spoke.

"This is one of those moments I told you about, Ethan."

So I took her, slowly and gently. She wept the first time, and then clung fiercely, crying out, the second. I clung too, shaking and gasping at the end, my eyes wetting when I thought first of Astiza, then of Napoleon, then of Miriam, and how long it would be before the French came again, as furious now as they'd been at Jaffa. If they got inside, they'd kill us all.

I turned my head so she couldn't see any tear or worry, and we slept.

Near midnight, I was jostled awake. I clutched a pistol, but then saw it was Mohammad.

"What the devil?" I hissed. "Can't we have some privacy?"

He put his finger to his lips and beckoned with his head. Come.

"Now?"

He nodded emphatically. Sighing, I climbed out, the floor cold, and followed him out to the main room.

"What are you doing here?" I grumbled, holding a blanket around myself like a toga. The city seemed quiet, the guns taking a rest.

"I'm sorry, effendi, but Sir Sidney and Phelipeaux said this shouldn't wait. The French used an arrow to fire this over the wall. It has your name on it."

"An arrow? By Isaac Newton, what century are we in?"

A small piece of burlap was tied to the arrow. Sure enough, a tag, with fine pen, read, "Ethan Gage." Franklin would have admired the postal efficiency.

"How do they know I'm here?"

"Your electric chain is like a banner announcing your

presence. The whole province is talking about it, I would guess."

True enough. So what could our enemies be sending me that was so small?

I unwrapped the burlap and rolled its content onto the palm of my hand.

It was a ruby ring, its jewel the size of a cherry, with a tag attached that read, simply, "She needs the angels. Monge." My world reeled.

The last time I'd seen the jewel, it had been on Astiza's finger.

CHAPTER 15

Mohammad was watching me closely. "This ring means something to you, my friend?"

"This is it? No other message?" Monge undoubtedly was Gaspard Monge, the French mathematician I'd seen at Jaffa.

"And it is not just the size of the jewel, is it?" Mohammad pressed.

I sat down heavily. "I knew the woman who wore it." Astiza was alive!

"And the French army would catapult her ring for what reason, exactly?"

What reason indeed? I turned the ring over, remembering its origin. I'd insisted Astiza take it from the subterranean treasure trove we'd found under the Great Pyramid, despite her protestations that such loot was cursed. Then we'd briefly forgotten it until she was trying to climb the tether of Conte's runaway balloon into my wicker basket, a desperate Count Silano clinging to her ankles. She remembered the curse and pleaded with me to get the ring off, but I couldn't. So, rather than drag me down within range of

French soldiers, she cut the tether and fell with Silano, screaming, into the Nile. The balloon shot up so tumultuously that I didn't see their landing, there was a volley from the French troops, and by the time I peered into the sun-dazzled waters . . . nothing. It was as if she'd vanished from the earth. Until now.

And the angels? The seraphim we'd found. I'd have to take them back from Miriam. "They want me to come looking."

"So it is a trap!" my companion said. "They fear you and your electrical magic."

"No, not a trap, I think." I didn't flatter myself that they considered me such a formidable enemy that they had to lure me outside the walls simply to shoot me. What I did suspect is that they hadn't given up our mutual quest for the Book of Thoth. If there was one way to enlist me again, it was the promise of Astiza. "They simply know I'm alive, because of the electricity, and they've learned something I can add to. It's about what I was searching for in Jerusalem, I'm guessing. And they know that the one thing that would make me come back to them is news of this woman."

"Effendi, you cannot mean to leave these walls!"

I glanced back to where Miriam was sleeping. "I have to."

He was baffled. "Because of a woman? You have one, right here."

"Because there's something out there waiting for rediscovery, and its use or misuse will affect the fate of the world." I thought. "I want to help the French find it, but then steal it from them. For that I need help, Mohammad. I'll have to escape through Palestine once I have Astiza and the prize. Someone with local knowledge."

He blanched. "I barely escaped Jaffa, effendi! To go amid the Frankish devils . . ."

"Might give you a share of the greatest treasure on earth," I said blandly.

"Greatest treasure?"

"Not guaranteed, of course."

He considered the matter. "What share?"

"Well, five percent seems reasonable, don't you think?"

"For getting you through the Palestinian wilderness? A fifth, at least!"

"I intend to ask other help. Seven percent is the absolute maximum I can afford."

He bowed. "A tenth, then, is utterly reasonable. Plus a small token if we get the help of my cousins and brothers and uncles. And expenses for horses and camels. Guns, food. Hardly a pittance, if it's really from the greatest treasure."

I sighed. "Let's just see if we can get to Monge without being shot, all right?"

There was, of course, a nagging matter as we began our brisk planning. I'd just slept with the sweetest woman I'd ever met, Miriam, and was planning to take back my seraphim and sneak off to learn the truth about Astiza without leaving the poor woman so much as a word. I felt like a cad, and hadn't the faintest idea how to explain myself without sounding caddish. It wasn't that I was disloyal to Miriam, I was simply also loyal to the memory of the first woman, and loved them both in different ways. Astiza had become to me the essence of Egypt, of ancient mystery, a beauty whose quest for ancient knowledge had become my own. We'd met when she helped try to assassinate me, Napoleon himself leading the little charge that captured her. Then she'd saved my life, more than once, and filled my empty character with purpose. We'd not just been lovers, we'd become partners in a quest, and nearly died in the Great Pyramid. It was perfectly reasonable to go looking for Astiza—the ring had ignited memories like a match to a trail of gunpowder—but a trifle awkward to explain to Miriam. Women can be grumpy about this kind of thing. So I'd go find the meaning of Astiza's ring, rescue her, put the two of them together, and then . . .

What? Well, as Sidney Smith had promised, it's splendid how these things work out. "So convenient it is to be a reasonable creature," Ben Franklin had said, "since it enables one to do everything one has a mind to do anyway." Old Ben had entertained the ladies himself, while his wife stewed back in Philadelphia.

"Should we wake your woman?" Mohammad asked.
"Oh no."

¤   ¤   ¤

When I asked Big Ned to come along, he was as hard to convince as a dog called for a walk by its master. He was one of those men who do nothing by halves; he was either my most implacable enemy or my most faithful servant. He'd become convinced I was a sorcerer of rare power, and was merely biding my time before distributing the wealth of Solomon.

Jericho, in contrast, had long since given up all talk of treasure. He was intrigued when I woke him to explain that the ruby ring had belonged to Astiza, but only because the distraction might keep me away from his sister.

"So you must take care of Miriam while I'm gone," I told him, trying to salve my conscience by leaving him in charge. He looked so pleased that for a moment I considered whether he'd somehow sent me the ring himself.

But then he blinked and shook his head. "I can't let you go alone."

"I won't be alone. I have Mohammad and Ned."

"A heathen and a lunkhead? It will be a contest to see which of the three leads you into disaster first. No, you need someone with a level head."

"Who is Astiza, if she's alive. Smith and Phelipeaux and the rest of the garrison need you more than I do, Jericho. Defend the city and Miriam. I'll still cut you in when we've found the treasure." You can't dangle wealth in a man's mind and not have him think nostalgically about the prospect, however slim.

He looked at me with new respect. "It's risky, crossing French lines. Maybe there's something to you after all, Ethan Gage."

"Your sister thinks so too." And before we could quarrel about *that* issue, I set off with Mohammad and Ned. We'd be caught in cross fire if we simply strolled outside the walls, so we took the boat Mohammad had fled Jaffa in. The city was a dark silhouette against the stars, to give the French as few aiming points as possible, while the glow of enemy camp-fires produced an aurora behind the trenches. Phosphorescence was silver in our wake. We landed on the sandy beach behind the semicircle of French lines and crept to their camp the back way, crossing the ruts and trampled crops of war.

It's easier than you might guess to walk into an army from its rear, which is the province of the wagon masters, sutlers, camp followers, and malingerers who aren't used to reaching for a gun. I told my compatriots to wait in a thicket by a tepid stream and marched in with that superior air of a savant, a man who has an opinion on everything and accomplishment in none. "I have a message for Gaspard Monge from his academic colleagues in Cairo," I told a sentry.

"He's helping at the hospital." He pointed. "Visit at your own peril."

Had we already wounded that many? The eastern sky was beginning to lighten when I found the hospital tents, stitched together like a vast circus canvas. Monge was sleeping on a cot and looked sick himself, a middle-aged scientist-adventurer whom the expedition was turning old. He was pale, despite the sun, and thinner, hollowed out by sickness. I hesitated to wake him.

I glanced about. Soldiers, quietly moaning, lay in parallel rows that receded into the gloom. It seemed too many for the casualties we'd inflicted. I bent to inspect one, who was twitching fitfully, and recoiled at what I saw. There were pustules on his face and, when I lifted the sheet, an ominous swelling at his groin.

Plague.

I stepped back hastily, sweating. There had been rumors it was getting worse, but confirmation brought back historic dread. Disease was the shadow of armies, plague the hand-maiden of sieges, and only rarely confined to one side. What if it crossed the walls?

On the other hand, the disease gave Napoleon a tight deadline. He had to win before plague decimated his army. No wonder he had attacked impetuously.

"Ethan, is that you?"

I turned. Monge was sitting up, tousled and weary, blinking awake. Again, his face reminded me of a wise old dog. "Once more I've come for your counsel, Gaspard."

He smiled. "First we thought you dead, then we guessed you were the mad electrician somehow inside the walls of Acre, and now you materialize at my summons. You may indeed be a wizard. Or the most baffled man in either army, never knowing to which side you belong."

"I was perfectly happy on the other side, Gaspard."

"Bah. With a despotic pasha, a lunatic Englishman, and a jealous French royalist? I don't believe it. You're more rational than you pretend."

"Phelipeaux said it was Bonaparte who was the jealous one at school, not he."

"Phelipeaux is on the wrong side of history, as is every man behind those walls. The revolution is remaking man from centuries of superstition and tyranny. Rationalism will always triumph over superstition. Our army promises liberty."

"With the guillotine, massacre, and plague."

He frowned at me, disappointed at my intransigence, and then the corners of his mouth twitched. Finally he laughed. "What philosophers we are, at the end of the earth!"

"The center, the Jews would say."

"Yes. Every army eventually tramps through Palestine, the crossroads of three continents."

"Gaspard, where did you get this ring?" I held it out, the stone like a bubble of blood in the paleness. "Astiza was wearing it when I last saw her, falling into the Nile."

"Bonaparte ordered the arrow missive."

"But why?"

"Well, she's alive, for one thing."

My heart took off at full gallop. "And her condition?"

"I haven't seen her, but I've had word. She was in a coma, and under the care of Count Silano for a month. But I'm told she's recovered better than he has. He entered the water first, I suspect, she on top of him, so he broke the surface. His hip was shattered, and he'll limp for the rest of his life."

The beat of my pulse was like drums in my ears. To know, to know . . .

"Now she cares for him," Monge went on.

It was like a slap. "You must be joking."

"Takes care, I mean. She hasn't given up the peculiar quest you all seem to be on. They were furious to hear you'd been condemned at Jaffa—that was the work of that buffoon Najac; I don't know why Napoleon wouldn't listen to *me*—and horrified that you'd been executed. You know something they need. Then there were rumors you were alive, and she sent the ring. We saw your electrical trick. My instructions were to inquire about angels. Do you know what she means?"

Once more I could feel them pressing my skin. "Perhaps. I must see her."

"She's not here. She and Silano have gone to Mount Nebo."

"Mount what?"

"East of Jerusalem, across the Jordan River. There Moses finally spied the Promised Land, and died before he could enter it. Now why are they so interested in Moses, Ethan Gage?" He was watching me carefully.

So Monge, and probably Bonaparte, didn't know everything. What kind of game were Silano and Astiza playing? "I have no idea," I lied.

"And what do you know about these angels of yours that makes them as anxious to find you as you are to find them?"

"I have even less idea of that," I said truthfully.

"You've come alone?"

"I have some friends, waiting in a safe place."

"No place is safe in Palestine. This is a pestilential country. Our friend Conte has devised elaborate wagons to transport more siege artillery from Egypt, since the perfidious British captured our guns at sea, but it's been a running skirmish to get them here. These people don't know when they are beaten."

If Napoleon was expecting big guns, time was short. "What happens at Mount Nebo?"

Monge shrugged. "If you'd confide in your fellow savants, Gage, perhaps we could illuminate your future with more precision. As it is, you keep your own counsel, and end up in trouble. It's like your goose chase over the Pascal's triangle that was inscribed on your medallion—say, did you finally get rid of that old toy?"

"Oh yes." Monge had become convinced my medallion in Egypt had been a modern fraud. Astiza, out of his hearing, had called him a fool. He was not a fool, but burdened by the certainty that comes with too much education. The correlation between schooling and common sense is limited in the extreme. "There's nothing to confide. I was simply conducting electrical experiments when you sent this ring over our walls."

"Experiments that killed my men."

The voice made me jump. It was Bonaparte, moving out of the shadows! He seemed to be everywhere, always. Did he sleep? He looked sallow, restless, and his gray eyes cast their cold hold, as they did toward so many men—like a master to his steed. Again I marveled at his knack of seeming bigger than he is, and how he exuded a sense of seductive energy. "Monge is right, Gage, your proper place is on the side of science and reason—the revolution's side."

We were enemies, I had to remind myself. "So are you going to try to shoot me again?"

"That is what my army was trying to do yesterday, was it not?" he said mildly. "And you and your electrical sorcery helped best us."

"After you tried to shoot or drown me at Jaffa at the advice of that madman Najac. There I was, facing eternity, and when I look up you are reading cheap novels!"

"My novels are not cheap, and I have an interest in literature as I do in science. Did you know I wrote fiction as a youth? I had dreams of being published."

Despite myself, I was curious. "Love or war?"

"War, of course, and passion. One of my favorites was called *The Masked Prophet*. It was about a Muslim fanatic in the eighth century, fancying himself the Mahdi, who goes to war with the caliph. Prophetic in its setting, no?"

"What happens?

"The hero's dreams are doomed when he's blinded in battle, but to keep his affliction secret he covers his face with a mask of brilliant silver. He tells his men he had to cover his face so the Mahdi's radiance wouldn't blind those who look upon him. They believe him. But he cannot win, and pride will not allow surrender, so he orders his men to dig a gigantic trench to swallow the enemy charge. Then he invites his followers to a feast and poisons them all. He drags the bodies into the trench, sets fire to the corpses, and runs into the flames himself. Melodramatic, I admit. Adolescent morbidness."

This was the imagination at work in the Holy Land? "If you don't mind me asking, what was your point?"

" 'The extremes to which the mania for fame can push a man' was my closing line." He smiled.

"Prophetic as well."

"You think my story was autobiographical? I'm not blind, Ethan Gage. If anything, I'm cursed by seeing too well. And one thing I see is that now you *are* at your proper place, on the side of science you never should have left. You think yourself different than Count Silano, and yet you both want to know—in that way, you are exactly alike. So is the woman you're both drawn to, all of you curious as cats. I could order you shot, but it's more delicious to let the three of you solve your mystery, don't you think?"

I sighed. "At least you seem more genial than when we last met, General."

"I have a clearer sense of my own direction, which always settles one's mood. I haven't given up seducing you, American. I still hope we can remake the world for the better."

"Better like the slaughter at Jaffa?"

"Moments of ruthlessness can save millions, Gage. I made clear to the Ottomans the risk of resistance so this war can end quickly. If not for fanatics like Smith and Phelipeaux, traitor to his own nation, they would have surrendered and no blood would be shed. Don't let yourself be trapped in Acre by their folly. Go, learn what you can with Silano and Astiza, and then make a scholar's decision of what to do with it. I'm a member of the Institute myself, remember. I will abide with science. Won't I, Gaspard?"

The mathematician gave a thin smile. "No one has done more to marry science, politics, and military technology, General."

"And no one has worked harder for France that Doctor Monge here, who I have nursed myself as ailments assail him. He is steadfast! Learn from him, Gage! Now, given your strange history, you will understand that I must assign you an escort. You have an interest in keeping an eye out for each other, I believe?"

And out the shadows stepped Pierre Najac, looking as disheveled and murderous as when I'd left him.

"You must be joking."

"On the contrary, guarding you is his punishment for not dealing more intelligently with you before," Bonaparte said. "Isn't it, Pierre?"

"I will get him to Silano," the man growled.

I'd not forgotten the burns and beatings. "This torturer is nothing more than a thief. I don't need his escort."

"But I do," Napoleon said. "I'm tired of you wandering off in all directions. You'll go with Najac or not at all. He's your ticket to the woman, Gage."

Najac spat. "Don't worry. After we find whatever it is we're looking for, you'll have your chance to kill me. As I'll have a chance to kill *you*."

I looked at what he was carrying. "Not with my rifle, you won't."

Napoleon was puzzled. "Your rifle?"

"I helped make it in Jerusalem. Then this bandit stole it."

"I disarmed you. You were a captive!"

"And now an ally once again, whether I want to be or not. Give it back."

"I'll be damned if I will!"

"I won't help if you won't return it."

Bonaparte looked amused. "Yes, you will, Gage. You'll

do it for the woman, and you'll do it because you could no more give up this mystery than pass a promising game of cards. Najac captured you, and he's right. Your gun is a prize of war."

"It's not even that good," the scoundrel added. "It shoots like a blunderbuss."

"A weapon's accuracy depends on the man who wields it," I replied. I knew the piece shot like the very devil. "What do you think of its telescope?"

"A stupid experiment. I took it off."

"It was a gift. If we're searching for treasure, I need a spyglass."

"That's fair," Napoleon adjudicated. "Give that to him."

Grudgingly, Najac did so. "And my tomahawk." I knew he must have it.

"It's dangerous to let the American be armed," Najac warned.

"It isn't a weapon, it's a tool."

"Give it to him, Najac. If you can't control the American with a dozen men when all he has is a hatchet, perhaps I should send you back to the constabulary."

The man grimaced, but gave it up. "This is an instrument for savages, not savants. You look like a rustic, carrying it about."

I hefted its pleasing weight. "And you look like a thief, brandishing my rifle."

"Once we find your damned secret, Gage, you and I will settle once and for all."

"Indeed." My rifle was already nicked and marked—Najac was as much an oaf with firearms as he was unkempt in clothing—but it still looked as slim and smooth as a maiden's limb. I longed for it. "Do me a favor, Najac. Escort me from a distance where I won't have to smell you."

"But within rifle shot, I promise."

"Alliances are never easy," Bonaparte quipped. "But now, Najac has the rifle and Gage the glass. You can aim together!"

The annoying joke made me want to discomfit the general.

"And I suppose you want me to hurry?" I gestured at the sick.

"Hurry?"

"The plague. It must be panicking your troops."

But I could never get him off-balance. "It gives them urgency. So yes, make haste. But do not concern yourself too deeply with my campaign timing. Greater things than you know are afoot. Your quest is not just about Syria, but Europe. France herself waits for me."

CHAPTER 16

I'd assumed we'd travel directly to Mount Nebo with Najac's band of cut-throats, but he laughed when I suggested it. "We'd have to cut our way through half the Ottoman army!" Ever since Napoleon had invaded Palestine, the Sublime Porte of Constantinople had been gathering soldiers to stop the French. Galilee, Najac informed me, was swarming with Turkish and Mameluke cavalry. Gallic liberation was not being embraced in the Holy Land with any more enthusiasm than it had been in Egypt. Now General Jean-Baptiste Kléber, who had landed with Bonaparte on the beach in Alexandria nearly a year ago, would take his division to brush these Muslims away. My companions and I would accompany his troops eastward to the Jordan River, which flows southward from the Sea of Galilee to the Dead Sea. Then we'd strike south on our own, following the fabled Jordan until it passed by the foot of Mount Nebo.

Mohammad and Ned were not happy at having to march with the French. Kléber was a popular commander, but he could also be an impetuous hothead. Yet we had no choice. The Ottomans were directly in our path and in no mood to differentiate between one group of Europeans and another. We'd rely on Kléber to bludgeon a path through.

"Mount Nebo!" Mohammad exclaimed. "It's for ghosts and goats!"

"Treasure, I'd guess," Ned said shrewdly. "Why else would our magician here be signing on again with the frogs? The hoard of Moses, eh, guv'nor?"

For a lummox, he guessed entirely too much. "It's a meeting of antiquity scholars," I said. "A woman I knew in Egypt is alive and waiting. She'll help solve the mystery we tried to answer in the tunnels beneath Jerusalem."

"Aye, and I hear you already have a pretty bauble."

I shot a look at Mohammad, who shrugged. "The sailor wanted to know what prompted our expedition, effendi."

"Then know this is bad luck." I took the ring from my pocket. "It's from the grave of a dead Pharaoh, and such plunder is always cursed."

"Cursed? That's a life's wages right there," Ned said in wonder.

"But you don't notice me wearing it, do you?"

"Wouldn't match your color," Ned agreed. "Too gaudy, that is."

"So we march with the French until we can break free. There's likely to be a scrape or two. Are you willing?"

"A scrape without a scrap of steel between us, except that sausage chopper of yours," Ned said. "And you do have a poor choice of escorts, guv'nor. That Najac character looks like he'd boil his children, if he could get a shilling for the broth. Still, I likes being outside the walls. Felt boxed, I did."

"And now you will see the real Palestine," Mohammad promised. "The whole world wishes to possess her."

Which was exactly the problem, as near as I could tell.

Were we French allies—or prisoners? We were weapon-less except for my tomahawk, with no freedom of move-ment, guarded by both escorting chasseurs and Najac's gang. Yet Kléber sent a bottle of wine and his compliments, we were given good mounts and treated as guests of the march, riding ahead of the main column to escape the worst of the dust. We were prized dogs on a leash.

Ned and Najac took an immediate disliking to each other, the sailor remembering the fracas that had killed Tentwhistle and Najac jealous of the giant's strength. If the villain came near us he'd swing his coat wide to display the two pistols crammed in his sash, reminding us he was not to be trifled with. In turn, Ned announced loudly that he hadn't seen a frog so ugly since a mutant croaker in the privy pond behind Portsmouth's sleaziest brothel.

"If your brain was even half the size of your bicep I might be interested in what you have to say," Najac said.

"And if your pudding was even half the size of your flapping tongue, you wouldn't have to look so hard for it every time you drop your breeches," Ned replied.

Despite the quarreling, I relished our release from Acre. The Holy Land arouses uncommon passion, well watered in the north and bright spring green. Wheat and barley grew like wild grass, and broad paint strokes of color came from red poppies and yellow mustard. There was purple flax, golden chrysanthemum in natural bouquets of twisted stems, and tall Easter lilies. Was this God's garden? Away from the sea the sky was the blue of the Virgin's scarf, and light picked out the mica and quartz like tiny jewels.

"Look, a yellow bunting," Mohammad said. "The bird means summer is coming."

Our division was a blue snake slithering through Eden, the French tricolor heralding our improbable penetration of the Ottoman Empire. Drifts of sheep divided like the sea for our passage. Light field guns bounced in the sun, their bronze winking like a signal. White covered wagons swayed. Somewhere to the northeast was Damascus, and to the south, Jerusalem. The soldiers were in a good mood, happy to get away from tedious siege duty, and the division had money enough—captured at Jaffa—to eat well, instead of stealing. At the end of the second day we climbed a final ridge and I had a glimpse of the Sea of Galilee, blue soup in a vast green and brown bowl, far, far below. It is a huge lake sunken below sea level, hazy and holy. We didn't descend but instead followed ridges south to famous Nazareth.

The home of the Savior is a gritty, desultory place, its

main road a dirt cart track and its traffic mainly goats. A mosque and a Franciscan monastery stand brow to brow, as if keeping an eye on each other. We drew water from Mary's Well and visited the Church of the Annunciation, an Orthodox grotto with the kind of gewgaws that give Protestants indigestion. Then we marched down again to the rich, lazy vale of the Jezreel Valley, the breadbasket of ancient Israel and a thoroughfare for armies for three thousand years. Cattle grazed on grassy mounds that once were great fortresses. Carts clattered on roads that Roman legions had traversed. My companions were impatient at this military meandering, but I knew I was experiencing what few Americans can ever hope to see. The Holy Land! Here, by all accounts, men come closer to God. Some of the soldiers crossed themselves or muttered prayers at sacred places, despite the revolution's official atheism. But when evening fell they sharpened their bayonets, the rasping as familiar as crickets as we fell asleep.

As anxious as I was to see Astiza, I also felt uneasy. I had not, after all, managed to save her. She was once more somehow entangled with the occult investigator Silano. My political alliances were more confused than ever, and Miriam was waiting in Acre. I practiced first lines for all of them, but they seemed trite.

Mohammad meanwhile warned that our three thousand companions were not enough. "At every village there are rumors the Turks are massing against us," he warned. "More men than stars in the sky. There are troops from Damascus and Constantinople, Ibrahim Bey's surviving Mamelukes from Egypt, and hill fighters from Samaria. Shi'a and Sunni are joining together. Their mercenaries range from Morocco to Armenia. It's madness to stay with these French. They are doomed."

I gestured to Najac's scoundrels. "We have no choice."

General Kléber, of course, was trying to find this Turkish host instead of evade it, hoping to flank it by coming down from the Nazarene highlands. "Passion governs," old Ben liked to say, "and never governs wisely." And indeed Kléber, competent as generals go, had chafed as a subordinate to

Napoleon for a full year. He was older, taller, stronger, and more experienced, and yet the glory of the Egyptian campaign had been won by the Corsican. It was Bonaparte who was featured in the bulletins sent home on the Egyptian campaign, Bonaparte who was growing rich on spoils, Bonaparte who was making possible great new archeological discoveries, and Bonaparte who ruled the mood of the army. Even worse, at the Battle of El-Arish at the beginning of the Palestinian campaign, Kléber's division had performed indifferently, while his rival, Reynier, had won Napoleon's praise. It didn't matter that Kléber had the stature, bearing, and shaggy locks of the military hero that Bonaparte lacked, and that he was a better shot and a better rider. His colleagues deferred to the upstart. None would admit it, but for all his faults, Bonaparte was their intellectual superior, the sun around which they instinctively revolved. So this independent foray to destroy Ottoman reinforcements was Kléber's chance to shine. Just as Bonaparte had broken camp in the middle of the night to strike the Mameluke at the pyramids before they were fully ready, so Kléber decided to set out in the dark to surprise the Turkish camp.

"Madness!" said Mohammad. "We're too far away to surprise them. We'll find the Turks just as the sun is coming up in our eyes."

Indeed, the path around Mount Tabor was far longer than Kléber had anticipated. Instead of attacking at 2:00 a.m., as planned, the French encountered the first Turkish pickets at dawn. By the time we had drawn up ranks for an assault, our prey had time for breakfast. Soon there were swarms of Ottoman cavalry dashing hither and yon, and Kléber's ambition began to be tempered by common sense. The rising sun revealed that he had led three thousand troops to assault twenty-five thousand. I do have an instinct for the wrong side.

"So the ring *is* bad luck," Mohammad muttered. "Is it possible Bonaparte is still trying to execute you, effendi, but merely in a more complicated way?"

The three of us gaped at the huge herd of menacing cavalry, horses half swallowed by the tall spring wheat as their riders pointlessly fired guns in the air. The only thing that prevented us from being overrun immediately was the enemy's confusion; no one seemed to be in charge. Their army was stitched from too many corners of the empire. We could see the rainbow colors of the various Ottoman regiments, great trains of wagons behind them, and tents pitched bright as a carnival. If you want a pretty sight, go see war before the fighting starts.

"It's like the Battle of the Pyramids all over again," I tried to reassure. "Look at their disarray. They have so many soldiers they can't get organized."

"They don't need organization," Big Ned muttered. "All they need is stampede. By barnacle, I wish I were back on a frigate. It's cleaner, too."

If Kléber had proved rash in underestimating his opponents, he was a skilled tactician. He backed us up a hill called Djebel-el-Dahy, giving us the high ground. There was a ruined Crusader castle called Le-Faba near the top that overlooked the broad valley, and the French general put one hundred of his men on its ruined ramparts. The remainder formed two squares of infantry, one commanded by Kléber and the other by General Jean-Andoche Junot. These squares were like forts made of men, each man facing outward and the ranks pointing in all four directions so that it was impossible to turn their flank. The veterans and sergeants stood behind the newest troops to prevent them from backing and collapsing the formation. This tactic had baffled the Mamelukes in Egypt, and it was about to do the same to the Ottomans. No matter which way they charged, they would meet a firm hedge of musket barrels and bayonets. Our supply train and our trio, with Najac's men, were in the center.

The Turks foolishly gave Kléber time to dress his ranks and then made probing charges, galloping up near our men while whooping and swinging swords. The French were perfectly silent until the command rang out to "Fire!" and then there was a flash and rippling bang, a great gout of white smoke, and the closest enemy cavalry toppled from their horses. The others steered away.

"Blimey, they have more pluck than sense," Ned said, squinting.

The sun kept climbing. More and more enemy cavalry poured into the gentle vale below us, shaking lances and warbling cries. Periodically a few hundred would wheel and charge toward our squares. Another volley, and the results would be the same. Soon there was a semicircle of dead around us, their silks like cut flowers.

"What the devil are they doing?" Ned muttered. "Why don't they really charge?"

"Waiting for us to run out of water and ammunition, perhaps," Mohammad said.

"By swallowing all of our lead?"

I think they were waiting for us to break and run—their other enemies must be less resolute—but the French didn't waver. We bristled like a hedgehog, and they couldn't get their horses to close.

Kléber stayed mounted, ignoring the whining bullets, slowly riding up and down the ranks to encourage his men. "Hold firm," he coached. "Hold firm. Help will come."

Help? Bonaparte at Acre was far away. Was this some kind of Ottoman game, to let us sweat and worry until they finally made the penultimate charge?

Yet as I sighted through the scope that Sir Sidney had given me, I began to doubt such an attack would come. Many Turks were holding back, inviting others to break us first. Some were sprawled on the grass to eat, and others asleep. At the height of a battle!

As the day advanced, however, our endurance sapped and their confidence grew. Powder was growing short. We began to hold our volleys until the last second, to give precious bullets the surest target. They sensed our doubt. A great shout would go up, spurs would be applied to horses, and waves of cavalry would come at us like breakers on a beach. "Hold . . . hold . . . let them come . . . fire! Now, now, second rank, fire!" Horses screamed and tumbled. Brilliantly costumed janissaries tumbled amid clods of earth. The bravest would spur onward, weaving between their toppling fellows, but when they reached the hedge of bayonets their horses would rear. Pistols and muskets pocked our ranks, but the carnage was far worse on their side. So many horse carcasses littered the fields that it was becoming difficult for the Turks to hurtle past to get at us. Ned, Mohammad, and I helped drag French wounded into the center of the squares.

Now it was noon. The French injured were moaning for water and the rest of us longed for it. Our hill seemed dry as an Egyptian tomb. The sun had halted its arc across the sky, promising to beat down on us forever, and the Turks were taunting each other on. A hundred French had fallen, and Kléber gave orders for the two squares to join into one, thickening the ranks and giving the men badly needed reassurance. It looked like all the Muslims in the world were massed against us. The fields had been trampled into soil and dust rose in great pillars. The Turks tried sweeping over the crest of Djebel-el-Dahy and coming down on us from above, but chasseurs and carabiniers in the old Crusader castle forced them to diverge and they spilled uselessly down both sides of our formation, letting us thin them by firing into their flanks.

"Now!" A volley would roar out, smoke acrid and blinding, bits of wadding fluttering like snow. Horses, screaming and riderless, would go galloping away. Then teeth would tear at cartridges, pouring in precious powder. The ground was white with paper.

By midafternoon my mouth was cotton. Flies buzzed over the dead. Some soldiers fainted from standing in place too long. The Ottomans seemed impotent, and yet we could go nowhere. It would end, I supposed, when we all died of thirst.

"Mohammad, when they overrun us pretend you're dead until it's over. You can emerge as a Muslim. No need to share the fate of addled Europeans."

"Allah does not tell a man to desert his friends," he replied grimly.

Then a fresh cry rose up. Men claimed they'd spied the glimmer of bayonets in the valley to the west. "Here comes *le petit caporal*!"

Kléber was disbelieving. "How could Bonaparte get here so soon?" He gestured to me. "Come. Bring your naval spyglass." My English telescope had proven sharper than standard French army issue.

I followed him out of the comfort of the square and onto the exposed slope of our hill. We passed a ring of bodies of fallen Muslims, some groaning in the grass, their blood a scarlet smear on the green wheat.

The Crusader ruins gave a panoramic view. If anything, the Turks looked even more numerous now that I could see farther over their ranks. Thousands trotted this way and that, gesturing as they argued what to do. Hundreds of their comrades already carpeted the hill below us. In the distance their tents, supplies, and thousands of servants and camp followers were visible. We were like a blue rock in a sea of red, white, and green. One determined charge and surely they would crack our formation open! Then men would run, and it would be the end.

Except they hadn't yet. "There." Kléber pointed. "Do you see French bayonets?"

I peered until my eye ached. The high grass billowed in the west, but whether from the passage of infantry or wind I didn't know. The lush earth had swallowed the antlike maneuvering of armies. "It could be a French column, because the high grass is moving. But as you say, how could it come so quickly?"

"We'll die of thirst if we stay here," Kléber said. "Or men will desert and have their throats cut. I don't know if there are reinforcements that way or not, but we are going to find out." He trotted back down, with me following.

"Junot, start forming columns. We're going to meet our relievers!"

The men cheered, hoping against hope that they were not simply opening themselves to being overrun. As the square dissolved into two columns, the Turkish cavalry became more animated. Here was a chance to swoop down on our flanks and rear! We could hear them shouting, horns blaring.

"Forward!" We began marching downhill.

Turkish lances waved and danced.

Then there was a cannon shot in the distance. The businesslike crack was as French as a shouted order in a Parisian restaurant, so distinct are calibers of ordnance. We looked and saw a plume of smoke drift off. Men began crying with relief. Help was indeed coming! The French began to cheer, even sing.

The enemy cavalry hesitated, peering west.

The tricolors rippled as we tramped down Djebel-el-Dahy, as if on parade.

Then smoke began rising from the enemy camp. There were shots, faint screams, and the triumphant wail of French bugles. Napoleon's cavalry had broken into the Turkish rear and was sowing panic. Precious supplies began to go up in flames. With a roar, stored ammunition exploded.

"Steady!" Kléber reminded. "Keep ranks!"

"When they come at us, crouch and fire on command!" Junot added.

We saw a small lake by the village of Fula. Our excitement grew. There was an Ottoman regiment in front of it, looking irresolute. Now the officers galloped up and down the columns, giving orders to ready a charge.

"Strike!" With a cheer, the bloodied French swept the rest of the way down the hill and toward the Samaritan infantry that garrisoned the village. There were shots, a plunge of bayonets and clubbed muskets, and then the enemy was running. Meanwhile Turks were fleeing from whatever had appeared in the west as well. Miraculously, in minutes an army of twenty-five thousand was collapsing into panic, fleeing east before a few thousand Frenchmen. Bonaparte's cavalry galloped past us, giving chase toward the valley of the Jordan. Ottomans were hunted and slain all the way to the river.

We plunged into the Fula pond, slaking our thirst, and then stood wet and dripping like drunken men, our cartridge pouches empty. Napoleon galloped up, beaming like the savior he was, his breeches gray from dust.

"I suspected you'd get yourself into trouble, Kléber!" he shouted. "I set out yesterday after reading the reports!" He smiled. "They ran at the crack of a cannon!"

CHAPTER 17

With his instinct for the political, Bonaparte immediately named our near-disaster the Battle of Mount Tabor—a much more imposing and pronounceable peak than modestly sloping Djebel-el-Dahy, though several miles distant—and proclaimed it "one of the most lopsided victories in military history. I want the full details dispatched to Paris as soon as we can."

I was certain he hadn't been as prompt in relaying news of the massacre at Jaffa.

"A few more divisions and we could march to Damascus," Kléber said, intoxicated by his improbable victory. Instead of being jealous, he now seemed dazzled by his commander's timely rescue. Bonaparte could work miracles.

"A few more divisions, General, and we could march to Baghdad and Constantinople," Napoleon amended. "Damn Nelson! If he hadn't destroyed my fleet, I would be master of Asia!"

Kléber nodded. "And if Alexander hadn't died in Babylon, or Caesar been stabbed, or Roland been too far behind . . ."

"For want of a nail the battle was lost," I piped up.

"What?"

"Just something my mentor Ben Franklin used to say. It's the little things that trip us up. He believed in attention to detail."

"Franklin was a wise man," Napoleon said. "Scrupulous attention to detail is essential to a soldier. And your mentor was a true savant. He'd be anxious to solve ancient mysteries, not for his own sake but for science. Which is why you'll now go on to meet Silano, correct, Monsieur Gage?"

"You seem to have brushed the opposition out of the way, General," I said amiably. Bonaparte sundered armies the way Moses parted the sea. "Yet we're still at the lip of Asia, thousands of miles from India and your ally there, Tippoo Sahib. You've not even taken Acre. How, with so few men, can you emulate Alexander?"

Bonaparte frowned. He did not like doubt. "The Macedonians were not much more numerous. And Alexander had his own siege, at Tyre." He looked pensive. "But our world is bigger than theirs, and events progress in France. I have many calls on my attention, and your discoveries may be more important in Paris than here."

"France?" Kléber asked. "You think of home when we're still fighting in this dung hole?"

"I try to think of everything, always, which is why I thought to bring relief to your expedition before you needed it, Kléber," Bonaparte said crisply. He clapped the shoulder of the general that loomed over him, great hair like a lion's mane. "Just be assured there's a purpose to what we're doing. Stand your duty and we'll rise together!"

Kléber looked at him suspiciously. "Our duty is here, not France. Isn't it?"

"And this American's duty is to finish, finally, what we brought him here for—to solve the mystery of the pyramids and the ancients with Count Alessandro Silano! Ride hard, Gage, because time weighs on all of us."

"I'm more anxious to get home than anyone," I said.

"Then find your book." He turned and stalked off with his staff of officers, finger jabbing as he fired off orders. I, meanwhile, was chilled. It was the first I'd heard him mention any book. Clearly, the French knew more than I hoped.

And Astiza had told them more than I wished.

So we were in it now, tools of Silano and his discredited Egyptian Rite of Freemasons. The Templars had found something and been burned at the stake by tormentors hoping to get it. I hoped my own fate would be kinder. I hoped I wasn't leading my comrades to destruction.

We dined on captured Turkish meats and pastries, trying to ignore the stench already rising from the dark battlefield. "Well that's it, then," Big Ned remarked gloomily. "If a horde like that can't stand against a few frogs, what chance do me mates have in Acre? It will be another bloody massacre, like Jaffa."

"Except that Acre has the Butcher," I said. "He won't let anyone run or surrender."

"And cannon and Phelipeaux and Sidney Smith," said Mohammad. "Don't worry, sailor. The city will stand until we get back."

"Just in time for the final sacking." He looked at me slyly.

I knew what the sailor was thinking. Find the treasure and run. I can't say I entirely disagreed.

¤   ¤   ¤

French cavalry were still pursuing the remnants of the shattered Ottoman army when we followed their trampled trail and dropped into the valley of the Jordan River. We were past the fields now, in dry goat country except for the groves and meadows along the river. Any number of holy men had followed this stream, John the Baptist holding court somewhere along its fabled banks, but we rode like a company of outlaws. Najac's dozen French and Arabs bristled with rifles, muskets, pistols, and swords. There were real outlaws as well, and we saw two different bands slink off like disappointed wolves after spying our ordinance.

We also passed drowned and shot bodies of Ottoman soldiers, bloated like balloons of cloth. We gave them wide berth to avoid the stink and took care to draw water only from springs.

As we rode south, the valley became increasingly arid and the British ships Ned called home seemed ten thousand miles away. One night, he crawled over to whisper.

"Let's ditch these brigands and strike out on our own, guv'nor," he urged. "That Najac keeps eyeing you like a crow waiting for a corpse's eyeball. You could dress these rascals like choirboys and they'd still frighten Westminster."

"Aye, they have the morality of a legislature and the hygiene of galley slaves, but we need them to lead us to the woman who wore the ruby ring, remember?" He groaned, so I had to settle him. "Don't think I haven't retained my electrical powers. We'll get what we're coming for, and pay this lot back too."

"I longs for the day to mash them. I hate frogs. A-rabs too, Mohammad excepted."

"It's coming, Ned. It's coming."

We trotted past a track Najac said led to the village of Jericho. I saw nothing of it, and the country was so brown it was hard to believe a city with mighty walls had ever been built here. I thought of the ironmonger and again was guilty for my desertion of Miriam. She deserved better.

The Dead Sea was as its name implies: a salt-encrusted shore and brackish, bright blue water that extended to the horizon. No birds thronged its shallows and no fish broke its surface. The desert air was thick, hazy and muggy, as if we'd advanced in season by two months in two days. I shared Ned's disquiet. This was an odd, dreamlike land, spawning too many prophets and madmen.

"Jerusalem is that way," Mohammad said, pointing west. Then, swinging his arm in the opposite direction, he said, "Mount Nebo."

Mountains rose precipitously from the Dead Sea shore as if in a hurry to get away from the brine. The tallest was as much a ridge as a peak, speckled with scrub pine. In rocky ravines, which would run with water only in a rain, pink oleander bloomed.

Najac, who'd said little in our journey, took out a signal mirror and flashed it in the morning sun. We waited, but nothing happened.

"The damn thief has gotten us lost," Ned muttered.

"Be patient, thickhead," the Frenchman snapped back. He signaled again.

Then a column of signaling smoke rose from Nebo. "There!" our escort exclaimed. "The seat of Moses!"

We kicked our horses and began to climb.

It was a relief to get out of the Jordan Valley and into less cloying air. We cooled, and the slope began to smell of scrub pine. Bedouin tents were pitched on the mountain's benches, and I could spy black-robed Arab boys tending wandering herds of scrubby goats. We followed a caravan track upward, hooves plopping in the soft dirt, horses snorting when they passed camel dung.

It took four hours, but finally we breasted the top. We could indeed see the Promised Land back west across the Jordan, brown and hazy from here, looking nothing like milk and honey. The Dead Sea was a blue mirror. Ahead, I saw no cave promising to hold treasure. Instead there was a French tent in a hollow, green grass next to it indicating a spring. The low ruins of something, an old church maybe, were nearby. Several men waited for us by a wisp of campfire smoke, the remains of the signal fire. Was Silano among them? But before I could tell I spied a person sitting on a rocky outcrop below the ruined church, away from the men, and guided my horse out of our file and dismounted.

It was a woman, dressed in white, who'd been watching our approach.

¤   ¤   ¤

She stood as I approached on foot, her tresses long and black as I remembered, falling from a white scarf to keep off the sun. Fabric and hair blew slightly in the mountain breeze. Her beauty was more tangible than I was prepared for, vivid in the mountaintop light. I'd turned her into a ghost and yet here she was, made flesh. I'd braced for disappointment, having polished her in my memory, but no, what I'd imagined was still here, the poised litheness, the lips and cheekbones worthy of a Cleopatra, the lustrous dark eyes. Women are flowers, giving grace to the world, and Astiza was a lotus.

She'd aged, however. Not poorly—it's a mistake to think age an insult to women, because her beauty simply had more character—but her eyes had deepened, as if she'd seen or felt things she would prefer she hadn't. I wondered if I'd changed the same way: how long since I'd looked in a glass? I touched my hand to stubble and was conscious, suddenly, of my travel-stained clothes. Her own gown was dust-dyed, and divided for riding. She wore cavalry boots, small enough that perhaps they'd been borrowed from some drummer. She was slim, a dancer's body, but again, we'd all narrowed. Her waist was cinched by a silk rope, holding a small curved dagger and a leather pouch. A water skin was on the rock.

I hesitated, my rehearsals forgotten. It was as if she'd risen from the dead. Finally, "I sent men asking." It sounded like an apology, awkward and without eloquence—but I *was* embarrassed, having floated away in the balloon when she hadn't. "They told me you'd disappeared."

"Do you have my ring?"

It was a cool way to begin. I took it out, the ruby bright. She plucked like a bird and slipped it quickly into the pouch at her side, as if it were hot. She still thinks it cursed, I thought.

"I'll use it as an offering," she said.

"To Isis?"

"To all of Them, including Thoth."

"I feared you dead. It's like a miracle. You look like a spirit or an angel."

"Do you have the seraphim?"

Her distance was disconcerting. "I find you through hell and high water and all you want is jewelry?"

"We need them." She was straining not to show emotion, I realized.

"We?"

"Ethan, I was saved by Alessandro."

Well, there was a sharp little knife in the ribs. She'd been clinging to the balloon's trailing tether, Silano locked around her so she couldn't climb, and finally she had cut the rope with my tomahawk so the airship could float out of musket range. I'd failed to haul her into the basket, or get rid of the nobleman-sorcerer who'd once been her lover. So were they a couple again? If so, I was damned if I could understand why they'd sent for me. If all they wanted were gold trinkets, I could have mailed the things. "You were almost killed by that bastard. The only reason you didn't get away is because he wouldn't let go."

She looked away over the valley, her tone hollow. "I don't remember our landing, just the fall. The last thing I remember is your face, looking down from the lip of the basket. It was the most awful thing I've had to do in my life. As I cut the tether I saw a hundred emotions in your eyes."

"Horror, if I recall."

"Fear, shame, regret, anger, longing, sorrow . . . and relief."

I was going to protest but instead I flushed, because it was true.

"When I swung that tomahawk I freed you, Ethan, from the burden thrust upon you: safeguarding the Book of Thoth. I freed you of me. Yet you didn't go to America."

"You can't cut the rope that binds us with a hatchet, Astiza."

So she turned back and looked at me again, her gaze fierce, her body trembling, and I knew it was all she could do to keep from flying into my arms. Why was she hesitating? Once again I understood nothing. And I couldn't reach out either, because there was an invisible wall of duty and regret we had to break down first. We couldn't properly begin because we had too much to say.

"When I woke, a month had passed and I was with

Silano, nursed in secret. The savants had given him research quarters in Cairo. As he mended his broken hip he continued to read every scrap of ancient writing that could be scoured for him. He's assembled trunks and trunks of books. I even saw him picking through blackened manuscripts that must have come from Enoch's burned library. He hadn't given up, not for an instant. He knew we hadn't emerged from the pyramid with anything useful, and he suspected the book had been carried elsewhere. So once again I became his ally so I could use *him* to get back to *you*. I hoped you might still be in Egypt, or someplace near."

"You said you expected me to go to America."

"I doubted, I admit. I knew you might run. Then we heard rumors about inquiries being made, and my heart quickened. Silano had Bonaparte jail the real messenger and sent his own man in his place to Jerusalem to discourage you. Yet it didn't work. And as the count began to piece together a new plan, and Najac left to spy on you, I realized that fate was conspiring to bring us all together again. We're going to solve this mystery, Ethan, and find the book."

"Why? Don't you just want to bury it again?"

"It can also be used for good. Ancient Egypt was once a paradise of peace and learning. The world could be that way again."

"Astiza, you've seen our world. Or has the fall knocked all sense out of you?"

"There's a church on the rise just above us, ruins now. It marks where Moses may once have sat, gazing at his Promised Land, knowing that for all his sacrifice he himself could never enter it. Your culture's old god was a cruel one. The building itself dates to Byzantine times. We've found a tomb of a Templar knight, as Silano's studies led him to expect, and in that tomb bones. Hidden in one femur was a medieval map."

"You broke apart a dead man's bones?"

"Silano found mention of the possibility while studying in Constantinople. Fleeing Templars came this way, Ethan, after their destruction in Europe. They hid something they'd found in Jerusalem in a strange city this map describes. Silano has discovered something else as well, something that may involve electricity and your Benjamin Franklin. Then we heard you'd been executed at Jaffa, but your body was missing. In desperation, I gave Monge the ring, wondering if he'd come across you. And now . . ."

"Were you *ever* in love with Alessandro Silano?"

She hesitated only a moment before answering. "No."

I stood there, hoping for more before I dared ask the next, most logical question.

"I'm not proud of that fact," she said. "He loved me. He still does. Men fall in love easily, but women must be careful. We were lovers, but it would be hard for me to *love* him."

"Astiza, you didn't need me here to carry two golden angels."

"Do you still love *me*, Ethan, as you said along the Nile?"

Of course I loved her. But I feared her, too. What had poor Talma called her, a witch? A sorceress? I feared the power she'd once more have over me when I admitted my attraction. And what of poor Miriam, still besieged in the walls of Acre?

Yet none of that mattered. All the old emotions were flooding back.

"I've loved you from the moment I pulled the wreckage off you in Alexandria," I finally confirmed in a rush. "I loved you when we were riding in the *chebek* up the Nile, and I loved you in Enoch's house, and I loved you even when I thought for a moment you'd betrayed me at Dendara Temple. And I loved you when I thought we were doomed in the Great Pyramid. I loved you enough to throw in with the damned British just in hopes of getting you back, and I loved you to throw in again, it seems, with the damned French. I loved even the *hope* of seeing you when I was in the valley down there, and all the long ride up the mountain, even when I had no idea what I'd say to you or what you'd look like or how you'd feel." I was losing all discipline, wasn't I? Women can rob a man of sense faster than Appalachian jug whiskey. And now, out of breath and hanging for hope, I waited for her to cut me dead with a word. I'd opened my chest to the muskets. I'd bent beneath the executioner's blade.

She gave a sad smile. "It would be hard to love Alessandro, but it was *not* hard for me to fall in love with you."

I actually swayed slightly, dizzy with joy. "Then let's leave now. Tonight."

She shook her head, her eyes wet. "No, Ethan. Silano knows too much. We can't leave him to this quest. We have to see it through, and seize the book when the time is right. We have to work with him, and then betray him. It's been my destiny since I met him in Cairo, and yours since you won the medallion in Paris. Everything has been leading up to this mountaintop, and the mountains beyond. We'll find it and *then* we will leave."

"*What* mountains beyond?"

"The City of Ghosts."

"What?"

"It's a sacred place, a mythical place. No European has been there, I think, since the Templars. Our journey isn't done."

I groaned. "By the greed of Benedict Arnold."

"So you and I must now be estranged, Ethan, to mislead him. You're angry I've partnered again with Alessandro, and we journey on as bitter ex-lovers. They must think us enemies until the very end."

"Enemies?"

And then she swung and slapped me, as hard as she could.

It sounded like a rifle shot. I glanced back. The others were looking down the slope at us. Alessandro Silano, tall, his bearing aristocratic, was watching most intently.

¤   ¤   ¤

Silano was not the lithe swordsman I remembered. He walked with a limp, and pain had hardened his handsomeness, turning Pan-like charm into a darker satyr of frustrated ambition. He was more rigid from the injury he'd suffered in the balloon fall, and his gaze had no seduction this time, only purpose. There was darkness in his eye, and a hard set to his mouth. He winced as he came down a goat path from the ruined Byzantine chapel to meet us, and didn't offer a hand or greeting. What would be the point? We were rivals, and my face still stung from Astiza's slap. I suspected Monge or other physicians had given him drugs for the pain.

"Well?" Silano asked. "Does he have them?"

"He wouldn't say," she reported. "He's not convinced he should help us."

"So you persuade by slapping him?"

She shrugged. "We have some history."

Silano turned to me. "We don't seem able to escape each other, do we, Gage?"

"I was doing just fine until you sent for me with Astiza's ring."

"And you came for her, as you did before. I hope she learns to appreciate it before you learn to tire of it. She's not an easy woman to love, American." He glanced at her, no more sure than me how much to trust her. She'd put him off, I could tell. They were allies, not lovers. It's not easy to live with something you can't have, and Silano was not a man to tolerate frustration. We would all have to watch each other.

"She told me you'd bring two small metal angels you found in the Great Pyramid. Did you?"

I hesitated, just to make him squirm. Then, "I brought them. That doesn't mean I'll use them to help you." I wanted to test how hostile he was. He could, of course, have me killed. "They're in a safe place until we've talked. Given our history, you'll forgive me if I don't entirely trust you."

He bowed. "Nor I you, of course. And yet partners need not be friends. In fact, sometimes it is better they are not: there is more honesty that way, don't you think? Come, I'm sure you're hungry after your journey. Let's eat, and I'll tell you a story. Then you can decide if you wish to help."

"And if I don't?"

"Then you can go back to Acre. And Astiza can follow or stay as she wishes." He began limping back up the path, then turned. "But I know what both of you will decide."

I glanced at Astiza, looking for reassurance that she despised this man, this diplomat, duelist, conjurer, scholar, and schemer. But her gaze was not of contempt but of sadness. She understood how captive we are to desire and frustration. We were dreamers in a nightmare of our own making.

We hiked to the roofless church, light picking out its rubble. There were heaps and hollows from excavation. Astiza showed me the opened stone sarcophagus where the Knight Templar's bones had apparently been found, concealed beneath the floor.

"Silano found references to this grave in the Vatican and the libraries of Constantinople," she said. "This knight was Michel de Troyes, who fled the arrests of the Templars in Paris and sailed for the Holy Land."

"There was a letter that said he laid his bones with Moses," Silano said, "and buried the secret within him. It took some time before we realized the reference meant the location must be Mount Nebo, even though the grave of Moses has never been found. I hoped to simply find the document in the knight's grave, but didn't."

"You hit the bones in impatience," Astiza said.

"Yes." The admission of emotion was reluctant. "And a crack in his femur showed a hint of gold. A slim tube had been inserted—his leg must have been butchered and its bone hollowed after his death—and within the tube was a medieval map, the names in Latin. It points to the next step. It was then that we sent for you."

"Why?"

"Because you're a Franklin man. An electrician."

"Electricity?"

"Is the key. I'll explain after supper."

By now there were twenty of us—Najac's men, my own trio, and Silano, Astiza, and several bodyguards that Silano traveled with. Evening had come on. These servants built a fire in a corner of the church's ruined walls and then left key members of the expedition alone. Najac sat with us, to my distaste, so I insisted Ned and Mohammad eat with us as well. Astiza knelt demurely, not at all her character, and Silano commanded the center position. We sat on sand drifting across old mosaics of Roman hunting scenes, animals rearing before spears thrust by noblemen in a forest.

"So, we are all together at last," Silano began, the warmth of the fire making a cocoon from the cold desert sky. Sparks flew up to mingle with the stars. "Is it possible Thoth meant unions like this, to solve the riddles he left for us? Have we unwittingly been following the gods all along?"

"I believe in one true God," Mohammad muttered.

"Aye," said Ned, "though you've got the wrong one, mate. No offense."

"As I believe in One," Silano said, "and all things, and all beings, and all beliefs, are manifestations of his mystery. I've followed a thousand roads in the libraries, monasteries, and tombs of the world, and all lead toward the same center. That center is what we seek, my reluctant allies."

"What center, master?" Najac prompted, like the trained dog he was.

Silano picked up a grain of sand. "What if I said this was the universe?"

"I'd say take it, and leave us the rest," Ned suggested.

The count smiled thinly, threw up the grain, and caught it. "And what if I said the world around us is gossamer, as insubstantial as the spaces between a spider's web, and all that sustains the illusion are mysterious energies we don't understand—that this energy may be nothing more than thought itself? Or . . . electricity?"

"I would say that the Nile you crashed into was no spiderweb, but instead substantial enough to break your hip," I replied.

"Illusion upon illusion. That is what some of the sacred writings maintain, all inspired by Thoth."

"Gold is mere spider's silk? Power grasps nothing but air?"

"Oh no. While we are but a dream, the dream is our

reality. But here, then, is the secret. Let us suppose the most solid things, the stones of this church, are matrices of almost nothing. That the tumble of a boulder or the fall of a star is a simple mathematical rule. That a building can encompass the divine, a shape can be sacred, and a mind can sense unseen energies. What becomes of beings who realize this? If mountains are mere web, might not they be moved? If seas are the thinnest vapor, might not they be parted? Could the Nile become blood, or a plague of frogs spawned? How hard to tumble the walls of Jericho, when they are but a latticework? How hard to turn lead into gold when both, essentially, are dust?"

"You're mad," said Mohammad. "This is Satan's talk."

"No. I am a scholar!" And now he pushed to his feet, Najac giving him a hand that he shook off as soon as he was able. "You denied me that title once, at a banquet before Napoleon, Ethan Gage. You insulted my reputation to make me seem petty." I reddened despite myself. The man forgot nothing. "Yet I've probed these mysteries for twenty years. I came to Cairo when it was still in the thrall of the Mamelukes, and explored old mysteries while you were frittering your life away. I followed the trail of the ancients while you hooked your opportunism to the French. I've tried to understand the enigmatic hints left behind for us, while the rest of you wrestled in the mud." He hadn't lost his high opinion of himself, either. "And now I understand what we're seeking, and what we must harness to find it. We have to catch the lightning!"

"Catch what?" Ned asked dubiously.

"Gage, I understand you have succeeded in using electricity as a weapon against Bonaparte's troops."

"As a necessity of war."

"I think we're going to need Franklin's expertise when we near the Book of Thoth. Are you electrician enough?"

"I'm a man of science, but I don't understand a word you're saying."

"It's why we need the seraphim, Ethan," Astiza broke in, more softly. "We think that somehow they're going to point to a final hiding point the Knights Templar used after destruction of their order. They brought what they'd found beneath Jerusalem to the desert and concealed it in the City of Ghosts. The documents are enigmatic, but Alessandro and I believe that Thoth, too, knew of electricity, and that the Templars set that as a test to find the book. We need to draw down the lightning like Franklin did."

"So I agree with Mohammad. You're both mad."

"In the vaults beneath Jerusalem," Silano said, "you found a curious floor, with a lightning design. And a strange door. Did you not?"

"How do you know that?" Najac, I was certain, had never penetrated to the rooms we'd explored, and had not seen Miriam's oddly decorated door.

"I've been studying, as you said. And upon this Templar door you saw a Jewish pattern, did you not? The ten *sefiroth* of the kabbalah?"

"What has that to do with lightning?"

"Watch." Bending to the dust on the floor by our fire, he drew two circles, their edges joined.

"All things are dual," Astiza murmured.

"And yet united," the count said. He drew another circle, as big as the first two, overlapping both. Then circles upon those circles, more upon more, the pattern becoming ever more intricate. "The prophets knew this," he said. "Perhaps Jesus did as well. The Templars relearned it." Then where circles intersected he began drawing lines, forming patterns: both a five-sided and a six-sided star. "The one is Egyptian and the other Jewish," he said. "Both are equally sacred. The Egyptian star you use for your nation's new flag. Do you not think this was the intent of the Freemasons who helped found your country?" And finally, at the interstices, he jabbed out ten points, which made the same peculiar pattern we'd seen in the Templar Hall under the Temple Mount. The *sefiroth*, Haim Farhi had called them. Once again, everyone seemed to be speaking ancient tongues I wasn't privy too, and finding import in what I would have assumed was mere decoration.

"Recognize it?" Silano asked.

"What of it?" I said guardedly.

"The Templars drew another pattern from this design," he said. From dot to dot he drew a zigzagging, overlapping line. "There. A lightning bolt. Eerie, is it not?"

"Maybe."

"Not maybe. Their clues tell us to harness the sky if we wish to find where the book is. The lightning symbol is in the map we found here, and then there is the poem."

"Poem?"

"Couplets. They're quite eloquent." He recited:

Aether cum radiis solis fulgore relucet
Angelus et pinnis indicat ore Dei,
Cum region deserta bibens ex murice torto
Siccatis labris arida sorbet aquas
Tum demum partem quandam lux clara revelat
Quae prius ignota est nec repute tibi
Opperiens cunctatur eum dea candida Veri
Floribus insanum qui furit atque fide

"That's Greek to me, Silano."

"Latin. Do they not teach the classics on the frontier, Monsieur Gage?"

"On the frontier, the classics make good fire starter."

"The translation of this document, which I found in my travels, explains why I was anxious to make your reacquaintance:"

When heaven blazes with the lightning of the sun's rays
And with his feathers the angel points out at
    God's command
When the desert, drinking from the twisted snail shell
Thirstily sucks up water with dried-out lips
Then at last the clear light reveals a certain part
Which formerly was both unknown,
    nor was it cognized in your estimation
Lingering, divine bright Truth awaits him
The fool crazy for flowers, who also trusts with faith

What the devil did that mean? The world could avoid a great deal of confusion if everyone just said things straight out, but that doesn't seem to be our habit, does it? And yet there was something about this phrasing that jarred a memory, a memory I'd never shared with either Astiza or Silano. I felt a chill of recognition.

"We must go to a special place within the City of Ghosts," Silano said, "and call down the flames of the storm, the lightning, just as your mentor Franklin did in Philadelphia. Call it to the seraphim, and see which part they point to."

"The part of what?"

"A building or cave, I'm guessing. It will become apparent if this works."

"The desert drinks from a snail shell?"

"From the thunderstorm's rain. A reference to a sacred drinking vessel, I suspect."

Or something else, I thought to myself. "And the flowers and faith?"

"My theory is that is a reference to the Templars themselves and the Order of the Rose and Cross, or Rosicrucians. Theories of the origin of the Rosy Cross vary, but one is that the Alexandrian sage Ormus was converted to Christianity by the disciple Mark in 46 A.D. and fused its teachings with that of ancient Egypt, creating a Gnostic creed, or belief in knowledge." He looked hard at me to make sure I'd make the connection with the Book of Thoth. "Movements fade in and out of history, but the symbol of the cross and the rose is a very old one, symbolizing death and life, or despair and hope. The Resurrection, if you will."

"And male and female," Astiza added, "the phallic cross and the yonic flower."

"Flower and faith symbolize the character required of those who would find the secret," Silano said.

"A woman?"

"Perhaps, which is one reason we have a woman along."

I decided to keep my own suspicions to myself. "So you

want to draw lightning down to my seraphim and see what happens?"

"In the place prescribed by the documents we've found, yes."

I considered. "What you're talking about is a lightning rod, or rather two, since we have two seraphim. We need metal to bring the energy down to the ground, I think."

"Which is why our tent poles are metal, to mount your angels on. I've been planning this for months. You need our help to find the city, and we need your help to find the hiding place within it."

"And then what? We cut the book in half?"

"No," Silano said. "We don't need Solomon to resolve our rivalry. We use it together, for mankind's good, just as the ancients did."

"Together!"

"Why not, when we have the power to do unlimited good? If the world's true form is gossamer, it can be spun and shifted. That's what this book apparently tells us how to do. And when all things are possible, stones can be shifted, lives lengthened, enemies reconciled, and wounds healed." His eyes gleamed.

I looked at his hip. "Made young again."

"Exactly, and in charge of a world finally run on reason."

"Bonaparte's reason?"

Silano glanced at Najac. "I am loyal to the government that commissioned me. And yet politicians and generals only understand so much. It is scholars who will rule the future, Ethan. The old world was the plaything of princes and priests. The new will be the responsibility of scientists. When reason and the occult are joined, a golden age will begin. Priests played that role in Egypt. We will be the priests of the future."

"But we're on opposite sides!"

"No, we're not. All things are dual. And we are linked by Astiza." His smile was meant to be seductive.

What an unholy trinity. Yet how could I accomplish

anything without playing along? I looked at her. She was sitting at Silano's side, not mine.

"She hasn't even forgiven me," I lied.

"I will if you help us, Ethan," she replied. "We need you to call down fire from the sky. We need you to harness heaven, like your Benjamin Franklin."

CHAPTER 18

The entrance to the City of Ghosts was a slit of sandstone canyon, tight and pink as a virgin. The sinuous passageway was no wider than a room at its base, the sky a distant blue line above. The walls rose as high as six hundred feet, at times leaning in like a roof, as if closing like a crack in an earthquake. The embrace was disquieting as we walked with packs down its shadowed floor. Yet if rock can be voluptuous, this rose and blue barbican was a seraglio of rolling flesh, carved by water into a thousand sensuous forms as pleasing to the eye as a sultan's favorite. Much of it was banded into layers of coral, gray, white, and lavender. Here rock dripped down like frozen syrup, there it puffed like frosting, and in yet another place it was a lace curtain. The sand and rock wadi formed a crude road that dipped downward toward our destination, like a causeway to some underworld in a satyr's dream. And nature wasn't the only sculptor here, I saw when I looked closely. This had been a caravan gate, and a channel had been carved into the canyon wall, its dark stain making clear that it had once been an aqueduct for the ancient city. We passed beneath a worn Roman arch that marked the canyon's upper entrance and strode silently, in awe, past niches in its walls that held gods and geometric carvings. Sandstone camels, twice life-size, sauntered with us as bas-relief on the sandstone walls. It was as if the dead had been turned to stone, and when we turned the canyon's final corner this ghostly effect was redoubled. We gasped.

"Behold," intoned Silano. "This is what is possible when men dream!"

Yes, here the book must reside.

¤   ¤   ¤

We'd been traveling to this place several days from Nebo. Our party had followed the Jordanian highlands, skirting green pastures on the high plateau and passing by the brooding ruins of Crusader castles, as forsaken as the Templars. Occasionally we dipped down into deep and hot mountain canyons that opened to sandy yellow desert to the west. Tiny streams were swallowed by the dryness. Then we'd climb up the other side and continue south, hawks wheeling in the dry thermals and Bedouins shooing their goats into side wadis, watching silently from a safe distance until we passed. The siege at Acre seemed a planet away.

As we rode I had plenty of time to think about Silano's Latin clue. The part about the angels pointing seemed somewhat plausible, though what forces were at play was beyond me. What had jarred my memory, however, were the words "snail shell" and "flower." The same imagery had been used by the French savant, and my friend, Edme François Jomard when we climbed the Great Pyramid. He'd said the pyramid's dimensions encoded a "golden number" or ratio—1.618, if I recalled—that was in turn a geometric representation of a progression of numbers called the Fibonacci sequence. This mathematical progression could be represented by an interconnected series of ever-growing squares, and an arc through the squares produced the kind of spiral seen in a nautilus shell, or, Jomard said, in the arrangement of flower petals. My comrade Talma had thought the young scientist half addled, but I was intrigued. Did the pyramid really stand for some fundamental truth about nature? And what, if anything, did that have to do with where we were going now?

I tried to think like Monge and Jomard, the mathematicians. "Then at last the clear light reveals a certain part which formerly was both unknown, nor was it cognized in your estimation," the Templars had written. This seemed like nonsense, and yet it gave me a wild idea. Did I have a clue that would allow me to snatch the Book of Thoth out from under Silano's nose?

We camped in the most defensible places we could find, and one evening we climbed a hillock to spend the night in the limestone remains of a Crusader castle, its broken towers orbited by swallows. The ruin was yellow in the low sun, weeds growing from the crevices between stones. We rode up through a meadow of wildflowers that waved in the spring wind. It was as if they were nodding at my supposition. *Fibonacci*, they whispered.

As we bunched at the half-fallen gate to lead our horses into the abandoned courtyard, I managed a whisper to Astiza. "Meet me under the moon, on the battlements as far from where we sleep as possible," I murmured.

Her nod was almost imperceptible and then, acting as if irritated, urged her horse ahead of mine to cut mine off. Yes, to the others we were bitter ex-lovers.

Our own trio had made a habit of sleeping a little apart from Najac's gang of cutthroats, and when Ned was deep into his lusty snores I crept away and waited in the shadows. She came like a ghost, wrapped in white and luminous in the night. I rose and pulled her into a sentry post out of sight of any others, milky moonlight falling through the arrow slit. I kissed her for the first time since our reunion, her lips cold from the chill, her fingers knotting in mine to control my hands.

"We don't have time," she whispered. "Najac is awake and thinks I've gone to relieve myself. He'll be counting the minutes."

"Let the bastard count." I tried to embrace her.

"Ethan, if we go too far it will spoil everything!"

"If we don't I'll burst."

"No." She thrust me away. "Patience! We're close!"

Damnation, it had been hard to stay on keel since leaving Paris. Too much exercise and too few women. I took a breath. "All right, listen. If this lightning trick really works, you need to help me separate from Silano. I need time to try something on my own, and then we must rendezvous later."

"You know something you haven't told us, don't you?"

"Perhaps. It's a gamble."

"And you're a gambler." She thought. "After we harness the lightning, tell him you'll trade your share in the book for me. Then I'll pretend to betray you, and go with him. We'll abandon you. Act frustrated."

"That won't be hard. Can I trust you?"

She smiled. "Trust has to come from within."

And with that she slipped away. We took care that the rest of the time we were as prickly as porcupines. I hoped it was truly a ruse.

We followed the old caravan tracks and I feared Ottoman patrols, but it was as if the clash at Mount Tabor had temporarily made Turkish forces disappear. The world seemed empty, primeval. We were trailed once by native tribesmen, tough little men on camels, but our party looked tough too, and poor to boot, hardly worth robbing. Najac rode to talk with them with his toughs, and they disappeared.

By the time we reached the city of the Templar maps, no one followed us at all.

We turned west and dropped from the edge of the central plateau toward the distant desert. Between us and that waste, however, was the strangest geologic formation I'd ever seen. There was a range of moonlike mountains, jagged and stark, and in front of them a boil of brown sandstone, lumpy and rounded. It looked like a frozen brew of brown bubbles, or wildly risen bread. There seemed no way in or around this odd formation, but when we came near we saw caves on it like a pox, a hundred-eyed monster. The sandstone, I realized, was dotted with them. Carvings of pillars and steps began to appear in the outcrops. We camped in a dry wadi, the stars brilliant and cold.

Silano said the paths we would tread the next morning were too narrow and precipitous for horses, so when the sky lightened we left them picketed at the canyon's entrance with some of Najac's Arabs as guard. I noted the horses were oddly nervous, neighing and stamping, and they shied from a wagon that had appeared at the edge of our camp sometime in the night. It was boxy but covered with tarpaulins, and Silano said its supplies included meat that made the animals skittish. I wanted to investigate, but then the morning sun lit the escarpment and picked out its cracklike canyon and welcoming Roman arch. We entered on foot and within yards could see nothing of the world behind. All sound disappeared, except the scuffle of our own feet as we descended the wadi.

"Storms have washed cobbles over what was once an ancient road," Silano said. "The flash floods boil most frequently this time of year, records say, after thunder and lightning. The Templars knew this, and used it. So will we."

And then, as I have described, we came after a mile to the canyon's other end, and gaped. Before us was a new canyon, perpendicular to the first and just as imposing, but this is not what amazed us. Instead, on the wall opposite' was the most unexpected monument I'd ever seen, the first thing to be on a par in glory with the immensity of the pyramids. It was a temple carved from living rock.

Imagine a sheer cliff hundreds of feet high, pink as a maiden's cheeks, and not on it but *in* it, carved into its face, an ornate pagan edifice of pillars and pediment and cupolas rearing higher than a Philadelphia church steeple. Sculpted eagles the size of buffalo crouched on its upper cornices, and the alcoves between its pillars held stone figures with angel wings. What drew my eye weren't these cherubim or demons, however, but the central figure high above the temple's dark door. It was a woman, breasts bare and eroded, her hips draped with Roman folds of stony cloth, and her head high and alert. I'd seen this form before in the sacred precincts of ancient Egypt. Cupped in her arm was a cornucopia, and on her head the remains of a crown made of a solar disc between bull's horns. I felt a shiver at this weird recurrence of a goddess who'd haunted me since Paris, where the Romans had built a temple to this same goddess on what is now the site of Notre Dame.

"Isis!" Astiza cried. "She's a star, guiding us to the book!"

Silano smiled. "The Arabs call this the Khazne, the Treasury, because their legends claim this is where Pharaoh hid his wealth."

"You mean the book is in there?" I asked.

"No. The rooms are shallow and bare. It's somewhere nearby."

We rode to the Khazne's entrance, splashing across a small stream that ran down the center of this new chasm. The canyon twisted away to our right. A broad staircase led to the dark pillared entry. We stood a moment in the cool of the temple's portico, looking out at the red rock, and then stepped into the room beyond.

As Silano said, it was disappointingly empty, as feature-less as the room that had held the empty sarcophagus in the Great Pyramid. The cliff had been hollowed into straight, sheer, boxlike inner chambers. A few minutes of inspection confirmed there were no hidden doors. It was plain as an empty warehouse.

"Unless there's a trick to this place, like its mathematical dimensions, there's nothing here," I said. "What's it for?" It seemed too large to live in and yet not big and luminous enough for a temple.

Silano shrugged. "It doesn't matter. We are to find the Place of High Sacrifice. If there's one thing we can confirm about this, it isn't high."

"Glorious, however," Astiza murmured.

"Illusion, like all else," Silano said. "Only the mind is real. That's why cruelty is no sin."

We came back outside, the canyon half in sunlight, half in shadow. The day was hazing. "We're lucky," Silano said. "The air is heavy and smells like storm. We won't need to wait, but must act before the tempest breaks."

This new canyon slowly broadened as we followed it, allowing us ever better glimpses of the maze of mountains we'd entered. Rock shot skyward like layer cakes, rounded loaves, and doughy castles. Oleander bloomed to reflect the strange rock. Everywhere the cliff walls were pierced with caves, but not natural ones. They had the rectangular shape of human doors, indicating people had once carved them. It was a city not built on the earth, but of it. We passed a grand semicircular Roman theater, its tiers of seats again carved from the cliff itself, and finally passed out to a broad bowl enclosed by steep mountains, like a vast courtyard surrounded by walls. It was a perfect hiding place for a city, accessible only by narrow and easily defended canyons. Yet it had room enough for a Boston. Pillars, no longer holding anything up, reared from the dirt. Roofless temples rose from rubble.

"By the grace of Isis," Astiza murmured. "Who dreamed here?"

One cliff wall was a spectacle to rival the earlier Khazne. It had been carved into the façade of a fabulous city, a riot of staircases, pillars, pediments, platforms, windows, and doors, leading to a beehive of chambers within. I began counting the entrances and gave up. There were hundreds. No, thousands.

"This place is huge," I said. "We're to find a book in this? It makes the pyramids look like a postbox."

"*You're* to find it. You and your seraphim." Silano had pulled out his Templar map and was studying it. Then he pointed. "From up there."

A mountain behind us that rose above the ancient theater was carved into battlements but appeared flat on top. Goat tracks led upward. "Up there? Where?"

"To the High Place of Sacrifice."

¤   ¤   ¤

A narrow footpath had been built from crude steps chiseled out of sandstone. It was muggy and we sweated, but as we climbed our view broadened, and more and more cliffs came into view that were pockmarked with doorways and windows. Nowhere did we see people. The abandoned city was silent, without the keening of ghosts. The light was purpling.

At the top we came out to a flat plateau of sandstone with a magnificent view. Far below was the dusty bowl of ruined walls and toppled pillars, enclosed by cliffs. Beyond were more jagged mountains without a scrap of green, as stripped as a skeleton. The sun was sinking toward looming thunderheads that scudded toward us like black men-o'-war. There was a hot, humid breeze that picked up funnels of dust and spun them like tops. The rock shelf itself had been precisely flattened by ancient chisels. At the center was an incised rectangle the size of a ballroom, like a very shallow and dry pool. Silano consulted a compass. "It's oriented north and south, all right," he pronounced, as if expecting this. To the west, where the storm was coming from, four steps led to a raised platform that appeared to be some kind of altar. On it was a round basin with a channel.

"For blood," the count told us. His cloak flapped in the wind.

"I don't see anyplace to hide a book," I said.

Silano gestured to the city far below, ten thousand holes pocking the sandstone like a lunatic hive. "And I see infinity. It's time to use your seraphim, Ethan Gage. They are made of holier metal than gold."

"What metal?"

"The Egyptians called it Ra-ezhri. Tears of the Sun. The finger of God is going to touch it, and then point to where we must go. What do we need to draw down the finger of Thoth? How can the essence of the universe give us a sign?"

He was crazy as a loon, but so was old Ben, I suppose, when he proposed to go kite-flying in a tempest. Savants are a balmy lot.

"Wait. What happens when we retrieve the book?"

"We study," Silano said shortly.

"We don't know if we can even read it," Astiza added.

"I mean who gets it," I insisted. "Someone needs to become the caretaker. It seems my seraphim are the critical tool, and my skill at setting them the key. And I'm not really on the French *or* the British side. I'm neutral. You should entrust it to me."

"You couldn't have found this place by yourself in a thousand years," growled Najac, "or care for a grocery list."

"And you couldn't find your right ear if you had a cord tied from it to your cockles," I replied with irritation.

"Monsieur Gage, surely the situation is plain by now," Silano said impatiently. "You join me, join the Egyptian Rite, and win a share of power."

"Join a man who in Egypt sent me my friend's head in a jar?"

He sighed. "Or, you can leave with nothing."

"And what claim of ownership do *you* have?" I had to play my part.

He looked around, amused. "Why, all the guns, most of the provisions, and the only hope of deciphering what we're about to find." Najac's men raised the muzzles of their weapons. It especially annoyed me to have to look down the barrel of my own rifle, in Najac's greasy hands. "I really don't know what Franklin saw in you, Ethan. You have such a slow grasp of the obvious."

I pointed to the building clouds. "It won't work without me, Silano."

"Don't be a fool. If you don't help, then no one gets the book and you have nothing. Besides, you're as curious as I am."

I looked at Astiza. "This is the deal, then. I help you set the seraphim. If it works, you *do* get the book. Take it, and be done with it."

"Guv'nor!" Ned cried.

"But I want Astiza in its place."

"She is not mine to give, monsieur."

"I want you to let us go, without harm or interference."

He glanced at her. She was avoiding both our eyes. "And you'll help if I agree?"

I nodded. "We'd better hurry."

"But it's her choice, not mine," he cautioned. Astiza's face was a mask.

"Her choice," I confirmed confidently. "Not yours. That's all I'm asking."

"Agreed." He smiled, the grin as cold as a beaver trap in a Canadian creek. "Then help us prepare."

I took a breath. Could I trust her? Would this work at all? I was gambling all on a Latin riddle. I fished my pyramid souvenirs out from my clothing and watched the sorcerer's eyes gleam as he seized them. "Use the clasps that attached them to Moses' staff to mount them on the top of your metal poles," I directed. "We're going to make a Franklin lightning rod." I'd noticed two holes drilled in the top of the leveled plateau, and Silano confirmed they were mentioned in the Templar documents, so we inserted them. But there was no connection between them.

I studied the flat plane. There were grooves in the sandstone rock, I saw, forming a six-pointed star. The poles were at opposite points.

"We need a connection between the poles," I said. "Metal strips, to conduct electricity. Do you have any?"

Of course not. So much for Silano's research! It was growing darker, thunder rumbling as the cloudworks swelled and mounted. Funnels of dust skittered on the valley floor far below, weaving and bending like drunks.

"I don't see what the rods will do, if isolated," I warned.

"The Templars said this will work. My studies are infallible."

The man had an ego to match Aaron Burr. So I thought of what could replace the metal strips, because my enemies were right: I was as curious as anyone. "Najac, do something beside scowl," I finally suggested. "Use your water bag to fill these grooves with water, and add some salt."

"Water?"

"Ben said it can help conduct electricity."

The water filled the little runnels until the star gleamed in the thick, green-purple light. The sun was swallowed and the temperature dropped. My skin prickled. More thunder, and I could see first tendrils of rain curling downward like feathers, evaporating before they touched the ground. Lightning stabbed to the west. I backed to the edge of the plateau. Ned and Mohammad followed me, but no one else seemed frightened. Even Astiza was waiting expectantly, hair swirling, her eyes on the sky and not me.

The storm swept down on us like a cavalry charge. There was a gusting wall of wind, hurling grit, and the clouds overran us, great bags of rain and thunder that glowed silver as they billowed and ballooned. Lightning flashed and struck the peaks around us, nearer and nearer, the thunder like artillery. Fat drops of rain hit, hot and heavy, more like molten lead than water. Our clothing shuddered, and the wind rose to a shriek. And then there was a blinding flash, an instantaneous roar, and the mountain quaked. One of the rods had been hit! My knees went weak. Sparks blazed, and bright blue light flashed from rod to rod along the wet star grooves, and then arced across space from angel to angel. The seraphim turned glowing white. They swung, the iron rods turning, and their wings pointed northeast, tilting toward each other so that lines drawn from each would meet about twenty yards away. The lightning bolt had passed, but the rods held power, everything bathed in a purple glow not too different than the one we'd seen in the chamber below the Temple Mount in Jerusalem. And then beams of light flowed from the wings of the seraphim, met in midair, and a single beam streaked like a rifle bullet, as if pulled, to strike a grand pillared doorway of another cliffside temple, two miles from where we stood. Sparks flew in a fountain.

"Yes!" Silano's henchmen cried.

The ray held a moment, like a momentary peek of sun into a dark cave, and then faded. The mountaintop went dark. Dazzled, I looked at our metal poles. The seraphim had melted, the tops of the poles flattened like mushrooms. Silano had his arms up in the air in triumph. Astiza was rigid, her gown soaked, water dripping from the tendrils of dark hair plastered on her cheek. The storm was moving on toward the east, but behind its flashing prow came more rain, cooler this time, a hiss to cleanse the air of ozone. It poured down. We could all feel the electricity in the air, our hair still dancing to it. Water was sluicing everywhere off the cliff tops.

"Did everyone mark that?" Silano asked.

"I could find it with my eyes closed," Najac promised, a note of greed in his tone.

"Satan's work," Big Ned muttered.

"No, Moses'!" Silano answered. "And that of the Knights Templar and all those who quest for truth. We are at God's work, gentlemen, and whether the god is Thoth or Jehovah or Allah, his guise is the same: knowledge." His eyes were alight with energy, as if some of the lightning had entered him.

I've nothing against knowledge—I sailed with savants, after all—and yet his words and look disturbed me. I remembered childhood sermons of Satan as serpent, promising knowledge to Adam and Eve in the Garden. What fire were we playing with here? Yet how could we allow so tempting an apple to go unpicked?

I looked at Astiza, my moral compass. But she had to avoid my gaze, didn't she? She looked awed—that something had really happened—and worried.

"Gentlemen, I believe we are about to make history," Silano said. "Down we go before nightfall. We'll camp in front of the temple that was illuminated and search it at first light tomorrow."

"Or with torches tonight," the eager Najac said.

"I appreciate your impatience, Pierre, but after a thousand years I don't think our goal is going anywhere. Monsieur Gage, as always your company has been intriguing. But I daresay neither of us will entirely regret our parting. You have made your bargain, so now I can say it. Adieu, frontiersman." He bowed.

"Astiza," I said. "Now you can come with me."

She was silent a long time. Then, "But I can't, Ethan."

"What?"

"I'm going with Alessandro."

"But I came for you! I left Acre for you!" I displayed more bluster than a barrister facing damning evidence for a guilty client.

"I can't let Alessandro have the book by himself, Ethan.

I can't walk away from it after all this suffering. Isis has brought me to this place to finish what I started."

"But he's mad! Look at his companions. They're the devil's spawn! Come away with us. Come with *me* to America."

She shook her head. "Good-bye, Ethan."

Silano was smiling. He'd expected this.

"No!"

"She has made her choice, monsieur."

"I only helped with the lightning to get you!"

"I'm sorry, Ethan. The book is more important than you. More important than *us*. Go back to the English. I'm going with Alessandro."

"You used me!"

"We used you to find the book: for good, I hope."

In mock frustration I jerked out one of the iron poles to use as a weapon, but Najac's gang raised their muskets. Astiza wouldn't look at me as Silano shepherded her off the plateau, wrapping her head with her scarf.

"Someday soon you will realize what you just threw away, Gage," Silano called. "What the Egyptian Rite could have given you! You will rue your bargain!"

"Aye," Najac growled, his pistol steady. "So go back to Acre and die."

I let the pole drop with a clang. Our acting had succeeded. If, indeed, Astiza was acting. "Then get off my mountain," I ordered, my voice shaking.

Smirking, they filed back down the trail, taking the melted seraphim and the rods with them, Astiza glancing back just once as she made her way down.

It was when they were out of earshot that Big Ned finally erupted. "By the saints, guv'nor, we're going to let that papist scoundrel steal our rightful treasure? I thought you had more grit!"

"Not grit, Ned, wit. Remember how I bested you at swords?"

He looked chastened. "Aye."

"That was by brain, not muscle. Silano doesn't know as

much as he thinks. Which means we have our own chance. We're going to find a trail off the back side of this mountain and do our own exploring, well away from that tribe of cut-throats."

"Away? But they know where this book of yours is!"

"They know where the lightning strike threw its light. But I don't think the Templars would be that obvious. I'm hoping they were students of the Great Pyramid."

He was baffled. "What do you mean, guv'nor?"

"I'm betting we've just witnessed a little misdirection. I am a gambling man, Ned. And the Great Pyramid incorporates a series of numbers known as the Fibonacci sequence. Surely you've heard of it."

"Blimey, no."

"The French in Egypt taught me about it. And this sequence, in turn, is a representation of some basic processes of nature. It's holy, if you will. Just the kind of thing Templars would be interested in."

"I'm sorry, guv'nor, but I thought this was all about ancient treasure and secret powers, not numbers and Templars."

"It's all those things. Now, there's a ratio that comes up in any geographic representation of the sequence, a pleasing proportion of a longer line to a shorter one that happens to be 1.61 and some-odd. It's called the "golden number" and was known to the Greeks and the builders of the Gothic cathedrals and to Renaissance painters. And it's encoded in the dimensions of the Great Pyramid."

"Gold?" Ned was looking at me as if I were daft, which perhaps I was.

I found a patch of dirt and drew. "Which means the book may really be at an angle to what we've just seen. That's what I'm betting, anyway. Now, let's suppose that the base of a pyramid is represented by the line we saw shooting across the valley here." I sketched a line pointing at the ruins where Silano and his team were headed. "Draw a line perpendicular to it, and it runs off more or less west." I pointed toward the rugged range where the storm had come from. "Somewhere along that new line is a point that would be represented if we completed a right triangle by drawing from where Silano is going to my other line going west."

"A point where?"

"Exactly. You have to know how long the third line, the sloping line, should be. Let's suppose it is 1.61 times, roughly, that of the line to Silano's Temple—the golden ratio, the physical embodiment of Fibonacci and nature, and the slope of the Great Pyramid itself. A pyramid built to incorporate fundamental numbers, the kind that go into snail shells or flowers. It's hard to gauge distance, yes, but if we assume the temple is two miles away, then our adjoining line is a little over three . . ."

He squinted, following my arm now as I left the temple where the lightning beam had struck and swung it from north to west. "I'm guessing it would strike my imaginary western line just about where that imposing ruin is."

We stared. On the floor of the valley was a wreck of an ancient building that looked like it had been battered by artillery for a hundred years. The dilapidation was actually just time and decay, yet it still stood higher than all the rubble around it. A line of old pillars, holding nothing, jutted up along what appeared to be an ancient causeway.

"You saw this angle where, effendi?" Mohammad tried to clarify.

"In the slope of the Great Pyramid. My friend Jomard explained it to me."

"You mean that Count Devil is going to the wrong temple?"

"It's just a guess, but the only chance I've got. Lads, are you willing to take a look and hope that the Templars cared for this number game as much as the ancient Egyptians did?"

"I've learned to have faith in you, effendi."

"And my, what a joke it would be to find the bloody book first," Ned laughed. "And some gold, too, I'm betting." And he gave me that wide, menacing smile.

CHAPTER **19**

We pretended to descend as if we were making for the entry canyon to leave the City of Ghosts. But after picking our way around some rocks, out of sight of Silano, we found a tricky descent down a wet, beautiful ravine on the west side of the mountain. We passed more caves and ruined tombs, next to spraying falls spawned by the rain—the desert was drinking its fill indeed, as the Templars had prophesized—until we were on the city's floor. It was dusk, the rain over. Using low hills as cover to keep out of sight of the others, we reached the large temple we'd seen just as it was getting dark. It was cool after the storm, stars beginning to stud the sky.

This structure was in worse repair than the Temple of Dendara I'd explored in Egypt, and much less impressive. Its roof was gone, and what was left was a windowless pen of rubble with minimal decoration. It was big—the walls seemed a hundred feet high, with an arch tall enough to sail a frigate through—but plain.

A tunnel leading downward was not hard to find. In one

corner on the inside of the temple there was a crater in the rubble, as if someone had dug in search of treasure, and at the bottom were rough boards weighted down with rocks. "Here it is then!" Ned quietly exulted. We threw the boards aside and found a set of sandstone stairs leading downward. Using dry brush to make crude torches, we lit one with steel and flint and descended. Yet we were soon disappointed. After thirty steps the staircase ended abruptly at what appeared to be a well, its sides of smooth sandstone. I took a rock and dropped it. Long seconds passed, and then there was a splash. I could hear water running below.

"An old well," I said. "The Bedouin closed it up so their goats and children wouldn't fall in."

Disappointed, we went back outside to explore the perimeter but found nothing of interest. Out in front, old pillars holding nothing up lined an abandoned causeway. More heaps of broken masonry marked ancient buildings, long collapsed. All looked picked over, pottery fragments everywhere. I'll tell you what history is: broken shards and forgotten bones; a million inhabitants thinking their moment is the most important, all turned to dust. From the cliffs around, caves were mute mouths. Weary, we sat.

"Looks like your theory didn't work, guv'nor," Ned said, dispirited.

"Not yet, Ned. Not yet."

"Where's the ghosts, then?" He peered about.

"Keeping their own counsel, I hope. Do you believe in them?"

"Aye, I've seen 'em. Lost shipmates stalk the deck on the darkest watches. Other wraiths, from wrecks unknown, call from passing swells. It gives a sailor a chill, it does. There was a baby that died in a rooming house I rented in Portsmouth, and we used to hear the cries when . . ."

"This is Satan's talk," Mohammad interrupted. "It's wrong to dwell on the dead."

"Yes, let's think of our purpose, lads. We need a way down. If there's one thing that goes with treasure hunting, it's grubbing in the earth."

"We should get miner's wages, we should," Ned agreed.

"In the morning, Silano is going to enter a temple where that lightning beam struck and either find something or not. I've bet not. But we need to find it ourselves and be well on our way before then."

"And what of the woman?" Ned asked. "Are you givin' her up, guv'nor?"

"She's supposed to steal away and meet us."

"Ah, you gambled on her, too? Now, women are bad bets."

I shrugged. "Life is nothing but gambles."

"I like the sound of the river," Mohammad remarked, to change the subject. He viewed gambling as Satan's device too, I knew. "You seldom hear it in the desert."

We listened. Indeed, there was a stream running down a channel next to the causeway, chuckling as it splashed.

"It's that storm. This place is parched like a bone most days, I figure," Ned said.

"I wonder where the water goes," Mohammad added. "We're in a bowl."

I stood. Where indeed? *The desert drinks its fill.* Suddenly excited, I clambered down the temple's broken stairs to the causeway and crossed it to the temporary stream, sparkling now in the starlight. It ran west toward the mountains and . . . there! Disappeared.

An old pillar lay like a chopped tree trunk across the river course, and under it the river abruptly ended. On one side a babbling brook, on the other dry sand and cobbles. I slid into the cool water, feeling it rush against my calves, and peered under the column. There was a horizontal crack in the earth like a sleepy giant's eyelid, and into this the water poured. I could hear the echo. Not a giant's eye, but its mouth. *Drinks its fill.*

"I think I've found our hole!" I shouted up to the others.

Ned jumped down beside me. "Slip into that crack, guv'nor, and you might be flushed to hell."

Indeed. Yet what if by some miracle I'd guessed right, and this was a clue to where the Templars had really hidden their Jerusalem secret? It *felt* right. I backed out from under the pillar and looked about. This was the only pillar that had fallen into the stream course. What were the chances it would have rolled precisely to where a cavern led downward? A cavern, moreover, that made its presence known only after a big thunderstorm?

I followed the column's trunklike length up the slope opposite from the temple. It had sheered off its base as if in an earthquake, its lower remnant jutting like a broken tooth. Intriguingly, the foundation platform seemed freer of debris than the surrounding landscape. Someone—centuries ago, now?—had cleared this: perhaps after setting aside their coat of medieval chain mail and a white tunic with a red cross.

"Ned, help me dig. Mohammad, get more brush for torches."

He groaned. "Again, guv'nor?"

"Treasure, remember?"

Soon we'd revealed a platform of worn marble under the column base. For just a moment I could visualize what this city must have been like in its heyday, the columns forming a shady arcade on either side of the central causeway, crammed with colorful shops and taverns, clean water gushing down to blue fountains, and tasseled camels from Arabia, humps laden with trade goods, swaying in stately march. There would be banners, trumpets, and gardens of fruit trees . . .

There! A pattern on the marble. Carved triangles jutted from the pillar's square base. There were actually two layers of paving, I realized, one an inch higher and overlapping the other. It made this pattern:

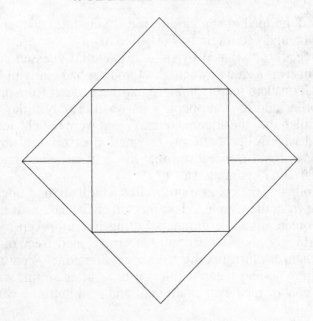

"Look for a symbol on this stonework," I told my companions. "Like a Masonic sign of compass and square."

We hunted. "Clean as a virgin's breast," Ned declared.

Well, the Templars were warrior-monks, not stonemasons. "No cross? No sword? No *sefiroth*?"

"Effendi, it's just a broken pillar."

"No, there's something here. Some way down to flower and faith, like the poem said. It's a locked door, and the key is . . . it's a square with a square. Four corners and four corners? That's eight. A sacred number? It's in the Fibonacci sequence."

The other two looked at me, blank.

"But two triangles too, three and three. Six. That isn't. Together they make fourteen, and that isn't either. Damn! Am I entirely off course?" I felt I was trying too hard. I needed Monge, or Astiza.

"If you could overlap the triangles, effendi, it would make the Jewish star."

Of course. Was it as simple as that? "Ned, help pull this

column base. Let's see if the triangles on this floor slide over each other."

"What?" Once more he looked at if I were a lunatic.

"Pull! Like you did on the altar beneath Jerusalem!"

Looking as if he was confirming his own damnation, the sailor joined me. By myself I don't think I would have budged the frozen stonework, but Ned's muscles bulged until they cracked. Mohammad helped too. Grudgingly, the base of the fallen pillar indeed began to move, the marble beginning to overlap. As the triangles crossed, they increasingly began to form the pattern of the Star of David.

"Pull, Ned, pull!"

"You're going to bring another lightning bolt, guv'nor."

But we didn't. The more the triangles overlapped, the smoother they slid. When they formed the star there was a click and the pillar base suddenly swung free, rotating out of the way on a single pin at its corner. The whole assembly had become weightless. As the base did so the six-sided star began to sink into the earth.

We gaped.

"Jump, jump, before it gets away from us!" I sprang and landed on the descending paving. After a moment's hesitation Ned and Mohammad did too, the Arab holding crude torches. We could hear the creak of ancient gears as we settled into the earth.

"We're going to hell," Mohammad moaned.

"No, men. The book and treasure!"

The sound of water was louder now, echoing into whatever subterranean chamber we were descending. We sank down a star-shaped shaft, our platform the six-sided star, and then it jerked and settled on the bottom. I looked up. We were in a well, far too high to climb out of. I could see only a few stars.

"How do we get back up?" Ned asked reasonably.

"Hmmm. I wonder if we should have left one of us on top? Well, too late now, lads. The book will tell us how to get out." I said it with more confidence than I felt.

A low horizontal passage led off from our peculiar shaft toward the sound of water. We crouched and followed it. In roughly the length of the fallen pillar above, we came to a cavern. There was a roar of water.

"Let's light a torch," I said. "Just one—we may need the others."

Yellow light flared. I gasped. The stream from the thunderstorm was spilling down from the slit I'd observed above, the desert drinking its fill. But that wasn't what caught my eye. The cavern we'd come to was man-made and shaped like a horn, or funnel, narrowing as it went down. Around its periphery a ledge wound, just wide enough for a man. We were clustered at its top. The ledge spiraled as it descended, and its pattern reminded me of the nautilus shell Jomard had shown me at the Great Pyramid, the one inspired by the Fibonacci sequence. *For the flower and faith.* At the funnel's bottom, the water was a swirling, turbulent pool.

"Whirlpool," Ned muttered. "Not the kind of thing you get back out of."

"No, it's another symbol, Ned. The universe is made of numbers somehow, and the Templars, or the people who built this city, were trying to memorialize it in stone. Just like the Egyptians. This is what the book is about, I'm guessing."

"Underground places built by madmen?"

"What's behind the everyday world we see."

He shook his head. "It's a sewer, guv'nor."

"No. A portal." *And faith.*

"Blimey, how did I get mixed up with you!"

"Indeed, we are in an evil place, effendi."

"No, this is a holy place. You two can wait here. I'm betting they wouldn't build all this if there wasn't something down there. Would they?"

They looked at me as if I belonged in an asylum, which wasn't far wrong. We were all crazy as loons, looking for a shortcut to happiness. But I *knew* I'd figured out the puzzle, that the mad Templars and their lightning had put their secret here, not where Silano was, and that if Astiza met us as promised I'd finally have it all—knowledge, treasure, and a woman. Well, two women, but that would be sorted out in due course. Again, I was gripped with guilt about Miriam, combined with sweet memory of her body and no little apprehension about her hurt. It's odd what one thinks about in tight times.

I lit another torch and descended, creeping down the spiral track like a careful snail. My compatriots stayed above, looking down on me. When I got to where the fall of water hit the pitch-black pool, my torch sputtered in the mist. How deep was this well? Too deep to retrieve whatever the Templars threw down here? For I'd no doubt they'd dropped their Jerusalem treasure down this funnel, trusting that surviving members would someday come back and reconstitute their order.

I gathered my courage. The water, as I said, was utterly dark, swirling like a drain, with green scum floating on its surface like curds. Its smell was musty as a coffin. But we couldn't get out the way we'd come, could we? So, setting my torch to one side where it promptly went out—my only light now was the dim torch of Ned and Mohammad above—I took a breath, prayed to all the gods I could think of, and plunged.

The water was chilly, but not shocking. I fell through ink. Soft, fibrous mats of algae brushed me as I fell, the slime of centuries. There may have been swimming things as well, white and pulpy in the dark—I imagined them, whether or not they were there—but I just kicked straight down, groping. I had two minutes to find what we sought, or drown.

The current started to hurry me. I began to panic, because it was increasingly apparent that fighting back upward would cost more time and breath than I had. I could not retreat, and I was being swept down and forward.

I noticed a peculiar glow. It came from ahead, not bright, but welcome enough after long seconds of utter blackness. I saw a bottom and it was reassuringly white, like a bottom of clean sand. Then I saw the true source of the paleness and almost swallowed water. The bottom was not sand, but bone.

I'd seen the frieze of skulls at the Templar chamber under Jerusalem, but this was a hundred times worse, an ossuary of the damned. Real skulls this time, pale and dim but recognizable enough, in gruesome tangle with arms, legs, and ribs. It was a reef of bone, bleached white, teeth as long as forefingers, sockets as blank as a grave. The whole was wrapped in fuzzed chain and chunks of stone.

This had been a sacrificial well or execution chamber.

The current swept me over this boneyard, pulling me toward a growing light. Was I hallucinating as my brain starved of air? No, it was real light, and I passed out of a short tunnel and saw it even brighter above me. While the current wanted to pull me on to wherever the river went, I kicked furiously upward.

I burst out of water with my last shrieking breath. Those bones! I spied and thrashed for a shelf of sandstone, grabbed, kicked, and flopped up out of the water like a played-out fish. For a while I just lay, gasping. Finally I got breath enough to sit up and look about. I was at the bottom of a sandstone shaft or well. High above, far out of reach, was the source of dim light. The underground stream I'd escaped ran past the shelf of rock and poured into another underwater tunnel. I shuddered. Might there be still more bones downstream, to be joined by mine?

I looked up to study the pale, silvery light of moon and stars. I couldn't see the sky so I surmised something was reflecting the night sky downward. The illumination was very dim, but it was light enough to see that the walls of the shaft were smooth, without crevice or foothold and too far apart to span with my body. There was no chance of climbing out. And what else?

Men watching.

Dripping, I rose slowly to my feet and turned about in this dim chamber. I was surrounded by men, I realized, huge brooding ones in medieval armor. They were helmeted, bearded, and had kite-shaped shields grounded at their armored feet. Except they weren't real men but sandstone statues, carved from the shaft walls to form a circle of eternal sentries: Templars. Perhaps they were representations of past grand masters. They were more than life-size, a good nine feet, and their gaze was grim. Yet there was something comforting about these companions as well, who would never let down their guard and yet stood back against the walls of the rock chamber as if they expected what they guarded was someday to be found.

And what was that? A stone sarcophagus, I saw, but not a lidless one like I'd seen in the king's chamber of the Great Pyramid. This was in the style of European churches, its lid the sculpted figure of a European knight. The sarcophagus was of limestone, and the Templar, I guessed, was perhaps that first one: Montbard, uncle of Saint Bernard. A guardian for all eternity.

The lid was heavy, and at first seemed firmly set in place. But when I gave it a hard enough shove it shifted slightly, with a scraping sound. Dust sifted from its edges. Straining, I pushed and pushed, until I had it ajar and could lower an edge onto the ground. Then I peered inside. A box inside a box.

The coffin was made of acacia wood, remarkably preserved. While opening it gave me pause, I'd come too far. I jerked open the lid. Inside was a skeleton of a man, not terrifying but instead looking small and naked in this ultimate exposure. His flesh had long since decayed away to bone and his clothes were wisps. His warrior's sword was a narrow, rusty tendril of its former might. But one skeletal hand gripped a marvel not corroded at all, but as bright and intricately decorated as the day it was forged. It was a golden cylinder, fat as an arrow quiver and long as a scroll. Its exterior was a riot of mythic figures, of bulls, hawks, fish, scarabs, and creatures so strange and unworldly that I'm at a loss to describe them, so different were they from anything I'd seen before. There were grooves and arabesque scrollwork, stars and geometric shapes, and the gold was so smooth and intricate that my fingertips stroked its sensuousness. The metal seemed warm. It was a life's fortune in weight, and priceless in design.

The Book of Thoth must be inside. But when I pulled to lift it away, the skeleton pulled back!

I was so startled I let go and the cylinder shifted slightly, settling deeper into the bones. Then I realized I'd simply been surprised by the object's weight. I lifted again and the cylinder came free like an anchor stone, supple, slick, and heavy. No lightning flashed. No thunder pealed. Without having realized I'd held it, I let loose pent-up breath. It was simply me in the gloom, holding what men had reportedly sought, fought, and died for over five thousand years. Was this, too, cursed? Of would it be my guidebook to a better world?

And how to open it?

As I studied the cylinder more carefully, recognition dawned. I'd seen some of these symbols before. Not all, but some had been on the ceiling at the Temple of Dendara, and others on the calendar device I'd studied in the hold of *L'Orient* before the French flagship blew up in the Battle of the Nile. There was a circle atop a line, just as on the calendar, and all the others: animals, stars, a pyramid, and Taurus the bull, the zodiacal age in which the Great Pyramid had been built. And not just a pyramid, but a small representation of a pillared temple. The cylinder, I saw, was jointed so that one could twist and align symbols, not unlike the circles of the calendar. So once more I tried what I knew: bull, five-sided star, and the symbol of the summer solstice, just as I'd done on the ship. But that was not enough, so I added pyramid and temple.

Perhaps I was smart. Perhaps I was lucky. Perhaps there were a hundred combinations that would open the cylinder. All I know is there was a click and it divided between pyramid and temple, like a sausage cut in two. And when I pulled the golden halves apart, what I expected was inside: a scroll, the ancient form of the book.

I unrolled it, my fingers trembling in my excitement. The papyrus, if that's what it was, was unlike any I'd seen or felt before. It was slicker, stronger, more tensile, and oddly shimmering, but of a material that seemed neither hide, paper, or metal. What was it? The writing was even stranger. Instead of the pictorial script or hieroglyphics I'd seen in Egypt, this was more abstract. It was angular and faintly geometric, but odder than script I'd ever seen, a riot of shapes, slashes, squiggles, loops, and intricate characters. I had discovered the secret of life, the universe, or immortality, if the lunatics chasing this thing were to be believed. And I couldn't read a word!

Somewhere, Thoth was laughing.

Well, I'd puzzled things out before. And even if the scroll proved indecipherable, its container was enough to pension a king of Prussia. Once more, I was rich.

If I could get out of this mouse hole.

I considered. A swim back against the current would be impossible, and even if I could do it I'd only climb back up to a shaft we had no means of ascending. Yet going downstream would suck me into an underground pipe with no guarantee of air. I'd barely survived such a sluice under the Great Pyramid, and didn't have the nerve to try it again. I'd seen no sign of this temporary river emerging anywhere.

What would Ben Franklin do?

I'd heartily tired of his aphorisms when I had to hear them everyday, but now I missed him. "Wise men don't need advice, fools don't take it." Clever, but hardly a help. "Energy and persistence conquer all things." Persistence how? Tunneling out like a miner? I inspected the chamber more closely. The Templar statues were rigid and unmoving, unlike the turning Madonnas under the Temple Mount. There were no designs on the cave walls, and no cracks, doors, or holes in which to insert the golden cylinder, in hopes it might serve as some kind of key. I tapped the shaft, but heard no hollows. I shouted, but the echo was useless. I beat the walls, just to see if something might give, but nothing did. How the devil did the Templars get in here? The tunnel would be dry between storms. Should I wait? No, more thunder had been growling and a stream like this could run for days. I kicked, wrenched, and howled, but nothing budged. "Never confuse motion with action," Ben had advised.

What else had he said? "Well done is better than well said." Yes, but not exactly useful in my present predicament, as near as I could tell. "All would live long, but none would be old." At the moment, even being old seemed preferable to dying. "In rivers and bad government, the lightest things swim to the top." Well, at least that had river in it. . . .

Swim to the top.

I looked up. If light was filtering down, there had to be a

way out. Impossible to climb without rope, ladder, or footholds. If only I had one of Conte's balloons . . . *swim to the top.*

What Ben did, different than almost all of us, was think first, and *then* act. Why is that so difficult? Yet finally I had an idea, a desperate one, and—just as important—no plausible alternative. I seized the lid of the sarcophagus that was leaning against the stone box and dragged it, screeching, to the edge of the water. Heaving, I got it upright like a door, balancing on one corner, to teeter above the underground river. As well as I could, I aimed at the dark hole into which the river disappeared downstream. And, with a grunt, shoved the lid out into the water! The force of the current rammed the lid against the mouth of the tunnel, sealing the water's outlet.

Instantly, the water began to rise.

It spilled across the sandstone platform, running over the boots of the Templar statues. This had better work! "Sorry, Montbard, or whoever you are." I heaved the acacia wood coffin up to the lip of the stone sarcophagus and tipped out its bones. They rattled into the limestone sarcophagus in a sacrilegious jumble, the skull looking up at me with what I swear was reproach. Well, I was cursed now. I balanced the wood box across the top of the sarcophagus, tucked the golden cylinder in my shirt, and climbed in as if it were a bathtub. The water was rising fast, almost a foot a minute. It crept past the Templar knees, topped the edge of the sarcophagus, and poured inside—and then floated me. I prayed to gods Christian, Jewish, and Egyptian. Glory, hallelujah!

My ark rose. As the well filled and the water deepened, I knew the increasing pressure might blow out the lid I'd jammed below, so I could only hope it would hold long enough. "He that lives upon hope will die fasting." My own advice is to pick and choose your aphorisms as convenient, so I hoped like the very devil. Up we bobbed, foot after precious foot. I realized my action would also back water into the spiral in the chamber behind, toward Ned and Mohammad.

I hoped they could swim.

The dim light grew as we climbed, and stars reflected in the black water. I found a rib or two that hadn't spilled out of my vessel and unceremoniously pitched them overboard, reasoning I wouldn't really care what happened to *my* bones once I didn't have need of them anymore. Up and up until I indeed saw a silvered disk, reflecting light from a slanted shaft. And on that shaft were sandstone stairs! I stood in my wobbling coffin, stretched for the first step, and boosted. Solid rock! Behind me, the water was still rising.

Then there was a thump, the water burped, and with a sucking roar it began falling, my coffin boat spiraling down with it. The lid that plugged the stream had cracked under the pressure and given way. Back out of sight the water swirled, pouring again out its drain, but I'd no time to watch it. I mounted the stairs, realizing this was the same well shaft we'd found in the ruined temple. We hadn't noticed the reflection from our angle, and if we hadn't cast aside the boards I would have had no light down there at all. I emerged between the stone walls, clambered over rubble, and raced back across the causeway to the base of the pillar where we'd first descended. "Ned! Mohammad! Are you alive!"

"By the skin of our teeth, guv'nor! That whole funnel filled with water and we was about to drown like rats! Then the water went down again!"

"How did you get up there, effendi? What's going on?"

"I just wanted to give you boys a bath is all."

"But how did you get out?"

"Ferry boat." I could see their upturned faces like little moons. "Wait. I've got an idea to try to get you up." The base of the fallen column, you will recall, had pivoted out of the way of the star-shaped paving to start the platform descending. Now I pushed it back, there was a click, and sure enough, the platform below began to rise up its star-shaped shaft, Ned and Mohammad hooting in joy like madmen.

Once they were up I got their help to shove the base back onto its rightful place, sealing the entry again. Then Ned hugged me as if I were his mother. "By Davy Jones, you is a wizard, guv'nor! Always you jump clear like a cat! And did you get the treasure?"

"There's no treasure, I'm afraid." Their faces fell. "Believe me, I looked. Just a Templar grave, my friends. Oh, and this."

Like a magician, I pulled out the golden cylinder. They gasped.

"Here, feel its weight." I let them hold it. "There's enough gold here to set all three of us up in decent style."

"But effendi," Mohammad said, "what of your book? Is it here? Is it full of magical secrets?"

"It's in there, all right, and it's the most peculiar thing I've ever seen. I'm sure we'll do the world a favor to keep it away from Silano. Maybe a scholar can make sense of it someday."

"A scholar?"

"I've finally got it, by the labors of Hercules, and I can't read a word."

They looked at me with consternation.

"Let's go get Astiza."

CHAPTER 20

The level exit from the City of Ghosts would take us past Silano's camp, which I dared not do. Instead, as the stars faded and the sky blushed, we first put the well's board back in place in the temple—I didn't want a falling child on my conscience—and then retraced our laborious route up and over the High Place of Sacrifice, pausing only at Ned's insistence to let him uproot a small, wizened pine tree. "At least it's a club," he explained. "A nunnery has more firepower than we has." While we hiked he peeled off branches with his meaty paws like a Samson to shape it. Up, over, and down we went, winded and weary by the time we reached the canyon floor at the ruined Roman theater. A mile or more behind us, I could see a campfire glow where Silano was camped. If Astiza had crept away, how long before her absence was noticed? To the east the sky was glowing. The higher peaks were already lit.

We hurried back up the city's main canyon toward the sinuous entry slit and came again to the façade of the first great temple we had seen, the Khazne. As the others knelt at the small brook to drink, I bounded up its stairs and into its dark interior.

"Astiza?"

Silence. Wasn't this to be our rendezvous?

"Astiza!" It echoed as if mocking me.

Damnation. Had I misread the woman again? Had Silano tumbled to our plan and held her captive? Or was she simply late or lost?

I ran back outside. The sky was brightening from gray to blue, and the tops of the cliffs were beginning to glow. We had to leave before the count realized I'd directed him to an empty hole! But I wasn't going to trade the woman I loved for a scroll I couldn't read. If we left without her, I'd be tortured with regret again. If we stayed too long, my friends might be killed.

"She's not here," I reported worriedly.

"Then we must go," Mohammad said. "Every mile we put between ourselves and those Frankish infidels doubles our chance of escape."

"I feel she's coming."

"We can't wait, guv'nor."

Ned was right. I could hear faint calls echoing down the canyon from Silano's group, though whether of excitement or outrage yet I couldn't tell. "A few minutes more," I insisted.

"Has she bewitched you? She's going to get us all caught, and your book!"

"We can trade away the book if we have to."

"Then what in Lucifer's privy did we come here for?"

Suddenly she appeared from around the bend, hugging the rock to minimize her chance of being seen, face pale, ringlets of dark hair in her eyes, breathless from having run. I rushed back to her.

"What took you so long?"

"They were so excited they couldn't sleep. I was the first to go to bed, and it was agony, waiting all night for them to quiet. Then I had to crawl in the canyon wadi past a sleepy guard, for a hundred yards or more." Her dress was filthy. "I think they've already noticed me gone."

"Can you run?"

"If you don't have it, I don't want to." Her eyes were bright, asking.

"I found it."

She gripped my arms, her grin like a child's waiting for a present. She'd dreamed of the book far longer than I had. I pulled the cylinder out. She sucked in her breath.

"Feel its weight."

Her fingers explored it like a blind man's. "Is it really in here?"

"Yes. But I can't read it."

"For Allah's sake, effendi, we must *go*," Mohammad called.

I ignored him, twisted the cylinder open, and unrolled part of the scroll. Once again I was struck by how alien the characters appeared. She held the book with both hands, bewildered, but reluctant to give it back. "Where was it?"

"Deep in a Templar tomb. I gambled there was a twist to their clues, and they required seekers to use pyramid mathematics to prove their knowledge."

"This will change the world, Ethan."

"For good, I hope. Things can't get much worse, from my perspective."

"Guv'nor!" Ned's shout broke us from our mutual trance. He had his hand to his ear, pointing. It was the echo of a gunshot.

I grabbed the book from her, twisted the cylinder shut, thrust it back in my shirt, and ran to where the sailor was looking. Sunlight was beginning to flood down the face of the temple, turning the cliff and carvings a brilliant rose. But Ned was pointing back the way we had come, toward Silano's camp. A mirror was winking as it tilted.

"They're signaling somebody." He pointed to the sandstone plateau the entry canyon cut in two. "Some devil on top there, ready to roll a rock."

"Silano's men are coming, effendi!"

"So we have to get those tethered horses away from the Arabs at the entrance. Are you up to it, hearties?" It seemed the sort of rallying cry Nelson or Smith might use.

"Home to England!" Ned shouted.

So we ran, swallowed in an instant by the tight entry canyon and absolutely blinded by its many curves. Our footsteps echoed as we charged uphill. Ned's arms pumped with his club. Astiza's hair flew out behind her.

There were shouts far above, and then bangs. We glanced up. A rock the size of a powder keg was ricocheting between the narrow walls as it came down, pieces flying off like grapeshot.

"Faster!" We sprinted, getting beyond the missile before it hit the canyon floor with a crash. Arabic was being shouted on the rim above.

On we jogged. Now there was a roar, and a flash of light. The bastards had rigged the whole canyon! Silano must have guessed we might outfox him and that he'd want to block our escape. An avalanche or rock blasted out by gunpowder sluiced down, and this time I pulled my companions back, all of us ducking under an overhang. The avalanche thundered down, shaking the canyon floor, and then we were running again through its concealing cloud of dust, clambering over the rubble.

Bullets whined, to no effect since we were invisible.

"Hurry! Before they set off another charge!" There was another explosion, and another deluge of rock, but this time it came down behind us where it would slow the pursuing Silano. We were more than halfway through this snake hole, I judged, and if all the Arabs were on top setting off gunpowder, there wouldn't be any left to guard the horses. Once mounted, we'd stampede the remainder and . . .

Panting, we rounded another bend in the canyon and saw our way blocked by a wagon. It was a caged contraption of the type I'd seen to transport slaves, and I guessed it was the one we'd seen shrouded near camp that the horses had shied from. There was a lone Arab by it, sighting at us with a musket.

"I'll handle this," Ned growled, hefting his club.

"Ned, don't give him an easy shot!"

Yet even as the sailor charged, there was a whistle in the air and a stone flicked by our ears with nearly the speed of a bullet, striking the Arab in the forehead just as he fired. The musket went off but the ball went wide. I looked back. Mohammad had removed his turban and used its cloth as a makeshift sling. "As a boy, I had to keep the dogs and jackals from the sheep," he explained.

We raced to tackle the dazed Arab and get past the wagon, Ned in the lead, Astiza next. Yet as the man groggily slid down, he released a lever and the back of the cage dropped with a bang. Something shadowy and huge rose and bunched.

"Ned!" I shouted.

The thing sprang as if launched by a catapult instead of its own hind haunches. I had a terrifying glimpse of brown mane, white teeth, and the intimate pink of its mouth. Astiza screamed. Ned and the lion roared in unison and collided, the club whacking down even as the predator's jaws crunched on his left forearm.

The sailor howled in agony and rage, but I could also hear the crack of the lion's ribs as the pine club smashed into its side, again and again, the velocity so powerful that it shoved the animal onto its side, taking Ned's arm, and him, with it. The two rolled, the human shouting and the cat snarling, a blur of fur and dust. The sailor reared up and the club struck again and again even as he was raked by the claws. His clothes were being shredded, his flesh opened up. I was sickened.

I had out my tomahawk, puny as a teaspoon, but before I could think things through and turn tail like a sensible man, I charged too.

"Ethan!" I heard Astiza only dimly.

Another stone from Mohammad sung by me and struck the cat, making its head whip, and the distraction was timed so exquisitely that I was able to dash into the melee and take a swipe at the lion's head. I connected with the brow of one eye and the cat let go Ned's arm and roared with pain and fury, its tail lashing and its hindquarters churning in the dirt. Now Astiza was charging too, a heavy rock held high over her head, and she heaved like an athlete so it came right down into the beast's bloody vision, crashing against its snout.

Our wild assault bewildered it. Against all expectation, the lion broke and ran, vaulting past the wagon cage that had brought it here. It raced up the canyon and then charged, I now saw, more of Najac's Arabs coming up to contest our way. Screaming at this reversal of their secret weapon, they turned and fled. The bloodied lion took one of them down, pausing to snap the man's neck, and then set off after the others and the freedom of the hills beyond.

The horses were screaming in terror.

We were in shock, hearts racing. My tomahawk's edge was stuck with blood and fur. Astiza was bent over, chest heaving. Astonishingly, all but Ned were unscathed. I could still smell the cat stink, that rank odor of piss, meat, and blood, and my voice was quavering as I knelt beside the giant sailor. His charge into the lion's jaws was the bravest thing I'd ever seen.

"Ned, Ned! We've got to keep going!" I was wheezing. "Silano's still coming, but I think the lion cleared the canyon for us."

"Afraid not, guv'nor." He spoke with difficulty, his jaw clenched. He was bleeding like a man flogged. He glowed with vivid blood. Mohammad was wrapping his turban cloth around the giant's mangled forearm, but it was pointless. It looked like it had been shredded by a machine. "You'll have to go on without me."

"We'll carry you!"

He laughed, or rather gasped, a sneezelike chortle between clenched lips, his eyes wide at the knowledge of his own fate. "Bloody likely."

We reached to lift him anyway, but he shrieked with pain and shoved us aside. "Leave me, we all know I'm not making it back to England!" He groaned, tears staining his cheeks. "He scraped me ribs raw, the leg feels like it's sprained or broken, and I weigh more than King George and his tub. Run, run like the wind, so it's worthwhile." His knuckles were white where he grasped the club.

"Ned, I'll be damned if I leave you! Not after all this!"

"And you'll be dead if you don't, and your treasure book in the hands of that mad count and his lunatic bullyboy. By

Lucifer, make my life mean something by *living*! I can crawl back to that rubble heap and catch 'em when they're coming across."

"They'll shoot you down!"

"It will be a mercy, guv'nor. It will be a mercy." He grimaced. "Had a feeling I wouldn't see England if I went with you. But you're a damned interesting companion, Ethan Gage. More than just a Yankee card sharp, you are."

Why do our worst enemies sometimes become our best friends? "Ned . . ."

"Run, damn your eyes! Run, and if you find me mums, give her a bit of that gold." And, shaking us off, he rose doggedly, first to his knees and then his feet, weaving, and began staggering back the way we came, his side a sheet of blood. "Christ, I'm thirsty."

I was transfixed, but Mohammad hauled at me. "Effendi, we must go. Now!"

So we ran. I'm not proud of it, but if we stayed to fight Silano's armed Frenchmen we'd lose for sure, and for what? So we hurtled past the Arab slumped at the wagon, leapt the one chewed by the lion, and on and on up the sloping canyon, our chests heaving, half expecting the maddened cat to leap out at us at every turn. But the lion was gone. As we came to the mouth of the canyon we heard the echo of shouts and then shots behind. There was screaming, a roaring scream a big man might make when subjected to unbearable pain. Ned was still buying us time, but with agony.

The horses were tethered where we'd left them the day before, but they were stamping with shrill neighs, eyes rolling. We saddled the three best, seized the line rope of the others, and began galloping back the way we'd come. There was more gunfire, but we were well out of range.

As we climbed to the highland plateau we looked back. Silano's group had emerged from the canyon and were following in dogged pursuit, but they were on foot. The gap was growing. We couldn't handle the extra horses, so except for three remounts we let the other horses go. It would take our pursuers time to recapture them.

Then, weeping and utterly drained, we set off north for Acre.

¤   ¤   ¤

At sunset we reached the Crusader castle where we'd camped before. I suppose we should have ridden farther, but after losing a night's sleep retrieving the book and fleeing through the canyons, Mohammad and I were reeling in our saddles. Astiza was little better. I'm a gambler, and I gambled Silano and Najac wouldn't retrieve their horses anytime soon. So we stopped, the castle stones briefly orange as the sun sank, and ate meager rations of bread and dates we found in the saddlebags. We dared not light a fire.

"You two sleep first," Mohammad said. "I'll keep watch. Even if the French and Arabs are stranded on foot, there are still bandits around here."

"You're as exhausted as us, Mohammad."

"Which is why you must relieve me in a few hours. That corner has grass for a bed and the stone will still be warm from the sun. I'll be up in the broken tower."

He disappeared, still my guide and guardian.

"He's leaving us alone on purpose," Astiza said.

"Yes."

"Come. I'm shivering."

The grass was still green and soft this time of year. A lizard skittered away into its hole when evening pulled down its shadow. We lay together in the wedge of warm stone, our first opportunity to be truly close since she'd slapped me in front of Silano. Astiza snuggled for warmth and comfort. She *was* shaking, her cheeks wet.

"Always it is so *hard.*"

"Ned wasn't a bad sort. I led him to disaster."

"It was Najac who put the lion there, not you."

And I who took Ned along, and Astiza who carried the ring. I suddenly remembered it and brought it out from her little purse. "You kept this even after saying it was cursed."

"It was all I had of you, Ethan. I meant to offer it back."

"Did the gods have a purpose, letting us find it?"

"I don't know. I don't know." She clung even tighter.

"Maybe it's good luck. After all, we have the book. We're together again."

She looked at me in amazement. "Hunted, unable to read it, a companion dead." She held out her hand. "Give it."

When I did she sat up and hurled it to the far corner of the ruined courtyard. I could hear it clink. A ruby, big enough to set a man for life, was gone. "The book is enough. No more, no more." And then she bent back down, eyes fierce, and kissed me, with electric fire.

Someday, perhaps, we'll have a proper bed, but just as in Egypt we had to seize the time and place given. It was an urgent, fumbling, half-clothed affair, our desire not so much for each other's bodies as for reassuring union against a cold, treacherous, relentless world. We gasped as we coupled, straining like animals, Astiza giving out a small cry, and then we slumped together in almost immediate unconsciousness, our tangle of linen drawn like a shell. I dimly pledged to relieve Mohammad as promised.

He woke us at dawn.

"Mohammad, I'm sorry!" We were struggling with as much decorum as possible to get dressed.

"It's all right, effendi. I fell asleep too, probably minutes after I left you. I checked the horizon. Nobody has come. But we must move again, soon. Who knows when the enemy will recover his horses?"

"Yes, and with the French in control of Palestine, there's only one place we can safely go: Acre. And they know it."

"How will we get through Bonaparte's army?" Astiza asked with spirit, not worry. She looked rejuvenated in the growing light, glowing, her eyes brighter, her hair a glorious tangle. I felt resurrected too. It was good to shed the pharaoh's ring.

"We'll cut toward the coast, find a boat, and sail in," I

said, suddenly confident. I had the book, I had Astiza . . . of course I also had Miriam, a detail I'd neglected to tell Astiza about. Well, first things first.

We mounted, and galloped down the castle hill.

¤ ¤ ¤

We dared not pause a second night. We rode as hard as we could push the horses, retracing our route to Mount Nebo and then descending to the Dead Sea and the Jordan, a plume of dust floating off our hooves as we hurried. The Jerusalem highlands, we assumed, were still swarming with Samaritan guerrillas who might or might not regard us as allies, so we pushed north along the Jordan and back into the Jezreel Valley, giving Kléber's battlefield there a wide berth. Vultures orbited the hill where we'd made our stand. My party was still weaponless, except for my tomahawk. Once we saw a French cavalry patrol and dismounted to hide in an olive grove while they passed by a mile distant. Twice we saw Ottoman horsemen, and hid from them too.

"We'll strike for the coast near Haifa," I told my companions. "It's only lightly garrisoned by the French. If we can steal a boat and reach the British, we'll be safe."

So we rode, parting the high wheat like Moses, the City of Ghosts as unreal as a dream and Ned's bizarre death an incomprehensible nightmare. Astiza and I had regained that easy companionship that comes to couples, and Mohammad was our faithful chaperone and partner. Since our escape, not once had he mentioned money.

We'd all been changed.

So escape seemed near, but as we rode northeast toward the coast hills and Mount Carmel that embraced Haifa, we saw a line of waiting horsemen ahead.

I scaled a pine to peer with my telescope, dread dawning as I focused first on one figure, then another. How could this be?

It was Silano and Najac. They'd not only caught up,

they'd somehow ridden around and put out this picket line to ensnare us.

Maybe we could creep by them.

But no, there were unavoidable open fields as we sprinted north, and with a cry they spotted us. The chase was on! They took care to keep between us and the coast.

"Why aren't they closing?" Astiza asked.

"They're herding us toward Napoleon."

We tried veering toward the Mediterranean that night, but a volley of shots sent us skittering back. Najac's Arabs, I suspected, were expert trackers and they'd guessed where we must go. Now we couldn't shake them. We rode hard, enough to keep them at a distance, but we were helpless without weapons. They didn't press, knowing they had us.

"We can go inland again, effendi, toward Nazareth or the Sea of Galilee," Mohammad said. "We could even seek refuge with the Turkish army at Damascus."

"And lose all we've gained," I said grimly. "We both know the Ottomans would take the cylinder in an instant." I looked back. "Here's our plan, then. We race them to the French lines, as if we're going to surrender to Napoleon. Then we keep going, right through their encampment, and run for the walls of Acre. If Silano or the French follow, they'll come under the guns of the English and Djezzar."

"And then, effendi?"

"We hope our friends don't shoot at us too." And we kicked for the final miles.

CHAPTER 21

We were on the coastal plain as the sun rose, the Mediterranean an enticing silver platter blocked by our enemies. When we galloped, our pursuers, who'd been conserving their own steeds, did too. I'd been looking at them through the glass and recognized some of the horses they'd recaptured. They had new ones as well. Silano must have pushed them brutally. Our rest at the Crusader castle had cost us dearly.

Our only hope was surprise. "Astiza! When we near the camp, hold your white scarf aloft like a truce flag! We have to confuse them!"

She nodded, leaning intently over the neck of her sprinting horse.

Behind us, we heard shots. I looked back. Our pursuers were well out of range, but trying to alert the French sentries that we were to be arrested. I was betting on confusion, helped by the fact that we had a woman.

The last mile passed in a dead run, our horses' foam-flecked, flanks heaving, our heads down as shots continued to pop behind us. The sentries were out, muskets raised, bayonets fixed, but uncertain.

"Now, now! Wave it now!"

Astiza did so, holding up one arm with the scarf trailing behind and straightening enough to give a look at her female torso, the wind flattening her gown against her breasts. The guards lowered their guns.

We thundered past. "Bandits and guerrillas!" I shouted. Najac's bunch looked like ruffians. Now the pickets were tentatively aiming at our pursuers.

"Don't slow!" I shouted to the others. We flashed by the hospital tents and jumped the tongues of wagons. There, was that Monge and the chemist, Berthollet? And was Bonaparte running out of his tent? We crashed through a campfire circle, men scattering and embers flying, and everywhere soldiers were standing from their morning breakfast and exclaiming and pointing. Their muskets were stacked in neat little pyramids, bayonets gleaming. Down the avenue-like corridor between a regiment's tents we pounded, dust swirling. Behind I could hear cries and argument as Silano's party reined up at the lines, pointing furiously.

We just might make it.

A sergeant aimed a pistol, but I swerved and the man was butted aside by the shoulder of my horse, the gun going off harmlessly. A quick-witted Mohammad snatched a tricolor and carried it, as if we were leading a charge on Acre all by ourselves. But no, now a hedge of infantry was forming between us and the city walls, still a mile distant, so we wove along the lines, leaping a dike of sand. Shots began to be fired. They buzzed past like insistent hornets.

Up on Acre's walls, horns were blowing. What would Smith think, when I'd deserted him without a word?

There, a kitchen unit, the men weaponless and preoccupied with cooking. I turned my horse and thundered through it, scattering them. Their numbers gave us cover from other fire. Then across a trench, galloping alongside the old aqueduct toward the city . . .

Then I was flying.

For a moment I didn't understand what had happened, and thought perhaps my horse had been shot or had suddenly burst its heart. I hit soft dirt and skidded, half blinded with dust. But as I rolled I realized Mohammad and Astiza had been thrown too, their horses screaming as the equine legs snapped, and I saw the rope that had been hastily staked to trip us. It snapped through the air, a cook hooting in triumph. Down, with our goal in view!

I got up, hands scraped raw, and ran back to the other two. More shots, balls humming past.

"The aqueduct, effendi! We can use it for cover!"

I nodded, pulling Astiza ruthlessly to keep up. She was wincing, her ankle twisted, but determined.

There was a stack of scaling ladders assembled for the next assault, and Mohammad and I seized one and threw it up against the old Roman engineering work. I pushed Astiza up from behind, rolling her over the top so we could collapse in the channel where water had run. It was a scrap of protection. Bullets pinged off the stone. "Stay low and follow this until we're under the British guns," I said. "Astiza, you go first with the scarf to signal them." The plucky woman had held onto the thing even when her horse went down.

She shoved it at me. "No, it's you they'll recognize. Run and get help. I'll follow as fast as I can."

"I'll stay with her," Mohammad promised.

I looked over the edge of the aqueduct. The entire French camp was boiling. Silano had talked his way in and was pointing. Najac appeared to be loading my rifle.

No time to tarry.

I ran, the channel less than three feet deep, shots whining and pinging. Astiza and Mohammad followed at a pained crouch. Thank Thoth a musket can barely hit the side of a barn! Ahead, more French soldiers in advance trenches were turning to the commotion and raising their own guns.

Then an English cannon boomed from Acre, throwing up a gout of earth, and the French instinctively ducked back into their own trenches. Then another gun, and another. No doubt the defenders had no idea yet who they were shooting to benefit, but had decided that any French enemy must be their friend.

Then there was another bark, a scream, and a ball struck the pillars of the aqueduct. French cannon! The entire structure quaked.

"Hurry," I yelled back at other two. I ran at a duck, waving the scarf like a madman and hoping for a miracle.

More puffs of smoke from a French battery, and more sizzles as balls sailed past, some bouncing over their own trenches. One hit, and the aqueduct shook again, and then again. A ball crashed through the upper rim, spraying me with rock splinters. I blinked and looked back. Astiza was hobbling grimly, Mohammad right behind. Another hundred yards! Cannon banged away on both sides, an entire battle swirling around our little trio.

Then Astiza cried out. I turned. Mohammad has jerked upright, stiff, his mouth round with surprise. His chest bloomed red, and he toppled over. I looked back. Najac was just lowering my rifle.

It was all I could do not to run back and kill the bastard.

"Leave him!" I shouted to Astiza instead. I'd wait for her.

But then the aqueduct between us exploded.

It was a perfect shot from big cannon. The French must have brought up new siege guns to replace the ones we'd captured at sea. The aqueduct heaved, ancient stone exploded in all directions, dust flew, and then there was a yawning gap between piers. Astiza and I were suddenly on opposite sides of a chasm.

"Jump down and I'll pull you up!"

"No, go, go," she shouted. "He won't kill me! I'll buy you time!" She ripped off part of her gown and began limping back, waving it frantically in surrender. The French fire slackened.

I cursed, but I had no means of stopping her. Heartsick, I turned and sprinted for Acre, fully upright now, gambling that speed would make me an elusive target.

If a longrifle were quicker to reload, Najac might have picked me off even then. But it would take him a full minute to get off another shot, and other bullets flew blind. I was beyond the forward French trenches now, to the point where the aqueduct's end crumbled into rubble before reaching the walls of Acre, and even as cannon fire rippled on both sides I swung over its broken lip and dropped to the sand. Dust puffed from my boots.

I heard the thunder of hooves and turned. Najac's Arabs were riding down the length of the aqueduct for me, I saw, bent over their steeds and heedless of English fire.

I sprinted for the moat. It was fifty yards away, the strategic tower looming like a monolith, soldiers on Acre's ramparts pointing at me. It would be a near-run thing. Legs pumping, I ran as I'd never run before, hearing the pursuing horsemen closing the distance. Now men up and down the Acre wall were firing over my head, and I heard horses neighing and crashing as some went down.

At the moat's end I slid over its edge like a Maine otter on a snow bank, tumbling to the dry bottom. The stench was nauseating. There were rotting bodies, broken ladders, and the abandoned weapons that make up the detritus of war. The breach in the tower had been sealed and there was no way up the wall. Men were peering down at me, but none seemed to realize yet who I was. No rope was offered. Not knowing what else to do, I ran down the moat's dusty course toward where it joined the Mediterranean. I could see the masts of British ships, and guns continued to go off above my head. Hadn't Smith said they were building a reservoir of seawater at the moat's head?

New shouts! I looked back. The damned Arab daredevils had spurred some of their horses down into the moat with me and now they were galloping along, heedless of the soldiers overhead trying to shoot them, determined to take me. Silano clearly knew I had the book! Ahead was the ramp over the moat by the Land Gate, and a black, moist seawall of the new reservoir beyond it. Trapped!

And then there was another explosion, straight ahead. A roar, pieces flying, and the black wall dissolved in front of me. The blast knocked me backward, and I stared stupefied as a wall of green seawater turned to foam and began rushing down the moat at me and my pursuers. I got to my knees just as the flood hit. It knocked me back the way I'd come, carrying me like a leaf in a gutter.

I was in a tumble of foam, unable to get proper breath, unsure what was up and down. I tumbled. The water swept me into a tangle with my pursuers and something big struck me, a horse I guessed, fortuitously knocking me toward air. We were being washed down the moat back toward the central tower, all of us tangled with half-decayed corpses and the flotsam of siege debris. I thrashed, coughing.

And then I saw my chain! Or *a* chain, at any extent, drooping down the tower wall like a garland, and when we swept by I grabbed it.

It plucked me out of the water like a well bucket and began dragging me up the rough tower walls, scraping like sandpaper.

"Hang on, Gage. You're almost home!"

It was Jericho.

Now bullets began banging off the wall around me and I realized I was a hanging target for the entire French army. One lucky shot and I'd fall off.

I tucked into a ball. If I could have shriveled any smaller I'd have disappeared.

Cannon boomed, and a ball that seemed big as a house crashed into the masonry a few yards from me, dissolving to shrapnel. The entire tower shuddered and I swung like a bead on a string. Grimly, I held on. Then another ball, and another. Each time the entire tower shook and the chain swayed, me dangling. Was this ever going to end?

I looked down. The flow of water was slowing but the Arab horsemen were gone, washed to who knows where. Wreckage dotted the water's surface. A man floated belly up, like a fish.

"Heave!" Jericho cried.

And then strong hands were grabbing me and I was dragged, wheezing, over the crenellation and onto the Acre battlements, half drowned, scraped, burned, cut, bruised, heartsick at the love and companions I had lost, and yet miraculously unpunctured. I had the lives, and bedraggled look, of an alley cat.

I sprawled, chest heaving, unable to stand. People clustered around: Jericho, Djezzar, Smith, Phelipeaux.

"Bloody hell, Ethan," Smith said in greeting. "Whose side are you on now?"

But I looked beyond them to the one who had instinctively caught my eye, hair golden, eyes wide and stunned, dress smeared with smoke and powder.

"Hello, Miriam," I croaked.

And then the French guns really started up.

¤   ¤   ¤

In my experience, it's when you need to collect thoughts most carefully that there are the greatest distractions. In this case it was a hundred French artillery pieces, venting frustration at my survival. I stood and looked out shakily. There was a lot of activity in Napoleon's encampments, units forming and moving to the trenches. I had, it seemed, something Bonaparte wanted back. Badly.

The wall was trembling under our feet.

Miriam was looking at me with an expression that was a cross between shock and relief, with a rising tide of indignation, a tributary of confusion, a reservoir of compassion, and more than a pitcher of suspicion. "You left with no word?" she finally managed.

It sounded worse the way she put it. "It was difficult to explain why."

"What was the Christian running from?" Djezzar wanted to know.

"It appears to be the entire French army," Phelipeaux observed mildly. "Monsieur Gage, they do not appear to like you very much. And we were thinking of shooting you as well, for desertion and treachery. Do you have any friends at all?"

"It's that woman, isn't it?" Miriam had developed a way of getting to the point. "She's alive, and you went to her."

I looked back. Was Astiza alive? I'd just seen my Muslim friend killed by my own gun, and Astiza turn back toward that villain Silano. "I had to get something before Napoleon did," I told them.

"And did you?" Smith asked.

I pointed at the massing troops. "He thinks so, and he's coming to get it." Realizing an attack might be imminent, our garrison's leaders began shouting orders, bugles sounding over the din of cannon.

I addressed Miriam. "The French sent me a sign that she might be alive. I had to find out, but I didn't know what to say to you—not after our night together. And she *was* alive. We were coming here together, to explain, but she's been recaptured, I think."

"Did I mean *anything* to you? At all?"

"Of course! I fell in love with you! It's just . . ."

"Just what?"

"I never fell out of love with her."

"Damn you."

It was the first profanity I'd ever heard Miriam use, and it shocked me more than a tirade of abuse from someone like Djezzar. I was searching for a way to explain, making clear that higher causes were at stake, but each time I started a sentence it sounded hollow and self-serving, even to me. Emotion had carried us away that night after the defense of the tower, but then fate and a ruby ring had drawn me off in a way I didn't anticipate. Where was the wrong? Moreover, I had a golden cylinder of incalculable value tucked in my shirt. But none of this was easy to put when the French army was coming.

"Miriam, it was always about more than just us. You know that."

"No. Decisions hurt people. It's as simple as that."

"Well, I've lost Astiza again."

"And me too."

But I could win her back, couldn't I? Yes, men are dogs, but women take a certain feline satisfaction in flogging us with words and tears. There is love and cruelty on both sides, is there not? So I'd take her scorn and fight the battle and then, if we survived, plot a strategy to paper over the past and get her back.

"They're coming!"

Grateful to have to face only Napoleon's divisions instead of Miriam's hurt, I climbed with the others to the top of the great tower. The plain had come alive. Every trench was a caterpillar of hurrying men, their advance fogged by the gun smoke of the furious cannonade. Other troops were dragging lighter field pieces forward to engage if a breach was effected. Ladders rocked as grenadiers crossed the uneven ground, and galloping teams hauled fresh cannonballs and powder to the batteries. A group of men in Arab robes had clustered near the half-destroyed aqueduct.

I snapped open my glass. They were the survivors of Najac's gang, by the look of it. I didn't see Silano or Astiza.

Smith hauled on my shoulder and pointed. "What the devil is that?"

I swung my glass. A horizontal log was trundling toward us, a massive cedar jutting from a carriage bed with six sets of wheels. Soldiers pushed from the sides and behind. Its tip was swollen, like a gigantic phallus, and coated, I guessed, with some kind of armor. What the devil indeed? It looked like a medieval battering ram. Surely Bonaparte didn't think he could start knocking against our ramparts with weapons centuries out of date. Yet the device's pushers were trotting forward confidently.

Had Napoleon gone mad?

It reminded me of the kind of makeshift contraption that might have delighted Ben Franklin, or my American colleague Robert Fulton, who prowled Paris with dotty ideas for things he called steamboats and submarines. And who else did I know who was an inveterate tinkerer? Nicolas-Jacques Conte, of course, the man whose balloon Astiza and I had stolen in Cairo. Monge had said he'd invented some kind of sturdy wagon to get heavy guns to Acre. This trundling log had all the markings of his makeshift ingenuity. But a battering ram? It seemed so backward for a modernist like Conte. Unless . . .

"It's a bomb!" I suddenly cried. "Shoot at its head, shoot at the head!"

The land torpedo had reached a slight downward incline leading to the moat and was beginning to accelerate.

"What?" Phelipeaux asked.

"There are explosives at the end of the log! We've got to set them off!" I grabbed a musket and fired, but if I hit the contraption at all my bullet bounced harmlessly off the metal sheathing at its tip. Other shots were fired, but our soldiers and sailors were still aiming for the men pushing alongside the wheels. One or two were hit, but the monster simply ran over them as they fell, the torpedo gathering speed.

"Hit it with a cannon!"

"It's too late, Gage," Smith said calmly. "We can't depress the guns far enough."

So I grabbed Miriam, brushing by her astonished brother, and pulled her to the rear of the tower before she could protest.

"Get back in case it works!"

Smith, too, was backing away, and Djezzar had already left to strut along the walls and cow his men. But Phelipeaux lingered, gamely trying to slow the rush of Conte's contraption with a well-aimed pistol shot. It was madness.

Then the rolling ram reached the lip of the moat and flew straight across, its snout crashing against the base of the tower.

The soldiers who'd been pushing ran, one pausing long enough to yank a lanyard. A fuse flared.

A few seconds, and then the device exploded with a roar so cacophonous that it blotted out my hearing. The air erupted with smoke and flame, and chunks of stone flew higher than the top of our tower, rolling lazily.

The edifice had shuddered under previous attacks, but this time it swayed like a drunk on Drury Lane. Miriam and I fell, me grabbing her in my arms. Sir Sidney held on to the tower's rear crenellations. And the front of the edifice dissolved before my eyes, sheering off and slipping into a hellish abyss. Phelipeaux and Jericho fell with it.

"Brother!" Miriam screamed, or at least that's the sound I interpreted her mouth making. All I could hear was ringing.

She ran for the lip until I tackled her.

Crawling over her squirming body, on a platform that was now half gone and dangerously leaning, I looked down into wreckage that was boiling smoke like the throat of a volcano. The front third of this strongest tower had simply peeled away, the rest of it exposed like a hollow tree and stitched together by half-destroyed floors. It was as if our clothes had been ripped away, leaving us naked. Bodies were entwined with stone in the rubble below, the moat filled to the brim with wreckage. A new sound impinged on my abused ears, and I realized that thousands of men were cheering, their roar just detectable in my addled state. The French were charging for the breach they had made.

Najac, I bet, would be with them, looking for me.

Smith had recovered his balance and had his saber out. He was shouting something the ringing in my ears made inaudible, but I surmised he was calling men to the breach below. I wriggled backward and hauled Miriam with me. "The rest of it may come down!" I shouted.

"What?"

"We have to get off this tower!"

She couldn't hear either. She nodded, turned toward the attacking French, and before I could stop her leaped off the edge I'd just crawled back from. I lunged, trying to grab her, and slid once more to the brink. She'd dropped like a cat to beams jutting from the tower floor below, and was climbing down the edges of the collapse toward Jericho. Swearing soundlessly to myself, I started to follow, certain the entire edifice would go over at any moment and bury us in a rock grave. Meanwhile bullets were bouncing like fleas in a jar, cannonballs were screaming in both directions, and ladders were reaching up like claws.

Smith and a contingent of British marines had half galloped, half bounded down the partially wrecked stairs behind us, and got to the breach when we did. They collided with French troops surging across the rubble in the plugged moat, and there was a blast of musket fire from both sides, men screaming. Then they were on each other with bayonet, cutlass, and musket butt. The French division commander

Louis Bon went down, fatally shot. The aide-de-camp Croisier, humiliated by Napoleon when he failed to catch some skirmishers the year before, hurled himself into the fray. Miriam dropped into this hell shouting frantically for Jericho. So there I dropped too, dazed, nearly weaponless, black from powder smoke, face-to-face with the entire French army.

They looked ten feet tall in their high hats and crossed belts, throwing themselves at us with the fury and frustration that comes from weeks of fruitless siege work. Here was the chance to finish things, as they had at Jaffa! They were roaring like surf in a storm, stumbling forward over carnage, the end of the shattered cedar log splayed outward like an opened flower. Yet even as they pressed they came under a deluge of iron, rock, and bomblets hurled by Djezzar's Ottomans above, which dropped them like wheat. If the French were determined, we were desperate. If they punched through the tower Acre was lost and all of us would certainly be dead. Royal Marines ran at them screaming, shooting, and chopping, the red and blue a mosaic of struggling color.

It was the most ferocious fight I'd been in, as hand-to-hand as Greek and Trojan, no quarter asked or given. Men grunted and swore as they stabbed, choked, gouged, and kicked. They surged and struggled like bulls. Croisier sank in the melee, shot and stabbed in a dozen places. We could see nothing of the wider fight, just this scrim on a hillock of rubble with the tower about to come down on top of us. I saw Phelipeaux, half buried, his back likely broken, somehow drag out a pistol from beneath himself and fire into his revolutionary enemies. A half-dozen bayonets entered him in reply.

Jericho had not just survived the fall, but dragged himself clear of the wreckage. His clothes were half burnt and blown off and his skin was gray with stone dust, but he'd found an iron bar, slightly bent, and strode into the oncoming French like Samson. Men backed from his maniacal energy as he whirled the staff. A fusilier came up behind with aimed musket, but Miriam had somewhere found an officer's pistol which she held with two hands and fired point-blank. Half the fusilier's head was blown away. A grenadier was coming from the other direction. I remembered my tomahawk and threw it, watching it spin before burying in the attacker's neck. He dropped like a cut tree and I pulled it back out. Then both Miriam and I managed to get hold of Jericho's arms and drag him backward a pace or two, out of the reach of the bayonets he seemed desperate to impale himself on. As we did so, fresh troops from Djezzar surged past to engage the French. A hedgerow of bodies was building. Smith, hatless, head bloodied, was slashing with his saber like a man possessed. Bullets whined, pinged, or hit with a thunk when they found flesh, and someone new would grunt and go down.

My hearing was back, dimly, and I shouted to Jericho and Miriam, "We have to get back behind our lines! We can help more from on high!"

But then something hummed past my ear, as close as a warning hornet, and Jericho took a bullet in his shoulder and spun like a top.

I turned and saw my nemesis. Najac was cursing, my own rifle planted butt first on the rubble as he began to reload, his bullyboys hanging back from the real fight but popping away over the heads of the struggling grenadiers. That shot was meant for me! They'd come for my corpse, all right—because they knew what was likely tucked in my shirt. And so I was seized with my own combat madness, an anger and awful thirst for vengeance that made me feel like my muscles were swelling, my veins engorged, and my eyes suddenly capable of supernatural detail. I'd seen the flash of red on the bastard's finger. He was wearing Astiza's ruby ring!

I knew in an instant what had happened. Mohammad had been unable to resist the temptation of the cursed jewel Astiza had flung away in the Crusader court. When we were sleeping he had pocketed it, ending his periodic demands for money. And so it had been he, not I, who'd been slain by Najac's longrifle shot as we fled along the aqueduct. The French brigand had checked to make sure the

Muslim was dead and then seized the stone for his own, not knowing its history. It was a confession of murder. So I picked up Jericho's iron bar and started for him, counting the seconds. It would take him a full minute to load the American long rifle, and ten seconds had already passed. I had to fight through a thicket of French to be on him.

The bar sang as I wielded it in a great arc, as possessed as a Templar for Christ. This was for Mohammad and Ned! I felt invulnerable to bullets, ignorant of fear. Time slowed, noise paled, vision narrowed. All I saw was Najac, hands trembling as he shook out a measure of powder into the rifle barrel.

Twenty seconds.

My bar swung into that thorn field of bayonets like a sickle clearing a trail. Metal rang as I batted it aside. Infantrymen sheered away from my madness.

Thirty seconds. The rifle ball was wrapped in its wadding and nervously fed into the muzzle opening with the short ramrod.

Najac's French and Arabs were screaming and firing, but I felt nothing but wind. I could see the ripples in the smoky air as the bullets sped, the glint of frantic eyes, the white of bared teeth, the blood spraying from somewhere across a young officer's face. The bar hit the ribs of a towering grenadier and he folded sideways.

Forty seconds. The stubborn ball was being rammed down.

I leapt across dead and dying men, using their bodies like rocks in a stream, my balance a spider's. Round me in a circle my bar sung, men scrambling as they had from Jericho, Smith running a chasseur through with his saber, one Royal Marine dying and two more sticking their prey with bayonets. The sky continued to rain debris from the walls above, and I saw blossoms of explosions behind Najac as grenades and shells went off. Even as I pressed forward, Ottoman and English reinforcements were surging behind me, clotting the breech with their numbers and blood. A tricolor wavered and went down, then rose again, swaying back and forth.

Fifty seconds. Najac didn't even take time to remove the ramrod but was fumbling to prime the pan with gunpowder and pull back the lock. There was fear in his eyes, fear and desperation, but hatred too. I was almost on him when one of his brigands rose before me, hands raised above his head with a scimitar, face distorted by howling, until my bar took him on the side of his skull and exploded it, bits of gore spraying in all directions. I could taste him in my teeth.

And now as I cocked my arm for a final swing, Najac's eyes wide with terror, there was a flash in the pan and a roar, a blast of heat and smoke, and my own rifle, ramrod still in it, fired straight at my breast.

I sat down hard, knocked backward. But before I could die, I swung low and my bar hit the thief in his ankles, shattering them. He went down too, troops surging over us, and realizing I still wasn't dead I crawled forward, wheezing, and seized him by the throat, cutting off his shrieks of pain. I squeezed so hard that the tendons in my own neck swelled with the effort.

His look was hopeless hatred. His arms thrashed, looking for a weapon. His tongue bulged out obscenely.

This is for Ned, and Mohammad, and Jericho, and all the other fine men you've cut down in your miserable, roach-scuttle of a life, I thought. And so I squeezed, as he turned purple, my blood dripping onto my squirming victim. I could see the ramrod sticking out from my chest. What was going on?

Then I felt his hands on my waist and a tug as he grabbed my tomahawk. Having failed to finish me with my own rifle, he wanted to stave in my temple with my own hatchet!

Hardly thinking, I leaned forward so the ramrod he'd fired was against his own chest and heart. Its tip was shattered and sharp as a knitting needle, and finally I realized what must have happened. When he'd fired, the arrow-like projectile had hit me all right, but exactly where the cylinder holding the Book of Thoth was tucked into my shirt. Its blunt head had stuck in the soft gold, knocking me backward but not breaking my skin. Now, as he worked my tomahawk free and cocked his arm to strike, I leaned into him so I was pushing the ramrod with the cylinder, straight against his chest. The effort hurt like hell but it cracked the devil's breastbone and then slid easily as a fork into cake. Najac's eyes widened as we embraced, and I pierced his heart.

Blood pumped up out of him as if from a well, a widening pool, and hissing like the viper he was, he died, my name a red bubble on his lips.

Cheering, but in English this time. I looked up. The French assault was breaking.

I jerked the ramrod out, swayed upward to my knees, and at long last reclaimed my custom rifle. This was the worst charnel yet, a ghastly tangle of limbs and torsos of men who'd died grappling with each other. There were hundreds of bodies in the breach, and scores more in the soggy moat in either direction, assault ladders shattered and the walls of Acre dented and cracked. But the French were retreating. The Turks were cheering too, their cannon barking to bid the French good-bye.

Smith's and Djezzar's men didn't dare pursue. They crouched, stunned by their own success, and then hastily reloaded in case the enemy came again. Sergeants began ordering a crude barricade at the tower's base.

Smith himself spied me and strode over, the bodies compressing slightly as he walked across them. "Gage! That was the nearest-run thing I ever did see! My God, the tower! Looks like she could come down in an instant!"

"Bonaparte must have thought the same, Sir Sidney," I said. I was gasping, trembling at every muscle, more exhausted than I'd ever been. Emotion had wrung me dry. I hadn't caught breath in a century. I hadn't slept in a thousand years.

"He'll see it rebuilt and braced stronger than ever by the next dawn, if British engineering has anything to do with it," the naval captain said fiercely. "By God, we've bested him, Ethan, we've bested him! He'll throw every cannonball he has at us now, but he won't come again after this thrashing. His men won't allow it. They'll balk."

How could he be so sure? And yet he was about to be proved right.

Smith nodded. "Where's Phelipeaux? I saw him lead the charge right into them. By God, that's royalist courage!"

I shook my head. "I'm afraid they've done for him, Sidney."

We picked our way over. Two bodies lay across Phelipeaux's so we dragged them aside. And miracle of miracles, the royalist was still breathing, even though I'd seen half a dozen bayonets pierce him like a haunch of beef. Smith pulled him up slightly, resting the dying man's head in his lap. "Edmond, we've turned them back!" he said. "The Corsican is finished!"

"What . . . retreated?" Though his eyes were open, he was blind.

"He's scowling at us right now from that high hill of his, the best of his troops gutted or sent running. Your name will know glory, man, because Boney won't take Acre. The republican tyrant has been stopped, and political generals like him don't last past a bad defeat." He looked at me, eyes gleaming. "Mark my word, Gage. The world will hear little of Napoleon Bonaparte, ever, ever again."

CHAPTER 22

And then Colonel Phelipeaux died. Did he really comprehend his victory as life leaked out his body? I don't know. But maybe he had a glimmer that it hadn't been in vain, and that in the violent insanity of this worst day of the siege, something fundamental had been won.

I went back to Najac's body, stooped, and took my rifle, my tomahawk, and the ring. Then I walked back through the rubble of the half-ruined tower. Shouting engineers were already beginning to lever aside stones, ready beams, and mix mortar. The tower would be patched yet again.

I went in search of Jericho and Miriam.

Fortunately, I didn't see the ironmonger's body among the long rows of defenders being laid mournfully to temporary rest in the pasha's gardens. I glanced up. The birds had disappeared in the cacophony, but I could see the veiled eyes of Djezzar's harem women looking down from their grilled windows. Splinters had been knocked from some of the woodwork, leaving yellow gashes in the dark-stained design. The pasha himself was strutting up and down his wall like a rooster, clapping his exhausted men on the shoulder and shouting out at the French. "What, you do not like my hospitality? Then come back and get some more!"

I drank at the mosque fountain and then walked dully through the city, smeared with blood and powder smoke, huddled civilians looking at me warily. My eyes, I supposed, were bright in the blackness of my face, but my stare was a thousand miles away. I walked until I reached the jetty with its lighthouse, the Mediterranean clean after the squalor of battle. I looked back. Cannon were still rumbling, and smoke and dust had created a pall in that direction, backlit to stormy darkness by a declining sun.

How had so much time passed? We'd sprinted for the wall in the morning.

I took out the pharaoh's ring that had meant grief for every person who'd touched it. Do curses really exist? Franklin the rationalist would doubt it. But I knew enough not to finger its ruby as I waded into the cool sea, to my knees, to my waist, the chill seizing my crotch, my chest. I bent and sank underwater, opening my eyes in the green gloom, letting the sea wash out some of the grit. I held my breath as long as I could, making sure I was finally ready to do what must be done. Then I surfaced, shaking the water from my wet, uncut hair, cocked my arm, and threw. It was a red meteor, heading for the cobalt that marked deep water. There was a plop and, simple as that, the ring was gone.

I shivered in relief.

¤   ¤   ¤

I found Miriam in the city hospital, its rooms jammed with the freshly wounded. Sheets were bright red, and pans of water pink. Basins held chunks of amputated flesh. Flies buzzed, feasting, and there were smells not just of blood but of gangrene and lye and the charcoal of braziers where surgical tools were heated before cutting. Periodically, the air would be pierced by screaming.

The building quaked from continuing artillery fire. As Smith had predicted, Napoleon seemed to be throwing everything he had at us in a last outpouring of frustration. Maybe he hoped to simply flatten what he couldn't take. Saws rattled on tables. Dust sifted down from the tile roof into wounded men's eyes.

Miriam was, I saw with relief, attending to a brother who was still alive. Jericho was pale, his hair greasy, his shirt gone, and the upper half of his torso wrapped in stained bandages. But he was alert and energetic enough to give me a skeptical glare as I came up to his pallet.

"Can't anything kill you?"

"I got the man who shot you, Jericho." My tone was dull from emotional overload. "We held the breach. You, me, Miriam, all of us. We held."

"Where in Hades' name did you go when you left the city?"

"It's a long story. That thing we were looking for in Jerusalem? I found it."

They both stared at me. "The treasure?"

"Of sorts." I reached inside my shirt and pulled out the golden cylinder. Sure enough, it was dented and nearly punctured where the ramrod had hit. My chest had a bruise the size of a plate. But both the book's metal sheath and my own body were intact. Their eyes widened at the gleam of metal, which I shielded from other hospital eyes. "It's heavy, Jericho. Heavy enough to build twice the house, and twice the forge, you left in Jerusalem. When the war's over, you're a rich man."

"Me?"

"I'm giving it to you. I have bad luck with treasures. The book inside, however, I intend to keep. Can't read a word, but I'm getting sentimental."

"You're giving me all the gold?"

"You and Miriam."

Now he scowled. "What, you think you can pay me?"

"Pay you?"

"For crashing into our lives and taking not just our home and livelihood but my sister's virtue?"

"It's not payment! My God, she didn't . . ." Wisely, I didn't finish. "Not payment, nor even thanks. Just simple justice. You'd be doing me a favor to take it."

"You seduce her, you take her, you leave without a word, and now you bring this?" He was getting angrier, not calmer. "I spit on your gift!"

Clearly he didn't understand. "Then you spit on the humble apology of your own future brother-in-law."

"What?" they said together. Miriam was looking at me in disbelief.

"I'm ashamed I had to go without explanation and leave both of you wondering these past few weeks," I said. "I know I seemed lower than a snake in a sewer. But I had a chance to finish our quest so I did, keeping this prize from the French who'd misuse it. They'll never get the book now, because even if they break through I can send it out to sea on Smith's ships. I finished what we started, and now I'm back to finish the rest. I want to marry your sister, Jericho. With your permission."

His face was churning with disbelief. "Are you completely mad?"

"I've never been saner in my life." The answer had been right before me, I'd realized. One god or another was showing me the sensible path by snatching Astiza away. We were poison for each other, fire and ice who ended up in peril whenever we got together, and the poor Egyptian woman was better off without me. Certainly my heart couldn't take losing her again. Yet here was gentle Miriam, a good woman who'd learned to blow a man's head off with a pistol but still set an example of a good, quiet life. That's what I'd really found in the Holy Land, not this silly book! So now I'd marry a proper girl, settle down, forget my pain over Astiza, and be done with battles and Bonaparte forever. I nodded to myself.

"But what about Astiza?" Miriam asked in wonder.

"I'm not going to lie to you. I loved her. Still love her. But she's gone, Miriam. I rescued her as I had before, and lost her again as I had before. I don't know why, but it's not meant to be. The last few hours of hell have opened my eyes to a thousand things. One is how much I love *you*, and how wonderful you'll be for me, and how good, I hope, I can be for you. I want to make an honest couple of us, Jericho. I seek your blessing."

He stared at me a long time, his expression inscrutable. Then his face twisted in a strange way.

"Jericho?"

It crinkled, and finally he burst into laughter. He howled, tears streaming down his face, and Miriam began laughing too, looking at me with something disturbingly close to pity.

What was going on?

"My blessing!" He roared. "As if I'd ever give it to *you*!" Then he winced, reminded by the pain of the hole in his shoulder.

"But I've reformed, you see . . ."

"Ethan." Miriam reached out and touched my hand with hers. "Do you think the world stands still while you go on these adventures of yours?"

"Well, no, of course not." I was more and more confused.

Jericho got himself under control, gasping and wheezing. "Gage, you have the timing of a broken chronometer."

"What are you telling me?" I looked from one to the other. "Do I have to wait until the war's over?"

"Ethan," Miriam said with a sigh, "do you remember where you left me when you went to find Astiza?"

"In a house here in Acre."

"In a doctor's house. A physician in this hospital." She opened her eyes, looking past me. "A man who found me in tears, confused and self-hating when he came home to finally snatch a few hours of sleep."

Slowly, I turned. Behind me was the Levantine surgeon, dark, young, handsome, and altogether more reputable-looking, despite his bloodstained hands, than a gambler and wastrel like me. By John Adams, I'd been played the fool once again! When the gypsy Sarylla had given me the Fool tarot card, she'd known what she was about.

"Ethan, meet my new fiancé."

"Doctor Hiram Zawani at your service, Mr. Gage," the man said with that kind of educated accent I've always envied. It makes them sound three times as smart as you, even if they don't have the sense of a dobbin. "Haim Farhi said you're not quite the rascal you seem."

"Doctor Zawani made an honest woman of me, Ethan. I was lying to myself about what I wanted and needed."

"He's the kind of man my sister needs," Jericho said. "No one should know that better than you. And you brought them together! You're a confused, shallow human being, Ethan Gage, but for once you did something right."

They smiled, as I tried to figure out if I'd been complimented or insulted.

"But . . ." I wanted to say she was in love with me, that surely she must have waited, that I had *two* women vying for my attention and my problem was sorting between them. . . .

In half a day, I'd gone from two to none. The ruby and the gold were gone, too.

Well, hang.

And yet it was liberating. I hadn't been to a good brothel since fleeing Paris, and yet here it was, the chance to be a free bachelor again. Humiliating? Yes. But a relief? I was surprised how much so. "It's splendid how these things work out," Smith had said. Lonely? Sometimes. But less responsibility, too.

I'd take ship home, give the book to the Philadelphia Library to scratch their heads over, and get on with my life. Maybe Astor had need of help in the fur trade. And there was a new capital being built in the swamps of Virginia, out of sight of any honest Americans. It sounded like just the kind of future den of opportunism, fraud, and skullduggery for a man of my talents.

"Congratulations," I squeaked.

"I *should* still break you in two," Jericho said. "But given what's happened, I think I'll just let you help us hock this." And he gave Zawani a peek at the gold.

¤   ¤   ¤

One day later the French, having used up much of their ammunition in a final furious bombardment that left their strategic plight unchanged, began to retreat. Bonaparte depended on momentum. If he couldn't surge forward and keep his enemies off-balance, he was hopelessly outnumbered. Acre had stopped him. His only alternative was to return to Egypt and claim victory, citing battles he'd won and ignoring those he'd lost.

I watched them skulk off with my glass. Hundreds of men, the sick and wounded who were unable to walk, were on wagons or slumped on horseback. If left behind they were doomed, so I spotted even Bonaparte walking, leading a horse that carried a bandaged soldier. They set fire to the supplies they couldn't take, great columns of smoke rising into the May air, and blew up the Na'aman and Kishon bridges. The French were so short of adequate animal transport and fodder that two dozen cannon were abandoned. So were crowds of Jews, Christians, and Matuwelli who had sided with the French in hopes of liberation from the Muslims. They were wailing like lost children, because now they could expect only cruel revenge from Djezzar.

The French vindictively began burning farms and villages along the path of their coastal retreat, to slow a pursuit that never came. Our dazed garrison was in no shape to follow. The siege had lasted sixty-two days, from March 19 to May 21. Casualties had been heavy on both sides. The plague that had riddled Napoleon's army had come inside the walls, and the immediate concern was to clear out the dead. It was hot, and Acre reeked.

I moved with dazed weariness. Astiza was gone again, captive or dead. I put the book in a leather satchel and hid it in the quarters I took at the Merchant's Inn, Khan a-Shawarda, but I bet I could have left it in the main market and not had it taken, so useless did its strange writing appear. Slowly, reports filtered back of Napoleon's retreat. He abandoned Jaffa, won at such terrible cost, a week after leaving Acre. The worst French plague cases were given opium and poison to hasten their deaths so they wouldn't fall into the hands of pursuing Samaritans from Nablus. The defeated soldiers staggered into El-Arish in Egypt on June 2, reinforcing its garrison, and then the bulk of the army went on toward Cairo. A thermometer put on the desert sands recorded a temperature of 133 degrees. When they reached the Nile the march stopped, men resting and refitting: Napoleon couldn't afford to present a defeated army. He reentered Cairo on June 14 with captured banners, claiming victory, but the claims were bitter. I learned that the one-legged artillery general Caffarelli had an arm shattered by a Turkish cannonball and died of infection outside Acre, that the physicist Etienne Louis Malus had sickened with plague in Jaffa and had to be evacuated, and that both Monge and his chemist friend Berthollet contracted dysentery and were among the sick evacuated by wagon. Napoleon's adventure was turning into a disaster for everyone I knew.

Smith, meanwhile, was anxious to finish his archenemy off. Turkish reinforcements from Constantinople had not arrived quickly enough to help Acre, but early in July a fleet arrived with nearly twelve thousand Ottoman troops, ready to sail on to Abukir Bay and regain Egypt. The English captain had pledged his own squadron in support of the attack. I had no interest in joining this expedition, which I doubted could defeat the main French army. I still had plans for America. But on July 7 a trade boat delivered to me a missive from Egypt. It was closed with red sealing wax with an image of the beaked god Thoth, and was addressed to me in a feminine hand. My heart beat faster.

When I opened it, however, the script was not by Astiza but in a strong male scrawl. Its message was simple.

I can read it, and she's waiting.
The key is at Rosetta.
Silano.

PART THREE

I arrived back in Egypt on July 14, 1799, one year and two weeks after I'd first landed with Napoleon. This time I was with a Turkish army, not a French one. Smith was enthusiastic about this counteroffensive, proclaiming it might finish Boney off. I couldn't help but notice, however, that he stayed offshore with his squadron. And it is difficult to say who had less confidence in this invasion's ultimate success: me or its aging, white-bearded commander, Mustafa Pasha, who limited his advance to occupying the tiny peninsula that formed one side of Abukir Bay. His troops landed, seized a French redoubt east of the village of Abukir, massacred its three hundred defenders, compelled the surrender of another French outpost at the end of the peninsula, and halted. Where the peninsula's neck joined the mainland Mustafa began erecting three lines of fortifications in anticipation of the inevitable French counterattack. Despite the successful defense of Acre, the Ottomans were still wary of meeting Napoleon in open field. After Bonaparte's ludicrously lopsided victory at the Battle of Mount Tabor, the pashas viewed every initiative on their part as disaster in the

making. So they invaded and dug furiously, hoping the
French would cooperatively expire in front of their trenches.
We could see the first French scouts of Bonaparte's rapidly
assembling blocking force peering at us from the dunes
beyond the peninsula.

Without being invited, I politely suggested to Mustafa
that he strike south and try to link up with the Mameluke
resistance my friend Ashraf had joined, a mobile cavalry
under Murad Bey. The rumor was that Murad had dared
come to the Great Pyramid itself, climbing to the top and
using a mirror to signal his wife kept captive in Cairo. It
was the gesture of a dashing commander, and I expected
these Turks would fare better under Murad's wily command than under cautious Mustafa. But the pasha didn't
trust the arrogant Mamelukes, didn't want to share command, and was terrified of leaving the protection of his
earthworks and gunboats. As Bonaparte had been impatient at Acre, the Ottomans had landed too quickly, with too
little force, in Egypt.

Yet things were in strategic flux. Yes, Napoleon's original grand strategic scheme had unraveled. His fleet had
been destroyed by Admiral Nelson the year before, his advance in Asia been halted at Acre, and Smith has received a
dispatch that the Indian sultan whom Bonaparte hoped ultimately to link up with, Tippoo Sahib, had been killed at the
siege of Seringapatam in India by the English general
Wellesley. Yet even as Mustafa landed, a combined
French-Spanish fleet had sailed into the Mediterranean to
contest British naval superiority. The odds were getting
complex.

I decided my own best gamble was to do my business
with Silano in Rosetta, a port on the mouth of the Nile, as
quickly as possible. Then I'd scuttle back to the Turkish
enclave before their beachhead dissolved and take a boat
going anywhere but here. If I succeeded, Astiza might come
with me. And the book?

Bonaparte and Silano were right. I felt ownership, and
was as curious as ever to hear what its mysterious writing
actually said. Could old Ben himself have resisted? "What

makes resisting temptation so difficult for people," he had written, "is that they don't want to discourage it completely." Somehow I had to get Silano's "key," once more rescue Astiza, and then decide for myself what to do with the secret. The only thing I was certain of is that if the text promised immortality, I wanted nothing to do with it in this world. Life is hard enough without bearing it forever.

While the Turks entrenched in the summer's oppressive heat, their tents a carnival of color, I hired a felucca to take me to the western mouth of the Nile and Rosetta. We'd sailed by the place during my first entry to Egypt the year before, but I didn't recall the town meriting particular attention. Its location gave it some strategic value, but why Silano wanted to meet there was a mystery; its convenience for me would be the last thing on the sorcerer's mind. The likeliest explanation was that his message was a lie and a trap, but there was just enough bait—the woman and a translation—to make me stick my head in the snare.

Accordingly, I had my new captain, Abdul, heave to midway in order to make an important modification to the sail, a thing he accepted as ample evidence of the balminess of all foreigners. I swore him to secrecy with the aid of a few coins. Then we once more passed from the blue sea to the brown tongue of the great African river.

We were soon intercepted by a French patrol boat, but Silano had sent a pass to give me entry. The lieutenant on the *chebek* recognized my name—my adventures and crisscrossing of sides had given me a certain notoriety, apparently—and invited me on board. I said I preferred to stay in my own craft and follow.

He consulted his paper. "I am then ordered, monsieur, to confiscate your baggage until such time as you meet with Count Alessandro Silano. It says this is necessary for the security of the state."

"My baggage is what you see on me, given that my exploits have left me penniless and without allies. Surely you don't wish me to disembark naked?"

"Yet there is a satchel you carry over your shoulder."

"Indeed. And it is heavy, because it is weighted with a

large stone." I held it over the side of the boat. "Should you try to take this meager belonging, Lieutenant, I will drop it into the Nile. Should that happen I can assure that Count Silano will have you court-martialed at best, or put under a particularly uncomfortable ancient spell at worst. So let us proceed. I'm here of my own volition, a lone American in a French colony."

"You have a rifle as well," he objected.

"Which I have no plan to discharge unless somebody tries to take it away. The last man who attempted to do so is dead. Trust me, Silano will approve."

He grumbled and looked at his paper a few times more, but since I was poised at the rail with rifle in one hand and the other propped over the river, confiscation was impractical. So we sailed on, the *chebek* herding us like a mother hen, and docked in Rosetta. It's a palm-shaded, well-watered farming town in the Nile Delta, made of brown mud brick except for the limestone mosque and its single minaret. I left instructions with my felucca captain and set off through the winding lanes toward a still unfinished French fort called Julian, the tricolor flapping above its mud walls and a crowd of curious street urchins following in my wake. These were halted at the gate by sentries with black bicorne hats and enormous mustaches. My notoriety was confirmed when these soldiers recognized me with a clear expression of dislike. The harmless electrician had become something between a nuisance and a threat, and they eyed me like a sorcerer. Tales from Acre must have filtered back here.

"You can't bring that rifle in here."

"Then I won't come. I'm here by invitation, not command."

"We'll hold it for you."

"Alas, you French have a habit of borrowing and not giving back."

"The count will not object," interrupted a feminine voice. And stepping from an alcove was Astiza, dressed modestly in a full-length gown, a scarf pulled over her head and wrapped around her neck so that her lovely but worried face was like a moon. "He's come to consult as a savant instead of as a spy."

Apparently she carried some of Silano's authority. Reluctantly, the soldiers let me through to the courtyard, and the main gate clicked shut behind me. Brick-and-board buildings lined the inner walls of the square, simple fort.

"I told him you'd come," she said quietly. The fierce sun beat down on the parade ground and it, and the scent of her—of flowers and spices—made me dizzy.

"And go, with you."

"Make no mistake, we are both prisoners, Ethan, rifle or not. Once more, we must forge a partnership of convenience with Alessandro." She gave a nod of her head to the walls and I saw more sentries watching us. "We need to learn if there's anything to this legend at all, and then make a plan what to do."

"Did Silano tell you to say that?"

She looked disappointed. "Why can't you believe I love you? I rode with you all the way to Acre, and it was a cannon shot that separated us, not choice. It was fate that brought us both together again. Just have faith a little longer."

"You sound like Napoleon. 'I have made all the calculations. Fate will do the rest.'"

"Bonaparte has his own wisdom."

And with that we came to the headquarters building, a one-story stucco structure with a shed roof of tile and a porch thatched with palm. It was cool and dim inside. As my eyes adjusted from the glare, I saw Silano waiting at a plain table with two officers. The older one I'd known since the French landing at Alexandria. General Jacques de Menou had fought bravely and later, by report, had converted to Islam. He was fascinated with Egyptian culture, but he was not a particularly commanding officer with his pencil moustache, round accountant's face, and balding pate. The other, a handsome captain, I didn't know. On either side of the room were closed doors, with locks.

Silano stood. "Always you are trying to escape me, Monsieur Gage, and always our paths entwine!" He gave a slight, courtly bow. "Surely you recognize destiny by now. Perhaps we're meant to be friends, not enemies?"

"I'd be more persuaded of that if your other friends didn't keep shooting at me."

"Even the best friends quarrel." He gestured. "General de Menou you know?"

"Yes."

"I didn't expect to see you again, *Américain*. How poor Nicolas was angry about his stolen balloon!"

"That came from the shooting part," I told the general.

"And this is Captain Pierre-Francois Bouchard," Silano went on. "He was in charge of construction at the fort here when his men dug up a piece of rubble. Fortunately, Captain Bouchard was quick to recognize its significance. This Rosetta Stone may change the world, I think."

"A stone?"

"Come. Let me show you."

Silano led us to the room on the left, unlocked its door, and ushered us inside. It was dim; the slit window looking out onto the courtyard draped for privacy. The first thing that caught my eye was the wooden coffin of a mummy. Brightly painted and remarkably preserved, it bore paintings that looked like a depiction of a soul's journey through the land of the dead.

"Is there a body inside?"

"Of Omar, our sentry," Menou joked. "He is tireless."

"Sentry?"

"I brought this downriver and told the soldiers we found it at this fort site," Silano said. "Fear surrounds these mummies, and this one is now reputed to haunt Rosetta. It's better than a cobra for keeping the curious out of this room."

I touched the lid. "Amazing how bright the colors are."

"Magic too, perhaps. We can't do the same now, just as we've lost the formula for the leaded glass in the medieval cathedrals. We can't match either beauty." He pointed to some paint pots in one corner of the room. "I'm experimenting. Maybe Omar in there will give me a hint one night."

"And you don't believe in curses?"

"I believe I'm about to control them. With this." Beside the wooden sarcophagus, something bulky, about five feet high and a little less than three feet wide, was shrouded with a tarpaulin. With a dramatic gesture, Silano whisked the cover off. I bent, peering in the dim light. There was writing in different languages. I'm not a linguist, but one block of words looked Greek, and another like writing I'd seen in Egyptian temples. A third script I couldn't identify but the fourth, at the top, just above the temple writing, made my heart beat faster. It was the same curious symbols I'd read on the scroll I'd found in the City of Ghosts. I realized what Silano had meant with his cryptic message. He could compare the Greek words to the secret ones of Thoth and possibly unravel the language!

"What's this text here?" I pointed to the one I didn't recognize.

"Demotic, the Egyptian language that followed the ancient hieroglyphs," Silano said. "My guess is that these are in order of time—the oldest language, that of Thoth, at the top, and the newest, Greek, at the bottom."

"When Alessandro brought me here I recognized what we'd seen on the scroll, Ethan," Astiza said. "See? I was *meant* to be captured again."

"And now you want me to help you decipher it," I summarized.

"We want you to give us the book so *we* can help *you* decipher it," Silano corrected.

"And I get?"

"The same that I offered before." He sighed, as if I were a particularly dim child. "Partnership, power, and immortality if you want it. The secrets of the universe, perhaps. The reason for existence, the face of God, and the world in your palm. Or, nothing, if you prefer not to cooperate."

"But if I don't cooperate, you don't have the book, right?"

I saw Menou make a small gesture. Captain Bouchard maneuvered behind me, and I noticed he had a pistol in his belt.

"On the contrary, monsieur," Silano said. He nodded and my satchel was yanked from my shoulder and roughly opened.

"*Merde,*" Bouchard said. He turned my leather bag upside down and a wooden rolling pin fell out, making a dent in the building's packed-earth floor. The general and the captain looked puzzled and Astiza stifled a laugh. Silano's look grew dark.

"You didn't really think I'd deliver it like Franklin's post, did you?"

"Search him!"

But there was no scroll. They even peered in my rifle barrel, as if I could have somehow stuffed it down there. They pried open the soles of my boots, checked the bottom of my feet, and grabbed at places that left me indignant.

"Are you going to look in my ears, too?"

"Where is it?" Silano's frustration was plain.

"Hidden, until we form a true partnership. If we Americans and French represent liberty and reason, then the translation is for all mankind, not the Egyptian Rite of renegade Freemasons. Or ambitious generals like Napoleon Bonaparte. I want it given to the institute of savants in Cairo for dissemination to the world. The British Academy, as well. And I want Astiza once and for all. I want you to give her up, Silano, to trade her for the book, no matter how much power you have over us. And I want her to promise to go with me, wherever I choose to go. Now and forever. I want Bonaparte to know we're all here, working together for him, so that none of us conveniently disappear. And I want the bloodshed to end. We've both lost friends. Promise me all that, and I'll fetch your book. We'll both have our dreams."

"Fetch it from where? Acre?"

"You can have it within the hour."

He bit his lip. "I've already had your felucca and wretched captain searched. They even hauled the boat to check its keel. Nothing!" Again, some of that impatient frustration I'd glimpsed the year before in Egypt broke through his urbane mask.

I smiled. "Such trust, Count Silano."

He turned to Astiza. "Do you agree with his condition for you?"

It was the second proposal I'd made in a month, I realized. Neither of them had been terribly romantic, but still . . . I must be getting old to want commitment from a woman, which meant commitment from me. "Yes," she said. She was looking at me with hope. I felt happy and panicked at the same time.

"Then damn it, Gage, where is it?"

"Do *you* agree to my conditions?"

"Yes, yes." He waved his hand.

"On your honor as a nobleman and a savant? These soldiers are your witness."

"On my word, to an American with more treacheries than I can count. The important thing is to break the linguistic code and translate the book. We'll enlighten the entire world! But not if you don't have it."

"It's on the boat."

"Impossible," Bouchard said. "My men searched every inch."

"But they didn't raise sail."

I led them out of the fort and down to the Nile. The sun was drawing low, warm light spilling through date palms that waved in the hot breeze. The green water looked soupy, egrets standing in its shallows. My boat captain had crawled into one corner of his beached craft, looking as if he expected execution any second. I couldn't blame him. I have a way of bringing bad luck to companions.

I snapped an order and the sail, bordered top and bottom by wooden booms, was cranked up the mast until it filled and turned in the wind.

"There. Do you see it?"

They looked close. Faint, in the horizontal light, was a strip from the bottom to the highest point of the sail with faint, odd characters.

"He sewed the thing into the cotton," Menou said with a certain admiration.

"It was on display all the way upriver," I announced. "Not one person noticed."

CHAPTER 24

We had two tasks. One was to use the Rosetta Stone to translate the symbols of Thoth's scroll into French. The second, even more time-consuming job, was to then actually translate the book and make sense of it.

Now that he had his hands on a scroll he'd been seeking for years, Silano exhibited some of that genteel charm with which he'd seduced the ladies in Paris. Lines disappeared from his face, his limp became less pained, and he was eagerly animated as he began charting symbols and trying to find connections. He had charm, and I began to understand what Astiza had seen in him. There was a courtly intellectual energy that was seductive. Even better, he seemed content to concede Astiza to me, even though I caught him looking at her longingly at times. She too seemed accepting of our treaty. What an odd triumvirate of researchers we'd become! I didn't forget the death of my friends at Silano's hands, but I admired his diligence. The count had brought trunks of musty books, and each educated guess would send one of us to another volume to check the plausibility of whether this grammar might work or that reference made sense. The dim prehistory when this book was supposedly written was slowly being illuminated.

Laboriously, we puzzled out chapter titles on the scroll.

"On the diaphanous nature of reality and bending it to one's will," read one. The disturbing promise excited me, despite myself.

"On Freedom and Fate," read another. Well, there was a question.

"On Teaming Mind, Body, and Soul."

"On Summoning Manna from Heaven." Had Moses read that? I didn't see any sections on parting the sea.

"On Life Everlasting, in Its Various Forms." Why hadn't that worked for him?

"On Underworld and Overworld." Hell and heaven?

"On Bending Men's Minds to One's Will." Oh, Bonaparte would like that one.

"On Eliminating Ills and Curing Pain."

"On Winning the Heart of a Lover." Now that could be sold faster than Ben's Almanac.

"On the Forty-Two Sacred Scrolls."

That last was enough to make me groan. This book, apparently, was just the first of forty-one other volumes, which my Egyptian mentor Enoch had claimed were but a sampling of 36,535 scrolls—one hundred for each day of the year—scattered around the earth. They were to be found only by the worthy when the time was right. Thank the saints that I wasn't particularly worthy! Just getting this first one had nearly killed me. Silano, however, was dreaming of new quests.

"This is astonishing! This book I'm guessing is a summary, a list of topics and first principles, with knowledge and mystery deepening with each volume. Can you imagine having them all?"

"The pharaohs thought even this one needed to be sealed away," I reminded.

"The pharaohs were primitive men who didn't have

modern science or alchemy. All human progress comes from knowledge, Gage. From fire and the wheel, our world is a culmination of a million ideas, shared and recorded. What we have here is a thousand years of scientific advancement, left by someone, a god or wizard or some exalted being from who knows where—Atlantis, or the moon—who started civilization and now can restore it. For five millennia the greatest library was lost, and now it's found again. This scroll will lead us to others. And then the wisest men, like me, can rule and put things in order. Unlike kings and tyrants, I will decree with perfect knowledge!"

No one was going to accuse Silano of humility. Stripped of his fortune by the revolution, forced to crawl back into favor by courting democrats who'd been mere lawyers and pamphleteers, the count was a man driven by frustration. Sorcery and the occult would win back what republicanism had taken away.

While we had some chapter headings, the actual text was proving tedious to piece together. Its construction was utterly foreign, and simply identifying words did not make the meaning clear.

"This is the work of whole universities," I told the count. "We'll spend the rest of our lives trying to puzzle this out here in Rosetta. Let's give it to the National Institute or the British Academy."

"Are you a complete fool, Gage? Letting a common savant have at this is like storing gunpowder in a candle shop. I thought you were the one who feared its misuse? I've studied the traditions around these words for decades. Astiza and I have labored long and hard to be worthy."

"And me?"

"You were necessary, oddly, to finding the scroll. Only Thoth knows why."

"A gypsy told me once I was a fool. The fool who sought the fool."

"That's the first time I've heard those charlatans be right."

And as if to prove the point, that night he had me poisoned.

¤   ¤   ¤

I'm not the most gentle and contemplative of men, and generally don't give much thought to God's creatures unless I want to hunt or trap or ride them. But there are hounds I've warmed to, cats I've appreciated for their mousing, and birds with feathers to take one's breath away. That's why I fed the mouse.

I stayed up later with the book than Silano and Astiza, puzzling whether this word fit that one, and if oddities such as "in your world, random chance is the foundation of fatalistic predetermination" made any sense at all. I finally took a brief break on our porch, the stars thick in the moist close darkness of the summer sky, and asked an orderly for some food to be brought. It took too long, but finally I was given a plate and went back inside to sit at our table and nibble at *fuul*, boiled beans mashed with tomatoes and onions. I spotted in a corner a periodic visitor that had amused me before, an Egyptian spiny mouse: so named because its hairs prick the mouth of any predator. Feeling companionable in the quiet night, I idly threw it some mash, even though the presence of such rodents was one reason we encased the book in a strongbox.

Then I bent back to work. So many choices! I marveled at the symbols, noticing suddenly how they seemed to shift and slide, rotate and tumble. I blinked, the words blurry. I was more tired than I realized! But if I could decipher where the sentence ended, or whether Thoth used sentences in the modern sense at all . . .

Now the scroll was wavering. What was going on? I looked over to the corner. The mouse, as big as a small rat at home, had flopped onto its side and was quivering, its eyes wide with terror. Foam was at its mouth.

I shoved my plate away and stood.

"Astiza!" I tried to cry, but it was a throttled mumble from a thick tongue, heard by no one but myself. I took a tottering step. That bastard Silano! He figured he didn't need me anymore! I remembered his threat of poisoned pig in Cairo, the year before. Then I was falling, not even sure what had happened to my legs, and hit the floor so hard that lights danced before my eyes. Through a haze I could see the mouse dying.

Men stole in the room to scoop me up. Yet how was he going to explain this murder to Astiza? Or did he plan to assassinate her too? No, he still wanted her. They hoisted, grunting, and carried me between them like a sack of flour. I was dizzy, but conscious—probably because I'd barely tasted the dish. They assumed I was dead.

We went out a side gate and down to the river and garrison privy, watered by a canal. Beyond it was a small lagoon off the main river, redolent of lotus and shit. With a swing back and forth they pitched my body, helpless as a baby.

With a splash, I went under. Did they mean to make it look like a drowning?

Yet the shock of the water revived me a little, and panic gave my limbs some motion. I managed to flop back to the surface and take a breath, treading water. The shallow dose was wearing off. My two would-be executioners watched me, curiously not very alarmed by my resilience. Didn't they realize I hadn't eaten enough poison? They were making no move to shoot me, or wade in after to finish me off with sword or ax.

Maybe I could paddle and find help.

It was then that I heard a big splash behind me.

I turned. There was a low dock in the lagoon, and with a rattle a chain was unreeling, its links snaking toward me. What the devil?

My escorts laughed.

Coming toward me in the dark were the protruding nostrils and reptilian eyes of that most loathsome and hideous of all beasts, the Nile crocodile. This prehistoric nightmare, armored in scales, thick as a log, a torpedo of muscle, can be astonishingly quick in and out of the water. It is old as dragons, as unfeeling as a machine.

Even in my fuddled state their plot came to me. Silano's scoundrels had chained the predator in this lagoon to dispose of me by eating me. I could hear the count's story. The American had used the privy, walked to the Nile to wash or gaze out at the night, the croc came out of the water—it had happened in Egypt a thousand times before—and snick, snack, I was gone. Silano would have stone, scroll, and woman. Checkmate!

I'd just processed this disagreeable scenario, acknowledging its ingenious perfidy with dull admiration, when the animal struck. It snatched me under, clamping my leg but not yet chewing it, and rolled us, in its time-honored habit of drowning its prey. The perfect horror of that vise, its long mouth of overlapping teeth, its mossy scales, the dim blankness of its expression, all somehow registered in my mind and shocked me into action despite the pain and poison. I freed my tomahawk from my belt as we whirled and struck the beast on his snout, no doubt surprising him with my little sting as much as he'd surprised me. His jaws snapped open, as if on a spring, releasing my leg, and I chopped again, hitting the roof of his mouth where the tomahawk lodged. The lagoon erupted as the crocodile writhed, and as it twisted I felt its chain slithering by me. Instinctively I grabbed. The animal and its chain carried me upward, my head broke water, and I seized breath. Then we dove again, the croc trying to turn to bite me, even as each snapping of its jaws must have driven the tomahawk painfully deeper. I dared not let his mouth get close. I pulled myself frantically forward on his chain until I got to where it made a necklace around the monster's neck, just before its forelegs. I hung on. Twist as it might, it couldn't bite me.

We dove, so I jabbed at its eyes. Now it thrashed like a bucking horse as I barely held on. We'd break surface and then submerge, wallow in the mud of the shallow bottom, and then surge upward again. I could hear the dock cracking and squealing behind as the beast yanked furiously on its chain. The laughter of my captors had stopped. My leg was bleeding, the blood making the crocodile's thrashing even more frantic as he smelled. I had no way to kill the beast.

So when our writhing brought us near the dock I let go and swam for it. No man has ever left the water that fast. I flew to get up on the wood.

The croc turned, wrapped in its own chain, and came after me, its snout crashing into the splintery dock. It bit, grunting at the pain of my tomahawk as it did so, snapping boards in two. The dock began to sink toward its snout as I scrabbled up its slope. I heard confused shouts from the men who'd thrown me in. Then I spied the post where the chain was wrapped and when a surging charge slacked the tension, I lifted its loop to release the animal, hoping it would swim away up the Nile.

Instead the crocodile exploded half out of the water, the loose chain singing like a whip. I ducked as it whickered by. The animal fell back into the lagoon, realized it was free, and suddenly was charging full tilt, but not toward me. His agonized eyes had spied the men on shore watching our struggle. The crocodile came out of the water after them, great feet splayed out as it charged, spray flying. Screaming, they ran.

A crocodile can gallop short distances as fast as a horse. He took one of my tormentors and broke him nearly in two with a furious snap of its jaws, then dropped that one and chased the next, straight toward the fort. The man was shouting a warning.

I didn't have much time.

I was damned if I'd leave it all to Silano. I'd kill him if I could, and if not I'd torment him with what he'd lost. I'd take the scroll and throw it into the deepest hole in the Mediterranean. Wounded by the animal's teeth, dripping blood, I limped up the path, following the trail of swept sand where the crocodile's mighty tail had thrashed. Cautiously, I paused at the small sally gate we'd come out of. The crocodile had smashed right through and was in the courtyard, men beginning to shoot. A cannon went off in alarm. I went inside myself but kept to the shadows, creeping around the perimeter to my quarters. There I grabbed my longrifle and peeked out the door. The crocodile was down, a hundred men blazing at it, chunks of another human trapped in its colossal jaws. Then I aimed, but not at the beast. Instead I put the sights on a lantern in the stables across the courtyard, which in turn weren't far from the magazine.

I was going to set the fort on fire.

It was one of the prettiest shots I ever made, breath held, finger squeezing. I had to fire the length of the parade ground, through an open window, and pluck down the lantern without extinguishing its wick. It fell, broke, and flames began to dance in the hay. A weird light began to illuminate the scales and saber-like teeth of the monster, even as men began shouting, "Fire, fire!" Horses were screaming.

No eyes were on me.

So I limped again and got back to the room where I'd been poisoned. Along the way, I seized one of the picks used for construction of the fort.

The scroll, damn him, was gone.

I glanced out. Flames were shooting higher and neighing horses were stampeding from the stable, adding to the chaos. I could hear officers shouting. "The magazine! Wet down the magazine!" I loaded and fired again, hitting someone trying to organize a chain of buckets from the fort's well. When he fell the bucket brigade scattered in confusion, not knowing what was going on. Shots went off as sentries fired in all directions.

Astiza burst in dressed in her nightclothes, her hair undone, eyes wide with confusion. She took in my bloody leg, soaked clothing, and the empty table where I'd had the scroll.

"Ethan! What have you done?"

"You mean, what has your ex-lover Silano done! He poisoned me and tried to feed me to that reptile out there! Don't think you wouldn't have been next, once he'd had you and tired of you. He wants that book all for himself. Not for science, not for Bonaparte, and certainly not for us. It's driven him mad!"

"I saw him running for the lookout tower with Bouchard. They slammed the door and locked themselves in."

"He's going to wait and let the garrison finish me. Maybe you, too." More shouting, and now bullets began pattering the headquarters building where we huddled.

"We can't let him disappear with that book!" she said.

"Then why did we find it in the first place?"

"Why do people learn anything? It's our nature!"

"Not my nature." I grabbed her. "Are you with me?"

"Of course."

"Then if we can't have the scroll, we'll break the key that translates it and give him a worthless book. Is there a way out of this rat hole?"

"There's an officer's armory behind that other door, and some powder inside."

"You think we can fight the whole garrison?"

"We can blow a hole through the back wall."

I smiled. "Lord, you are beautiful under pressure."

It was a heavy locked door but I fired once and then swung the pick. It gave way. This was not the main magazine, just the officers' arms, but by Thoth there were two kegs of powder. I uncorked one and set a trail of powder to the main room, then put both kegs against the outer wall. "Now we take the stone for ourselves."

"You can't take that! It weighs too much!"

I hefted the rolling pin I'd put in my satchel as a decoy and grinned. "Ben Franklin says I can."

Publishing always seemed a messy trade to me, but Franklin claimed it was like printing money. I slung my rifle over my shoulder and limped back to the room with the Rosetta Stone, lurid firelight outside throwing shadows. Soldiers in the courtyard had formed a long chain all the way down to the river, buckets passed over the tail of the dead crocodile. The shooting had slackened.

I took Silano's experimental paints from his pots and smeared some on my rolling pin. Then I ran it over the top part of the Rosetta Stone, coating the surface with paint but leaving the incised symbols paint-free. I did the same to the Greek.

"Strip to the waist, please."

"Ethan!"

"I need your skin."

"By the grace of Isis, men! Is that all you can think about at a time like . . ."

So I took her nightgown by the shoulders and tore, ripping it down her back as she shrieked. "Sorry. You're smoother than me." Then I kissed her, her rags held against her breasts, and backed her against the stone.

She twitched. "What are you doing?"

"Making you a library." I pulled her off and looked. Not perfect, some symbols lost at the indent of her spine, but still, a mirror image had been painted there. I pressed her again against the Greek, some carrying down onto the top of her buttocks. It was oddly erotic, but then women have quite lovely backs, and I did like the swell of the fabric draped on her hips. . . .

Back to work! While she stood there, too shocked to be angry yet, I attacked the monument, not to deface it but to truncate it. I had to aim for the middle of the hieroglyphics, hoping some savant wouldn't curse me years later. One blow, two, three, and then the granite began to crack! I took final aim and swung with all my might, and the top quarter of the Rosetta Stone broke free, taking all of Thoth's script and a portion of the hieroglyphics with it. The fragment crashed to the floor.

"Help me drag it."

"Are you completely mad?"

"We have the key script on you. We're going to destroy this piece. We can't move the whole stone, but we can get this into the armory."

"And then?"

"Blow it up when we blow the wall. It will make the book worthless until we steal it back!"

The stone was heavy, but we managed to tug, shove, and scrape it across the entry room and into the armory on the far side. I wedged it against the gunpowder kegs, figuring it would help direct their blast against the wall.

Then I retreated, took a candle, and lit the train of

powder. I glanced back. Astiza was crouched by the window, looking out. Men were shouting and running. The flames were growing brighter.

"Ethan!" she warned. Then the whole world erupted.

Fort Julian's magazine went first, a thunderous explosion that shot flaming debris hundreds of feet into the sky. Even sheltered as we were inside, the concussion knocked us sprawling. A moment later there was a second boom from the armory and debris rained out from it, too. Bits of the Rosetta Stone flew like shrapnel. Astiza's lovely torso would be the only record of Thoth. I touched her.

"The paint is already dry." I smiled. "You're a book, Astiza, the secret of life!"

"You'd better get this book a cover. I'm not running around Egypt naked."

I fetched an officer's cloak. My tomahawk I had to leave in the dead crocodile. With my rifle we pushed through the wreckage of the armory. The mud fort wall had breached, and we climbed over its rubble to the streets of Rosetta. Down at the end of the lane some laundry hung by a donkey cart, not far from a corralled and very frightened donkey.

CHAPTER 25

Fleeing at the pace of a donkey cart is not the swiftest way to avoid one's enemies, but it has the advantage of being so ridiculous as to be overlooked. Liberation of laundry allowed us to be more or less in Egyptian dress, my leg wound throbbing but tightly bound. My hope was that in the confusion caused by a rampaging crocodile, stampeding horses, and an exploding magazine, we might slip away. With any luck, the faithless Silano might assume I was in the belly of his gigantic reptile, at least until someone thought to slit open its stomach. If not that, he'd assume we were trying to slip by the patrol boats on the Nile. My vague plan was to slip by the French into the Ottoman camp, go to Smith's squadron offshore, and bargain from somewhere safe. If we'd lost the book, Silano had lost the ability to continue deciphering it.

The success of this scheme began to diminish as the sun rose and the day grew hotter. As we left the green flood plain of the Nile for the red desert toward Abukir, a grumble like thunder began to be heard, but in such a clear sky it was the thud of guns. A battle was underway, which meant unless the Turks won and the French broke, the entire Frankish army was in our way. It was July 25, 1799.

"We can't turn back," Astiza said. "Silano would spot us."

"And battles are confusing. Maybe a way will present itself."

We parked the donkey in the lee of a high sand dune and ascended to look out at the bay beyond. The panorama was heartbreaking. Once more, the atrophy of Ottoman arms was apparent. There was nothing wrong with the courage of Mustafa's men. What was lacking was firepower and tactical sense. The Turks waited like a paralyzed hare; the French bombarded and then attacked with their cavalry. We were spectators to a disaster, watching a headlong charge by Joachim Murat's troopers not merely breach the first Ottoman line, but knife through the second and third as well. The cavalry stampeded the entire length of the Abukir peninsula, spilling the defenders in a panic from their trenches, tents deflating as guy ropes were cut. We learned later that Murat himself captured the Turkish commander-in-chief in furious hand-to-hand combat, receiving a grazing wound on his jaw from Mustafa's pistol but chopping off a couple of the pasha's fingers with his sword in return. Bonaparte used his own handkerchief to bind the man's hand. In 1799, there was still chivalry.

The rest was slaughter, once the lines cracked. More than two thousand of the Muslim warriors were cut down on land and twice that many drowned as they plunged into the sea to try to reach their ships. A garrison in the fort at the end of the peninsula stubbornly held out, but was bombarded and starved into submission. For the price of a thousand casualties, three-quarters of them wounded, Bonaparte had destroyed another Ottoman army. It was exactly the triumph he needed to retrieve his reputation after the debacle at Acre. To a colleague he wrote it was "one of the most beautiful battles I ever saw," and to the Directory in Paris he described it as "one of the most terrible." Both were true. He had been resuscitated by blood.

So Astiza and I had a camp of boiling mad Frenchmen back at Rosetta and a victorious French army looting the remains of our allies in front. I'd fled from the jaws of a crocodile to military encirclement.

"Ethan, what do you think we should do?" I suppose it's flattering when women ask men things like that in the midst of military peril, but I wouldn't mind if they came up with their own ideas once in a while.

"Keep running, I think. I just don't know where."

So she did make a suggestion, plucky girl. "Remember the Oasis of Siwah, where Alexander the Great was declared a son of Zeus and Amon? Napoleon doesn't control it. Let's make for that."

I swallowed. "Isn't that a hundred miles across empty desert?"

"So we'd better get started."

We'd both end up mummified by heat and thirst, but where else could we go? Silano would kill us for sure, now. Napoleon too. "I wish our donkey didn't look so half-starved and addled-eyed," I said. "If we'd had time, I'd have looked for a better one."

No matter. A French patrol was waiting when we descended from the dune.

¤   ¤   ¤

Predictably, Napoleon was in a good mood that night. There's nothing like victory to settle him. Bulletins would be sent to France describing Bonaparte's victory in vivid detail. Captured standards were being readied for shipment for display in Paris. And I, his annoying mosquito, was safely bound, one leg chewed by a ravenous crocodile, my love trussed, my gun confiscated, and my donkey on its way back to its rightful owner.

"I've been trying to save you from witchcraft, General," I tried, without much spirit.

He'd uncorked a bottle of Bordeaux, part of the personal horde his brother had brought from France. "Have you now? With your beautiful viper by your side?"

"Silano is seeking dark powers that will lead you astray."

"Then thank God you blew up half my fort, Gage." He took a swallow.

It *did* sound bad when he put it that way. "That was simply a diversion." It would have been braver to be surly and defiant, I know, but I was trying to save our lives.

Count Silano had arrived gaping as if I'd walked from the tomb after three days. Now he said, "I am tired of trying to kill you, monsieur."

I smiled at them both. "I'm tired of it too."

"This piece of stone you destroyed," Bonaparte said. "It was a key to translate an ancient book?" Fortunately, there was enough dignity that no one thought to strip Astiza.

"Yes, General."

"And that book would tell us what, exactly?"

"Magic," Silano said.

"Does magic still exist?"

"We can make it exist. Magic is just advanced science. Magic and immortality."

"Immortality!" Bonaparte laughed. "Escape from the ultimate fate! But I've seen too many dead, so my immortality is not to be forgotten. Recollection is what we leave."

"We believe this book will help you achieve immortality in more literal ways," the count said. "You, and those who rise with you."

"Such as yourself?" He passed the bottle. "So you have incentive, my friend!" Napoleon turned to me. "It's annoying you broke the stone, Gage, but Silano has already deciphered some of the symbols. Perhaps he'll puzzle out the rest. And the stone remaining will allow the savants to focus on hieroglyphics. Depending on who ultimately wins here in Egypt, the piece will probably wind up someday in either Paris or London. Crowds will flock to it, never knowing a fourth text is gone."

"I could stay around to tell them."

"I'm afraid not." Napoleon reached into a leather binder and brought out a bundle of dated newspapers. "Smith sent me these as a gift when I let the Turks take off their wounded. It seems that while we've achieved glory in Egypt, events in

Europe have been rapidly unraveling. France is once more in peril."

It was then I confirmed that Bonaparte had clearly abandoned one goal, conquest of Asia, and adopted another, a return to Paris. He'd won what he could, and we'd found what he most wanted to find. Power, one way or another.

"France and Austria have been at war since March, and we've been driven from Germany and Italy. Tippoo Sahib died in India the same time we were repulsed at Acre. The Directory is in shambles, and my brother Lucien is in Paris trying to reform the imbecilic assembly. The British fleet will have to loosen its blockade soon to resupply at Cyprus. That's when I can return to put things right. Duty requires it."

That seemed shameless. "Duty? To leave your men?"

"To prepare the way. Kléber has dreamed of command since we landed here. Now he'll get it: I'll surprise him with a letter. Meanwhile I take the risk of evading the British fleet."

Risk! The risk was to be left with a marooned army in Egypt. The bastard was abandoning his men for the politics of Paris! Yet the truth was, I had a grudging admiration for the sly dog. We were two of a kind in some ways: opportunists, gamblers, and survivors. We were fatalists, always after the main chance. We both liked pretty women. And high adventure, if it was an escape from tedium.

It was as if he'd read my mind. "War and politics makes necessity," he said. "It is too bad we have to kill you, but there it is."

"There *what* is?"

"I feel as if I'm being driven toward an unknown goal, Ethan Gage, and that you represent as much of a dangerous obstacle now as you did assistance when I brought you to Egypt. Neither of us planned you'd end with the damned English, but there you were at Acre with your electricity. And now you've attacked Rosetta."

"Only because of Silano. He was the one with the crocodile . . ."

Bonaparte stuck out his hand. "Au revoir, Monsieur Gage. Under different circumstances we might have become firm partners. As it is, you've betrayed France for the last time. You've proven yourself entirely too much of a nuisance, and too able an enemy. Yet even cats have only nine lives. Surely you've used yours up by now?"

"Not unless you put it to the test," I replied morosely.

"I will leave it to Silano to be creative with you and your woman. The one who shot at me so long ago, in Alexandria."

"She shot at *me*, general."

"Yes. Why are the bad ones so beautiful? Well. Destiny awaits." And having disposed of us, off he marched, his mind on his next project.

¤   ¤   ¤

A decent man would simply shoot us, but Silano was a scientist. Astiza and I had crossed him enough that he thought we deserved some pain, and he was curious to use our environment. "Do you know sand alone can mummify a carcass?"

"How erudite."

So we were buried after midnight, but only to our necks.

"What I like about this is that you can watch each other burn and weep," he said as his henchmen finished packing sand around our bodies. Our hands had been tied behind our backs, and our feet bound. We had no hats, and were already thirsty. "There will be a slow increase in torment as the sun rises. Your skin will fry, and eventually crack. The reflected light and dust will slowly induce blindness, and as you watch each other you will gradually go mad. The hot sand will leach out any liquid you retain, and your tongues will swell so much that you will have difficulty breathing. You will pray for snakes or scorpions to make it faster." He stooped and patted me on the head, like a child or dog. "The scorpions like to go for the eyes, and the ants crawl up the nostrils to feed. The vultures will hope to get to you before you're completely eaten. But it is the snakes that hurt the most."

"You seem to know a lot about it."

"I'm a naturalist. I have studied torture for many years. It's an exquisite science, and quite a pleasure if you understand its refinements. It's not easy to keep a man in excruciating pain and yet coherent enough to tell you something useful. What's interesting about this exercise is that the body below the neck should be baked dry and preserved. It is from this natural process, I'm guessing, that ancient Egyptians got the idea of mummification. Do you know that the Persian king Cambyses lost an entire army in a sandstorm?"

"Can't say that I care."

"I study history so as not to repeat it." He turned to Astiza, her dark hair a fan on the earth. "I did love you, you know."

"You've never loved anyone but yourself."

"Ben Franklin said the man who loves himself will have no rival," I chimed in.

"Ah, the amusing Monsieur Franklin. Certainly I'm more faithful to myself than either of you have been to me! How many chances for partnership did I give you, Gage? How many warnings? Yet you betrayed me, again and again and again."

"Can't imagine why."

"I'd like to watch you beg before the end."

And I would have, if I thought it would do a lick of good.

"But I'm afraid that destiny tugs at me, too. I'm accompanying Bonaparte back to France, where I can study the book more deeply, and he's not a man to sit still. Nor is it safe to stray from the main army. I'm afraid we will not meet again, Monsieur Gage."

"Do you believe in ghosts, Silano?"

"I'm afraid my interest in the supernatural does not extend to superstition."

"You will, when I come after you."

He laughed. "And after you give me a good fright, perhaps we'll play a game of cards! In the meantime I'll let you turn into one. Or a mummy. Maybe I'll have someone dig you out in a few weeks so I can prop you in a corner like Omar."

"Alessandro, we do not deserve this!" Astiza cried.

There was a long silence. We could not see his face. Then, quietly, "Yes you do. You broke my heart."

And with that, we were left alone to fry.

Astiza and I faced each other, me south and she north, so that our cheeks could be equally roasted between dawn and sunset. It's cold in the desert at night and for the first few minutes after the sun broke the horizon, the warmth was not unpleasant. Then, as pink left the sky and it turned to summer's milk, the temperature began to rise, accentuated by the reflecting sand. My ear began to burn. I heard the first rustlings of insects.

"Ethan, I'm afraid," whispered Astiza, who was six feet from me.

"We'll black out," I promised, without conviction.

"Isis, call to me our friends! Give us help!"

Isis didn't reply. "It won't hurt after a while," I said.

Instead, the pain increased. I soon had a headache, and my tongue thickened. Astiza was quietly moaning. Even in the best of circumstances the summer sun in Egypt hammers one's head. Now I felt like Jericho's anvil. I was reminded all too sharply of the flight that Ashraf and I made into the desert a year before. That time, at least, we'd been mounted and my Mameluke friend had known how to find water.

The sand grew hotter. Every inch of skin could feel the rising heat, and yet I couldn't wiggle. There were sharp pricks, like bites, but I couldn't tell if something was already eating me or it was merely the heat gnawing into my sensations. The brain has a way of amplifying pain with dread.

Did I mention that gambling is a vice?

Sweat had half blinded me, stinging, but soon was leached out, leaving salt. My entire head felt like it was swelling. My vision blurred from the glare, and Astiza's own head seemed as much a blob as someone recognizable.

Was it even noon yet? I didn't think so. I heard a faint rumble. Was the fighting starting again? Maybe it would rain, as at the City of Ghosts.

No, the heat rose, in great shimmering waves. Astiza sobbed for a while, but then fell silent. I prayed she'd passed out. I was waiting for the same, that slow slide into unconsciousness and death, but the desert wanted to punish me. On and on the temperature climbed. My chin was burning. My teeth were frying in their sockets. My eyes were swelling shut.

Then I saw something scuttle by.

It was black, and I groaned inwardly. Soldiers had told me that scorpion stings were particularly painful. "Like a hundred bees at once," one had said. "No, no, like holding a hot coal to the skin!" chimed in another. "More closely like acid in the eye!" offered another. "A hammer to the thumb!"

More scuttling. Another one. The scorpions were approaching us, then backing off. I couldn't hear any signaling, but they seemed to pile into packs like wolves.

I hoped their assault would not wake Astiza up. I pledged to try as hard as I could not to scream. The rumbling was getting louder.

Now one arthropod came near, a monster in my ruined vision, as huge as the crocodile from this perspective. It seemed to be contemplating me with the dull, cold instinctive calculation of its tiny brain. Its cocked tail twitched, as if aiming. And then . . .

Slam! I jerked as much as my entrapment would let me. A dusty boot had come down, obliterating the creature. It twisted, grinding the scorpion into the dust, and then I heard a familiar voice.

"By the beard of the Prophet, can you never look after yourself, Ethan?"

"Ashraf?" It was a bewildered mumble.

"I've been waiting for your tormentors to go far enough

away. It is hot, sitting in the desert! And here the two of you are, in even worse shape than when I left you last fall. Do you learn nothing, American?"

Could it be? The Mameluke Ashraf had been first my prisoner and then my companion as we fled Cairo and rode to rescue Astiza. He'd saved us again in a skirmish on a riverbank, given us a horse, and then bid good-bye, joining the resistance forces of Murad Bey. And now he was here again? Thoth was at work.

"I've been tracking you for days, first to Rosetta, and then back again. I did not understand why you were disguised like a fellahin in a donkey cart. Then your Franks bury you alive? You need better friends, Ethan."

"Amen to that," I managed.

And I heard the blessed scrape of a spade, digging me out.

¤   ¤   ¤

I only dimly remember what came next. Crowding by a company of well-armed Mamelukes, explaining the rumble I'd heard. Water, painfully wet as we sucked it into our swollen throats. A camel knelt and we were tied onto it. Then a ride into the setting sun. We slept under a scrap of tent at an oasis, regaining our senses. Our heads were red and blistered, our lips cracked, our eyes like slits. We were helpless.

So at length we were tied on again and led even deeper into the waste, south and west and then east to a secret camp of Murad's. Women salved our burnt skin, and nourishment slowly restored us. Time was still a blur. If I climbed to the top of a nearby dune, I could just see the tips of the pyramids. Cairo was invisible, beyond.

"How did you know to find us?" I asked Ashraf. He'd already related his raids and battles that were wearing down the French.

"First we heard an ironmonger was inquiring about Astiza from distant Jerusalem," he said. "It was a curious report, but I knew you'd disappeared and suspected. Then Ibrahim Bey reported that Count Silano had ridden north and disappeared somewhere in Syria. What was going on? Napoleon was repulsed at Acre, but you did not come back to Cairo with him. So I believed you'd joined the English, and I determined to watch for you in the Ottoman invasion force. And yes, we saw flames in Rosetta, and I spied the two of you in your donkey cart, but French cavalry were too near. So I waited, until they buried you and the French finally drew off. Always I am having to save you, my American friend."

"Always I am in your debt."

"Not if you do what I suspect you must do."

"What is that?

"Word just came that Napoleon has sailed and taken Count Silano with him. You're going to have to stop them in France, Ethan. The servant women have told me of the mysterious signs on your companion's back. What are they?"

"Ancient writing to read what Silano has stolen."

"The paint is sloughing off, but there is a way to extend them longer. I've told the women to mix their pots of henna." Henna was a plant used to decorate the Arab women with intricate traceries of brown patterns, like an impermanent tattoo.

When they finished, Astiza's back looked oddly beautiful.

"Should this book be read at all?" Ashraf asked as we prepared to leave.

"If not, then its secret will die with me," she said. "I am the Rosetta key."

CHAPTER **26**

Astiza and I landed on the southern coast of France on October 11, 1799, two days after Napoleon Bonaparte and Alessandro Silano did the same. For both parties it had been a long voyage. Bonaparte, after patting mistress Pauline Foures on her fanny and leaving a note to Kléber informing him that he was now in command (he preferred not to face the general in person), had taken Monge, Berthollet, and a few other savants like Silano and hugged the frequently windless African coast to avoid the British navy. The route turned a routine sea voyage into a tedious forty-two days. Even as he crept homeward, French politics became more chaotic as plot and counterplot simmered in Paris. It was the perfect atmosphere for an ambitious general, and the bulletin announcing Napoleon's smashing victory at Abukir arrived in Paris three days before the general did. His way north was marked by cheering crowds.

Our voyage was also slow, but for a different reason. With Smith's encouragement, we boarded a British frigate a week after Bonaparte had left Egypt and sailed directly for France to intercept. His slowness saved him. We were off

Corsica and Toulon two weeks before Napoleon arrived and, learning there was no word of him, darted back the way we'd come. Even from a masthead, however, a lookout surveys only a few square miles of sea, and the Mediterranean is big. How close we came I don't know. Finally a picket boat brought word that he'd landed first in his native Corsica and then France, and by the time we followed he was well ahead of us.

If Silano hadn't been along, I'd have been content to let him go. It's not my duty to dog ambitious generals. But we had a score to settle with the count, and the book was dangerous in his hands and potentially useful in ours. How much did he already know? How much could *we* read, with Astiza's key?

If our hunt at sea was anxious and discouraging, the time it took was not. Astiza and I had rarely had time to take a breath together. It had always been campaigns, treasure hunts, and perilous escapes. Now we shared a lieutenant's cabin—our intimacy an issue of some jealousy among the lonely officers and crew—and had time to know each other at leisure, like a man and wife. Time enough, in other words, to scare any man wary of intimacy.

Except I liked it. We had certainly been partners in adventure, and lovers. Now we were friends. Her body ripened with rest and food, her skin recovered its blossom, and her hair its sheen. I loved to simply look at her, reading in our cabin or watching the bright sea by the rail, and loved how clothes draped her, how her hair floated in the breeze. Even better, of course, was slowly taking those clothes off. But our ordeals had saddened her, and her beauty seemed bittersweet. And when we came together in our cramped quarters, sometimes urgently and at other times with gentle care, trying to be quiet in the thin-walled ship, I was transported. I marveled that I, the wayward American opportunist, and she, the Egyptian mystic, got on at all. And yet it turned out we *did* complement and complete each other, anticipating each other. I began thinking of a normal life ahead.

I wished we could sail forever, and not find Napoleon at all.

But sometimes she was lost to me with a troubled look, seeing dark things in the past or future. That's when I feared I would lose her again. Destiny claimed her as much as I did.

"Think about it, Ethan. Bonaparte with the power of Moses? France, with the secret knowledge of the Knight Templars? Silano, living forever, every year mastering more arcane formulae, gathering more followers? Our task isn't done until we get that book back."

So we landed in France. Of course we couldn't dock in Toulon. Astiza conferred with our English captain, studied the charts, and insistently directed us to an obscure cove surrounded by steep hillsides, uninhabited except by a goatherd or two. How did she know the coast of France? We were rowed ashore at night to a pebble beach and left alone in the moonless dark. Finally there was a whistle and Astiza lit a candle, shielded by her cape.

"So the fool has returned," a familiar voice said from the brush. "He who found the Fool, father of all thought, originator of civilization, blessing and curse of kings." Men materialized, swarthy and in boots and broad hats, bright sashes at their waists that held silver knives. Their leader bowed.

"Welcome back to the Rom," said Stefan the gypsy.

¤   ¤   ¤

I was pleasantly astounded by this reunion. I'd met these gypsies, or "gyptians," as some in Europe called them—wanderers supposedly descended from the ancients—the year before when my friend Talma and I had fled Paris to join Napoleon's expedition. After Najac and his gutter scoundrels had ambushed us on the Toulon stage, I'd escaped into the woods and found refuge with Stefan's band. There I had first met Sidney Smith and, more agreeably, the beautiful Sarylla who had told my fortune, told me I was the fool to seek the Fool (another name for Thoth) and instructed me in lovemaking techniques of the ancients. It had been a pleasant way to complete my journey to Toulon, encapsulated in a gypsy wagon and safe from those pursuing my sacred medallion. Now, like a rabbit popping from a hole, my gypsy saviors were here again.

"What in the tarot are you doing *here*?" I asked.

"But waiting for you, of course."

"I sent word ahead to them on an English cutter," Astiza said.

Ah. Hadn't these same gypsies sent word ahead to *her*, of the medallion and my coming? Which almost led to my head being blown off by Astiza's former master, not the easiest of introductions.

"Bonaparte is ahead of you, and word of his latest victories just ahead of him," Stefan said. "His journey to Paris has become a triumph. Men hope the conqueror of Egypt may be the savior of France. With only a little help from Alessandro Silano, he may achieve everything he desires, and desire is dangerous. You must separate Bonaparte from the book, and safekeep it. The Templar hiding place lasted nearly five centuries. Yours, hopefully, will last five millennia, or more."

"We have to catch him first."

"Yes, we must hurry. Great things are about to happen."

"Stefan, I'm delighted and amazed to see you, but hurrying is the last thing I thought gypsies capable of. We ambled to Toulon about as fast as a grazing cow, if I remember, and your little ponies can't pull your wagons much faster."

"True. But the Rom have a knack for borrowing things. We're going to find a coach and a fast team, my friend, and drive you—a member of the Council of Five Hundred, let us pretend—at breakneck pace to Paris. I shall be a captain of police, say, and André here your driver. Carlo as your footman, the lady as your lady . . ."

"The first thing we're going to do back in France is steal a coach and four?"

"If you act as if you deserve it, it doesn't look like stealing."

"We're not even legally in France. And I'm still charged with murdering a prostitute. My enemies could use it against me."

"Won't they kill you regardless?"

"Well, yes."

"Then what is your worry? But come. We'll ask Sarylla what to do."

The gypsy fortune-teller who taught me more than my fortune—lord, I fondly remembered the yelps she made—was as beautiful as I remembered, dark and mysterious, rings glittering on her fingers and hoop earrings catching the firelight. I was not entirely glad to bump into a former paramour with Astiza in tow, and the two women bristled silently in that way they have, like wary cats. Yet Astiza sat quietly at my shoulder while the gypsy woman plied the cards of the tarot.

"Fortune speeds you on your way," Sarylla intoned, as her turn of cards revealed the chariot. "We will have no problem liberating a carriage for our purposes."

"See?" Stefan said with satisfaction.

I like the tarot. It can tell you anything you want to hear.

Sarylla turned more cards. "But you will meet a woman in hurried circumstances. Your route will become circuitous."

Another woman? "But will we be successful?"

She turned more cards. I saw the tower, the magician, the fool, and the emperor. "It will be a near-fought thing."

Another card. The lovers. She looked at us. "You must work together."

Astiza took my hand and smiled.

And she turned again. Death.

"I do not know who this is for. The magician, the fool, the emperor, or the lover? Your way is perilous."

"But possible?" Death for Silano, certainly. And perhaps I should assassinate Bonaparte too.

Another card. The wheel of fortune. "You are a gambler, no?"

"When I have to be."

Another card. The world. "You have no choice." She

looked at us with her great, dark eyes. "You will have strange allies and strange enemies."

I grimaced. "Everything's normal then."

She shook her head, mystified. "Wait to see which is which." She looked hard at the cards and then at Astiza. "There is danger for your new woman, Ethan Gage. Great danger, and something even deeper than that, I think. Sorrow."

Here it was, that rivalry. "What do you mean?"

"What the cards say. Nothing more."

I was disturbed. If Sarylla's original fortune hadn't come true, I'd have brushed this off. I am, after all, a Franklin man, a savant. But however I might mock the tarot, there was something eerie about its power. I was frightened for the woman beside me.

"There may be fighting," I said to Astiza. "You can wait for me on the English ship. It's not too late to signal them."

Astiza considered the cards and the gypsy for some time, and then shook her head. "I have my own magic and we've come this far," she said, pulling her cloak around her against the unaccustomed European chill of October, already reaching south. "Our real danger is time. We must hurry."

Sarylla looked sympathetic and gave her the tarot card for the star. "Keep this. It is for meditation and enlightenment. May faith be with you, lady."

Astiza looked surprised, and touched. "And you."

So we crept to a magistrate's house, "borrowed" his coach and team, and were on our way to Paris. I was awed by the lush green-gold of the countryside after Egypt and Syria. The last grapes hung round and fat. The fields were pregnant with yellow haystacks. Lingering fruit gave the air a ripe, fermented scent. Wagons groaning with autumn produce pulled aside as Stefan's men cried commands and cracked the whip as if we were really republican deputies of importance. Even the farm girls looked succulent, seeming half-dressed after the robes of the desert, their breasts like melons, their hips a merry bushel, their calves stained with wine juice. Their lips were red and full from sucking on plums.

"Isn't it beautiful, Astiza?"

She was more troubled by the cloudy skies, the turning leaves, and trees that formed unruly arbors over the highways.

"I can't see," she replied.

Several times we passed through towns with sagging decorations of tricolor bunting, dried flower petals on the roads, and wine bottles discarded in ditches. Each was evidence of Napoleon's passing.

"The little general?" an innkeeper remembered. "A rooster of a man!"

"Handsome as the devil," his wife added. "Black lock of hair, fierce gray eyes. They say he conquered half of Asia!"

"The treasure of the ancients is coming right after him, they say!"

"And his brave men!"

¤   ¤   ¤

We drove well into the night and rose before dawn, but Paris is a multiday journey. As we went north; the sky grew grayer and the season advanced. Our coach blew the highway's carpet of leaves into a rooster tail. Our horses steamed when we stopped for water. And so we were clattering onward in the dusk of the fourth day, Paris just hours ahead, when suddenly another fine team and coach burst out of a lane to our left and swerved right in front of us. Horses screamed and crashed, the teams dragging each other down. Our own coach tilted, balanced on two wheels, and then slid into a ditch and slowly went over. Astiza and I tumbled to one side in the coach. The gypsies leapt clear.

"Imbeciles!" a woman shouted. "My husband could have you shot!"

We shakily climbed out of the wreck. Our coach's front axel was broken, as were the legs of two of our screaming horses. Cavalry who were escorting whomever we'd collided with had dismounted and were moving forward with pistols to dispatch the injured horses and disentangle the others. Shouting at us from the window of her own coach was an impressively fashionable woman—her clothes would beggar a banker—with a frantic look. She had the hauteur of a Parisian, but I didn't immediately recognize her. I was an American, illegally back in France, still wanted for murder as far as I knew, who had not even obeyed the forty-day quarantine imposed on those traveling from the East. (Neither had Bonaparte.) Now there were soldiers and questions, even though her coach was in the wrong. I had a feeling being in the right wouldn't matter much here.

"My business is of paramount importance for the state!" the woman shouted in panic. "Get your animals away from mine!"

"*You* pulled out in front of *us*!" Astiza replied, her accent plain. "You are as rude as you are incompetent!"

"Wait," I cautioned. "She has soldiers."

Too late. "And you are as impertinent as you are clumsy!" the woman shrieked. "Do you know who I am? I could have you arrested!"

I went forward to head off a cat fight by making a bogus offer of later payment, just to get the harridan on her way. Our gypsies had wisely melted into the trees. Two pistol shots rang out, silencing the worst screams of the horses, and then the cavalrymen turned to us, hands on the hilts of their swords.

"Please, madame, it was just a simple accident," I said, smiling with my usual affable charm. "A moment more and you'll be on your way. And you're heading to?"

"My husband, if I can find him! Oh, this is disaster! We took the wrong turn and I missed him on the highway, and now his brothers will get to him first and tell their lies about me. If you've delayed me too much, you'll answer for it!"

I thought the guillotine had thinned out this kind of arrogance, but apparently it hadn't gotten them all. "But Paris is that way," I pointed.

"I wanted to meet him! But he's got past us and we were taking this lane to swing back. Now he'll already be home, and I not being there will confirm the worst!"

"What worst?"

"That I'm unfaithful!" And she burst into tears.

It was then that I recognized her features, somewhat famous in the Parisian social circles at whose fringes I'd moved. This was none other than Josephine, Napoleon's wife! What the devil was she doing on a dark road with night falling? And of course tears brought sympathy. I am nothing if not gallant, and weeping will disarm any gentleman.

"It's Bonaparte's wife," I whispered to Astiza. "When he heard she was an adulteress, on the eve of the Battle of the Pyramids, he nearly went insane."

"Is that why she's frightened?"

"We know how mercurial he is. He might put her in front of a firing squad."

Astiza considered, then moved swiftly to the coach door. "Lady, we know your husband."

"What?" She was a small woman, I now assessed, slim and finely dressed, neither homely nor particularly beautiful, her skin warm, her nose straight, her lips full, her eyes attractively wide and dark and, even in their desperation, intelligent. She had dark hair and finely sculpted ears, but her complexion was blotchy from crying. "How could you know him?"

"We served with Bonaparte in Egypt. We're hurrying ourselves, to warn him of terrible danger."

"You *do* know him! What danger? An assassination?"

"That a companion, Alessandro Silano, plans to betray him."

"Count Silano? He's coming with my husband, I heard. He's supposed to be a confidant and adviser."

"He's bewitched Napoleon, and has tried to turn him against you. But we can help. You're attempting to reconcile?"

She bowed her head, eyes wet. "It's been such a surprise. We had no warning he was coming. I rushed from my dearest friend to meet him. But these idiots took a wrong turn." She leaned out the carriage window and gripped Astiza's arms. "You must tell him that despite everything, I still love him! If he divorces me, I lose everything! My children will be penni-less! Is it my fault he goes away for months and years?"

"Then the gods have arranged this accident, don't you think?" Astiza said.

"The gods?"

I drew my companion back. "What are you doing?" I hissed.

"Here is our key to Bonaparte!" Astiza whispered. "He'll be surrounded by soldiers. How else are we going to get to him save through his wife? She's not faithful to him or any-thing else, which means she'll ally with anyone who suits her purpose. That means we have to enlist Josephine on our side. She can find out where the scroll is when she beds him, when men lose what little wits they have. Then we steal it back!"

"What are you whispering about?" Josephine called.

Astiza smiled. "Please, lady, our own carriage is ruined but it's imperative we reach your husband. I think we can help each other. If you'd let us ride with you we can help you reconcile."

"How?"

"My companion is a wise Freemason. We know the key to a sacred book that could give Napoleon great power."

"Freemason?" She squinted at me. "Abbot Barruel in his famed book said they were behind the revolution. The Jac-obins were all a Masonic plot. But the *Journal of Free Men* says the Masons are actually Royalists, plotting to bring back the king. Which are you?"

"I see the future in your husband, lady," I lied.

Josephine looked intrigued, and calculating. "Sacred book?"

"From Egypt," Astiza said. "If we ride we can be in Paris by dawn."

Somewhat surprisingly, she assented. She was so rattled by Napoleon's reappearance and his undoubted fury at her adulterous ways that she was eager for any help, no matter how improbable. So we left our own stolen coach a wreck, half its horses shot, our gypsies hiding, and took hers to Paris.

"Now. You must tell me what you know or I will throw you out," she warned.

We had to gamble. "I found a book that conveys great powers," I began.

"What kind of powers?"

"The power to persuade. To enchant. To live unnaturally long, perhaps forever. To manipulate objects."

Her eyes were wide and greedy.

"Count Silano has stolen this book and fastened onto Bonaparte like a leech, draining his mind. But the book hasn't been translated. Only we can do so. If his wife was to offer the key, on the understanding that Silano must be displaced, then you'd get your marriage back. I'm proposing an alliance. With our secret, you can get into your husband's bedchamber. With your influence, we can get back our book, dispose of Silano, and help Napoleon."

She was wary. "What key?"

"To a strange, ancient language, long lost." Astiza turned on Josephine's coach seat and I gently unlaced the back of her dress. The fabric parted, revealing the intricate alphabet in henna.

The Frenchwoman gasped. "It looks like Satan's writing!"

"Or God's."

Josephine considered. "Who cares whose it is, if we win?"

Was Thoth finally smiling on us? We raced toward Bonaparte's house on the newly renamed Rue de la Victoire, a tribute to his victories in Italy. And, with no plan, no confederates, and no weapons, we drew this ambitious social climber into our confidence.

What did I know about Josephine? The kind of gossip Paris thrived on. She grew up on the island of Martinique, was half a dozen years older than Napoleon, two inches shorter, and a tenacious survivor. She'd married a rich young army officer, Alexandre de Beauharnais, but he was so embarrassed by her provincial manners that he refused to present her to the court of Marie Antoinette. She separated from him, returned to the Caribbean, fled a slave revolt there to return to Paris at the height of the revolution, lost her husband to the guillotine in 1794, and then was imprisoned herself. Only the coup that ended the Terror saved her head. When a young army officer named Bonaparte called to compliment her on the conduct of her son Eugene, who had asked for help in retrieving the sword of his executed father, she seduced him. In desperation she gambled on this rising Corsican and married him, but then slept with everyone in sight while he was in Italy and Egypt. Some whispered she was a nymphomaniac. She'd been living with a former officer named Hippolyte Charles, now a businessman, when the alarming news arrived of her husband's return. With the revolution having allowed divorce, she was now in danger of losing everything at the very moment Bonaparte was seeking ultimate power. At thirty-six, with discoloring teeth, she might not have another chance.

Her eyes widened at Astiza's explanation of supernatural powers. A child of the Sugar Isles, tales of magic weren't alien to her.

"This book can destroy men who possess it," Astiza said, "and wreck nations in which it is unleashed. The ancients knew this and hid it away, but Count Silano has tempted fate by stealing it. He's bewitched your husband with dreams of unlimited power. It could drive Napoleon mad. You must help us get it back."

"But how?"

"We'll safeguard the book if you give it to us. Your knowledge of it will give you tremendous influence over him."

"But who are you?"

"My name is Astiza and this is Ethan Gage, an American."

"Gage? The electrician? Franklin's man?"

"Madame, I am honored to make your acquaintance and flattered that you have heard of me." I took her hand. "I hope we can be allies."

She snatched it away. "But you are a murderer!" She looked at me doubtfully. "Of a cheap adventuress! Aren't you?"

"A perfect example of Silano's lies, the kind that can entrap your husband and ruin his dreams. I was the victim of an unjust accusation. Let us help get this kind of poison away from your husband, and your married bliss will return to normal."

"Yes. It is Silano's fault, not mine. This book contains terrible power, you say?"

"The kind that can enslave souls."

She thought carefully. Finally she sat back and smiled. "You're right. God is looking out for me."

¤   ¤   ¤

The Bonaparte house, bought by Josephine before they were married, was in the fashionable part of Paris known as Chaussée d'Antin, a once-marshy area where the rich had built charming homes called "follies" over the past century. It was a modest two-story abode with a rose garden at the end of its bloom and a terrace that Josephine had covered with a wooden roof and hung with flags and tapestries: a respectable home for striving, midlevel functionaries. Her carriage pulled into a gravel drive under linden trees and she got out, nervous and flustered, plucking at her cheeks. "How do I look?"

"Like a woman with a secret," Astiza assured her. "In control."

Josephine smiled wanly and took a breath. Then we entered.

The rooms were a curious mix of feminine and masculine, with rich wallpaper and lacy curtains but hung with maps and plans of cities. There were the mistress's flowers, and the master's books, heaps of them, some just unpacked from Egypt. Her neatness was apparent, even as his boots were discarded in the dining room and his greatcoat thrown over one chair. A staircase led upward.

"He is in his bedchamber," she whispered.

"Go to him."

"His brothers will have told him everything. He will

hate me! I am a wicked, unfaithful woman. I can't help it. I love love so. I thought he would be killed!"

"You are human, as is he," I soothed. "He's not a saint either, trust me. Go, ask forgiveness, and tell him you've been busy recruiting allies. Explain how you've persuaded us to help him, that his future depends on the three of us."

I didn't trust Josephine, but what other weapon did we have? I was worried that Silano might be lurking about. Summoning her courage, she mounted the twenty steps to the floor above, tapping on his door. "My sweet general?"

It was quiet for a while, and then we heard pounding, and then weeping, and then sob-wracked pleas for forgiveness. Bonaparte, it seemed, had locked the door. He was determined for divorce. We could hear his wife pleading through the wood. Then the shouting quieted and there was quieter talk, and once I thought I heard the click of a lock being turned. Then, silence. I took the stairs down to the basement kitchen and a maid found us some cheese and bread to eat. The staff clustered like mice, awaiting the outcome of the storm above. We dozed, in our weariness.

Near dawn, a maid roused us. "My mistress wants to see you," she whispered.

We were led upstairs. The maid tapped and Josephine's voice replied "Come in" with a lightness I hadn't heard before.

We entered, and there the victor of Abukir and his newly faithful wife lay side by side in bed, covers to their chin, both looking as satisfied as cats with cream.

"Good God, Gage," Napoleon greeted. "You're still not dead? If my soldiers could survive like you, I could conquer the world."

"We're only trying to save it, General."

"Silano said he left you buried! And my wife has been telling your stories."

"We only want to do what is best for you and France, General."

"You want the book. Everyone does. Yet no one can read it."

"We can."

"So she says, with a record of what you helped destroy. I admire your cleverness. Well, rest assured one thing good has come from your long night. You've helped reconcile me to Josephine, and for that I am in a generous mood."

I brightened. Maybe this would work. I began glancing around for the book.

Then there were heavy steps behind and I turned. A troop of gendarmes was mounting the stairs. When I looked back, Napoleon was holding a pistol.

"She's convinced me that instead of simply shooting you, I should lock you in Temple Prison. Your execution can wait until you stand trial for that whore's murder." He smiled. "I must say, my Josephine has been tireless on your behalf." He pointed to Astiza. "As for you, you will disrobe in my wife's dressing room with her and my maids watching. I've summoned secretaries to copy your secret."

CHAPTER 27

There was irony in being imprisoned in a "temple" first built as headquarters for the Knight Templars, then used as a dungeon to hold King Louis and Marie Antoinette before they were beheaded, and finally serving as an unsuccessful jail for Sidney Smith. The English captain had escaped in part by signaling a lady he'd bedded through the prison windows, which was resourcefulness after my own heart. Now, eighteen months later, Astiza and I got to experience the accommodations ourselves, our lodgekeeper the portly, greasy, obsequious, officious, dim, but curious jailer Jacques Boniface, who'd entertained Sir Sidney with legends of the Knights.

We were driven there in the jail's iron wagon, watching Paris through iron bars. The city seemed drab in November, the people apprehensive, the skies gray. We were watched in turn, like animals, and it was a depressing way to introduce Astiza to a great city. All was foreign to her: the great cathedral steeples, the clamor of the leather and linen and fruit markets, the cacophony of neighing horse traffic and sidewalk merchants, and the boldness of women wrapped in fur and velvet strategically opened to give a glimpse of breast and ankle. Astiza had been humiliated by her stripping to copy the key, and didn't speak. When we alighted alongside the outer keep, in a cold and treeless courtyard, something caught my eye at the compound gate. There were people staring through the grillwork, always glad to see wretches even less fortunate than they, and I was startled to spy one head of bright red, wiry hair, as familiar as a bill of rent and as pesky as an unwanted memory. Could it be? No, of course not.

Temple Prison, which dated from the thirteenth century, was a narrow, ugly castle that rose two hundred feet to the peak of its pyramidal roof, its tower cells lit by narrow barred windows. They opened on the inside to galleries around a central atrium, climbed by a spiral staircase. It says something for the efficiency of the Terror that the prison was largely empty. Its royalist inmates had all been guillotined.

As prisons go, I've seen worse. Astiza and I were allowed to stroll the parapet around the roof—it was much too high to try to jump or climb from—and the food was better than in some of the *khans* I'd experienced near Jerusalem. We were in France, after all. If it wasn't for the fact that we were shut up tight, and that Bonaparte and Silano seemed intent on mastery of the world, I might have welcomed the rest. There's nothing like treasure hunting, ancient legends, and battles to make one appreciate a good nap.

But the Book of Thoth pulled on us, and Boniface was a gossip who enjoyed relating the machinations of a city at war and under strain. Plots and conspiracies were fried quick as a crêpe, each cabal looking for "a sword" to provide the necessary military muscle to take over the government. The Directory of five leading politicians was constantly reshuffled by the two legislative chambers. And the Council of the Ancients and the Council of Five Hundred were raucous, pompous assemblies who wore Roman mantles, indulged in shameless graft, and kept an orchestra on hand to punctuate legislation with patriotic songs. The economy was a wreck, the army was beggared for supplies, half of western France was in a revolt fueled by British gold, and most generals had one eye on the battlefield and the other on Paris.

"We need a leader," our jailer said. "Everyone is sick of democracy. You're lucky to be here, Gage, away from the turmoil. When I go into the city I never feel safe."

"Pity."

"Yet people don't want a dictator. Few seek the return of the king. We must preserve the republic, but how can anyone take the reins of our fractious assembly? It's like controlling the cats of Paris. We need the wisdom of Solomon."

"Do you now?" We were sharing supper in the confines of my cell. Boniface had done the same with Smith because the jailer was bored and had no friends. I suppose his company was supposed to be part of our torture, but I'd taken an odd liking to him. He showed more tolerance of his prisoners than some hosts show guests, and paid better attention. It didn't hurt that Astiza remained quite fine to look at and that I, of course, was uncommonly good company.

Now he nodded. "Bonaparte wants to be a George Washington, reluctantly accepting stewardship of his country, but he hasn't the gravity and reserve. Yes, I've studied Washington, and his stoic modesty is a credit to your young nation. The Corsican arrived thinking he might be swept into the Directory by popular acclaim, but his superiors received him with coldness. What is he doing back from Egypt without orders? Have you two seen *Le Messenger*?"

"If you will recall, Monsieur Boniface, we are confined to this tower," Astiza said gently.

"Yes, yes, of course. Oh, that brave periodical denounced the Egyptian campaign! Made a mockery of it! An army abandoned! Soldiers thrown uselessly at the ramparts of Acre! Bonaparte humiliated by the man once imprisoned here, Sir Sidney Smith! The newspapers are a voice for the assembly, you know. It's all over for Napoleon."

Talma had told me that Bonaparte feared hostile newspapers more than bayonets. But what no one knew was that Napoleon had the book, and that Silano once again had the full code to read it. So much for bargaining with Josephine, the scheming slut. That woman could seduce the pope, and reduce him to beggary in the process.

When I asked Boniface about the Knight Templars who'd built this place, it was like turning the handle on a pump. Facts and theories gushed out. "Jacques de Molay himself was grand master here and then tortured! There are ghosts here, young people, ghosts I've heard shrieking in winter storms. The Templars were burned and beaten until they admitted to the worst kinds of abominations and devil worship, and then they were sent to the stake. Yet where was their treasure? The rooms you're confined in were supposed to be stuffed, yet when the French king arrived to pillage them, they were empty. And where was the rumored source of Templar power? De Molay would say nothing, except when he went to the stake. Then he prophesized king and pope would be dead within the year. Oh, the shiver in the crowd when he prophesized that! And it was true! These Templars were not just warrior-monks, my friend, they were magicians. They'd found something in Jerusalem that gave them strange powers."

"Imagine if such power could be rediscovered," Astiza murmured.

"A man like Bonaparte would seize the state in an instant. Then we'll see things change, let me tell you, for better *and* worse."

"Is that when our trial will be?"

"No. That's when you'll be guillotined." He gave a Gallic shrug.

Our jailer was eager to hear our adventures, which we cautiously edited. Had we been inside the Great Pyramid? Oh yes. Nothing to see.

And Jerusalem's Temple Mount?

A Muslim holy site now, with Christian access prohibited.

What about rumors of lost cities in the desert?

If they are lost, how could we find them?

The ancients could not raise their great monuments without colossal secrets, Boniface insisted. Magic had been lost with the priests of yore. Ours was a pale modern age, stripped of wonder, mechanical and cynical. Science was subduing mystery, and rationalism was trampling wonder. Nothing like Egypt!

"Yet what if it were found again?" I hinted.

"You know something, don't you, American? No, don't shake your head! You know something, and I, Boniface, am going to get it out of you!"

¤   ¤   ¤

On October 26, our jailer brought electrifying news. Lucien Bonaparte, age twenty-four, had just been elected president of the Council of Five Hundred!

I knew Lucien had been working on his brother's behalf in Paris long before Napoleon left Egypt. He was a gifted politician. But president of France's most powerful chamber? "I thought you had to be thirty years old to hold that post?"

"That's why Paris is buzzing! He lied of course—had to, in order to comply with the Constitution—but everyone knows the lie. Yet they elected him anyway! This is Napoleon's doing, somehow. The deputies are frightened, or bewitched."

More intriguing news followed. Napoleon Bonaparte, who'd been snubbed by the Directory, now was to have a banquet in his honor. Was public opinion turning? Had the general been wooing the city's politicians to his side?

On November 9, 1799—18 Brumaire on the new revolutionary calendar—Boniface came to us goggle-eyed. The man was a walking newspaper. "I don't believe it!" he exclaimed. "It's as if our legislators are under the spell of Mesmer! At half past four this morning, the Council of Ancients was roused out of bed and sleepily assembled in the horse ring of the Tuileries, where they voted to remove themselves outside the city to the estate of Saint-Cloud to deliberate there. The decision is insane: it separates them from support of the mob. They did this willingly, and the

Five Hundred will follow them! All is confusion and speculation. But more than that has Paris holding its breath."

"What?"

"Napoleon has been given command of the city's garrison, with General Moreau removed! Now troops are moving
to Saint-Cloud. Others are manning barricades. Bayonets
are everywhere."

"Command of the garrison? That's ten thousand men.
The army of Paris was what kept everyone, including
Bonaparte, in check."

"Exactly. Why would the chambers allow this? Something odd is going on, something that leads them to vote the
opposite of what they asserted just hours or days before.
What could it be?"

I knew what, of course. Silano had made progress trans-
lating the Book of Thoth. Spells were being said and wo-
ven, and minds were being clouded. Bewitched indeed! The
entire city was being entranced. Astiza and I looked at each
other. There was no time to waste. "Mysteries of the East,"
I said suddenly.

"What?"

"Jailer, have you ever heard of the Book of Thoth?"
Astiza asked.

Boniface looked surprised. "But of course. All students
of the past have heard of the Thrice Great, ancestor of Solomon, originator of all knowledge, the Way and the Word."
His voice had shrunk to a whisper. "Some say Thoth created an earthly paradise we've forgotten how to maintain,
but others say that he's the dark archangel himself, in a
thousand guises: Baal, Beelzebub, Bahomet!"

"The book has been lost for thousands of years, has it
not?"

Now he looked sly. "Perhaps. There are rumors the Templars . . ."

"Jacques Boniface, the rumors are true," I said, standing
from the rude table where we shared a jug of cheap wine,
my voice deepening. "What charges are filed against Astiza
and me?"

"Charges? Why none. We don't need charges to hold you in Temple Prison."

"Yet don't you wonder why Bonaparte has confined us here? You can see for yourself we're friendless and helpless. Confined us but not yet killed us, in case we may be useful yet. What is an odd pair like us doing in Paris at all, and what do we know that is so dangerous to the state?"

He looked at us warily. "I have wondered these things, yes."

"Perhaps—allow the possibility, Boniface—we know of *treasure*. The greatest on earth." I leaned forward across the table.

"Treasure?" It was a squeak.

"Of the Knights Templar, hidden since that Friday the thirteenth, 1309, when they were arrested and tortured by the mad king of France. Keeper of this keep, you are as trapped as us. How long do you want to be here?"

"As long as my masters . . ."

"Because *you* could be master yourself, Boniface. Master of Thoth. You and we, who are the true students of the past. *We* wouldn't give sacred secrets to ambitious tyrants like Bonaparte, as Count Alessandro Silano is doing. We'd reserve them for all mankind, would we not?"

He scratched his head. "I suppose so."

"But to do so we must move, and quickly. Tonight is Napoleon's coup, I think. And it depends on who holds a book that was once lost, now recovered. The Templars hid their wealth all right, in a place they reasoned no man would ever dare look," I lied.

"Where?" He was holding his breath.

"Under the Temple of Reason, built on the Isle de la Cité exactly where the ancient Romans built their temple to Isis, goddess of Egypt. But only the book will tell us *exactly* where it is."

His eyes goggled. "Notre Dame?" Poverty will make you believe anything, and a jailer's wage is criminal.

"You'll need a pick and courage, Monsieur Boniface. The courage to become the richest, most powerful man in the world! But only if you are willing to dig! And only one man can lead us to the precise spot! Silano lives only for his own greed, and we must capture him and do what's right, for Freemasonry, Templar lore, and the mysteries of the ancients! Are you with me?"

"Will it be dangerous?"

"Just get us to Silano's chambers and then you can hide in the crypts of Notre Dame while we decipher the secret. Then together we'll change history!"

¤   ¤   ¤

In calmer times I might not have persuaded him. But with Paris on the edge of a coup, troops erecting barricades, legislative assemblies panicking, generals crowding in glittering array into Napoleon's house, and the city dark and apprehensive, anything could happen. More importantly, the Catholic priesthood had been shut down by the revolution and Notre Dame had become a grand ghost, used only by devout old women and swept out by the poor for welfare. Our jailer could get into its crypts easily enough. While Bonaparte was addressing thousands of men in the garden of the Tuileries, Boniface was assembling trenching tools.

To let us out was a blatant violation of the responsibilities of his office, of course. Yet I warned him he'd never find the book, or read it, without us. That he'd spend the rest of his days as jailer of Temple Prison, gossiping with the condemned instead of inheriting the wealth and power of the Knight Templars. That evening Boniface reported that Bonaparte had stormed into the Council of the Ancients when they balked at his demands to disband the Directory and appoint him first consul. His speech had been volcanic and nonsensical, by all accounts, so much so that his own aides pulled him away. He was shouting gibberish! All seemed lost. And yet the deputies did not order his arrest or refuse to meet. They instead seemed inclined to meet his demands. Why? That evening, after Napoleon's mesmerized troops had cleared Saint-Cloud's Orangerie of the

Council of Five Hundred, some of the deputies leaping from windows to get away, the Ancients passed a new decree dictating that a "temporary executive committee" led by Bonaparte had replaced the nation's Directory.

"All seemed lost to his plotters a dozen times, and yet men wilted before his will," our jailer said. "Now some deputies from the Five Hundred are being rounded up to do the same. The conspirators will take the oath of office after midnight!"

Later, men said it was all bluff, bayonet, and panic. But I wondered if that gibberish included words of power that hadn't been spoken for nearly five thousand years, words from an ancient book that had been buried in a City of Ghosts with a Knight Templar. I wondered if the Book of Thoth was already in motion. If its spells still had power, then Napoleon, new master of the most powerful nation on earth, would soon master the planet—and with him Silano's Egyptian Rite. A new rule of occult megalomaniacs would commence, and instead of a new dawn, a long darkness would fall upon human history.

We had to act.

"Have you discovered where Alessandro Silano is?"

"He's conducting experiments in the Tuileries, under Bonaparte's protection. But word is that he is away tonight, aiding the conspirators in their takeover of the government. Fortunately, most of the troops have marched to Saint-Cloud. There are a few guards at the Tuileries, but the old palace is largely empty. You can go to Silano's chambers and get your book." He looked at us. "You are certain he has the secret? If we fail, it could mean the guillotine!"

"Once you have the book and treasure, Boniface, you will *control* the guillotine—and everything else."

He nodded uncertainly, the stains from his last half-dozen suppers a mottled scramble on his shirt. "It's just that this is risky. I'm not sure it's the right thing."

"All great things are difficult, or they would not be great!" It sounded like something Bonaparte would say, and Frenchmen love that kind of talk. "Get us to Silano's chambers and we'll take the risk while you go ahead to Notre Dame."

"But I am your jailer! I can't leave you by yourself!"

"You think sharing the world's greatest treasure won't bind us more tightly than the strongest chain? Trust me, Boniface—you won't be able to get away from us."

Our route through Paris was a mile and a half, and we went on foot instead of coach so that we could skirt the military checkpoints erected in the city. Paris seemed to be holding its breath. There were few lights, and those people on the streets were clustered, trading rumors of the attempted coup. Bonaparte was king. Bonaparte had been arrested. Bonaparte was at Saint-Cloud, or the Luxembourg Palace, or even Versailles. The deputies would rally the mob. The deputies had rallied to Bonaparte. The deputies had fled. It was a paralyzed chatter.

We passed city hall to the north bank of the Seine, and theaters dark instead of lively. I had fond memories of their lobbies crowded with courtesans, courting business. Then we followed the river westward past the Louvre. The great spires and buttresses of the cathedrals on the Isle de la Cité rose against a gray sky, illuminated by a shrouded moon. "That is where you must prepare the way for us," I said, pointing toward Notre Dame. "We'll come with the book and a captured Silano."

He nodded. We ducked into a doorway while a company of cavalry clattered by.

Once I thought I sensed a figure following us and whirled, but it was only to catch a skirt disappearing into a doorway. Again, a flash of red hair. Had I imagined her? I wished I had my rifle, or any weapon, but if we were stopped with a gun we might be jailed. Firearms were prohibited in the city. "Did you see a strange woman?" I asked Astiza.

"Everyone in Paris looks strange to me."

We passed by the Louvre, the river dark and molten, and at the Tuileries Gardens turned and followed the great façade of the Tuileries Palace, ordered by Catherine de Medici two centuries before. Like many European palaces it was a great pile of a place, eight times too large for any sensible need, and moreover had been largely abandoned after the construction of Versailles. Poor King Louis and Marie Antoinette had been forced to move back to it during the revolution, and then the edifice had been stormed by the mob and left a wreck ever since. It still had the air of ghostly abandon. Boniface had a police pass to get us by one bored, sleepy sentry at a side door, explaining we had urgent business. Who didn't these fretful days?

"I wouldn't take the woman up there," the soldier advised, giving Astiza a gander. "No one does anymore. It's guarded by a spirit."

"A spirit?" Boniface asked, paling.

"Men have heard things in the night."

"You mean the count?"

"Something moves up there when he's gone." He grinned, his teeth yellow. "You can leave the lady with me."

"I *like* ghosts," Astiza replied.

We climbed the stairs to the first floor. The architectural opulence of the Tuileries was still there: vast halls opening one to another in a long chain, intricately carved barrel ceilings, mosaic-like hardwood floors, and fireplace mantels with enough gewgaws to decorate half of Philadelphia. Our footsteps echoed. But the paint was dirty, the paper was peeling, and the floor had been cracked and ruined by a cannon the mob dragged through here to confront Louis XVI back in 1792. Some of the grand windows were still boarded up from being broken. Most of the art had disappeared.

On we went, room after room, like a place seen endlessly through mirrors reflecting each other. At last our jailer stopped before a door. "These are Silano's chambers," Boniface said. "He doesn't allow the sentries to come near. We must hurry, because he could return at any time." He looked around. "Where is this ghost?"

"In your imagination," I replied.

"But *something* keeps the curious away."

"Yes. Credulity for silly stories."

The door lock was easily picked: our jailer had had plenty of time to learn how from the criminals he housed.

"Fine work," I told him. "You're just the man to penetrate the crypts. We'll meet you there."

"You think me a fool? I'm not leaving you until I'm sure
this count really has anything worth finding. So long as we
hurry." He looked over his shoulder.

So we passed together through an anteroom and into a
larger, shadowy chamber and then stopped, uncertain. Silano had been busy.

Catching the eye first was a central table. A dead dog lay
on it, lips curled in a snarl of frozen pain, its fur daubed
with paint or shorn bare. Pins tied together with filaments
of metal jutted from the carcass.

"*Mon dieu,* what is that?" Boniface whispered.

"An experiment, I think," replied Astiza. "Silano is toy-
ing with resurrection."

Our jailer crossed himself.

The shelves were jammed with books and scrolls Silano
must have shipped from Egypt. There were also scores of
preservative jars, their liquid yellow like bile, filled with
organisms: saucer-eyed fish, ropey eels, birds with beaks
tucked in their wet plumage, floating mammals, and parts
of things I couldn't entirely identify. There were baby limbs
and adult organs, brains and tongues, and in one—like
marbles or olives—a container of eyes that looked disturbingly human. There was a shelf of human skulls, and an
assembled skeleton of some large creature I couldn't even
name. Stuffed and mummified rodents and birds watched
us from the shadows with eyes of glass.

Near the door a pentagram had been painted on the
floor, inscribed with odd symbols from the book. Parch-
ment and plaques with odd symbols hung on the walls,
along with old maps and diagrams of the pyramids. I spied
the kabbalah pattern we'd seen beneath Jerusalem, and
other jumbles of numbers, lines, and symbols from arcane
sources, like a backward, twisted cross. All was illuminated by low-burning candles: Silano had been gone for
some time, but obviously expected to be back. On a second
table was an ocean of paper, covered with the characters
from the Book of Thoth and Silano's attempts at French

translation. Half was crossed out and spattered with dots of ink. Additional vials held noxious liquids, and there were tin boxes with heaps of chemical powder. The room had a weird smell of ink, preservative, powdered metal, and some underlying rot.

"This is an evil place," Boniface muttered. He looked as if he'd made a pact with the devil.

"That is why we must get the book from Silano," Astiza said.

"Leave now if you're afraid," I urged.

"No. I want to see this book."

The floor was mostly covered with a grand wool carpet, stained and torn but no doubt left by the Bourbons. It ended at a balcony that overlooked a dark space. Below was a ground floor, paved with stone, that had large double doors leading outside like a barn. A coach and three carts were jammed into it, the carts heaped with boxes. So Silano was still unpacking. A wooden stair led to where we were, explaining why this particular apartment had been chosen. It was convenient for shipping things in and out.

Like a wooden sarcophagus.

The coffin from Rosetta had been lost in the shadows but I saw it now, leaning upright against the wall. The tracery of ancient decoration was gray in the dim light, but familiar. Yet there was something oddly forbidding about the case.

"It's the mummy," I said. "I'll bet the count has spread word. This is the spirit the sentry was talking about, the thing that keeps men from snooping in this room."

"A dead man is in there?"

"Thousands of years dead, Boniface. Take a look. We'll all be like that, someday."

"Open it? No! The guard said it comes alive!"

"Not without the book, I'll guess, and we don't have that yet. The key to the fortune under Notre Dame might be in that sarcophagus. You've sent men to execution, jailer. You're afraid of a wood box?"

"A casket."

"Which Silano brought all the way from Egypt without trouble."

So the goaded jailer screwed up his courage, marched over, and swung the lid open. And Omar, guardian mummy, face almost black, sockets eyeless and closed, teeth grimacing, slowly leaned out and fell into his arms.

Boniface shrieked. Linen wrappings flapped by his face and musty dust puffed into his eyes. He dropped Omar as if the mummy was on fire. "It's alive!"

The trouble with miserly pay for public servants is that you don't get the best.

"Calm yourself, Boniface," I said. "He's dead as a sausage, and he's been dead for several thousand years. See? We call him Omar."

The jailer crossed himself again, despite the Jacobin animosity to religion. "This is a mistake, what we're doing. We'll be damned for it."

"Only if we lose our courage. Listen, the hour grows late. How much risk can you tolerate? Go to the church, pick its locks, and hide our tools. Hide, and wait for us."

"But when will you come?"

"As soon as we get the book and answers from the count. Start tapping on the crypt floors. There has to be a hollow somewhere."

He nodded, regaining some of his greed. "And you promise to come?"

"I won't be rich unless I do, will I?"

That satisfied him and, to our relief, he fled. I hoped it was the last I'd ever see of him, since to my knowledge there wasn't a scrap of treasure under Notre Dame and I had no intention of going there. Omar the mummy had done us a favor.

I looked at the corpse warily. It *would* stay still, wouldn't it?

"We have to find the book fast," I told Astiza. The trick was to finish before the count came back. "You take that side's shelves, I'll take this one."

We flew along the books, spilling them out, searching for *the* book somewhere behind. Here were volumes on alchemy, witchcraft, Zoroaster, Mithras, Atlantis, and Ultima Thule. There were albums of Masonic imagery, sketches of

Egyptian hieroglyphs, the hierarchy of the Knights Templar, and theories about Rosicrucians and the mystery of the Grail. Silano had treatises on electricity, longevity, aphrodisiacs, herbal cures, the origin of disease, and the age of the earth. His speculation was boundless, and yet we didn't find what we were looking for.

"Perhaps he takes it with him," I guessed.

"He wouldn't dare do that, not on the streets of Paris. He's hidden it where we wouldn't think—or dare—to look."

Dare to look? At Rosetta, Omar had served as sentry. I considered the poor tumbled mummy, its eroded nose to the floor. Could it be?

I rolled him over. There was a slit in its wrappings and his torso, I realized, was hollow, vital organs removed. Grimacing, I reached inside.

And felt the slick, tightly wrapped scroll. Clever.

"So the mouse has found the cheese," said a voice from the doorway.

I turned, dismayed we weren't ready. It was Alessandro Silano, striding toward us erect and young, years flushed away, a drawn rapier flicking back and forth as he strode. His limp was gone and his look was murderous. "You're a hard man to kill, Ethan Gage, so I'm not going to repeat the indulgent mistake I made in Egypt. While I wanted to dig up your mummified corpse and toast it in my future palace, I was also hoping I'd someday have this chance—to run both of you through, as I will right now."

CHAPTER 28

Astiza and I were both weaponless. The woman, for lack of something better, picked up a skull. For little more reason than to hold what we'd come for, I scooped up Omar and his eternal grin, the Book of Thoth still inside. He was light and fragile. The bandages were like old paper, rough and crumbly.

"It's fitting that we're back here in Paris where it all began, isn't it?" the count said. His rapier was a lethal wand, twitching like the tongue of a snake. With his free hand he undid the cord at his neck to let his street cloak fall. "Have you ever wondered, Gage, how different your life would be if you'd simply sold the medallion to me that first night in Paris?"

"Of course. I wouldn't have met Astiza and taken her away from you."

He gave her a quick glance, her arm cocked to throw the skull. "I'll have her back to do with as I wish, soon enough." So she hurled the bone. He knocked it away with the hilt of his rapier, his lips in a sneer, the skull making a loud clack as it fell. And he kept coming past the tables toward me.

He looked younger, yes—the book had done *something*

for him—but it was an odd youthfulness, I realized, as if
he'd been stretched. His skin was tight and sallow, his eyes
bright and yet shadowed by fatigue. He looked like a man
who hadn't slept for weeks. Who might never sleep again.
And because of that, his eyes had a hint of madness.

There was something terribly wrong with this scroll
we'd found.

"Your study smells like hell, Alessandro," I said. "Which
god are you apprentice to?"

"It's simply a preview of where you're going, Gage.
Right *now*!" And he thrust.

So I held up my macabre shield. Omar was penetrated,
but the mummy trapped the point. I felt guilty about putting
the old boy through all this, but then he was past caring,
wasn't he? I shoved the mummy at Silano, twisting his
wrist, but then his sword slipped entirely through the carcass and along my own side. Damn, that hurt! The rapier
was like a razor.

Silano cursed and swung with his free arm—he'd regained his old litheness—and struck me a blow, knocking
me back and wrestling the Egyptian cadaver away from me.
He staggered to one side, his sword still entangled, but he
groped inside the body's cavity and triumphantly pulled out
the scroll. Now I had no shield at all. He held the book
above his head, daring me to lunge so he could skewer me.
Astiza had crouched, waiting for a chance.

I looked around wildly. The wooden sarcophagus! It was
already leaning upright, so I grabbed it and wrestled the
unwieldy box around to protect me. Silano had his sword
free now, poor Omar almost broken in two, and he thrust
the scroll into his shirt and came at me once again. I parried with the casket, letting the sword stab through the old
wood but twisting, now knocking him backward and snapping the rapier in two. He kicked at the coffin angrily,
smashing the decrepit wood, and when it fell apart something wedged inside broke free.

My rifle!

I dove for it, but when I reached out the broken sword
slashed across my knuckles like the bite of a snake, so

painful I couldn't get a grip on my gun. I rolled clear as Silano was kicking shattered wood aside to get at me. Now he'd produced a pistol, his face twisted with rage and loathing. I threw myself back against the shelves just as the gun went off, feeling the wind of the bullet as it sped past. It hit one of his noxious glass jars at the end of the room and the vessel shattered. Liquid splashed onto the floor by the balcony and something hideous and pale went skittering. A poisonous smell arose, a stench of combustible fumes, to mix with the smell of gunpowder.

"Damn you!" He fumbled to reload.

And then old Ben came to my aid. "Energy and persistence conquer all," I remembered again. Energy!

Astiza was under the table, creeping toward Silano. I took off my coat and threw it at him for distraction, and then tore off my shirt. The count looked at me as if I were a lunatic, but I needed bare, dry skin. There's nothing better for creating friction. I took two steps and dove forward toward the jar that had broken, hitting the wood carpet like a swimmer and skidding on my torso, gritting my teeth against the burn. Electricity, you see, is generated by friction, and the salt in our blood turns us into temporary batteries. As I slid to the end of the room, I had a charge.

The broken jar had a metal base. As I slid I thrust out my arm and extended my finger like Michelangelo's God reaching toward Adam. And when I came near, the energy I'd stored leapt, with a jolt, toward the metal.

There was a spark, and the room exploded.

The fumes of Silano's witch's brew became a fireball, shooting over my cringing body and ballooning toward the count, Astiza, and down toward the carts, coaches, and boxes below where the preservative had dripped. The puff of the blast threw the table's papers up in a whirlwind, singeing some, while below me the storage area caught fire. I struggled up, my hair singed and both sides burning—one from the scrape of the sword and the other from my slide on the carpet—and eyed my rifle. There was preservative on my remaining clothes, and I swatted out a puff of flame on my breeches. A dim, smoky haze filled the room. Silano, I saw, had fallen, but now he too was struggling upward, looking dazed but groping again for his pistol. Then Astiza rose behind him and wrapped something around his neck.

It was the linen wrapping from Omar!

I crawled toward my gun.

Silano, writhing, lifted her off her feet but she hung grimly on his back. As they clumsily danced the hideous mummy bounced with them, a bizarre ménage à trois. I got to my gun and snapped a shot, but there was just a dry click.

"Ethan, hurry!"

The powder horn and shot bag were there, so I began to load, cursing a rifle's laborious ramming for the first time.

Measure, pour, wadding, ball. My hand was trembling. Astiza and Silano spun by me. The count was turning red from her choking but he had her hair and was twisting to get at her. Starter ram, now the hammering with the longer one . . . damn! The pair had crashed against the balcony railing, breaking part of it free. Fire rose below. The attached mummy continued its dance. The count twisted Astiza to his front, shielding himself as he eyed my rifle and struggled to lift his pistol clear. Smoke thickened against the ceiling. My one shot had to be perfect! He'd pulled the wrappings off his own throat and was tightening them on hers. He lifted his gun.

I threw out the ramrod, put a pinch of powder in the pan, my barrel coming up, Silano firing but his aim spoiled by Astiza, whom he twisted to hurl into the flames, just enough to expose his neck as they strained . . .

"He's going to burn me!"

I fired.

The ball hit his throat.

His scream was a bloody gargle. His eyes went wide in shock and pain.

And then he smashed through the balcony railing and down into the flames below, taking my woman with him.

"Astiza!"

It was the plunge from the balloon all over again. She gave a cry and was gone.

¤   ¤   ¤

I ran to the end of the study and peered down, expecting to see her in flames. But no, the mummy had snagged on one of the broken balustrades, its rib cage and dried muscles still tight after millennia. Astiza was hanging by its linen wrappings, her feet kicking above the hot fire.

Count Silano had disappeared into the holocaust, writhing on the makeshift pyre. The book was at his breast.

To hell with the cursed book!

I grasped the bandages, hauled, got her arm, and pulled her up. I wasn't going to let her drop with Silano again! As I dragged her across the lip of the balcony Omar broke free and fell, turning into a torch as his linens caught the flames. He banged down to burn with his master. I looked. His broken limbs were moving, as in agony! Was he somehow still alive? Or was it a trick of the heat?

He'd not been a curse but a savior. Thoth had smiled on us after all.

And the book? As Silano's clothes burned away, I could see the scroll curling on his dissolving chest. The flames were growing hotter as the count's flesh bubbled, and I backed away.

Astiza and I clung. There were church bells, shouts, a clatter of heavy wagons. The Paris fire brigade would be here soon. By the time they arrived, the secrets men had coveted for thousands of years would have turned to ash.

"Can you walk?" I asked her. "We don't have much time. We have to flee."

"The book!"

"It's gone with Silano."

She was weeping. For what, I wasn't sure.

Below, I heard the carriage doors being opened and water pumped. We slowly limped to the door we'd entered by, bloody and singed, stepping over a mess of glass, fluid, bone, books, and ruined papers.

The hall was smoky. For a moment I hoped the fire would push any pursuers away until we could make our escape.

But no, a platoon of sentries was pounding down the hall.

"That's him! That's the one!" It was an annoyingly familiar voice I hadn't heard for a year and a half. "He owes me rent!"

Madame Durrell! My former landlady in Paris, who I fled in unseemly circumstances, had been the red-haired mystery woman who'd haunted the periphery of my vision since I'd returned to Paris. She'd never been a believer in my character and at our parting had accused me of attempted rape. I'd deny it, but really, all you had to do is look at her. The pyramids are younger than Madame Durrell, and in better shape, too.

"Am I never to be free of you?" I groaned.

"You will when you pay what you owe me!"

"Creditors have better memories than debtors," Ben liked to say. From experience, I knew he was right. "And you've been following me like one of Fouché's secret policemen?"

"I spied you in the prison wagon, where you belonged, but I knew you'd be out somehow, and up to no good! Oui, I kept an eye on Temple Prison, let me assure you! When I saw you enter the palace with that corrupt jailer I ran for help. Count Silano himself said he would confront you! Yet by the time I get back here the whole place is in flames!" She turned to the soldiers. "This is typical of the American. He lives like a wilderness savage. Try getting him to pay you!"

I sighed. "Madame Durrell, I'm afraid I've lost everything once again. I cannot pay you, no matter how many policemen you have."

She squinted. "What about that gun there? Isn't that the one you stole from my apartment, the one you tried to shoot me with?"

"I did not steal it, it was mine, and I shot the lock, not at you. It's not even the same . . ." But Astiza put her hand on my arm and I looked past my old landlady. Bonaparte was coming down the corridor with a cluster of generals and aides. His gray eyes were ice, his features stormy. The last time I'd seen him that angry was when he'd heard of Josephine's infidelities and annihilated the Mamelukes at the Battle of the Pyramids.

I braced for the worst. Bonaparte's command of the language of the drill field was legendary. But, after glowering, he shook his head in grudging wonder. "I should have guessed. Have you indeed discovered the secret of immortality, Monsieur Gage?"

"I'm just persistent."

"So you follow me for two thousand miles, set fire to a royal palace, and leave my firemen to find two bodies in the ashes?"

"We were preventing worse things from happening, I assure you."

"General, he owes me rent!" Madame Durrell piped up.

"I would prefer you refer to me as first consul, madame, a post to which I was elected at two o'clock this morning. And how much does he owe you?"

We could see her calculating, wondering how far she dared inflate the true total. "One hundred livres," she finally tried. When no one erupted at this absurdity, she added, "With fifty, for interest."

"Madame," Napoleon said, "Were you the one who sounded the alarm?"

Durrell puffed herself up. "I was."

"Then another fifty livres as a reward for that, as a gift from the government." He turned. "Berthier, count out two hundred for this gallant woman."

"Yes, General. I mean Consul."

Madame Durrell beamed.

"But you must never breathe a word of this to anyone," Bonaparte lectured her. "What has gone on here tonight involves the security of France, and our nation's fortunes rely on your discretion and courage. Can you handle such a burden, madame?"

"For two hundred livres I can."

"Excellent. You are a true patriot." His aide pulled her away to count out some money, and the new ruler of France turned back to me. "The bodies were burned beyond recognition. Can you identify them to me, Monsieur Gage?"

"One is Count Silano. It seems we could not renew our partnership."

"I see." He tapped his foot. "And the second?"

"An old Egyptian friend named Omar. He saved our lives, I think."

Bonaparte sighed. "And the book?"

"A victim of the same conflagration, I'm afraid."

"Was it? Search them." And we were searched, roughly, but there was nothing to be found. A soldier confiscated my rifle yet again.

"So you betrayed me to the end." He peered up at the smoke beginning to dissipate, frowning like a landlord at a leak. "Well, I have no need of the book any longer, given that I have France. You should watch what I do with her."

"I'm sure you'll not sit still."

"Unfortunately, you are long overdue to be shot, and France will be safer when that happens. Having left it to others before this night, without success, I think I'll tend to it myself. The Tuileries Gardens are as good a place as any."

"Napoleon!" Astiza pleaded.

"You will not miss him, madame. I am going to shoot you too. And your jailer, if I can find him."

"I think he's looking for treasure in the crypts of Notre Dame," I said. "Don't blame him. He's a simple man with imagination, the only jailer I ever liked."

"That idiot lost Sidney Smith from Temple Prison too," Napoleon grumbled. "Whom I then had to face at Acre."

"Yes, General. But his tales encouraged all of us to keep looking for your book."

"Then I'll shoot you twice, to make up for him."

We were marched outside. Wisps of smoke were rising into a predawn gray sky. Once more I was much the worse for wear—exhausted, slashed by a rapier, scraped raw to make friction, and sleepless. If I truly have the devil's luck, I pity the devil.

Bonaparte stood us up against a decorative wall, the season having taken most of the flowers. It is there in an ominous November dawn that my story should end: Napoleon master, the book gone, my love doomed. We were too exhausted to even beg. Muskets were raised and hammers drawn back.

Here we go again, I thought.

And then came a sharp command. "Wait."

I'd closed my eyes—I'd had quite enough of staring down musket barrels at Jaffa—and heard the crunch of boots on pea gravel as Napoleon came over. What now? I opened them warily.

"You're telling the truth about the book, aren't you Gage?"

"It's gone, General. I mean, First Consul. Burned."

"It did work, you know. Parts of it. You can put men under a spell and get them to agree to extraordinary things. It's a criminal waste what you've done, American."

"No man should be able to enchant another."

"I despise you, Gage, but I'm impressed by you as well. You're a survivor, like me. An opportunist, like me. And even an intellectual like me, in your own odd way. I don't need magic when I have the state. So what would you do if I let you go?"

"Let me go? You'll excuse that I wasn't thinking that far ahead."

"My position has changed. I *am* France. I can't indulge in petty revenge, I must think for millions. There will be an election next year in your United States, and I need help improving relations. You're aware our two nations have been dueling at sea?"

"Most unfortunate."

"Gage, I need an envoy in the Americas who can think on his feet. France has interests in the Caribbean and Louisiana, and we've not given up hope of recovering Canada. There are strange reports of artifacts in the west that might interest a frontiersman like you. Our nations can be enemies, or we can help each other as we did during your revolution. You know me as well as anyone. I want you to go to your new capital, the one they call Washington, or Columbia, and explore some ideas for me."

I looked beyond him at the line of executioners. "An envoy?"

"Like Franklin, explaining each nation to the other."

The soldiers grounded their arms. "Delighted, I'm sure." I coughed.

"We'll waive the charge of murder against you and overlook this fiasco with Silano. Fascinating man, but I never trusted him. Never."

That's not what I remembered, but there was a limit to argument with Napoleon. I felt life returning to my extremities. "And?" I nodded toward Astiza.

"Yes, yes, you're as bewitched by her as I am with Josephine. Any man can see that, and God pity us both! Go with Astiza, see what you can learn, and remember—you owe me two hundred livres!"

I smiled as affably as possible. "If I can get my rifle back."

"Done. But we'll confiscate your ammunition, I think, until I'm well out of range." As they handed back my empty long rifle, he turned and contemplated the palace. "My government will begin in the Luxembourg, of course. But I've a mind this could be my home. Your fire is an excuse to start remodeling: This very morning!"

"How fortunate I could be of assistance."

"You realize that it's because your character is so empty that it's not worth the bullets to kill you?"

"I couldn't agree more."

"And that France and America share the same interests against perfidious Britain?"

"England does have a way of being overbearing at times."

"I don't trust you either, Gage. You're a rascal. But work with me and maybe something will come of it. You've yet to make your fortune, you know."

"I'm well aware of that, First Consul. After nearly two years of adventure, I don't have a penny to my name."

"I can be generous to friends. So. My aides will find you a hotel, well away from that horrid landlady of yours. What a Medusa! I'll start you on a small allowance and count on you not to risk it at cards. We'll dock some until I get my livres back, of course."

I sighed. "Of course."

"And you, lady?" he addressed Astiza. "Are you ready to see America?"

She'd looked troubled as we talked. Now, she hesitated and then slowly, sadly, shook her head. "No, Consul."

"No?"

"I've been searching my heart these long dark days, and I've realized I belong in Egypt as much as Ethan does not. Your country is beautiful but cold, and its forest shadows the soul. The American wilderness would be worse. This isn't my place. Nor do I think we've found the last trace of Thoth or the Templars. Send Ethan on your mission, but understand why I must return to Cairo and your institute of savants."

"Madame, I cannot guarantee your safety in Egypt. I don't know if I'll be able to rescue my army."

"Isis has a role for me, and it's not across the ocean." She turned. "I'm sorry, Ethan. I love you, as you've loved me. But my quest is not entirely over. The time hasn't come for us to settle down together. It will, perhaps. It will."

By the swamps of Georgia, could I never succeed with women? I go through Dante's inferno, finally dispose of her former lover, get a respectable job from the new government of France—and now she wants to leave? It was insane!

Or was it? I was in no mood to nest just yet, and really had no idea where this next adventure might take me. Nor was Astiza the type of woman to trail docilely in my wake. I, too, was intrigued to learn more about ancient Egypt, so maybe she could start that path while I ran Bonaparte's errands in America. A few diplomatic dinners, a quick look at a sugar isle or two, and I'd be free of the man and ready to plan our future.

"Won't you miss me?" I risked.

She smiled sadly. "Oh, yes. Life is sorrow. But life is also destiny, Ethan, and this stay of execution is a sign that the next door must be opened, the next path taken."

"How do I know we'll see each other again?"

She smiled sadly, regretfully, and yet sweetly, and kissed me on the cheek. Then she whispered. "Bet on it, Ethan Gage. Play the cards."

HISTORICAL NOTE

If we learn more from our mistakes than our successes, then Napoleon's 1799 campaign in the Holy Land was education in the extreme. His attacks were impatient and ill-prepared at Acre. He alienated most of the indigenous population. The massacre and subsequent execution of prisoners at Jaffa were to plague his reputation the rest of his life. Scarcely better were reports that he was guilty of mercy-killing his own troops by distributing opium and poison to dying plague victims. He would not experience such an embarrassing military and political setback until his invasion of Russia in 1812.

And yet, by the close of 1799, Bonaparte had not just survived a military debacle; the Corsican had so adroitly manipulated public opinion back in France that he found himself first consul of his adopted nation, on his way to becoming emperor. Modern politicians who seem coated with Teflon (meaning that nothing critical sticks to them) cannot compare to the slickness of Napoleon Bonaparte. How could he achieve such turnaround from such disaster? That's the mischievous mystery at the center of this book.

For fiction readers curious about such things, much of this novel is true. The tragedy of Jaffa, the Battle of Mount

Tabor, and the siege of Acre went much as described, although I have taken liberties with details. Ethan Gage and his electrified chain are an invention, and so is Napoleon's battering-ram torpedo. But Sir Sidney Smith, Phelipeaux, Haim Farhi, and Djezzar were real. (In reality, Phelipeaux died of exhaustion or sunstroke in the siege, not bayonets.) Acre and Jaffa—the latter now a suburb of Tel Aviv—retain some of the architectural flavor of 1799, and it's not hard to imagine Gage's sojourn in the Holy Land. While the strategic tower and walls of the siege of Acre are gone—they were replaced after the battle with new ones by Djezzar because of the extensive damage—there's abundant romance in walking the ramparts of this lovely Mediterranean town. To the east, a highway to Galilee cuts by the foot of the hill where Napoleon had his headquarters.

For readers interested in the history of Bonaparte's Syrian campaign, I recommend *Napoleon in the Holy Land* by Nathan Schur and *Bonaparte in Egypt* by J. Christopher Herold. Evocative documentary watercolors made by the English artist David Roberts in 1839 are collected in a number of art books.

While I've imagined some of my subterranean vaults under Jerusalem's Temple Mount—a necessity since even long-visited chambers such as Solomon's Stables have been closed to visitors by Muslim authorities—Jerusalem is riddled with caves and tunnels. They include a dark, thigh-deep subterranean waterway from the lower Pool of Siloam that this author dutifully waded through to get a feel for the underground adventure I describe. Underground gates to long-secret tunnels under the Temple Mount exist: You can see at least one as a tourist. The Temple Mount is kept off-limits to archeologists because of fear that discovery could ignite religious strife. Explorers have been chased off by angry mobs in the past, but doesn't that lend credence to the idea that there might still be revelations there? Just don't show up with a shovel. You might ignite a holy war.

Some readers will recognize that the "City of Ghosts" is in fact the breathtaking Jordanian ruin of Petra, built by the Nabataean Arabs shortly before Christ and ultimately administered by the Romans. At the time Gage visits, it was indeed a lost city that would stun the first nineteenth-century Europeans to see it. While I've taken some obvious liberties, much is as I've described it. There is a High Place of Sacrifice.

The Tuileries Palace in Paris was begun in 1564 and burned down in 1871. It served as the palace of Napoleon and Josephine beginning in February of 1800, three months after he seized power. Temple Prison was also real, but has since been demolished. And yes, Notre Dame is built on the site of a Roman temple to Isis.

The lore of the Knights Templar, kabbalah symbolism, and the idea of a Book of Thoth are all real. More on Thoth can be found in the prequel to this novel, *Napoleon's Pyramids*. My suggestion that Thoth's book was found by the Templars is made up—but then what *was* the source of their astonishingly quick and overwhelming rise to power after they excavated under the Temple Mount? Just what did they find? Where *is* the biblical Ark of the Covenant? What secrets *did* ancient societies acquire? There is always more mystery.

I should wryly note that it may come as a surprise to the British Museum that the Rosetta Stone, proudly displayed after British troops confiscated it from the French in 1801, is in fact missing its topmost and most important piece. After reading this novel, the curators may want to put a small index card on the stone's glass case apologizing for the omission and assuring that strenuous efforts are being made to find the fragments blown to pieces by a renegade American in Rosetta in 1799. But that is only a suggestion—as is the idea that archeologists keep an eye out for the remaining 36,534 Books of Thoth.

If, that is, they are worthy.

ACKNOWLEDGMENTS

This author relied on the careful scholarship of a host of historians to craft this tale, plus the evocative archaeological preservation work that makes Israel and Jordan such rewarding places to visit. I thank in particular guides Paule Rakower and Professor Dan Bahat in Israel, and Mohammed Helalat in Jordan. Diane Johnson of Western Washington University provided the Templar Latin epigram, and Nancy Pearl brought to my attention the anecdote of Napoleon ripping out the pages of novels and passing them on to his officers. At HarperCollins, special thanks to my editor, Rakesh Satyal, copyeditor Martha Cameron, production editor David Koral, editorial assistant Rob Crawford, publicist Heather Drucker for her hard work getting the word out, and the many others who make publication of a book possible. Kudos of course to Andrew Stuart, the agent who keeps me in business. And, as always, thanks to my first reader, Holly.

BOOKS BY WILLIAM DIETRICH

THE EMERALD STORM—COMING SUMMER 2012!
An Ethan Gage Adventure
ISBN 978-0-06-198920-9 (hardcover)

Action and adventure from around the world, with a magical Spanish treasure, the fate of England, and the first successful slave revolt in history hanging in the balance.

THE BARBARY PIRATES
An Ethan Gage Adventure
ISBN 978-0-06-219141-0 (paperback)

Swashbuckling hero Ethan Gage finds himself in a desperate race with the Barbary Pirates, a powerful band of Muslim outlaws from North Africa.

THE DAKOTA CIPHER
An Ethan Gage Adventure
ISBN 978-0-06-219143-4 (paperback)

Ethan Gage is sent by newly-elected Thomas Jefferson on a mysterious and perilous quest to the edge of the American frontier.

THE ROSETTA KEY
An Ethan Gage Adventure
ISBN 978-0-06-219157-1 (paperback)

Our beloved hero continues his pursuit of Napoleon and a precious Egyptian relic whose owner has the power to rule the world.

NAPOLEAN'S PYRAMIDS
An Ethan Gage Adventure
ISBN 978-0-06-219148-9 (paperback)

In the first installment, American adventurer Ethan Gage travels with Napoleon's great expedition to solve a 6,000 year old riddle.

BLOOD OF THE REICH
ISBN 978-0-06-198919-3 (mass market)

Two American adventurers must stop the Nazis from acquiring a mythical substance that promises them immortality and world domination.

HADRIAN'S WALL
A Novel of Roman England
ISBN 978-0-06-056372-1 (mass market)

William Dietrich evokes a lost world of Roman ideals and barbaric romanticism in this novel about the final great clash of Roman and Celtic culture.

THE SCOURGE OF GOD
A Novel of the Roman Empire
ISBN 978-0-06-073508-1 (mass market)

On the plains of Hunuguri, Attila the Hun gathers the most menacing army the Roman Empire has ever faced.

Available wherever books are sold, or call 1-800-331-3761 to order.